THE THINGS WE CAN CHANGE

The Things We Can Change

A LEGACY OF LIGHT
BOOK TWO

Kyah Merritt

Northern Horizon Books

Copyright

Copyright © 2020 Kyah Merritt
All rights reserved.
ISBN: 978-1-7355459-4-3
Cover art created using postermywall.com
Published by Northern Horizon Books

Contents

Copyright		iv
Introduction		1
1	Kadesh	2
2	The Strong Bull	12
3	Pain	21
4	The Endless Journey	31
5	Separation	39
6	Home	49
7	Rest	57
8	Bruises	66
9	Alone	75
10	The Judgment of Pharaoh	84
11	The Sole Companion	94
12	Friends	104
13	Usermontu	115
14	Recovery	125
15	Maya	135

16	Teamwork	145
17	Healing	154
18	The Other General	164
19	One Perfect Day	172
20	Mosquitoes	180
21	Fever	191
22	Investigations	203
23	Suspicion	211
24	Trying	221
25	Possibilities	231
26	Waiting	239
27	The Secret	247
28	Sorrow	257
29	The Gift	262
30	Power Play	273
31	Plans	282
32	Treason	293
33	Offers	303
34	Love	312
35	Possibilities	323
36	Hope	331
37	The Last Game	339
38	Philosophical Differences	349
39	Desperation	354

Author's Note	364
Glossary	377
Locations	379
Ankhesenamun's Queens List	381
Calendar	383
Lyrics	384
Selected Resources	385
Acknowledgments	387

Introduction

Far back in the mists of time (or at least 2011), at the age of sixteen, I wrote a short school paper about Pharaoh Tutankhamun and his unexpected death, which, at that point, was believed to have been the result of a chariot accident. In 2014, a new "virtual autopsy" of his remains strengthened the theory that he had lived with a clubfoot and several other physical challenges, which made a chariot wreck somewhat less likely, but presented the opportunity for other types of drama. Then, in 2015, Spike TV produced a highly-fictionalized biographical miniseries simply titled *Tut*.

My earlier interest in this historical figure, the compelling new information about him, and the entertaining Shakespearean soap opera converged in a story of my own. Through 2018-20, this story grew into a piece of historical fiction that has captivated me, kept me company through the coronavirus pandemic— this generation's historical event— and taught me more about Egyptian history, the Bible, and myself, than I ever could have dreamed.

During the writing process, I found more kinship with Tutankhamun and his family than I ever would have expected. And I am honored, grateful for, and moved by the experience of getting to know a person who was, in some ways, very much like me, and whose family was, in some ways, very much like mine. I hope my readers will be as intrigued as I have been as I seek to answer the questions of this famous Pharaoh's life and death.

1

Kadesh

It took the caravan of Egyptian soldiers fifteen days to get to Kadesh, fifteen days spent feeling the breeze in their faces as they rode in an open cart, laughing and chatting, polishing knives and swords, dreaming of the heroes they were about to become, imagining the brand-new experience they were riding into. Days spent with other young men, the Pharaoh thinking about anything and everything but his argument with the Queen, letting the anger he still felt fade into the back of his mind. Awful as it was, it was a strange novelty not to see her every hour of every day, a strange relief at not having to deal with the tension that remained between them, not yet. So for now, he was glad to be apart for the first time in forever; glad for the chance to cool his head.

Although... it was strange. For three or four days, he was caught up in the newness of the landscapes through which they were traveling; a scenery of trees and flowers not exactly like the ones at home in Egypt, and in the distance... in the distance to the north, he could see for the first time the towering peaks of the Mitanni's mountains, as high and cold as the Canaanite mountain range they had just traveled past. He had been caught up in the strange newness of the different peoples and languages they had encountered in every town they stopped in; the human people who were just like the Egyptians, and yet, were not Egyptians.

But now... He was still excited; of course he was. But now, he was beginning to feel the strenuous weariness of travel, of a constant, bumpy ride that was making his foot ache more than usual. He could ignore it, but the pain was there. Just like the pain in his heart. And now that his anger had cooled, he missed his sister. The sister he was even now riding away from, and might not see again for weeks.

He consciously ignored the pain in his foot, blocked it out. He was a warrior. And warriors did not let little aches and pains distract them from their duty. Just like they did not allow themselves to be distracted by homesickness. Or the things that remained unresolved at home.

Meanwhile, Ankhesenamun found that the palace was quiet without her brother. The Queen went about her days, reading her histories, chatting with Meresankh, occasionally seeing Amenia and Mutnedjmet. Brooding over the last, regrettable conversation she had had with Tutankhamun. She wondered if she really had held him back. Still feeling the prick of anger when she remembered the hateful words he'd spoken, her guilt twisted in her stomach as she experienced what felt suspiciously like relief to be apart for a brief space. Yet she hoped, amid it all, that he would be home soon. When he came home, they would talk. Apologies would be made for what needed to be apologized for. And they would forgive one another.

They were whispering, Ay, Maya, Nakhtmin. She avoided them; limited her conversations with them to brief greetings in the hallways. But in their conspiratorial postures, their furtive manner, the way that their eyes would flicker shiftily whenever someone walked too close past their whispered conversations, she could tell better than her brother that something was up. Politics were indeed taking place. Politics, she feared, of the worst sort.

The Pharaoh remembered the conversation they had had, he and his sister, just before he had gone. "Who's going to run the country while you're gone?" she had asked. A question worth asking. He had left the running of his nation to the Grand Vizier, the man who had essentially been in charge since Tutankhamun's coronation at nine years old. Maybe he had reservations about the old man's vision for the future of Egypt. But until Tut got home, Ay would keep things stable. And Tut put the politics of the palace out of his mind. It was all under control.

One day as they stopped for lunch, the Pharaoh looked up from gazing at the new scenery to see General Horemheb walking over with his plate of beef and beans. Tut had just started his; for being so simple, it really was quite good, and, as always, Semerkhet had tested it for poison. Semerkhet, who had been quiet during the trip, fetching things for the Pharaoh a little stiffly, his demeanor more formal than the attitude of friendship Tut had come to cherish. He seemed... annoyed by something. Or hurt.

As he ate, Tutankhamun had been half-wondering what was bothering Sem. But he put those questions aside as the General paused a few yards from where Tut sat on a camp stool, somehow managing to bow without dropping his plate. For a moment, the Pharaoh envied him his ability to walk and carry something in both hands at the same time.

"Glorious Lord?" Horemheb asked.

"Sit down, General," Tut said, nodding at an empty seat near his own. Carefully, Horemheb sat down, balancing his plate on his knee. And the Pharaoh remarked to see how his face was shining.

"I've waited so long for this day, Your Majesty," he said, his voice seeming to ache with pride. "Your time has come! Finally you're ready to lead us in glorious victory as the warrior King. A campaign like this will show the world that the Pharaoh is strong and powerful, that Egypt is strong and powerful... this is exactly why I didn't want you to cut the military budget. I grew up hearing stories of your grandfather's great armies and victories, but during the dark days of your father's reign, I wondered if I would ever have the chance to be part of a campaign like those of Amenhotep the Great. I've waited all my life to release the power of Egypt against her enemies. The time has finally come. The time to protect our neighbors, the Mitanni, from the threat of Hattusa and wipe the Hittites off the face of the Earth!"

Horemheb's hand went to his dagger as he spoke, and he gripped the hilt until his knuckles went white. "And having you here, leading us to victory, will be so meaningful," he continued. "So meaningful. Every soldier will be so inspired by your presence, and thanks to your courage, the gods will be with us. This will be an easy win— a guaranteed win, because you are here to lead us."

The Pharaoh's heart swelled with pride even as Horemheb's words made his head spin. He was the heroic warrior King of conquest, leading his nation to victory. His prayers were being answered. And his dreams were coming true.

Tut enjoyed a series of friendly conversations with Horemheb as the journey went on, learning more about the other man as he felt the friendship he'd hoped to establish with the General beginning to blossom. He remembered the days they'd shared when he'd been twelve, thirteen, when Horemheb had taught him to shoot his bow and arrow. He had honed that skill as a hunter. But now... now, he was going to employ it on the battlefield.

"It's such an honor to fight," Horemheb said one day. "For my country... for my Pharaoh... for my dear wives." He smiled as he spoke, and Tut's heart warmed as he recognized the same love that he felt for Ankh. "I may not yet be the husband I aspire to become," Horemheb continued, "and we may not yet have developed the friendship you share with the Queen, but they mean everything to me. And I could never... never bear to lose them. Even as we stand ready to take back Kadesh from the Hittites, I would give up everything, do anything, fight Anubis himself, to protect them if they were ever in danger."

The Pharaoh smiled. "They know," he said simply. "They know."

After a fortnight on the road, the caravan reached the army camp at Kadesh, a city of tents dotted through a valley that cut into the barren land a short march from a dry, sandy plain, the plain that was to be their field of battle. The world here seemed to exist in shades of gray and tan; sand, gravel, and rocks were all there was to see. Few trees provided shade from the glare of the desert sun; the only color in the bare landscape came from the people. And the Pharaoh marveled at the size of the army he commanded, lines of tents stretching out into the invisible distance like the river of guests on Tribute Day.

"Do you want to see the camp?" a deep voice said. The Pharaoh almost jumped as a large hand came to rest on his shoulder, and he looked round to see General Horemheb standing beside him, a proud smile on his face.

"Show me," Tut said, feeling his heart quicken with excitement. With a nod, Horemheb began to walk, and grasping his walking-stick, Tutankhamun followed him.

Slowly they strolled through the camp, hearing the mooing of the cattle that would provide the beef for Egypt's finest soldiers, watching the steam and smoke rising from the cooking pots and outdoor ovens that were churning out enough beans, lentils, and flatbread to feed an army, passing by the sacks of wheat and kegs of beer that would continue to sustain them tomorrow.

"It takes an army to feed an army," Horemheb said conversationally, pointing out the cooks who were busily ladling hot beans into bowls for lunch. They passed the paddocks of fattened cattle, the massive casks of fresh water that they had carried with them all the way from Memphis.

A narrow river flowed past the camp, and a few men were kneeling beside it, proudly doing their own laundry and that of their brothers-in-arms. Even here, the ripple effect of one small act mattered.

They continued their journey, walking along the endless row of tents, where soldiers sat checking their armor, sharpening their weapons.

"They're preparing for tomorrow," the General explained. He pointed to one man who sat on his cot, bent over a papyrus. "He's writing to his family," Horemheb said solemnly. "A letter he hopes will never be sent."

The Pharaoh just nodded. The men he commanded were ready to lay their lives down for the glory of Egypt. And he… he was ready to lead them.

So many new sights, sounds, smells… The Pharaoh's head spun as he experienced life in an army camp for the first time, eating new foods, learning new songs, meeting new people. Things he had never experienced; things he had never imagined. Things that were finally his. His prayers were being answered. He had become the warrior King.

The excitement in Tut's heart seemed to glow brighter with every new thing the General showed him. And with everything Horemheb showed him, taught him, he could feel the friendship he had hoped to forge growing stronger. He was— he was spending more time with Horemheb than with Semerkhet. Semerkhet, with whom he had barely spoken since they'd left Memphis.

He still wished he knew what was bothering Sem. But as the glory of conquest that Horemheb promised him made his heart soar, he was sure that whatever it was, it couldn't be that important.

This felt like the first days that he had truly been able to call Sem his friend. And as he spent more and more time with Horemheb and less and less with Semerkhet, he wasn't sure that was a bad thing.

Life in the camp was exciting… but not every one of the new experiences was enjoyable. It was the Pharaoh's first time camping, and there were discomforts to get used to— sleeping in a camp bed, eating very plain food, his nightly wash being limited to a quick rinse with a damp cloth, no palace conveniences, and very little privacy. Compared with the palace, the army camp was loud, smelly, crowded, and full of strangers. And the excitement that still glowed in Tut's heart argued with the small part of him that was looking forward to going home.

But one day… one day, Tutankhamun looked over to see Horemheb speaking with someone Tut thought he recognized, a servant who might have been the Grand Vizier's secretary. The secretary handed the

General a papyrus scroll, which Horemheb unrolled. And Tut saw the General's expression change as he tucked the scroll into his belt before offering a stiff bow to the Vizier's secretary.

He did not look very happy as he walked away.

Tut stood in his tent on the twenty-third of Athyr, hands resting firmly on his cane while Semerkhet finished fastening his armor of leather scales, some of which were plated with metal. Semerkhet's armor was similar, but not quite as fancy. Then the valet placed the blue *khepresh,* the war crown, on the King's head. Their wigs were neat; their nails were painted blood-red with henna. They looked like warriors.

In mere hours, they would be on the battlefield. In mere hours, they would be men.

"Are you ready, Master?" Semerkhet asked, picking up one of the Nubian shields from Tribute Day, the leopard-skin one. Today, it would see action. Semerkhet's voice was stiff; his manner was still that of the uncomfortable formality that had returned since their departure from Memphis. But the Pharaoh barely noticed.

"Yes."

Tut's heart pounded with excitement; he had never imagined actually having the opportunity to fight. Every time he and Semerkhet had gone hunting or racing spun through his mind. If he could bow-hunt from a moving chariot, he could participate in combat archery from a moving chariot.

But before they could gather their supplies and make their way out to their chariot, a shadow in the opening of the tent stopped them.

"Glorious Lord?" a familiar deep voice said.

Tutankhamun looked down at Horemheb, who had dropped to one knee, eyes respectfully lowered— a more dramatic gesture of respect than he had offered the Pharaoh since the beginning of the journey. Tut gestured with his free hand, and slowly, the General rose. Inclining his head to Horemheb, Semerkhet stepped back to continue sorting through the shields and ensure that the Pharaoh's quiver was sufficiently stocked with arrows.

"Yes, General?" Tut asked.

Horemheb gave a heavy sigh as he looked at the Pharaoh, gazing into his face but carefully avoiding direct eye contact. "My Lord..." he said in a soft, halting voice that made Tut immediately wonder what was wrong, "I want to remind you... that this is voluntary. You've made a brave choice making the journey here; you've been brave... enough. Just by coming here, you've already led us into battle. You are ready to be King, but battle... battle is... is something you can't imagine if you've never experienced it. You don't..." Horemheb swallowed. "You don't have to ride out." The General closed his eyes almost sadly. "If you... oversee the battle from your tent; if you inspire us with a speech and then step back, we will still be telling the truth when we report that you led us to glorious victory." He swallowed again. "If you choose to fight, I can't protect you from everything that might happen."

Tut's heart began to pound as Horemheb's baffling words washed over him.

"What?"

He looked at the General in confusion; the General who just the other day had been celebrating the glorious victory to which the Pharaoh was going to lead them. And he felt anger pounding in his temples. What had happened to their growing friendship? Did— did anything Horemheb had said over the past week even matter, or had everything been a lie? Did all the moments they had spent together over the past years, the trust and camaraderie that had grown between them as Horemheb had taught the Pharaoh everything Tut knew about hunting, riding a chariot, and now, being a soldier, mean anything at all?

"You told me that my time had come, and that I was going to lead us to glorious victory! What changed?" All at once, Tut thought back to what he'd overheard. "What did the Vizier's secretary say that changed the glorious, easy win you were talking about?"

Horemheb's jaw tightened as Tut spoke. And the air changed. All at once, the Pharaoh realized he was entering a political thicket, and he knew that his sister would tell him to slow down, listen carefully, and analyze everything he learned. So he looked at Horemheb. And waited for what he would say.

Horemheb gave a deep sigh, as if though he was considering what he was about to say. Then he looked steadily into the Pharaoh's eyes and said, "My Lord… you're not strong enough."

Tut sighed, frustration rising again. Now even the General was trying to hold him back, tell him he couldn't do it, that it was too dangerous for the poor, delicate boy.

"Yes, I am," he said firmly, straightening his war-crown with the hand that wasn't gripping the handle of his walking-stick. He was taller than Horemheb. And he could use that as he made the final decision. "And I'm going to prove it. I am *so… sick…* of people telling me I'm not strong enough for this or that… Anubis, I'm the Pharaoh! I'm not going to let them call me the Great Coward— not going to let them depose me because they think someone else is stronger. I'm going out there today, General. I'm going to fight. Because I *am* strong enough."

He'd come too far to back down now. It was too late to change his mind, standing here mere yards from the battlefield. And he wasn't going to do that. He had his pride, after all. And how could he continue leading Egypt if he came home unscathed because he had not even fought? And he had to keep his promise to the Mitanni, to the people of Amurru, to defend them from the Hittites.

Even if it meant riding out into battle.

He had to defy his court's expectations. And show everyone that he was stronger… in this capacity… than any of them had thought. Worthy to lead. Worth listening to. Only then could he get the schools built, the economic inequality between the different social classes corrected, the slave trade ended. Only then could he tell himself that he deserved to rule. Only after he had shown them what he was made of.

He sighed, releasing some of the anger. And he looked at the General, who still looked like he was half-hoping that the Pharaoh would turn back. "I'm ready. I have to do this. For Egypt. For the Mitanni. For Amurru. And for myself."

Horemheb's face fell. Then he bowed. "So be it." Crossing the tent, he took the silver trumpet. And with an uncomfortable expression that almost looked like regret, he was gone.

Tut watched him go. And he shook his head. Horemheb knew something. And the General seemed worried about Tut. Like there were things going on that were outside even the great warrior's control. Things that he feared. Things that made him wish the Pharaoh would stay safe inside his tent.

The Pharaoh shook his head, letting go of the questions, the worries, the doubts that any of this was a good idea. Outside the tent, he could hear soldiers marching by, some talking, some chanting. They were assembling. Regardless of what Horemheb was worried about, regardless of whatever message the Vizier's secretary had given him, it was time to go. Time to be the warrior King.

2

The Strong Bull

Semerkhet got Tut's bow and quiver for him, put his walking-stick away, helped the Pharaoh into their chariot, and took his position as charioteer, the large Nubian shield on his arm. This was one of their chariots from home, beautifully gold-plated. Stormy and Flash, too, were decorated, elaborate feather plumes of red and blue on their heads, their black manes braided, fringed, striped blankets on their silky, chestnut backs.

The Pharaoh knew these horses; they were the same ones that had taken him and Semerkhet out on all those hunting trips over the past season. And the same ones that Semerkhet had raced to victory time and time again. This would be the same, wouldn't it? Just another hunting trip, just another joyride, with the wind in his face and the thunder of hooves and wheels rumbling in his bones? If he could bow-hunt from a moving chariot, he reminded himself, he could fight from a moving chariot.

His stomach flip-flopped as he realized the depth of the lie he was telling himself. This would be just like every other time he'd ridden in his chariot. Of course it would.

Wouldn't it?

Tut nodded. Time to go inspire his loyal troops. He had to hang on to the side of the chariot, but he could still look reasonably awe-inspiring.

They rode out to hear him being announced by a bull-voiced sergeant. "All hail Pharaoh Tutankhamun, Lord of the Two Lands, the Strong Bull, Ruler of Truth, He who has Pacified the Two Lands, the Living Image of Amun! All life, prosperity, and health!" The hair on the back of Tut's neck stood up as Horemheb and another officer raised their instruments to their lips, one of silver and one of bronze, and raised their warlike cry to the sky in an eerie harmony.

His army of ten thousand stood before him in neat ranks a hundred deep, foot soldiers and chariot-archers cheering, stamping, pounding their shields with their swords. Their hair was tidy; their nails were painted red. They were going to fight for their country looking their best. Few wore any sort of armor; Tut saw a few breastplates, but it seemed that most intended to march or ride into battle bare-chested, some even barefooted. He wished he had their courage.

A year ago, this crowd would have intimidated him. It still did, just slightly, but right now, he was more frightened of what they were all about to ride into. But it was time to go. His chance to turn back had passed. There was nothing to do but keep moving forward.

He cleared his throat. Time for an inspiring speech.

"Men!" he cried. Within seconds, their shouts had stilled. "I stand before you Pharaoh of all Egypt, ready to lead you in glorious victory against our enemies! Today we push out the Hittites and reclaim Kadesh for Egypt! Today we use the strength and might of Egypt's armies to defend our neighbors against this common threat! Today we usher in a new era of peace and prosperity for ourselves and those to come! Let us fight today so that Egypt may stand strong and powerful, and none will ever dare encroach on her borders again!"

They bellowed their approval, shouting themselves hoarse as they gazed up at their Pharaoh whose armor gleamed in the morning sun.

They rode out together onto the broad, open plain that was to be their field of battle, Tutankhamun resting one hip against the side of the chariot as Semerkhet drove. He held his bow aloft, an arrow nocked. Time to fight.

The strong Pharaoh was ready to ride into battle.

Ankhesenamun closed her eyes, pausing as she walked down the hall to lunch. Something was happening. Far away, in Kadesh, something was happening. She shuddered, putting her arms around herself. She could almost hear him screaming.

Men screamed, fell, died. Swords slashed and hacked, arrows and spears whistled through the air, shields clattered. Horses galloped and swerved, powerful kicks sending soldiers to their deaths, falling to the sting of an arrow, the thrust of a spear, or a well-placed strike with a sword. Tut's heart pounded as he pressed his body against the side of the chariot, struggling to stay upright while Semerkhet skillfully, confidently navigated through the chaos. His legs shook; he struggled with his bow and arrow. All around him, real people were really dying. Egyptian, Hittite. And all because he had followed Ay's advice and given the order to attack. This was not what he had imagined. This was not the great and glorious conquest depicted in Grandfather Thutmose's portraiture. This was real blood and guts.

Twenty thousand men fought for their lives on that battlefield, Egyptians and Hittites clashing over the city in their midst; the city that represented control of the lands between their nations. Whoever won the city of Kadesh held the power to invade the bitter enemy that lay across the desert. And on that day, ten thousand Egyptians and ten thousand Hittites fought for that power.

A sea of men roared and churned, ebbing and flowing as one army gained ground, then lost it to the other. All was chaos; Tut caught flashes of arms, legs, hands, feet; glimpsed the sun reflecting off the point of a spear or the shadow of a shield. Horses neighed furiously as chariots raced through the storm of battle; angry faces and faces full of fear flashed past as men moved in for the kill or fell to their own deaths. The power around the Pharaoh took his breath away; the strength and force of the men who fought alongside him. And he was stunned to think that he was one of them.

The world had become a nightmare, a nightmare of sweat and blood and the screams of the wounded, the gasps of the dying. All around the Pharaoh was death— death, and fear, and hatred. Bleeding men lay wounded on the ground, their screams for help barely audible over the roar of the battle, a few hanging on long enough to be rescued by their compatriots, others finding an unmerciful death under the pounding hooves of the horses whose chariots sped wildly through the madness.

Like an ocean, the battle roared. And like an ocean, it ebbed and flowed, with Tut and Sem fighting their way through pockets of action before finding an instant of relief in an unexpected moment of rest. Tutankhamun would raise his bow to fire at a Hittite across the battlefield, and then the chariot would swerve as Semerkhet dove to protect them from a hail of unexpected arrows. And Tut's mind seemed to ache as he forced himself to maintain the perfect focus that would keep him alive, his body already flagging as he pushed his hands and arms to continue handling his bow, commanded his shaking legs to remain firm even as his foot seemed to moan with pain.

What have I done? the Pharaoh wondered as they drove along, his heart pounding in terror, his stomach twisting and churning. With every breath he took in the dust that the men and horses were kicking up into the air, dust that tasted like blood. *This is not strength. What kind of Pharaoh leads their people to do this? I should have been a King of peace. This is not what I wanted to do, wanted to be. This is all wrong. I want to go home.* He shook his head. *Just a few months ago, we reached out to the Kingdom of Hattusa in peace, and now we're at war. How did this happen? Sweet Osiris, what have I done? And what do I do now?*

The chariot bounced and veered this way and that as they rode through the melee, careening through the field, struggling to avoid every arrow, every sword. With fumbling fingers, Tut nocked an arrow, glancing around and attempting to decide which unlucky Hittite's life he would attempt to end. He felt a wrenching in his gut when the man fell from his horse with a cry that carried all the way across the battlefield.

Tut clung to the chariot as it jogged and swayed through the raging sea of men, the very ground rumbling with the pounding hooves of hundreds of galloping horses and speeding chariots, hundreds of running soldiers. It felt like an earthquake. An earthquake that screamed. Or a thunder-hailstorm. With kicked-up stones and drops of blood as hail and rain, the flight of burning arrows as lightning, the rumbling of horse-hooves and the screams of the dying as thunder.

Just another hunting trip, he told himself over and over. *Just another joyride. Just the same.*

But it was not the same.

A clattering by Tut's ear startled him; turning his attention to it for half a heartbeat, he realized that it was the sound of arrows bouncing off the shield Semerkhet held, protecting himself and the Pharaoh, defending his Lord and Master. Tut let his mind switch back to his bow and arrow. He didn't have to worry about what Sem was doing. His valet would protect them both.

Ten others the Pharaoh managed to kill that hour, ten random strangers, men of Hattusa; sons, he knew, probably brothers, possibly fathers. Why, why, why had he ever listened to Ay? What was all this loss of life accomplishing that they could not have achieved through a meeting of the kings? Why had he called upon all his brave soldiers to sacrifice themselves when other options had remained?

Couldn't they have defended their neighbors, and their own borders, through diplomacy?

But now was not the time for philosophical musings. Now was the time to fight, kill, and survive. He took a bead on another random stranger, catapulting him into eternity. Twelve now dead at the Pharaoh's hand. *This is just like hunting,* he tried to tell himself for what might have been the hundredth time. *Only I'm hunting people.*

And they were hunting him at the same time.

Tutankhamun whizzed along in his chariot through the chaos of the battle, chasing a general of the Hittites. The Hittite chariot whipped around a corner and Tut and his valet followed, Semerkhet slapping the horses' backs with the reins to make them race along even faster. If Tut closed his eyes, he could pretend they were only hunting, hurtling after an ostrich…

Out of nowhere, one of the trumpets sounded. In a heartbeat, all the Egyptian soldiers that surrounded Tut and Semerkhet retreated, leaving them completely exposed. Tut looked around wildly to see what had happened to see General Horemheb holding the silver trumpet. They locked eyes for an instant, and the General looked rather horrified.

"AAAAGH!" Tutankhamun's world spun upside-down as an arrow struck Stormy, sending him neighing in agony to the ground. Flash ran into him, collapsing beside him, and before Tut could do anything the whole chariot had tipped. With a dizzying crash, he fell to the ground, the weight of the entire metal chariot and an injured horse digging into his broken legs as the battle continued to rage around them.

The air left Semerkhet's lungs as he flew through the air, jumping clear of the falling chariot. The King was screaming, he was screaming, the horses were screaming, everyone was screaming. Then there was a thud, a solid thud as his body hit the ground. The pain hit him half a second later.

Semerkhet opened his eyes, shaking his head. He searched his body with his mind; he hurt, but nowhere did he feel the searing pain he remembered from having broken his wrist as a little boy. Just bruises. Slowly he sat up, looking down at his body with slightly fuzzy vision, his ears ringing. Bruises and scrapes… yes. To be expected. Especially with the way that his shoulder had mashed into the shield strapped to his arm. Ooh. He looked at his right knee. That was rather bad.

But he would deal with it later. He had to find the King. With a grunt of pain, he got up, struggling to his feet. He could stand, and walk. Good.

Where was his Master?

No… no… no… Terrible memories of that deadly hippopotamus hunt flashed through Sem's mind as he clawed his way through the melee, stomach turning at what he knew he might find. He'd been gored; Nedjes had been gored, and by the time they had made it to his side, he was no longer struggling. He'd bled out, floating silently in the water with a red stain slowly spreading over the waters like in that story no one was allowed to talk about. No one could survive a wound to that part of the leg.

Part of Semerkhet's heart had died when they'd found his baby brother dead. And another part of it would die if it happened again.

Suddenly, the prayers he had barely noticed he was praying were answered. And his entire heart seemed to light up as he saw a familiar face twisted in pain, the Pharaoh lying broken on the ground.

Tutankhamun lay there on the ground, feeling his legs throb, fiery pain bringing tears to his eyes as he lay there flat on his back with the chariot on top of him, looking straight up at the smoke-clouded sky, watching arrows arc through the air far above him, hearing the battle still roaring around them.

The sound seemed to grow louder and softer, the light around him grow brighter and dimmer, as he struggled to remain conscious. He could feel his left cheek stinging and blood trickling down his face, hot, then sticky and cold. With every breath, his legs hurt all the way down to his toes. In the roaring distance, cries of "To the King!" rang through the smoky air.

A young man fought his way through the raging conflict, dropping to his knees beside the King and pulling him into his arms. Semerkhet was at his side, dirty, streaked with blood and a few bruises and scrapes of his own. Was that blood on his right knee? Tut's blurry eyes couldn't tell. Semerkhet's hand found his, and the Pharaoh latched on, clinging to it as though he were drowning.

"Your Majesty," Semerkhet murmured, weeping into Tut's hand.

Tutankhamun smiled weakly, leaning into the arm that was supporting his head and shoulders. "Sem." Oh, he couldn't talk. His legs hurt him too much. He struggled against wanting to pass out; his legs were on fire…

Semerkhet's strong, warm hand was the only thing keeping him present, connecting him to the real world. "I'm right here, Master. I'm right here."

"Th-thtay wiff me."

Semerkhet nodded, tears sparkling in his eyes, making his kohl run all over his face. Gently, Tut felt his friend begin to rock him. "Hold on for me."

The King nodded back, focusing on being awake. "Y-yeth." He paused, a question forming in his mind. "You're not hurt."

Semerkhet shook his head, mouth twisting, forehead crinkling as he shook his head and closed his eyes, a single tear escaping and rolling down his dirty cheek. "I jumped. I know I shouldn't have…"

Tut shook his head in response, trying to smile. "No. 's good."

Semerkhet knelt on the dirty ground beside his Pharaoh, gathering his friend into his arms as best he could, hugging him to his heart as though he would never let him go. Alive. Hurt, but still alive. Praise be. Then, as the sounds of chaos all around them wrenched him back to the reality of the present moment, Semerkhet began to gingerly examine his brother. Carefully he looked him over, and his gut tightened as he saw the chariot lying awkwardly on its side, concealing whatever might be left of his Master's smashed legs. Would he ever walk again?

Semerkhet just held him tighter. Whether or not he ever walked again, he was alive. And they would get him home.

The din around them seemed to have faded. Tut tried to look around, and discovered that in the moments since his fall, several dozen of his men had formed a solid wall of shields around them, protecting their fallen King. They were the same men who had just retreated, now defending him for all they were worth. Horemheb was nowhere to be seen.

"We must get him to safety. Oh, Amun, preserve him... My Lord, can you hear me?"

A soldier moved into Tut's limited field of view, behind Semerkhet's tear-streaked face, the new figure bending fearfully over him. "I... I hear you," the injured King murmured.

Now a third face moved fuzzily into the Pharaoh's field of view. A terrified servant was bending over him, touching his shoulder apprehensively with a shaking hand. As he squinted through the pain, Tut thought it might have been Raherka.

"My Lord, we have to get the chariot off you. It will be painful, but we need you to just hang on." Tut nodded, closing his eyes and preparing himself. Semerkhet held his hand even tighter.

"One, two, three!" With a grunt, ten men heaved the broken chariot off the King's legs.

Tut blacked out.

3

Pain

The Pharaoh came to with a shudder. There. That was actually better. Now that the chariot was off his legs, all that awful weight was gone, the metal digging into what was left of his legs. Of course, now he could see them better when he made the effort to lift his head. They were twisted and mangled and covered in blood. He could swear that both of them were broken. Tut was bleeding. He really was just a boy.

Noncombatant servants and soldiers alike worked tirelessly to get the cart ready as others continued to defend the few yards around the King. Tut watched quietly from where he lay on the ground with Sem at his side, suffering his whole world, the burning pain in his legs so all-consuming that he could barely breathe. His lame foot had started to go numb. He shook it and bit back a scream as the movement shot agony through his broken leg.

"What is it?" Semerkhet cried, staring down into his face as he heard him cry out.

"My… my leg," he moaned, feeling sweat beading on his forehead. "Tried to move."

Tut tried to stay awake, stay with Semerkhet, but he just couldn't do it. He wavered in and out of awareness, but he always knew Sem was with him, and he always hurt. He could never get away from that.

"Stretcher!" someone was bellowing through the continued din. To move him with, Tut supposed. He wasn't walking anywhere anytime soon. Beside them someone was attending to Stormy and Flash— if attending was the right word. Both were injured beyond recovery, thrashing and giving agonized whinnies, and one of the servants held a knife, preparing to cut their throats and end their suffering. Tut shuddered. His failure to be a King of peace had condemned even his innocent horses, Sem's beloved racers, to death.

"Cart ready!" came a desperate yell. Semerkhet looked over, then back down at the King. Two more men had arrived through the mayhem, carrying an empty stretcher between them. The shield-bearing soldiers who encircled the Pharaoh made a space, letting the stretcher-bearers into the circle of protection. Carefully they set the litter down next to the King, ready for him to ride in for the short journey to the cart.

"Kamose and I will get you into the stretcher," Semerkhet said as a tall, strong soldier hurried over, looking amazed that he had been called upon to help the Pharaoh while remaining horrified that the Pharaoh had been injured. "Are you ready?"

Tut nodded, knowing that the pain was about to get much, much worse. Carefully, Semerkhet got out from under the Pharaoh, whose head and shoulders he had been supporting in his lap, then slipped a shield under Tut's feet and lower legs as delicately as he could. That would allow him to bear some of the Pharaoh's weight without disturbing the broken bones more than necessary. Then Semerkhet and Kamose bent over the King, Kamose putting his hands under Tut's arms while Sem got a firm grip on the shield. "One, two, three!"

Tut passed out again from the pain. Some time later, he opened his eyes in one of the army tents. It was quiet, so quiet after the din of the battle, but in the distance, he thought he could hear someone crying; someone chanting a prayer.

He had completely missed his moments in the stretcher. And whatever ride he had apparently taken in the cart.

"You're safe," Semerkhet said gently, patting his shoulder. The servant's wig was tangled and askew, and his makeup was in a terrible state. Tut just nodded and went back to sleep.

Ankhesenamun sat in her private sitting room, a nagging worry nibbling at her. Out of the corner of her eye, she saw movement, and she looked to see Bastet softly padding into the room. She looked up at the Queen, and Ankh remarked at the intelligence in the cat's eyes. The way that she seemed to be… communicating.

"What is it, kitty?" Ankh said softly. Lightly the cat jumped up onto the Queen's chair, curling up beside her. Ankh picked her up; held her in her arms like a baby. "What's going on out there?" Bastet rubbed her face against Ankh's neck, making soft, chirrupy cat noises. Ankh shuddered at the meaning with which Bastet was talking to her. "Something happened, didn't it?" she whispered, holding Bastet closer. She shook her head. "Something's happening."

Meresankh stood up straight as she heard what sounded like a sob.

"What's wrong, My Lady?" she asked, hurrying to the Queen's side. She was sitting in her chair with the Pharaoh's cat in her arms, tears running down her cheeks. "Are you thinking about the Pharaoh?"

The Queen nodded, letting the cat go and reaching out. Slowly Meresankh offered her hand, and her Mistress took it, holding it tightly as if she needed her handmaiden's strength.

"I just… I think something's happened," Ankh whispered through her tears, wiping her eyes with her free hand so her makeup smeared. "Bastet… I just get a sense that… she knows something. And something's happening."

Meresankh felt a quickening in her heart, a Light glowing strong. "My Lady…" she whispered, "would you like me to pray?"

The Queen just nodded. And still holding her hand, Meresankh bowed her head.

Two scouts went ahead on the fastest horses in the cavalry, a letter tucked safely into one of their saddlebags. They would deliver the news to the palace that the Pharaoh was coming home wounded.

Semerkhet watched them ride away from the camp, soon disappearing into a cloud of dust on the southern horizon. And he prayed to the gods and goddesses of his people that the messengers would get there as fast as the wind.

He hoped the gods were listening.

Semerkhet winced as he held the King's shoulders, pressing his Pharaoh's arms into the thin mattress he lay on. At Tutankhamun's feet, the doctor was preparing to set his legs and place them in splints made of bark. And he needed the King's valet to hold him down.

But Tutankhamun did not move, even as Semerkhet shuddered to hear the broken bones snap back into place; watch the doctor carefully wrap his legs in linen bandages and put on the splints. The poppy-based painkiller the doctor had given him was working. And that was a blessing.

As the Pharaoh slept, unwelcome thoughts crept into Semerkhet's mind. Thoughts of two beautiful chestnut horses lying broken on the ground, screaming and thrashing in pain. And thoughts of a knife; a knife meant to end their suffering.

Biting his lip, he pushed the thought away. There was not time for that right now.

But there was a hole in his heart. A hole in the exact shape of Stormy and Flash.

Faces moved fuzzily in and out of Tutankhamun's field of view as he lay flat on his back, trying to breathe as the pain consumed him. The camp doctor splinted his legs without him ever having been aware of it. And they gave him medicine that made his thoughts fuzzy; dulled the pain while dulling his mind. All he wanted to do was sleep. At least through keeping him asleep, his body was able to protect him from his suffering. And the medicine would help with that.

The doctor was standing over him, helping him sip the bitter medicine as Semerkhet's warm arm helped him sit up slightly. Dimly Tut saw someone else come into the tent, another soldier he didn't recognize. He was tall, and wiry, and proud-looking, with a hooked nose and a lined face. And really quite old for a soldier. He looked almost like he could have been Horemheb's father.

"Commander Seti," the doctor said, inclining his head respectfully. The commander looked down at the King as Semerkhet bent over him, dabbing his face and neck with a cool, damp cloth, but Tut didn't see the anxious concern he would have expected. He saw something that looked almost like contempt.

"The other soldiers are in pain too," the commander said, nodding at the little bottle of poppy medicine. "And some of them are hurt much worse than he is. Praise the gods my son is not hurt, but if he had been, I would expect to be able to give him something for it."

The doctor picked up the little bottle, hiding it in his hand. "He is the Pharaoh," he said shortly. "He gets as much as he needs."

Seti inclined his head, but there was bitterness in his capitulation. "Of course." The commander turned on his heel and left the tent, his red cloak swishing behind him.

Tutankhamun just closed his eyes and let the medicine take effect.

Ankhesenamun didn't sleep that night. Something was wrong. Something had happened. And she was afraid for her brother.

He'd been gone just over two weeks… about the length of time it would take for them to get to Amurru. And surely, almost immediately after arriving in Amurru, he would have joined the campaign.

The cat purred again, hopping up onto the bed beside her and regarding her quietly.

And Ankh shuddered. But not just with the cold of the Athyr night.

"Is he hurt?" she whispered to the cat.

She just gave a long, slow blink, looking up at her boy's sister.

Ankhesenamun had to fight back the tears.

She stared at the ceiling, Bastet in her arms, and waited for morning.

"Where'th… Horemheb?" Tut asked during a brief lucid moment.

"The campaign isn't over," the doctor said gently. "The effort to reclaim Kadesh goes on."

Tut just nodded, feeling himself drifting off again.

Three days later, on the twenty-sixth of Athyr, Semerkhet squinted at the southern horizon, imagining the scouts getting closer and closer to the palace, carrying the message that the Pharaoh had been wounded. And then he turned his attention to the task at hand— getting his Master into the cart that would carry them home.

The loyal people of Amurru wept for the Pharaoh as they gathered to watch him leave their lands, wounded in the war he had agreed to fight to free them from the Hittites and make them Egyptian again. And they prayed to their own gods that he would be healed.

They rode out of Kadesh, out of Amurru, through Canaan, through the land of the former slaves who had thrown Egypt into chaos in the days of Tut's grandfather, Amenhotep the Third. And fuzzily, Tutankhamun remembered the stories his father, his mother, and later on, Ankh, had told him; stories of I-AM, of ten plagues, of a war waged between the gods of Egypt and the God of the Hebrews, between falsehood and Truth, between darkness and Light. And lying in the dark longing for the touch of the Sun on his face, Tut wondered what was true.

Sometimes they fed Tut spoonfuls of thin porridge or gave him sips of water out of a bowl, which splashed down his chin onto his chest. Occasionally he felt a cool cloth dabbing at his face, his scalp, his neck, gently washing away the sweat and soothing the burning pain of his cheek. Someone had taken off his armor, and he lay there in his under-tunic.

He slept to protect himself from the pain.

Semerkhet held his Pharaoh tight, using one arm to keep his Master's head and shoulders from sliding off his lap. And he tried to breathe. Another brother, hanging between life and death. Another friend he couldn't bear to lose.

Tutankhamun's head moved on the rolled-up cloak Sem had slipped under his head for a pillow. And his eyes opened a little, just enough for Semerkhet to know he was awake.

"Hey," Semerkhet said. He had never imagined saying that to his Master.

The Pharaoh blinked. "Hmm?"

"You have to pull through; you hear me?" he said, not gently. Unshed tears ached in his dry throat. "You can't leave me. I've already lost one baby brother. Can't lose another one." He slipped his hand into Tut's and squeezed it, feeling himself give a little smile as his friend squeezed it back. "So don't you go anywhere. I'm bringing you home."

Vaguely, his Master smiled. And his grip on Semerkhet's hand slackened as he slipped back into sleep.

Sem sat there as Tut went back to sleep, listening to his steady breathing, feeling his Master's weight on his own painful legs. And one by one, the unshed tears began to fall.

And the pain he remembered filled his heart again. Because in speaking so frankly to his Pharaoh, he had spoken the truth.

He could not lose another brother.

As the Pharaoh surfaced from sleep, he realized he was crying. It was dark; was he in bed? He rooted with his face, groped with his hands, clung to his mother when he finally found her.

"Mommy," he moaned through his tears, and heard a gentle, soothing shushing from above as he was rocked. Gently a hand wiped away his tears. She was there. And she would take care of his leg, like she'd taken care of every other bump or bruise he'd ever gotten. "Mommy, my leg hurts. I wanna go home."

Only it wasn't his mother. Or his nurse Hetty. The person who held him was tall and muscular, without any soft, yielding, motherly curves. This was a boy. A familiar boy.

He was in Semerkhet's lap.

"It's all right," he heard Semerkhet murmur, still rocking him. "We're going home."

He sighed, surrendering. His mother, his nurse, couldn't come to him. But Semerkhet was here. That would have to be enough. But somehow, he knew it would be.

What could Semerkhet do, right here, right now? The Pharaoh had started to cry, a great big nineteen-year-old boy weeping in his arms like a toddler, and his valet had gently hushed him as he would a toddler. Semerkhet had nothing but sympathy for him, but how could he keep him calm for the rest of the endless trip home? And how could he keep himself calm?

The words of a lullaby echoed in his mind. Semerkhet gave a little smile. And he began to sing.

Semerkhet shook his head as he looked down at the Pharaoh sleeping in his lap. What was happening? Here he was, a lowly servant, actually holding the god-king in his lap as the Pharaoh tried to sleep. The Morning and the Evening Star, who could have someone executed for sneezing, the Lord of the Two Lands who could disintegrate someone with a mere glance, was sleeping under his watch.

In just over a year of service, he never would have imagined letting his Master rest his head and shoulders in his lap. Although… He bit back a sarcastic chuckle. He never would have imagined his Master going into battle.

It was all so strange. Even his best friend from childhood, he never would have imagined holding in his lap like this. But maybe… just maybe… a big brother could hold his baby brother this way.

Baby brother. Semerkhet's heart ached with thoughts of Nedjes; how when they had carried him home, he had already been still and silent. There had been no opportunity to fetch a doctor, get him home and to bed, hold him and comfort him. One bite from that hippopotamus and it had all been over.

How he had missed his younger brother over the next months; how he had longed to have someone to guide, to protect, to teach, to help raise into a strong young man. What he wouldn't have given for one more day with Nedjes, who would be fourteen now.

And yet, sitting here in the darkness of the cart watching the Pharaoh sleep, Semerkhet felt a warmth in his heart. And he knew that he still had a little brother.

They stopped that night, in the city of Sidon. And they traded out the six horses that the driver had been pushing as hard as he could for nearly a hundred miles, replacing them with a fresh team. By the order of the Pharaoh they traded them out, to a little old man who claimed he'd been the greatest charioteer from Thebes to Carchemish, back in his day. They took a few minutes to stretch their legs, have a proper drink, and relieve themselves, Semerkhet stretching broadly as his stiff muscles complained at having spent the past five hours sitting with half a Pharaoh resting on his knees.

After the valet had installed Raherka to sit at the Pharaoh's side, Semerkhet and the other men ate their dinner huddled around a campfire on the outskirts of town, wolfing down the bread and lentils they'd bought and hoping that the medicine they'd bought from the town magician would keep the Pharaoh's leg attached for one more day. And when he returned to his friend's side, Semerkhet patiently fed Tutankhamun as much of the thin porridge as he would eat; porridge mixed with poppy medicine that Sem fervently hoped would help his friend continue to rest. Even though he could only guess at how many drops he should add to the Pharaoh's paltry meal.

The nights were getting cooler, bordering on chilly. As the day ended, Semerkhet made sure his Master was warmly tucked in with the only blanket. It wasn't a very nice blanket; it was scratchy, riddled with holes, and smelled like the last eight people who had used it, but it would keep him warm. Of course, that meant that there wasn't a blanket for Semerkhet. But he didn't need one. As long as his Pharaoh was provided for, he was satisfied. Even as he shivered.

After a fitful night of rest, they hitched up the fresh team and began all over again.

4

The Endless Journey

At some indeterminate point the next day, the twenty-seventh of Athyr, Semerkhet sat absentmindedly stroking the Pharaoh's head, staring into space. He could hardly believe what they had been through. And he could hardly believe they were both still alive.

He tried to pray, that his Master would be able to hang on until they got home. He was almost too tired to attend to to Whom he was praying, but he was grateful to feel an answering warmth in his heart. He had been heard. By Someone.

As they drove on and on, Semerkhet found himself drifting off every few hours. But his sleep was not restful. Whenever he closed his eyes, he was plunged into nightmares of what they had just survived. And he could see from the fitfulness of the drowse in which his Master lay that the Pharaoh, too, was dreaming.

In the dark and the quiet, Semerkhet thought. And inside his heart, an ember of anger began to smolder. And not at himself, for failing to be hurt worse than his Master. At the Pharaoh.

Because it was the Pharaoh's decision that had brought them to Kadesh; thrown them into battle. The Pharaoh's decision that had put him in danger… put Semerkhet in danger. The Pharaoh's decision that had very nearly killed both of them.

And the worst part? He had not even asked. And Semerkhet had never had the chance to express his opinion on the matter.

The Pharaoh had forced them both to go. And look where it had gotten them.

Semerkhet could see Meresankh's beautiful face in his mind, hear her kind voice, see the dimple in her cheek and her sweet smile. He ached for wanting to be by her side. And his heart ached when he thought of how afraid she must be for him. She had no idea if he had even lived; if he was ever coming home.

Would he ever see her again?

Occasionally Tut wondered if they had won the battle against the Hittites, and if he would ever know. Sem was always with him, exchanging decorum for friendship as he stroked the King's head, held his hand, even held him in his lap as he tried to sleep, softly humming to him. Dimly Tut wondered if he would ever be able to thank Semerkhet properly, and hoped he knew how grateful he was.

Then it hit him. He wasn't just grateful that his friend had saved his life… he was ashamed for forcing that friend to risk *his* life.

Because that was what he had done. Tut swallowed as he felt tears of shame prickling in his fuzzy, itchy eyes.

"I'm tho thorry," he whispered.

Sem looked down at him with a concerned frown. "About what?" he asked softly.

Tutankhamun blinked away the tears. "I'm tho thorry I… brought you here. All tho wrong… and I forthed you into it. Put you in danger when you couldn't thay *no*. And I'm… thorry."

"That's my job," Semerkhet said, shaking his head gently. "I'm your valet."

Tut shook his head. "No. You're my brother."

"I shouldn't have jumped," Semerkhet whispered through tears as Tut lay on his back on his cot with Sem kneeling beside him. He had been so cold, but Sem had found him a blanket, and now he was wrapped up tight. Even if the blanket was a little scratchy... and a little smelly... it was warm. "It should have been me. How could I try to save myself when you fell? How could I do that?" He swallowed, sniffing back tears. "Can you ever forgive me?"

Tut reached up and took his hand, letting him know he was listening. He could smell the sweat on Semerkhet's body and his own, the blood on their tunics, the smoke of campfires and burning arrows. Every muscle in his bruised, scraped-up body ached.

"It'th all right," he choked. "Glad you're all right. And thith way... you can get me home thafely."

"And what will they say when they find out I didn't give myself up to save you? I'll be court-martialed, and there's no way I can defend myself. Legally it is as if I shot the h-horse." Semerkhet's voice shook as he said the word *horse*, and the Pharaoh shook his head. He knew why. After swallowing hard, Semerkhet went on. "I will be executed for dereliction of duty for not getting hurt when you were."

Tutankhamun shook his head. "No. I'll tell them you didn't do anything wrong. Did everything you could. Thith wath not your fault." He paused. "Just glad you're all right. And— ath your Pharaoh, I'm ordering you to be glad too."

Semerkhet sniffled again with a choked chuckle. That was all. But it was enough.

Every time he woke up, Tut could see a little more clearly. And for that he was grateful. But now, as he peered up at his friend's face through the dimness of the covered cart, he felt his heart aching. Because although his friend had apparently had the chance to wash the dirt, blood, and smeared makeup off his face, Tut realized that Sem's eyes were red and puffy. Had he been crying?

Semerkhet tried to breathe slowly as the pain in his knee wore on, spiking every time the cart jolted over a rock or pothole. He couldn't let the Pharaoh know how much pain he was in. Not yet, anyway. Not til they got home.

But Semerkhet was forgiven. Forgiven for anything he had or had not done that may in some way have contributed to what had happened. And he... he would forgive the Pharaoh for the big heart and impulsive sense of adventure that had gotten them here.

And he was responsible for getting his Pharaoh home safely, protecting him through whatever came next. Because Semerkhet had a sense that it was not going to be easy. Even if his Master got better. But the valet had been ordered to be glad that he was all right. Sem almost chuckled. He would try.

He had killed twelve men, Tut mused in the silence once he found himself being able to think again. Twelve men who had not needed to die. And he had caused the deaths of hundreds more, Egyptians and Hittites, by ordering this attack when they had still had other options. Even their mission of defending the Mitanni and the people of Amurru just might have been accomplished through words, through letters, rather than swords and shields. When... if... if he did not survive, would his heart balance with the Feather of Ma'at, or would the blood on his hands tip him into the mouth of Ammut, the crocodile-lion-hippopotamus who devoured the hearts of the unworthy?

The King of peace had failed.

And the brother of the Queen had failed. Because Tutankhamun wondered if the weight of the terrible words he had said to his sister would doom him for eternity.

Semerkhet wrapped the warm, woven blanket around his shoulders, rubbing its softness against his cheek. Finally he was warm, burrowed inside the warmth and shielded from the cold night. And that was not all— the people of Megiddo, where they had spent the previous night, had given each man two blankets, so not only did Semerkhet have one to wrap himself in, he had one to lay out on the floor of the cart and make himself a little bed. Now his aching joints would be nicely padded as he lay against the hard wood. And the Pharaoh was warmly tucked in, weary young face looking almost peaceful as he slept, his face all that was visible.

The other thing that they had gotten in Megiddo was more poppy, and the expertise of a village granny in how much to give the Pharaoh. Now Semerkhet knew the correct dose, carefully balanced so that it would keep Tut asleep and away from his pain without either leaving him to awaken an hour later thrashing in such agony that he might unset his broken legs, or sending him so deeply to sleep that he might stop breathing. And Semerkhet would be able to use that knowledge to help make the rest of this endless journey that much easier for the Pharaoh.

Semerkhet sang constantly. Marching songs, mushy love ballads, old lullabies, nursery rhymes for the youngest of young children. He sang to keep himself sane. And whenever Tut woke up, he was still singing. So even if Tut could not open his eyes, he knew his friend was at his side.

Hours... or were they long days and endless nights... or weeks... months... years? passed meaninglessly in the shadowy confines of the covered cart, hearing the wheels turning, the horses' hooves on the ground, Semerkhet's humming. Sometimes they paused, but it was never long before they were moving again, the endless rumble of the cart beginning again. With no sun to tell day from night, Tut slept when he could, lay awake when he couldn't, mumbled plaintively when he was hungry or thirsty. Would they ever get home? Would they ever get anywhere? Or would he be trapped here for the rest of his life, for the rest of eternity, groaning in pain every time the wheels of the cart jolted over a rock?

Azzati, Rafah. All Egyptian cities, full of people who were loyal to the Pharaoh, who were happy to feed a squadron of weary soldiers and barter one lathered, half-killed team of horses for a fresh one. And they had been forewarned that the caravan of the wounded Pharaoh would be passing through in need of food and lodging; the scouts had left that message at every town they passed. And at each successive town, the scouts had left the message of where they were bound next, so the caravan could follow the same route home. Thankfully the scouts wore armbands officially issued by the palace; armbands that would prove to the inhabitants of this village or that city that they really were on an urgent mission, not just dehydrated.

The men would get up and stretch whenever they stopped, taking a moment to work out the stiffness of being confined to a cart or a saddle. And at each town they passed through, they also accepted the gifts, ornate or humble, that the people had gathered to give to the poor Pharaoh.

When they took a break, Semerkhet would help Tut reposition himself; decide whether he wanted to rest his head and shoulders in Semerkhet's lap or whether he wanted the few inches of space he could get. Sem would also help him take a few sips of water— trying to drink anything while the cart was in motion was futile; with all the jostling, the precious water would only have spilled. Semerkhet never took much for himself; only enough to moisten his mouth, his dry lips. And of course, he would try to get his friend to eat a few spoonfuls of the poppy porridge. Anything to keep him asleep until they got home.

The main driver and two or three soldiers who could drive took turns as the days passed, giving one another time to rest. And every day, every night, every hour, they got closer. Closer to home.

On the twenty-eighth of Athyr, Ankhesenamun sat thinking, wondering, worrying. At the sound of a footstep, she looked up.

"My Lady?"

It was a guard, standing at attention in the doorway of the Queen's bedroom.

She got up, heart pounding. Was there news?

"Yes?"

"I have news," he said. His face was solemn. The Queen began to feel lightheaded.

"The Pharaoh has been wounded."

And Meresankh had to lead her to her chair.

Ankh didn't eat. Didn't sleep. Just lay on her bed, her wig tangled, her makeup smudged, the cat in her arms, and thought of him. Wept. Prayed. Waited.

For good news or bad. She waited.

Bastet had been right.

But even as she prayed, she felt no answering warmth. Only the emptiness of her own breaking heart.

"He's been wounded," Ankh whispered to her handmaiden. They sat together on the Queen's bed like Ankh and Tut had so many times—would they ever sit together like that again? Meresankh's arm was around her; in this moment of fear and grief, rank ceased to matter; boundaries had fallen away. The cat was curled up against the Queen's leg. In some strange way, she seemed to understand that something had happened to her boy. Hadn't she been the one who had told Ankh in the first place?

"And they really don't know anything else?" Meresankh asked. She was wearing the little silver necklace Semerkhet had given her, and she kept reaching up to run her fingers over it. "Whether he's…"

The Queen shook her head, red, puffy eyes filling with tears for what might have been the hundredth time today. "No. Just that he's on his way home."

"And Semerkhet?"

Ankh shook her head. "Didn't hear anything."

Meresankh sighed, looking into her own thoughts as she continued to stroke the necklace. And she held the Queen, and rocked her, as they waited for news.

Meresankh closed her eyes with a shudder as she held the Queen close. What a strange thing, to sit here with her, an arm around her shoulders. Just as if they were friends. To her surprise, she felt herself giving a tiny smile as her heart warmed. Yes. They were friends.

A shivering sob shuddered through the Queen, and Meresankh held her even tighter, one arm around her shoulders, the other hand slowly creeping over to the Queen's. The moment Meresankh touched her hand, the Queen grabbed her handmaiden's, clinging to it like she was drowning. Meresankh held it tighter. The Queen was her friend. And she would do everything she could to comfort her.

Meresankh thought of Semerkhet as she felt the cool metal of her necklace resting against her collarbone. And she closed her eyes against the tears. There was nothing either of them could do but wait for news.

Except that there was. Meresankh felt herself smiling as a familiar peace gently touched her heart, peace from the Lord of Light Himself, known to her as I-AM and to her Queen's father as the Aten. She would pray without ceasing until the Pharaoh came home… or they received news. She would pray for the Pharaoh to get well. And she would pray for an opportunity to speak to her Queen about the Truth she possessed.

5

Separation

"I shouldn't... have let... him go," Ankh whispered through dry lips as she sat in one of the chairs in her private sitting room, rocking the cat in her lap like she had rocked her baby brother when they were seven and two, eight and three. "I should have stopped him. Should have told him *no*." She held Bastet closer, burying her face in her warm, gray fur. "I promised Mother and Father I would keep him safe... and I haven't. I've broken my promise." She looked up, tears slowly trickling down her face. "And what... if I've killed him?"

From where she sat in the other chair, Meresankh reached out, gently taking her Queen's hand. And the Queen squeezed it gratefully. Her handmaiden paused, as if she was considering what to say. Even... asking what to say. Then she sighed, half a little smile coming to her face.

"Can anyone stop a nineteen-year-old boy when he gets an idea?"

And a chuckle washed away a tiny part of the Queen's fear. For just a moment.

It wasn't her fault. She knew it wasn't. Ankh repeated it to herself over and over, the truth that she had tried to stop him from going; had told him it wasn't safe. She had done everything in her power to counsel her baby brother not to go to Kadesh.

It had been his choice.

It was like she had thought to herself after the argument she had had with Tutankhamun just before he had left for Kadesh. She had set him free from her control... and from her motherly protection.

He was an adult now. And his decisions were his own.

Even... She put her arms around herself, shivering. Even if they killed him.

But oh, she regretted that fight. And now, she was forced to wonder... if they would ever have the chance to make up.

Meresankh thought of Semerkhet, the strong, faithful valet who took such good care of his Pharaoh and one day, would be such a good husband, such a good father.

If he ever came home.

She prayed. And she waited.

Ankh sat beside her handmaiden, worn out with tears. The Queen's grief was wearing her down. Her eyes were red and puffy, her nose raw from blowing it so much, her throat sore. And she had stopped wearing makeup, because all her crying just made it run down her face.

Her dress was wrinkled from being slept in; her wig was tangled and askew. And her body was confused at the way she had practically stopped sleeping; stopped taking regular meals. Eating and sleeping were not important right now.

"How can you be so calm?" the Queen asked through dry lips. "I can't eat... can't sleep... I never stop praying, but it feels so... empty." She sniffled. "But you look... calm. Like... you're not even afraid. What's your secret?"

Meresankh gave a little smile. And again Ankhesenamun remarked to herself to see the light in her handmaiden's eyes; the Light that reminded her of her parents.

"Well, My Lady," the handmaiden said slowly, as if she was wondering exactly how to say what she wanted to express, "I'm not afraid... because I know my prayers are being heard."

The Queen sniffled again. "How do you know? I don't feel like mine are being answered at all."

Meresankh paused. "My Lady... who do you pray to?"

Ankh shrugged. "To Amun-Ra, Isis, Horus... all the gods of the temples, who we've worshiped for centuries. The priests brought us back to them after my father died... brought us back to the truth."

Meresankh swallowed. She looked like she was thinking very hard. Then she gave a little smile. "My Lady... what if the Truth is what you've left behind? What if—" She glanced at the window, where a single ray of sunshine was gently streaming in, "what if your father found the truth, in the Aten..." She paused. "In I-AM?"

Ankh shuddered, drawing back and staring at her handmaiden. "Is that what you believe? Is that why you don't go to any of the festivals?"

Meresankh just smiled. And the Light shone in her eyes.

Ankh shook her head, confusion filling her heart and mind. Aten? Real? I-AM? Real? And... one and the same? It made no sense; ran completely counter to everything she knew to be true. And yet... her handmaiden had so much peace... and right now, she had none at all.

What could be the harm in letting Meresankh continue to pray... in her own way? Because whatever the Queen believed; whatever she doubted... her handmaiden had found something.

Ankhesenamun gave a deep sigh. And she smiled at Meresankh. "I... you've given me a lot to think about. But I would... appreciate it if you would pray for the Pharaoh."

Meresankh smiled and squeezed her Queen's hand. "I have been, My Lady. And I always will."

Dreams chased the Queen. *A thousand things that might have happened; the angry cries of warriors and shrill neighs of horses, clash of swords on shields and whistle of arrows through the air, screams of pain, smells of smoke and dust and blood. She saw him cut down by a sword, saw him thrown from his chariot and crushed beneath the horses' hooves, saw him fall riddled with arrows, saw him taken prisoner, bruised, beaten...*

When she woke, the dreams ended. But the thoughts did not. And she was left to mull over a thousand terrible things that might have happened until morning finally came and brought her closer to learning the truth.

Ankh looked up from sitting at her desk, staring into space on the twenty-ninth of Athyr. Meresankh stood there, unrolling a large papyrus map.

"Where are they now?" she asked, laying the map out on the desk. "Show me."

The Queen rubbed her tired eyes and bent over the map. "Here's Kadesh," she said, pointing, "and here's us. Now, the fastest couriers can ride about as far as Per-Bast in a single day, and since this is… is an emergency, they'll push the horses as hard as they have to. I imagine they'll trade them out when they can, when they stop at a town for food. And the scouts only took three days to get here." Ankh's eyes moved over the cities speckled over the landscape captured on the map. "The scouts said that by their best guess, the caravan would be in the city of Rafah by the time the scouts got here." She sighed. "Probably take them another two or three days to get home."

Meresankh gave her a hopeful little smile. "But they will."

Three times a day sometimes, Meresankh would bring the Queen the map. And they would point at the cities, estimating where the Pharaoh and his valet were at that very moment. And every day, they got closer.

What would the Queen do if he didn't come home, or if when they brought him home, he was still and silent? What would she do?

Then, there were no more cities. Long days passed traveling through bare desert; the desert that had seemed so exciting on the trip north. A cold night spent, the twenty-ninth of Athyr, with nothing but the light of a campfire, the faithful soldiers who had had abandoned

Horemheb to guard their way home taking watches through the long hours of darkness as jackals and hyenas yelped in the distance. The next night, as the terrain was smooth and the moon was bright, they rode through the night, drivers relieving one another hour by hour so each could get a wink of sleep. They found safety in continuing to move, past endless dunes lit silver by the moon god Khonsu's rays; dunes and valleys that might hide bandits that would like to slit their throats.

Finally they passed Per-Amun, a sign that they were getting somewhere. South, still south they journeyed, again finding towns where they could buy food and medicine from loyal Egyptians. Avaris, Per-Bast, cities Tut had visited before. Slowly but surely, they were getting closer to home.

As they got closer to home, and Tut could think more and more clearly, he thought of whom he was traveling toward. His beloved Queen; his loving big sister. He thought of the last conversation they had had, the one before they had said goodbye. He thought of her face as she had left the room. He thought of how he had hurt her. And how much he regretted every painful word he had said.

And he prayed and prayed to Whoever was listening that he would have the chance to apologize.

Another sudden thought popped into his mind. A thought that made Tut's eyes open wide as he stared up into his friend's face, heart pounding with anxiety.

"Are you hurt?" he asked through dry lips.

Semerkhet shook his head with a reassuring smile. "I'm all right," he said gently, reaching up to run a hand over Tut's head. Then he winced. But the smile returned. "I'm a little banged up," he admitted, "but it's nothing for you to worry about. Getting you home is all we're worried about."

Tutankhamun smiled, closing his eyes again. Sem might have some bumps and bruises, but he wasn't in danger. Soon they would be home. And the doctor would see them.

Semerkhet tried to keep track of roughly where they were; whenever the cart stopped, he asked the driver their current location. The trip had been long and miserable… but Semerkhet smiled when the driver told him it was almost over. They were passing through On, and would be home the next morning. The month of Sholiak was beginning, the fourth and final month of the Season of Inundation. Every day, a little more of the heat seemed to fade, and each night was chillier than the last. The cooler half of the year was beginning.

As they got closer to home, Tut and Sem had more chances to properly look at one another. And they chuckled. Because they could see the beards the two of them were growing; the stubble that had developed over the weeks they had spent away from their toiletries. And they knew that their heads also needed to be shaved. Just one more thing to look forward to about getting home.

"I'm thorry," the Pharaoh said again. Semerkhet opened his eyes as his friend's voice gently roused him from the drowse into which he had fallen.

"About what?" he asked softly.

Even in the dimness of the cart, Sem could see Tut frowning. "For ignoring you. I could thee thomething wath bothering you, but I never athked you what it wath. I'm thorry if I made you feel left out."

Semerkhet shook his head even as his heart warmed with gratitude. "It's all right," he said gently. "It's all right."

Tutankhamun swallowed loudly. "I thought… I thought Horemheb wath my friend."

There were a thousand ways that Semerkhet could have replied, but he did not. Just let the Pharaoh's words hang in the air between them.

"But you're my friend," Tut continued a moment later. "You're my friend."

And Semerkhet felt his heart melt as his friend went back to sleep.

Ankhesenamun paged through the Queens List again, carefully wiping away her tears so as not to let them fall on the delicate papyrus. This was the only copy, after all. And she found what her mother had written for her and her sisters about Pharaoh Hatshepsut.

As she read the familiar story of Hatshepsut's journey from Royal Daughter to Great Royal Wife to Lady of the Two Lands, Ankh's heart began to ache. Because she could see the similarities. Married to her frail younger brother, Hatshepsut had been left widowed without a son. As regent, she had guided her stepson and nephew, Thutmose the Third, as she had guided his father, her own baby brother. And before too long, seeing that her wisdom and experience were what Egypt needed, she had arranged for her own crowning, reigning for twenty-two successful years with her daughter Neferura beside her, fulfilling the duties of Queen much as Meritaten had done during the reign of her mother, Pharaoh Smenkhkare. It was all so familiar. So beautifully, painfully familiar.

Slowly Ankh rolled the papyrus back up, putting away the wise words of the past. And she swallowed. Could she do that? Succeed her little brother as Pharaoh in her own right, despite the fact that they had no son?

If she had to… could she do that?

This journey was impossibly different from the joyful ride that had taken the boys to Kadesh. Then they had been pumped, aching to get there as quickly as possible. They had been singing, smiling, laughing. Because they were going to be heroes.

Only… they weren't heroes. They were veterans now, yes, but heroes… not the glorious ones they might have hoped to become. On the battlefield, they had indeed become men. But they were roughed-up and worse, making their slow way home before victory was secure. Not cowards, not for a moment, but… neither of them was exactly Thutmose the First.

Semerkhet adjusted his painful legs, hearing the sleeping Pharaoh give a drowsy moan as Sem bumped him. The journey to Kadesh had flown by, because they had thought there would be glory at the end of it. This journey… was stretching out into eternity, days and nights blurring meaninglessly together. And there was no glory at the end of it. At the end of this journey… there was the uncertain hope that the Pharaoh would very simply be alive when they got home. And for Sem, another thing was certain. That he would be arrested.

He would live to get home, he knew. But would his Master? And even in returning home, would Semerkhet ever see Meresankh again?

"We should be home in the morning," Semerkhet said out of nowhere. The King opened his eyes, and somehow, he found himself giving a little smile. *Home.* The word sounded good.
"Good." And he drifted off again.

Sem thought of the past year, the fourteen months since Nedjes had died on his first hunt, leaving Semerkhet and his father alone in the world. Father had emotionally capsized, turning to drink. And he had blamed his older son for the loss of the precious thirteen-year-old, the favorite son, the miracle baby born to him and his sainted wife after so many years of trying.
Sem had spent a week navigating the irrational blame placed on him by his father for not having protected Nedjes, the drunken bellows that it should have been him that drowned, the deafening pounding on his locked bedroom door in the middle of the night that made him pray that he would not have to strike his own father in self-defense. By the end of that week, he had known that he could no longer remain in his childhood home. So he began searching for a job.
One month after Nedjes' death, Semerkhet had begun work at the palace, moving his small wagonload of possessions to his new home in the staff quarters while his oblivious father slept off a hangover. The note he had left would have to be enough.
First Semerkhet had served as a low-ranking footman, fetching and carrying for Hetepheres, the ancient nurse who still looked after the

Pharaoh even though he was a teenager. And when she had passed away after many, many years of service at the palace, Semerkhet had been promoted, rising to the rank of Attendant of the Lord of the Two Lands, the personal valet of the Pharaoh.

And somehow, over the months… he had become friends with his Master. And now Semerkhet sat in this cart beside his injured little brother as they made this long, long journey home.

"Shouldn't be much longer," Sem said after the dark had gone on what felt like an improbably long time. "Would you like me to put your wig back on you? Might not want a bare head with all the people who will want to see you right away. Show them… show them the Pharaoh is going to be all right. They do think you're a god, after all."

Tut gave a little smile. Sem was right. They would be surrounded by anxious servants and courtiers the moment they arrived at the palace. And it would be good to look his best. His best… under the circumstances, at least.

"Fank you," he lisped, giving a nod. And he tried to lift his head as Semerkhet slipped the familiar wig into place. As dirty and tangled as it was, it would make him look like a Pharaoh.

Ankhesenamun sat still as Meresankh put the finishing touches on her makeup after getting her dressed, in a long-sleeved dress and warm, yellow outer robe, one of the first times she had worn an outer robe this season. This morning, the second morning of the month of Sholiak, it was chilly.

She had spent enough days in the same dress, face unadorned by makeup, wig looking worse by the hour. Spent enough time grieving without even knowing whether the news was good or bad. She had needed that time, but she couldn't sit there, wait there, forever. She had to be strong, had to be Queen, even as she waited to find out what the rest of her life would look like. So today she had taken a deep breath and gotten her day going just like she always had, in the distant past before all this had begun.

I have a country to lead, she told herself, squaring her shoulders. *I need to be ready to do this all myself. It's possible that when they bring him home... he'll already be gone. Maybe I've seen him for the last time. If he comes home dead, then I will mourn, but until I find out, I should save my strength. Egypt needs me. Even if I may be leading alone.*

"My Lady?" A guard appeared in the doorway of her room.
The Queen looked up. And her heart began to pound.
"Yes?"
The guard gave the ghost of a smile. "The Pharaoh is home."
Ankhesenamun took off running, Bastet at her heels.

6

Home

What felt like years later, gentle hands found their way under his body, and slowly, Tutankhamun was settled into a stretcher, then carried from the cart to a sled and gently laid down again. Out of the corner of his eye he saw Semerkhet climbing stiffly out of the cart, and he thought he caught a glimpse of a pained grimace; heard a brief grunt of pain. He focused his gritty eyes and saw the familiar outlines of the palace; heard the birds singing in the gardens. Early-morning sunlight was turning everything pink and yellow; all the white alabaster sparkling dazzlingly, so bright after so long in the dimness of the cart, so bright that he kept blinking, his eyes stinging. At the temple, the priests would be greeting the sunrise with morning prayers. They were home.

"Darling!" A shriek echoed through the courtyard and Tut felt the movement stop. Sobbing and panting, Ankh scrambled up onto the sled and sat beside him, gathering him desperately into her arms and placing his head on her lap, bending to kiss him over and over as she hugged him as though she would never let him go. "How bad are you— where are you—" She pulled away the blanket, revealing the splints on both his legs.

Eyes half open, squinting in the dazzling brightness, tired mouth finding its way into a smile, he groped for her hand. She gave it to him. He had never realized how small and soft her hand was before. Or how warm. He was so cold. "Darling..." she whispered, her body shaking as she sobbed. "I heard... I was so worried... didn't know if you were..."

"Ankh," he choked, squeezing her hand as hard as he could as he squinted at her through tired, fuzzy, watering eyes. His first thought was that he was glad she was safe.

"We'll get you home," she whispered, stroking his face. Tears spilled from her sparkling eyes; her makeup was running all over her pretty brown face. He kept blinking in the brightness, eyes struggling to focus. "You'll be all right."

In the distance, Tut heard more feet, more voices, loud and frightened. The staff had realized he was home. Slowly the sounds rose in volume as more servants gathered, running toward them as the sled bearing the Pharaoh moved closer and closer to the palace.

Suddenly they came into view like a swarm of locusts. Every servant in the palace seemed to have converged on them. Gasping, whispering, weeping in confusion and breathless concern, they crowded around the sled and its occupants, trying to catch a glimpse of the King, waiting for their instructions. Tut felt Sem squeeze his hand— had he been walking alongside the sled?— and saw him begin to walk toward the palace, pointing this way and that as he directed the other servants. The King knew he'd caught a flash of red on Semerkhet's leg as his friend turned around, and as he walked away, he was definitely favoring his right leg. The cloud of worried staff began to disperse, following the valet inside to prepare the palace for the wounded Pharaoh.

They began moving again, slowly. It was like riding in the palanquin, the Pharaoh thought with almost a smile, only a thousand times less fun. Tut could hear, far away, that many of the servants who were still walking with them were crying as they chanted prayers together. And someone was running toward the temple to tell the priests what had happened. Was he going to die? As they moved, Ankh continued stroking his wig, caressing his head, kissing his hands, trying to comfort him. He gave her a little smile and closed his eyes, trying to go away to a place without pain.

It felt good to rest in her lap. Warm, safe, loved. He was too tired, in too much pain, for very elaborate thoughts, but he was glad he was with Ankh. And glad he was home.

Meresankh ran out of her Queen's room, wig-comb still in her hand. She could hear loud voices; sobs, even. The Pharaoh was home. And the sobs were happy enough, and few enough, for her to be sure that he was alive. The other servants weren't tearing at their wigs, beating their chests, or striking their heads against the ground as they would if he had come home dead. Her prayers had been answered.

Her heart began to pound as she joined the crowd, hurrying along as other servants jostled her from the sides, bumped into her from behind. Had Semerkhet come home too?

Thank you for protecting the Pharaoh, she prayed breathlessly inside her heart as she ran. *Please let Semerkhet be safe. Let him be home.*

Ankh clutched her husband to her heart as they rode toward the palace. He was alive. Alive. Glory be. Heavy and solid in her lap, blinking up at her and trying to hold her hand. The weight of the pyramids seemed to lift from her shoulders. He was alive. And he was home.

Morning had barely broken, and in early Sholiak, the daybreak was chilly. But the Pharaoh had a blanket over him, and his sister's warm lap to lie in. And he would keep her warm too, until they got inside.

It was so bright. He kept his eyes shut as they moved, not ready for the sun after so many hours in the dimness of the cart. It would be dimmer in the palace. And it wouldn't be long before his eyes readjusted.

Semerkhet got out of the cart, blinking in the bright early-morning sunlight, wincing as he forced his right knee to walk. It took him a moment to get his balance after so many hours of cramped stillness in the cart; he had to get his circulation going again. All around him other servants were crowding, whispering, pointing, trying to get a glimpse of the Pharaoh, some starting to cry. He squeezed his Master's hand and began leading, calling for the others to follow him into the palace. And once he was there, he began administrating, directing the others to call the doctor, alert the priests, get the furniture moved so the stretcher would fit into the room. He had a role to play. And he would play it.

In the middle of the crowd, Meresankh kept squinting in the early-morning sunshine, trying to pick Semerkhet out of the crowd. He was there somewhere, even if she hadn't found him yet. Had to be. Of course he was.

She kept looking, kept squinting, putting her arms around herself as she shivered. It was chilly this morning. Men and women rushed around, some she recognized, a few she didn't. Still no Semerkhet.

Her heart began to pound as she sent up a frantic prayer. Could it be that…

A flapping of fabric caught her eye; someone else was getting out of the cart that had brought the Pharaoh home. And relief hit Meresankh square in the heart. Semerkhet was home.

Her prayer of fear turned into a prayer of thanks. Her beloved was home. Her prayers had been answered.

After what felt like hours, the large sled finally came to a halt. The same gentle, careful hands lifted the King and slowly carried him inside on the stretcher, Ankhesenamun running alongside, trying to keep her hand in his limp one. He could hear her delicate little sandals flapping on the ground as she hurried along. "I'm right here; I'm right here, darling," she kept saying. He knew that; he'd never once forgotten that she was right beside him, but he appreciated her reminding him.

They were inside the palace now, and it was comfortably dim after the brightness of morning. Everyone who wasn't carrying the King was running around the room like so many locusts, moving things, bringing things in, clearing a path to the royal bedroom, preparing a soft bed to lay him on. And Semerkhet was directing them all. Three other servants dashed away to summon the doctors. They would help him, Tutankhamun reflected as the people carrying him slowly transferred him to the bed, thickly padded with all the pillows they could find. All his furniture had been hastily moved, but how else would they have gotten the stretcher into the room? Everyone was whispering to one another, and Tut thought he could hear someone crying. For him?

Ankh was by his side in an instant, sitting at his head, letting him lay his head in her lap as before. She took his ruined wig off him and started bathing his head with a cold, wet cloth that had appeared out of nowhere, in the hands of one of the servants. That felt nice. Then there was a shallow cup of water, and he drank until he was satisfied, Ankh gently helping him lift his head. Semerkhet was there too, not saying a word, but standing at the foot of the bed as if silently guarding him. Tut knew he would be faithful to the end.

He sank into the soft bed, exhausted, aching body filling with relief. Somehow he had never truly realized just how wonderfully soft his bed was. Even after Tribute Day, he had never fully appreciated it.

Someone at his other end had hold of one leg. Tut opened one eye, lifted his head a little, and tried to focus on what they were doing. They were just elevating his splinted legs and putting pillows under them so he'd be more comfortable until the Chief Physician came in. Wasn't that thoughtful. For some reason the movement didn't hurt all that much.

No one spoke. The servants stared at the injured Pharaoh with large, worried eyes, some with makeup running down their faces with their tears, but no one said a word. Shepset, Kamose, Tentamun, Nuya, all torn from their day's work by the sudden emergency. Not Kahotep, but he was retired. They watched him, heartbroken, terrified by what had happened, but they did not speak to him. They were too afraid. Of what had happened, and of him. Meresankh's gossiping campaign had not been as effective as he had hoped.

Tut heard the sound of tiny, furry feet padding into the room; heard a questioning chirrup. He opened one eye again to see Bastet coming to see him.

"Hello, kitty," he whispered as she approached, pausing to sniff the bruised hand he held out to her. She looked up at him, and he thought he saw real concern on her face. Somehow, in some cat way, she understood. Bastet walked up to the bed, legs moving like a tiny lioness, then gracefully hopped up beside her Master, curling up softly against his chest. Tut closed his eyes again, feeling her warmth, her breathing, her soft, gray fur, her gentle presence. He lifted a hand and laid it on the soft, warm fur of her back, feeling her purr.

He was home. Ankhesenamun held her husband tight, feeling his warmth, his aliveness. Hurt, but alive. Glory be; praise all the gods from Amun to Aten. He was home.

Tut felt her holding him; felt her warmth, her strength, her steady breathing. She was so small, so soft. She held him tight, supporting him, comforting him. Sometimes she rocked him. Safe in his wife's arms, Tut was surprised to find himself smiling. Because he was home.

But that didn't mean that every single part of his body didn't hurt. Because it did.

He was home. But he was hurt, in pain, broken legs supported only by the simple splints put on by the army doctor. The Queen sat up a little straighter, biting her lip as her brother groaned at the movement.

"Sorry," she whispered, running a gentle hand over his right cheek, the side of his face that was less badly beat-up than the other. "Where is the Chief Physician?" she asked the room at large in a voice that was gentle but commanding. "The Pharaoh is wounded."

"The Chief Physician will be here momentarily, Your Majesty," Raherka said quickly, offering a deep bow. "He is preparing his materials."

Ankhesenamun nodded. "Thank you, Raherka. In the meantime, can someone at least make some more chamomile tea?"

"I'm thorry," Tut whispered, the word coming out as a lisp. "Tho thorry... I should have lithened... and everything I thaid... I do need you... I'm tho..."

"Sh-sh-shh," Ankh hushed him, rocking him again, even as his apology touched her heart like a soothing balm. "You're home safe. And that's all that matters."

Half a minute later, she smiled down at him again. "But thank you." She paused. "I'm sorry too. If I ever made you feel like I was holding you back."

He just shook his head with a little smile, even as he was grateful for her words. Forgiven, he raised his face for a kiss, and forgiving, she gave him a kiss on the forehead.

The doctors came in ten minutes after Tut had been installed in bed. Finally. The Chief Physician strode across the polished stone floor faster than Tutankhamun had ever seen him move his overweight self anywhere, white robes billowing behind him, sandals flapping on his fat feet, flanked by four nervous other doctors.

"O Great Morning Star, I am so sorry this has befallen you—" He prostrated himself on the floor for an instant, groveling on his knees, then, recognizing the urgency of the situation, popped back up again, faster than Tut had ever seen him do it. Why, of all times, were things funny now? Especially when it hurt to laugh?

"Get up, man!" the Queen all but snapped. "My husband is wounded. Stop wasting time!"

"Yes, My Lady; yes, My Lady," the doctor groveled. And the Pharaoh almost laughed again. His sister would take care of him no matter what.

Tut hardly attended to what the doctor said, but Ankh listened to him intently, staring at him and hanging on every word, blue beads jingling as she nodded in response to every bit of instruction. She would take care of it for him. Right now he just needed to rest.

The Physician took the Pharaoh's bruised wrist between his fingers, checking his pulse, peered into each of his eyes, made sure that even despite the pain of moving them, he was able to feel and move his legs and feet, as well as his hands and arms. He checked the interior of Tut's mouth, peeked into his ears, checked that his arms and torso were relatively undamaged. He had to get a clear picture of Tut's injuries in order to treat him.

Then the examination seemed to be over. Dimly Tutankhamun heard the doctor say, "The abrasions and bruises I can treat, and I can contend with the broken bones." Those were the three categories into which doctors arranged injuries and illnesses— curable, contend-able, and pain control.

The Chief Physician left, having placed new wooden splints on each leg with the help of the others, which Tut had barely noticed. He also had a poultice of chamomile and onions tied to each leg, as well as a smaller one over the scrapes on his face (without the onion). There was also a salve they could use later for the bruises and scrapes that covered every inch of his body, made with everything from rosemary to comfrey to daisy leaves, blended together with a base of coconut oil. But despite all this care, every breath still brought pain.

7

Rest

The doctor turned away from the King and saw Semerkhet leaning against a chair, trying to rest his right leg.

"Let me see that, young man," he said, beckoning. Gratefully Semerkhet sat down in the chair, letting the doctor examine his knee and dab it clean with a cloth. To Sem's relief, there was no evidence of infection; the area was just extremely raw. Finally the doctor bandaged it, leaving Semerkhet with his own little jar of the same salve he had made up for the King. The valet allowed himself a little smile. It felt good to be looked after. And much to his surprise and delight, the doctor had treated him as though he were every bit as much a person as the Pharaoh. Maybe his Master's new philosophy was wearing off on the people around him.

Later on an old maidservant came and washed the Pharaoh, dabbing his face, head, arms, hands, and feet with a damp cloth. For a moment he thought it was Rahonem, but this woman was plumper, her hands sure but not quite as gentle, without the experience of a doctor. As she methodically moved the rag over his bruised, scraped body, he felt like a piece of clothing or furniture being washed, not a person being bathed.

It was nothing like when Sem helped him with his shower, a moment of care and connection.

She didn't say anything; avoided his eye and acted as though she was afraid to touch him, but had to. All he could do was vaguely try to smile at her. And at some point, someone changed him into a fresh sleeping-tunic, taking away the torn, dirty garment that was still flecked with the blood of Egyptian and Hittite warriors. Slipping into a drowse, he never noticed who had done it. Being moved, jostled around, in order to be washed, was exhausting.

He did notice, however, that this anonymous person had taken a moment to grease him up with his favorite moisturizer. And what a relief it was. His skin had been so itchy, and his lips and the backs of his hands had been cracked and bleeding. But now, over his arms, his hands, his torso, even his knees, he could feel the ointment soaking into his thirsty skin. It felt good to be clean. And it felt good to breathe in the familiar fragrances of spikenard and frankincense.

Semerkhet hurried around the room fetching, carrying, making himself as useful as possible as he directed the other servants a mile a minute. The King did notice, however, that he was moving a bit stiffly, and with the tiniest bit of a limp, as if he were in pain. And the doctor had had a look at him, too, after splinting Tut's legs, and now there was a bandage on Sem's right knee, right where Tut had seen a flash of red. Had he been bleeding all the way home, but chosen to conceal it from the Pharaoh?

Then there was a soft knock at the door, and Semerkhet hurried over, taking just a moment to greet someone before returning to his Lord and Master. The Pharaoh smiled, even though he could have had Sem punished for having mixed-up priorities. Tut could see that Meresankh was glad Semerkhet had come home safely.

Meresankh forced herself to wait; to hang back until the hubbub had passed. The Pharaoh came first in all things, and he had to be cleaned up and put to bed before anyone could even think about anything else. She stood at the door of the Pharaoh's room, waiting.

Finally all was quiet. And she took her chance. Quietly, she knocked on the door.

It flew open, and there he was, her Semerkhet, tall, and strong, and alive. Laughing for sheer joy, she flew into his arms, feeling him pick her up and swing her around, then bend down and kiss her.

"I'm home," he whispered, holding her tight.

"You're home," she whispered back.

And he was back in the room, going back to work. Five seconds was all he had.

Meresankh sighed, heart still pounding for joy. He was home. Alive… and hurt. There was a bandage on his right knee, a nasty bruise on his left knee and one on his upper arm, and various scratches on his limbs. But what did that matter, now that he was home, now that she saw he was alive?

The other thing she had noticed… something that made her almost chuckle… was that he needed to shave.

The valet smiled, heart warming inside him. He had been bad, he knew, taking a moment for himself at a time like this, but he had had to do it. And it had taken only about five seconds. He had had to greet Meresankh… and let her kiss him.

Then Tutankhamun suddenly noticed how quiet it had become. The servants, having finished their sudden flurry of work in helping him get settled, had disappeared, returning to their daily work and fearfully leaving their god-king in peace. His sister held his hand, watching him carefully, and she helped him take a sip of water when he wanted. But she was quiet for the moment. She knew he didn't feel like talking.

The stillness… was beautiful. After nearly a week of the constant rumbling and creaking of the cart as it crunched and bumped over the rough roads, the soft quietness embraced him; welcomed him like the softness of the bed he was comfortably sinking into. And he smiled. He felt better already.

Semerkhet sat in a chair on the other side of the bed, silently guarding his Master. He didn't say much, but Tut was grateful that he could feel his brother's presence. Because that was what he was. His brother.

Ankh and Sem sat on each side of the bed, each holding one of the Pharaoh's hands. He didn't want to talk, but they wanted him to know they were near. They guarded him, keeping an eye on the door, admitting only the doctor. Curious servants stood there in the doorway, trying to peek in, get just a glimpse of the injured god-king, but Semerkhet kept them out. The Pharaoh needed to rest.

Then Tut woke up for a few minutes, and they gave him a little chamomile tea. And Ankh got up from her chair and sat beside him on the bed, letting him rest his head in her lap.

Ankhesenamun gazed down at the sleeping husband whose head was resting in her lap, feeling his warm, living weight on her legs. Gently she stroked his head; the fine hairs that were growing on his usually-shaved scalp. And, shaking her head with the smallest of chuckles, she admired the scraggly young beard that was growing on his chin and jawline. Her baby brother was growing up.

Tutankhamun was home. He was safe. His wounds were treated, he was clean, and the bed was very comfortable. Nice and warm on this cool Sholiak day, after those cold nights in that cart. His sister's lap was also very comfortable, as were her soft little arms that were wrapped around him. He actually smiled as he realized that as of now, it was cool enough to snuggle; cool enough to wrap up in blankets. But with every breath he took, he was still in pain.

He closed his eyes and tried to rest.

Meresankh hurried down to her Granny's workshop. And she told her that the Pharaoh was alive and ready to begin his recovery, and that Semerkhet was all right too. Together they rejoiced, and together they prayed for the Pharaoh and for Semerkhet to recover. And together they smiled as they felt the warmth touch their hearts. Just like always, they knew they had been heard.

Even on a day like this, the first day she had seen her husband in nearly a month and the first day she had seen him after not being sure she ever would again, Ankh needed a moment. The shock of almost losing him had been unbearable, but the shock of having him back was also overwhelming. Delightfully so, but after six solid hours of doctors flapping around the room, servants scurrying about, and the combined stress and confusion coalescing in an exhausting vibe that hung so heavily in the air she could almost see it, she needed a short break. So she had kissed him, squeezed his hand, and walked across the hall to her own room. Now she was lying back in her favorite chair with her feet up.

She needed time to readjust. Even readjusting to the happiest thing that had ever happened to her was not going to be accomplished in the space of a heartbeat.

Meresankh poured her a cup of tea. Ankh took it with a sigh, slowly sipping at it. The peppermint was refreshing, and she had not realized how thirsty she had gotten.

"He's safe."

The handmaiden smiled. "Our prayers have been answered."

The Queen nodded, her blue beads clinking. Whichever god had answered them, hers or Meresankh's, they had been. "They have." Then she looked at Meresankh. She, too, had just welcomed her beloved home from war. "How is Semerkhet?"

Meresankh grinned, and Ankhesenamun saw the dimple in her cheek. Just for an instant, because it disappeared as the handmaiden gave a sigh, her face growing serious. "He's alive," she said slowly. "I only saw him for a few seconds, but he was walking." Meresankh swallowed, her eyes flickering to her Lady's face. "How is the Pharaoh?" she whispered.

The Queen shrugged with a tired smile. "Home," she said. "Alive. It's..." She sighed, looking down. "It's going to be a long recovery. But he's safe now, so it can start." She sighed again, now looking up to smile at her friend. "Thank you for your prayers," she whispered.

Meresankh smiled, boldly extending her soft little hand. The Queen took it gratefully, and they shared a sisterly clasp. "Always, My Lady."

There were many more things Meresankh wanted to say, but she bit her tongue; held them back. Their Pharaoh was injured, after all— the Morning and the Evening Star, the Lord of the Two Lands, seen by his people as a god among men. And Semerkhet... well, he was just Meresankh's boyfriend. Right now... right now, Meresankh had to defer; defer completely. The Morning and the Evening Star lay wounded— she could keep her concerns about her own one true love within her own heart. And as she had spoken with the Queen, Meresankh had felt I-AM gently restraining her from saying very much about Semerkhet.

As much as she wanted to share her thoughts and feelings with her friend, her sister, the time was not right. Because her Queen was hurting. And how unkind would it be to rejoice in front of her because Semerkhet had only gotten a few scrapes and bruises? Would that... would that even suggest that he possessed a level of bravery that the Pharaoh did not— that the fact that Semerkhet was a better warrior in some way had allowed him to come home safe while her Queen's husband was wounded?

Meresankh had no information on the battle, and had no idea if or how bravery or combat skills had played into who had been wounded and who had not. But it was not something to talk about right now. That she knew. And she would express continual concern for their Pharaoh while saying very little about Semerkhet, until her Queen gave her a sign that she was free to speak.

The chattiest member of the palace staff would wait in prayerful silence until I-AM told her the time was right.

Ankh sipped her tea. Coming home from battle wounded. Not anything she ever would have expected to happen to her husband, her baby brother. Now the legs that had always struggled to get him around were broken. And the recovery would be long and hard. Who knew what lay ahead of them; how the other politicians might try to take back their power while the Pharaoh lay recovering. Who knew what battles lay before them.

But through it all, she knew there was purpose. Still undiscovered, still waiting to be uncovered, shrouded in shadow. But it gave her hope to think that it was there. Hope... in what she had not yet seen with her own eyes, but was waiting for with as much perseverance as she could muster.

She sent up a prayer of thanks that he was home... and felt it echo back to her in empty silence. And she wondered, like she sometimes wondered about Tawaret's impassive unresponsiveness, how many of her prayers were even heard.

Semerkhet sat quietly with his Pharaoh while the Queen took a well-deserved break in her chambers. They were home. His tired mind could hardly believe it. Home. Safe. And they were both alive.

Sem looked down at his Master, drowsing in the bed. The Pharaoh's face was bruised, scraped, and scratched; so were his arms, one of which was wrapped gently around the snoozing cat. And his broken legs had been carefully splinted. Now he could begin to heal.

They were holding hands. The Pharaoh didn't want to talk, but he needed to know that his friend, his brother, was near. So Semerkhet gave him his hand, and he fell asleep holding it.

Before the Queen had excused herself, Semerkhet had poured himself a cup of tea, and he sat there sipping it, the gentle chamomile helping him melt into the chair as a wave of drowsiness overtook him, even in the middle of the morning. What heavenly relief to be able to drink as much tea as he wanted, finally relieving the thirstiness that had ached in his throat for the past week. Someone had even been kind enough to bring in a footstool, and gratefully, he rested his tired feet, feeling his body truly relax for the first time in a month.

The valet lay his head back in his chair, closing his eyes for a moment. He wasn't going to go to sleep... but he was grateful to be able to rest for a few minutes.

The Pharaoh rested as much as he could that afternoon. His pain was surprisingly minimal; he could actually ignore it well enough to go to sleep. And he was so tired. He napped on and off, and whenever he opened his eyes, Semerkhet was there. He got Tut water when he wanted it; adjusted his pillows and blankets when they got out of place. But mostly, he was simply there, holding Tut's hand, the warmth of his strong hand making the Pharaoh feel safe, reassured, connected. And Tut was grateful.

Sometime later, Tut opened his eyes to see Ankh coming into the room. Apparently she had taken a little break. That was probably good, he thought. What a day it was for her with him suddenly being home. She had something balanced in her hands; something that smelled delicious.

"Dinnertime," she said softly, sitting down beside him. Now he could see what she was carrying— a bowl of broth. Semerkhet got up to sample it, then handed it back to the Queen with a nod.

Tut smiled and opened his mouth, and carefully his sister spooned in a bite. His stomach groaned appreciatively as the rich, warm broth made its way down his throat, the first real food he had had in days.

That was all it was, broth. That was probably good, though; he had hardly eaten anything since his fall. It would be wise to start slowly.

He smiled as he ate. "Tastes good," he whispered. "Nithe treat after poppy gruel and lukewarm water out of a leather skin."

Ankh smiled and shook her head sympathetically, blue beads jingling. "You have as much as you want."

He took another bite, savoring the rich, warm, beefy flavor. There were onions in it too, for flavor. For something so simple, it was delicious.

Tut finished the broth in silence. When it was gone, Ankh set the bowl aside and used a bit of linen to wipe away the few stray drops of broth that had stayed behind in his peach-fuzz teen moustache.

"Now let's get you tucked in. It's been a long day."

The King nodded with a yawn. He tried to think back to where he had been when he had woken up this morning— in a horse-cart a few miles outside Memphis. That seemed years ago. And the time before he had gone to Amurru felt a lifetime ago.

But he was home now. And it was time for bed.

Semerkhet slept on the floor that first night home. He was stiff, sore, and exhausted, knee throbbing. And, although he had been able to wash his hands and face and relieve his hunger and thirst with as much soup and tea as he wanted, he was itchy and sweaty and still smelled like smoke and blood. But it was more comfortable than the cart, and at least he had enough blankets to be warm. And those little bits of discomfort were not even worth bothering about. Because his Pharaoh was alive. And they were home.

The Pharaoh slept in his sister's lap, warm and safe in his own soft bed. He was clean, and bandaged, and his stomach was full.

So that meant that he could really, truly rest. And he slept long and deeply, getting a good, solid, restful, healing night's sleep for what felt like the first time in years.

Ankhesenamun slept in her husband's room, sitting on the bed with his head in her lap. It wasn't comfortable, but she relished it; being able to hold him, feeling his strong, warm, living weight in her lap, his steady breathing, his strong heartbeat. He was home.

8

Bruises

Every inch of his body hurt. The King craned his neck to look down at his own body the next morning; his sleeveless under-tunic revealed an impressive assortment of bruises and scrapes running all the way down each arm from his aching shoulders to his hands. Peeking under his tunic, he could see more bruises on his chest and stomach, and he could feel more on his back and shoulders. And of course, his legs were broken on the inside as well as beaten up on the surface. He hadn't seen a mirror yet, but he knew that he had a large scrape on the left side of his face, and the area around his left eye felt swollen. There was very little of him that wasn't going to slowly turn purple, then green, before the bruises finally healed.

Coming home after Tribute Day, he had thought he had been in pain. What he wouldn't give to have that day back. What he wouldn't give to have his old problems back. He would celebrate the things that used to burden him.

A reasonably good night's sleep had left the Queen feeling refreshed— although with a stiff neck. Tut had fallen asleep in her arms, and she'd slept beside him all night, keeping him as comfortable as possible even as she struggled to drift off. And now she was ready; ready to readjust and to devote all her energy to taking care of her brother, her husband, her brave warrior.

They had a long road ahead of them.

The Queen's stomach twisted as she dipped an alabaster spoon into the little ceramic jar of bruise salve the doctor had prepared. She let it melt in her hand, ready to dab it gently onto her husband, who sat quietly on the bed, splinted legs dangling off the side. That was a good sign; he was able to sit up, at least for a few minutes. All he had on at the moment was his loincloth, so she could get to all the bruises, but she felt like she could hardly see any of him. Almost every inch of his warm, brown skin was mottled with purple bruises. And that black eye would take awhile to heal.

Even a year ago, she had been sorry for the daily pain he had to contend with. She had never imagined something like this. At least there was something she could do. Except… that even this might make the pain worse.

"All right," she said, taking a deep breath, "just tell me if it hurts." He nodded, and, with her own wince, she got started.

Carefully she smeared the salve onto his skin, watching his face. He closed his eyes, then squeezed them shut as his jaw tightened. She bit her lip, wondering if she should stop.

"Is that too much?" she asked softly as she smoothed the ointment over his left arm, touching him as lightly as she could.

He shook his head, eyes still closed. His shoulders had stiffened, rising to just below his ears, and his hands had slowly clenched, knuckles white. A little crease had formed between his eyebrows, which had drawn together.

"It'th all right," he muttered through set teeth. But there was pain in his voice; a tightness just like she could see in his shoulders. She bit her lip again. She hated seeing him become more tense because of something she was doing, rather than relaxing at her touch. But this needed to be done. And although the doctor, or Semerkhet, could do it just as easily, why not her?

She moved on to his right arm, carefully covering the purple bruises in the healing salve. It smelled good; smelled like every flower in the garden and every herb in the kitchen all at once. "Well…" she said with a little smile, "another day or two and they won't hurt so much, and then… putting it on might be kind of nice."

Tut opened his eyes and smiled. "I'll look forward to that."

Then Ankh giggled. "You suppose there are any crocodile eyeballs in it?"

He just chuckled. And a tiny bit of the tension melted away as they laughed together.

"I'm juth glad," Tut said a moment later, "that I can fink again; talk again. Now that I don't need the poppy, I'm really starting to feel like mythelf again."

"I'm glad," Ankh said sincerely. And she kissed him on the forehead.

Tut looked up at his wife as he lay with his head in her lap, trying to rest as she stroked his head, rubbed his hands, hummed to him. He was rather tired from sitting up for the few minutes that had somehow felt like a very long time. "I'm thorry I didn't listen," he whispered again, his weariness even after such a good night's sleep bringing out his lisp. He knew he was forgiven for the harsh words he'd spoken, but there was more. "Thorry I jumped ahead without talking to you first. Like you said. And like I thaid I would. Let you… protect me."

She shook her head with a frown, blue beads echoing her disagreement. "No, no. Don't worry about that. Don't even think about it. No one could have known what would happen."

"No…" And as he thought back to the dim memory he had of Horemheb's trumpet blowing and every single soldier retreating, he hoped she was right.

Then she gave a little smile. "And you are growing up."

He bit his lip as his heart warmed. Now it ached even more.

"He's doing a bit better," the Queen said, walking into her chambers the morning after the Pharaoh had come home.

Meresankh set aside the wig she was untangling and smiled up at her Mistress. "Oh, that is good to hear," she said with a smile. But even so, it was a quiet smile. A smile that didn't want to be too excited about anything at this stage. Even the Pharaoh.

"He's... he's not out of danger, but the first night... he's through the first night. And the first night is always the most important." Happy tears glimmered in Ankhesenamun's eyes, and she opened her arms, pulling Meresankh in for a brief hug. "He's going to make it," she whispered.

Meresankh hugged her back. "Oh, glory be," she whispered back. Slowly Ankh let her go, and they stepped apart with heavy sighs of joy and gratitude.

Then the Queen gave half a little smile, and she extended her hand. Meresankh took it with a smile, waiting for what Ankh was going to say next.

"I just wanted to say..." she said softly, "that it's all right. It's all right to be happy around me, that Semerkhet doesn't have any broken bones. I'm... I'm happy for you; I really am. I'm very happy that all he has is bruises. So please... don't worry. And please..." She smiled at her handmaiden. "Be happy."

Meresankh squeezed the Queen's hand and grinned. "Yes, My Lady."

Ankh paused, looking out the window with a sigh. Then she looked at her friend again. "Do you have any information about the battle?" she asked. "Anything at all?"

Meresankh shook her head. "No, My Lady. I've hardly seen Semerkhet since he's been back, and he hasn't told me anything."

"Talk to him," Ankh said earnestly. "Ask him what happened. Because I want to know. And I don't... I don't know if the Pharaoh remembers anything. But I know Semerkhet could tell us exactly what happened. And I want to know."

"I will," Meresankh said with a smile. "So do I."

"How were things while I wath gone?" Tut asked when his sister came into the room after a short break.

He looked up to see Ankh shrug. "Odd," she said finally with a slow nod. "A lot of whispering. I stayed out of it, and none of them said anything to me other than to say hello in the hallway. Ay, Maya, they did seem secretive... What *is* going on?" She frowned at him, face darkening. "Why won't you tell me? When we first worked on the new budget, we did it together. You've always told me everything. I've always been right there, helping you. And now... I don't know, but I know there's something you're not telling me." She swallowed. "I want to help. What could there be that you don't want to tell me?"

Tut shook his head. "I'm not sure mythelf," he said softly. "And I don't want to make any accusations before I am."

She sighed, her frown almost accusing. "We've always shared everything. Why won't you trust me with this?" Her longing to learn his secrets ached in her voice.

He shook his head and gave her a little smile. "I trust you most of all. But for now, I need you to trust me. It's not that I don't trust you; I want to keep you thafe."

Ankh shook her head. "I'm supposed to keep *you* safe. Not the other way around. I'm the one who's supposed to be protecting you. I'm the one who says 'it's just politics.' That's my line. Not yours."

"And you are keeping me safe," he said with another little smile. "I'd be lost without you. And I know that'th not my line, but it's all I can say... You've always kept me safe, and now it's my turn to keep you thafe." He looked down and squeezed her hand, smile fading. "I don't want to... be without you."

She shuddered. She knew what he meant.

"I wish I was Pharaoh instead of you," Ankh whispered. "Then I could keep you safe."

He just smiled and squeezed her hand.

Tut sighed. "It's strange... Something I can't quite catch, can't quite remember, thomething thomeone thaid that was important... If I'm keeping a secret from you, it's because I don't know myself. But when I figure it out, I'll tell you."

Ankh nodded solemnly and bent to kiss him on the forehead. She didn't look satisfied; she looked resigned for the moment.

"Promise?"

He smiled. He knew she would hold him to it.

"Promise."

Semerkhet went to the doorway of the Pharaoh's room, opening the door to set a basket of dirty laundry in the hallway for pickup by the Handlers of Royal Linen. Someone was waiting for him.

"Meresankh," he said with a smile. He set the basket on the floor and opened his arms, dirty as he still was, and she hugged him, holding him tight.

"Can I come in?" she asked.

"Of course," the Queen said from inside the room, where she sat at the Pharaoh's side.

"Tell us what happened," Meresankh said, pulling Semerkhet back into the Pharaoh's room. "Both of us."

"All three of uth," the Pharaoh chimed in from where he sat in the bed, awake for the moment. "I'm sure there are plenty of thingth I don't remember."

Semerkhet sighed. And he took his customary seat at the Pharaoh's other side. "Well... we traveled for two weeks, and after we got to the camp in Kadesh, we spent the next few days preparing. And then, one morning... it was time to ride out. The Pharaoh made a speech..." He looked proudly at his friend, "and we rode out. I drove the horses, and he fought as an archer. And it was... well, I can hardly say that it was going well, but the Pharaoh was protecting us in one direction and I was holding our shield in the other direction and driving, and we were... we were fighting the Hittites." His stomach turned within him as he remembered all the implications of the phrase "fighting the Hittites." "And the mighty hunter has proven himself to be a mighty warrior. But then..."

Semerkhet swallowed, looking down at his hands, clenched in his lap. And pain filled his heart as he remembered. "Something happened that neither of us could have accounted for. A trumpet sounded, and the next thing we knew, our men had retreated. And before we could do anything… a Hittite arrow struck one of the horses, and the whole chariot crashed to the ground."

Ankhesenamun had been gazing intently into Semerkhet's face with every word he spoke, eyes growing wider and wider. Now she gasped, clutching her skirt with one hand and Meresankh's hand with the other as tears came to her eyes.

"And then?" Meresankh whispered as she patted the Queen's shoulder.

Semerkhet swallowed. "And then… I jumped." His face fell as guilt twisted inside him, and he clenched his hands until his nails bit into his palms. "I… I saved my own life. And I fell… and I rolled… and I looked to see if I was alive. And then…" He looked up again, tears sparkling in his eyes. "I found the Pharaoh. And I… I held him… I waited with him while the same men who had abandoned us protected us with their shields. And they brought a stretcher to carry him off the field… and the camp doctor splinted his legs… and we spent another horrible week in that cart… and I helped as much as I could… and finally, we made it home."

Meresankh flew over and threw her arms around Semerkhet. Smiling back his tears, he held her close, delighting in feeling her close to him, the sweet, soft, little friend he had missed so much.

The Queen was also wiping away tears, makeup smearing on her face. And she reached out and gratefully touched Semerkhet's shoulder, just for an instant.

"You saved his life," she whispered.

Semerkhet dipped his head. "I did my duty."

Ankhesenamun lay back in her chair as Meresankh went back to her day's work and Semerkhet tidied what needed tidied, which wasn't much. Semerkhet had saved her brother's life. And he had brought him home safely, despite his own pain. He had done everything possible to bring Tut home. And he had succeeded.

And Ankh was grateful.

Semerkhet had saved the Pharaoh's life, Meresankh thought as she polished the Queen's jewelry with a soft cloth. He had defended him and heroically overseen his journey home, bringing him home alive. And all while being hurt himself.

I-AM had truly used Semerkhet in a miracle.

Then she chuckled as a sudden realization hit her. She had never been in the Pharaoh's room before. But… the Queen had invited her in, and she had comported herself appropriately, listening to Semerkhet's story and then excusing herself; not standing around gawking.

But what a thing, all the same. Meresankh shook her head. She never would have thought of walking into the Pharaoh's room.

Semerkhet had saved his life. Tutankhamun's mind was filled with dim memories of the battle and its aftermath, but he could hardly put it in order. He knew that Sem had been with him every moment since his injury, but he hadn't known every piece of what his valet had done.

His friend had jumped. Kept himself alive so that he could save the Pharaoh. And Tut was incredibly grateful.

The Pharaoh was safe. Semerkhet sat watching him lying there in bed, the Queen tending to him. And he realized just how tired he was. And how dirty. His Master was so flexible and forgiving; surely he wouldn't mind if his valet slipped out for just a minute or two to freshen up?

The Pharaoh's eyes were closed; Sem wasn't sure if he was awake or asleep. But he could ask the Queen's permission to take a short break. Very quietly Semerkhet got up, offering the Queen a questioning smile, raising his eyebrows, and nodding at the door. She responded with her own smile and a nod, and, with a brief bow and a whispered wish for his Master's well-being, he crept out the bedroom door and into the hallway.

He ran straight into six frowning, spear-bearing guards. Two of them grabbed his arms with large, unfriendly hands while a third snapped cold, heavy iron manacles onto his wrists.

"You're coming with us."

9

Alone

"My Lord." Tutankhamun opened his eyes as he heard Ay's voice. The Vizier hurried into the room, robes flying behind him, grandfatherly face a picture of concern. The Queen got up, walking across the room to give them a moment without being too far away. "My Lord." The Vizier sat down on the edge of the bed, taking one of Tut's hands in his gnarled old claw. Looking at their entwined hands, Tut noticed again that he even had purple bruises on his wrist and forearm, and a scrape on the back of his hand.

Bastet jumped off the bed with a snort, scurrying under the Queen's chair. The Vizier took a deep, shuddering breath and began pouring out a breathless torrent of words with a speed and intensity Tut had never heard him use before. "I am so sorry to have put you in danger… It was never my intention that your first battle should actually result in injury… that you should have fallen when Horemheb ordered the retreat… Thank the gods you're so brave. I am so glad you're safe."

Tut tried to smile at his penitent Vizier. "You didn't know," he said, shaking his head. "No one could have known. I knew the risks… I put myself in danger." Now that he was home, now that he had had some water and a good, long, solid night's sleep, he was starting to be able to speak clearly again.

"But I told you to go; I advised you, and I told you you would be safe," Ay insisted, looking disconcertingly upset, almost as if he were about to choke up. In fact, if he squinted, Tut almost thought the Vizier's eye makeup was smudged, as if he had indeed actually been crying. Or was it just a trick of the light?

Ay was still clinging to the Pharaoh's hand as he lamented his irresponsibility, all his wrinkles flexing as he bewailed his decision, the loose skin at his throat wobbling. "I told you you would be safe... I'm a liar. This is all my fault. I did this. I do not deserve to be Grand Vizier; how shall I live with myself if my actions have killed the Morning and the Evening Star?"

"But they haven't," Tut said, shaking his head again as he tried not to let his face show how delighted he would in fact be to see Ay retire as Grand Vizier. "And the doctors will take good care of me. They already have. See the splints they put on?" He nodded at his legs.

Ay bent and examined them. "Ah, yes. Very well done, I must say." He heaved a massive sigh, lined old face twisting. "My heart bleeds seeing you like this... You're like my own son..."

"And you are a very wise grandfather."

Ay gave a slightly choked chuckle. "Oh, Great Morning Star, what would we ever do without you?" He sighed again. "Please accept my sincerest apologies," he said softly. "And my best wishes for your recovery. I shall pray at the temple for you. It is my fondest wish to see you grow to become as great a Pharaoh as your grandfather."

Tut inclined his head. "Thank you, Vizier. Be at peace. I hold you blameless."

"Thank you, Glorious Lord, thank you," Ay whispered, bowing to the floor as he left the room. Tut could never remember him having done that since the Pharaoh's coronation; actually dropping to his knees, clasping his hands before his heart, and nearly touching his forehead to the floor. "I can never repay your undeserved mercy. All life, prosperity, and health, a thousand, thousand times." And he was gone, slipping from the room like a shadow. Setting down the jewelry she'd been fiddling with, Ankh came and sat down again.

Tut looked over at Bastet, who was oozing out from under the chair. With another rather vicious snort, she sat down, licking herself huffily as if the Vizier's visit had dirtied the entire room. Did she know something?

Heart bleeds... own son... Somehow Ay's words hearkened back to what he had said after Pentu had died. Interesting.

Meresankh tried to get on with her day, tidying the Queen's room, organizing her jewelry. It was hard; she kept trying to sneak peeks into the Pharaoh's room just to see how he was. The Queen was sitting with him, taking care of him. Meresankh didn't see Semerkhet. Where was he?

He'd done so much for the Pharaoh. Saved his life; brought him home safely while burdened with his own pain. But as brave as Semerkhet had been, and as proud as she was of him, Meresankh still wondered why she hadn't seen him since that morning.

She prayed that he was all right.

It was so difficult to tell what time it was. Tutankhamun lay quietly in bed, every part of his body sore, his eyes sensitive after so many hours, so many days, lying in the dark of the cart that had carried him home. But when it seemed to him that perhaps this second day home had gone on long enough, Ankhesenamun came in with a bowl of soup.

"Dinnertime," she said with a little smile, sitting down on the edge of the bed. He smiled, trying to sit up a little.

"Smells good."

"Nuya tested it," she said, stirring it. She sighed. "Semerkhet must be really tired."

Tut nodded. Now a nagging worry was beginning to prickle in the back of his mind. "Must be."

She spooned up a bite for him and he sipped it, smiling as the warm broth slowly made its way down to his stomach.

Suddenly it struck him who he would expect to have feeding him soup. The person who was inexplicably absent.

"Where *is* Sem?" he asked.

His sister spooned up another bite. "Haven't seen him for a couple hours. He's probably resting. He looked pretty beat-up too…" She glanced at his splinted legs, then bit her lip as if she hoped it hadn't been disrespectful to compare Semerkhet's wear and tear to her brother's injuries.

Tut nodded. "I hope he's getting some good rest."

But there was something odd. Because if Semerkhet was in any way mobile, which he was, Tut would expect his valet to come in and tell him goodnight. Especially on a night like this. And even if Sem had had two broken legs like the Pharaoh did, he still would have sent a message by another servant. "Suppose I'll see him in the morning."

"I'm sure we will. Now drink up."

In a cold jail cell almost a mile from his Master's chambers, Semerkhet sat on a thin blanket on a hard wooden bench. His handcuffs had been removed once he was locked in, but now one of his ankles was shackled to the cold, dripping stone wall. The only source of light was a small oil lamp in a recess across the room, which offered a faint glimmer and created flickering shadows but brought no warmth to the cell. There were no windows. And there was no sound. Only the cold. And the dark.

An empty terracotta plate and bowl sat next to him; he was still hungry after eating the bowl of flavorless gruel and the piece of plain flatbread that had been provided to him. At least he had been allowed a second cup of water, even if it wasn't cold. At least he had been fed at all. And at least he had a blanket, thin and tattered as it was. It was colder in this dungeon than it had been on all those cold nights in the cart.

A terrible throb in his knee made him wince, squinting down at it in the flickering dark. The bandage was still in place, and he couldn't see any blood seeping through it. That, at least, was a good thing. It wasn't a puncture wound, wasn't like an animal bite or a stab wound, and his kneecap was intact, but it was the worst scrape he had ever had. And the pain was ongoing and quite unpleasant... although not nearly, nearly as severe as the pain his Master was going through, with two badly broken legs and bruises on every inch of his body. Sem had bruises too, though. Especially on his arm and his shoulder.

He wrapped the thin blanket around his shoulders, huddling up inside it and trying to distract himself from the pain in his knee. And the temptation to unwrap the bandage and see how it was. The area didn't feel hot, and there was no obvious pus. So he had no outright evidence that it was infected. But on the other hand... the doctor had looked at it a good twelve hours ago. And it very much needed checked again. At the very least, he didn't want the bandage to get stuck.

Semerkhet sighed. Even if he did uncover his knee, there wasn't enough light for him to see if it was healing properly or not, and he had no clean water, no more of the doctor's ointment, and no clean bandages. There was nothing to do about his knee right now. There was nothing to do but think... about what had happened.

Exactly as he had dreaded, he had been arrested the moment he left the Pharaoh's bedroom that morning, handcuffed, and dragged away to the dungeons. All because he had failed to die. What if he had died, he wondered as he shivered, pulling the tattered blanket closer around himself. Would the Pharaoh's safety really have been preserved? Or would he have died too? Was it just possible that surviving in the way he had was the only thing that had allowed Semerkhet to then keep his Master alive?

He thought of his Pharaoh. In bed, he was sure, with the cat at his side. Hopefully sleeping, resting, beginning to heal. But surely wondering what had happened to his valet. And missing him, just as Semerkhet missed him. He should be there, taking care of him. But that wasn't possible.

This is not how I imagined the second night home would go, he thought. *I thought I would be by his side, taking care of him. I knew I would be arrested, but I had hoped it would at least be later.* He thought of how strange it was that he had actually become friends with the Pharaoh. A year ago, he would never have imagined that even being possible.

And he thought of Meresankh. Sweet, loving Meresankh, the small, sweet love whom he had missed every day since beginning the journey to Amurru. And was still missing. He had only gotten to spend a few minutes with her since coming home. She didn't know where he was; what had happened. He pictured her, sitting in her room, soft, dimpled little fingers gently stroking the necklace he had given her as she wondered and worried.

And for the first time, he had the space and time to think of the horses, Stormy and Flash. The beautiful, graceful, swift horses he had raced to victory so many times, whom he had loved as much as the Pharaoh loved his cat. Now they were dead, put down after breaking too many bones to recover. He shook his head. Everyone he loved and cared about was being taken away. Even his horses.

The Queen would certainly put it together, he thought. When Semerkhet didn't reappear, she and the Pharaoh would realize what had happened. And they would tell Meresankh. Although of course, what was yet to happen remained to be seen.

Silently he prayed that all three of them were all right. He directed his prayer to Thoth— they were all going to need wisdom. But this time, he felt no answering warmth as he prayed.

Semerkhet swallowed. Oh, for one glimpse of Meresankh's sweet, round face; one touch of her hand. Or one sound of her voice, that confident, cheerful voice that loved to tell stories. But he could not see Meresankh, could not hear her, could not touch her. He was alone in the dark, and Meresankh and his Master were far away.

And would he ever see them again?

Meresankh went to bed and tried to sleep. What a big two days. The Pharaoh was home. Hurt, but alive. And Semerkhet was home too, also hurt, but not as badly. And alive. Praise be.

It was rather strange, though, that she hadn't seen him since that morning.

She stroked her little silver necklace and tried to sleep as worries followed one another through her mind, even though he was home.

Her prayers brought her peace, as they always did, but it was a peace of being heard... not a peace that she would receive what she had asked for. Even as she held tight to her faith, the future remained uncertain.

Ankh closed her eyes, her brother sleeping in her lap again that second night home. Whatever his secret was, it could wait.

Tutankhamun tried to rest that night, his head still resting on Ankhesenamun's lap. She had taken such very good care of him today, tenderly dabbing some of the doctor's bruise salve onto his back and arms, her tiny, delicate fingers working as gently as they possibly could. It still hurt, but what could she do? And then she had patiently fed him soup for the second time in two days. He was so blessed to have a sister and wife like her. And again, she was sleeping in the bed with him, sitting in the same spot where she had spent a large portion of the day, her presence making him feel safe. She wouldn't think of moving, and he was grateful that she didn't mind sleeping upright under an invalid...

In the middle of the night, a stab of pain woke him at the same moment as a realization. Ay had said he hadn't meant for Tut to fall when Horemheb ordered the retreat... but that didn't make sense. Ay hadn't been there.

How could he possibly have known?

He closed his eyes again and tried to go back to sleep as his mind reeled and his broken bones burned with pain.

An hour or two later, a knock at the door woke him again. He sat up with a yawn, pulling his blankets closer around himself. The pain was gone, and when he pulled the blankets away from his legs, they were perfectly fine— or at least, as fine as they ever were. And there were no bruises on his arms or his chest. Strange. Had the battle in Kadesh been nothing more than a nightmare?

"Who is it?" he called to his visitor. Slowly the door opened, and in stepped—

"Pentu?" Tut gasped, heart leaping. "But you—"

The young Vizier smiled sadly as he walked up to the bed.

"You know I'm not really here," he said softly in his high, gentle voice. "I'm here with a message. Trust yourself and the Queen. No one else. If they'd kill me, if they'd send you off to die, they'll stop at nothing. Keep yourselves safe."

Tut grasped Pentu's hand, eyes filling with tears. He'd never actually touched Pentu's hand before; it felt very small and thin, but strong, almost like Ankh's. "I'm so sorry I couldn't protect you," he whispered. "I never wanted anyone to die... especially you. And you're the one I need most. And..." He swallowed. "And Meritaten."

Pentu bowed his head. "I always had my suspicions. You confirmed them."

"Actually... This is weird, but... you were the one who helped us solve the mystery; find out that she was murdered," Tut said. "With her, and with you, Ay told us that it was overnight ague. But you were both so strong and healthy, and it was the wrong season." His eyes flickered. "What was it really, if I may ask?"

Pentu shook his head. "You don't want to know, Your Majesty." He swallowed. "But I may be at a bit of a disadvantage in the afterlife. So will My Lady Meritaten."

The King shuddered.

"I have to leave now," Pentu said, slowly walking back towards the door. "Be careful, all of you. You, the Queen, and Semerkhet and Meresankh. They're not just good servants; they're good friends, friends you can trust."

Tut nodded. "I know. Ankh and I are so grateful for them."

"There's still a chance that you can get the General on your side," Pentu said as he put his hand on the doorknob, "if you can make him grateful for the... opportunities you've given him. But watch out for Nakhtmin."

"I know. Little jackal."

Pentu chuckled. "I never could say that before, but I agree; he is a little jackal." He sighed, looking at the floor, then back up at the King. "And Your Majesty..." he said softly, "please take care of Usermontu. He's my friend."

The Pharaoh nodded. "I will. Thank you for coming to see me. Even if this is just a dream."

Pentu smiled. "Just don't come see me too soon." And he was gone, carefully closing the door behind him.

Tut rolled painfully over in bed, the cat arching her back as he disturbed her. The door was closed; he and Ankh were alone in the room, his sister breathing slowly and quietly as she lay back against the headboard of the bed, still half sitting up even though Tut was no longer in her lap. Had that been a dream? The searing pain in his legs and the aching in his arms and torso told him that it had been. And that Kadesh had been no mere nightmare.

He shook his head and closed his eyes again. Dream or no dream, he had received a message.

10

The Judgment of Pharaoh

"Where is Semerkhet?" Tut asked the third morning home. He had not seen his valet since the previous morning, and Sem had not reappeared this morning as he and the Queen had hoped.

Another servant hurried forward to answer his question. With a little smile, the King recognized him as Raherka, one of the two who had kept him from being hurt that time he'd tripped over the cat... back when he could actually walk. What good days those had been. And Raherka, of course, had also been the first to rush to his side on the battlefield at Kadesh.

"In the palace dungeon, Son of Ra, awaiting sentencing. He is to be brought before you today so you can approve his execution. The stake is being prepared for him to be burned."

Tut's eyes snapped open as his heart began to pound. Without thinking, he pushed himself up with his elbow, sitting up in bed.

"What? On what charge? And by whose authority?"

"Numerous charges, O Great Morning Star. Treason, cowardice, dereliction of duty... in the eyes of the law, he all but fired the arrow that caused your fall. And by the authority of the Grand Vizier, for the harm that came to you through the decisions of the accused."

"We'll see about that," Tut said, squaring his shoulders. "Let the trial begin immediately."

Quickly the Pharaoh called for Nuya to put his eye makeup on and help him shave the stubble that had been growing since the morning of the battle, as well as the short hair under his wig. Then he had the scribe bring him one of his wigs and a circlet, as well as the false beard of magnificence, a warm, red outer robe to cover his sleeping-tunic, and a ring. Tut was going to be dispensing justice, and he wanted to look the part, even if he couldn't quite manage the double crown. It felt odd to have someone other than Semerkhet helping him put on his finery, but… Semerkhet was the reason he was putting the beard on.

He also called for a red sash from his storage room. He folded it up carefully and set it beside him for the proper moment.

As he looked in the mirror at his completed ensemble, the King shook his head. He hadn't actually looked at himself since his injury. Dark purple bruises were blooming down the badly-scraped-up left side of his face. And no one had told him he had a black eye. At least… He gave a wry chuckle. At least he hadn't lost any teeth. Checking his arms, he saw that the bruises and scrapes were just as visible as they had been yesterday. Oh, well. A battle-scarred Pharaoh was one with authority.

Ankh came in, having slipped out to get dressed. And he hugged her and told her that this morning, he needed a bit of space, as he had a meeting. With a questioning smile, she nodded, kissing him on the forehead and returning to her own room.

As she left, a question popped into his mind. Shouldn't he ask her what to do before proceeding? He opened his mouth to ask Nuya to call her back, then closed it.

He didn't need to ask her what he should do. Because he knew. She had taught him well. And now he possessed enough good judgment of his own to do this himself. He knew he did.

The day would come, she had told him, that he would have the confidence in his own abilities to no longer have to ask her what to do. And now that day… that day had come.

And he smiled to think of how proud she would be.

"Get up."

Semerkhet opened his eyes, wondering where he was and why his neck, and his knee, hurt so much. Then it all came flooding back. Getting home, getting arrested... getting put in the dungeon. "Get up," he heard again, more insistently. A uniformed guard, one of the ones who had arrested him, stood over him, large, rough hand gesturing impatiently. Sem remembered just how hard those hands had been, clamped around his upper arms. Did he have bruises on his biceps? "Get a move on."

"What's going on?" Semerkhet mumbled, rubbing his eyes. His stomach was rumbling; his meager dinner had worn off and his body was demanding breakfast.

"You're being brought to trial before your execution."

Any remaining sleepiness fell away in an instant as the word hit his ears like the hard ground outside Kadesh. He sat bolt upright, heart pounding, mouth dry as sand. The thin blanket slipped off his body, slithering to the floor. "What?"

The guard looked at him in annoyance, as if he was surprised Semerkhet wasn't up on the details of his sentencing. "You're being charged with treason, dereliction of duty, and cowardice in the face of danger to the Pharaoh. You're to be burned at the stake. Let's go."

"B-burned?" Semerkhet stuttered.

"Better than it could be, for letting the Pharaoh fall out of his chariot like that. Now come on." Before Semerkhet could do more than think of trying to get away, the guard grabbed his arm, hauling him to his feet and putting the cold, heavy manacles back onto his wrists, then removing the chain that attached Sem's leg to the wall and placing shackles on his ankles. Semerkhet winced as he put weight on his still-bandaged knee, then began limping out of the cell beside the enormous guard, who was dragging him along by his elbow. A moment later, Sem was flanked by six guards in identical uniforms, all carrying long spears. Apparently he was a high-ranking criminal.

He had no choice but to shuffle along with them, heart pounding as his legs shook under him, the heavy chains weighing him down and clinking grimly with every step he took. Slowly they walked the many halls that led back to the more familiar areas of the palace, the rooms where he worked every day.

Could his Master save him?

Ten minutes later, there was a formal knock at the bedroom door. The Pharaoh looked up, his heart beginning to pound.

"Come in," Tut said in his most formal tone. Slowly, the door began to open, and six spear-bearing guards entered, leading Semerkhet, barefoot, wearing a plain white tunic and chains. His wig looked worse than ever, and Tut could see that he had, indeed, been rather bruised up, too, and still had a bandage on his right knee. The valet's eyes darted around the room as if he had never been in it before; he kept stumbling as if he was shaking too hard to keep his balance— and as if he was in pain. Behind the prisoner and the guards walked the Priest of Ma'at, the leader of the justice system (other than the Pharaoh, of course), Usermontu, and Ay, wearing flowing white robes and elaborate collars, bald heads gleaming in the lamplight. The Viziers needed to be present at a royal sentencing.

There were a lot of people, but the Pharaoh hardly noticed. All he could think of was his friend.

"Semerkhet!" Tut cried, sitting up as he forgot his injuries. Heart leaping, he beckoned to his friend, waving his bruised hands. "C'mere!" An instant later, he fell back in pain as his sudden movement sent searing pain through his broken legs and bruised torso. "Bring the prisoner to me," he gasped. Slowly he sat up again.

"You heard the Pharaoh; move!" a guard said, roughly shoving Semerkhet forward. He stumbled across the room, almost tripping, and stood shaking from head to foot, quite close to the Pharaoh's bed. The bedroom was large, but not that large; with ten people standing in a little crowd, trying not to bump into any of the furniture, space was running low. Bastet hissed at the gathering and scurried under the bed.

Tut swallowed, stiffening his resolve to be the dignified, commanding Pharaoh as he looked at his shaking friend, the friend he wanted to throw his arms around. The god-king did not hug his best friend, or a servant, in front of this group. Not until he had used his authority as Pharaoh to hopefully, somehow, make all this go away.

"What charges are being brought against this man?" Tut asked the room at large in the most imperious voice he could muster with the horrible throbbing in his legs and the aggravated aching in the rest of his body. Silently Semerkhet stared at Tut, pleading with his Pharaoh to save him. Tut locked eyes with him for just a moment, asking him to trust.

The Priest of Ma'at spoke up. "Treason, dereliction of duty, and cowardice in the face of danger to the Pharaoh, O King for Whom the Sun Rises."

"What evidence has been obtained that this man failed in his duty?" Tut asked.

The Priest of Ma'at looked disdainfully down his nose at the shivering Semerkhet, as if he did not think such an unworthy piece of dirt even deserved to step foot in the Pharaoh's chambers.

"He failed to save your life at the expense of his own, Glorious Lord. When the Hittite arrow struck your horse, he did nothing to break your fall. In fact, the coward jumped, abandoning his place at your side and clearly placing higher value on his own life than that of the Living Image of Amun." He gave a simpering smile, confident that his argument had swayed the Pharaoh and Semerkhet would be executed within the hour.

"If the arrow of the Hittite warrior caused my fall, should not the archer be considered responsible for my injuries?" Tut asked in his most formal tone.

"The Hittite archer has been reported to have been immediately killed by ten of your men, Great Morning Star. He was hacked into numerous little pieces, which were burned, and the ashes thrown into the river." Somehow the Priest made it sound as though he felt the punishment had been lax.

Tut raised an eyebrow. Talk about vengeance. "Then can we not consider justice to have been served? Or should we punish my horses for being injured, or the chariot-builder for designing my chariot so that it was subject to being overturned with great force, or the gods themselves for placing a stone where one of my horses might trip over it after being shot? As I remember, the arrow flew from the side on which Semerkhet stood, protecting me with his shield. If he had stayed where he was, he would have landed on me during the crash, probably making my injuries even more severe. There was no way he could have broken my fall.

"The fact that he was acting as my shield-bearer also prevented the arrow from hitting me directly, which would have had a much greater chance of killing me instantly. Must we lay blame for my injuries when they clearly took place in open warfare, in a battle I joined by my own free will? If anyone is responsible for my wounds, it is me. I chose to fight— I believed Ay when he said..."

Tut stopped and swallowed, suddenly feeling dizzy. He did not finish what he had been about to say— *I believed Ay when he said I would not be hurt; I followed my Vizier's counsel and rode into battle. Great gods, I've been murdered.* Ay stood there among those gathered, watching him, regarding him pleasantly, waiting for what he would say next. Tut shook his head. He would deal with that later. "I... I chose to fight," he finished, hoping no one had noticed his pause. "And that is all that matters."

The court stood in silence. Usermontu had not spoken a single word, but the Pharaoh thought he looked proud. The old man was on his side. If only Pentu were here too. He, too, would be sure to agree with the King's decisions.

Tutankhamun cleared his throat, ready to pass judgment. He sat up as straight as he could in the bed, taking up as much space as possible, giving himself the most commanding presence he could.

"Be still. Pharaoh speaks. Semerkhet has been a good and faithful servant. He has always served me well, and he is a good man. And he, too, was injured; just look at his knee. He did not fail me, and he did everything he could in the wake of my fall. He disobeyed no direct order; he relied on his own best judgment. He did not abandon me, and I see no evidence of cowardice. It was his actions, in fact, his care, that kept me alive during the journey home. Saving his own life first was the only thing that enabled him to save mine. He has fulfilled his duties toward me. Furthermore," he continued, "as his Master, I alone am responsible for deciding upon consequences for his actions. And as Pharaoh," he said mildly, "I alone have the power to declare the death penalty." Out of the corner of his eye, Tutankhamun saw Ay fidgeting with his staff, shifting his weight uncomfortably.

Tut maintained eye contact with Semerkhet as he spoke, watching his friend and servant stand in awe as the Pharaoh set him free of the consequences of his circumstances. "Semerkhet is blameless in what has happened. We declare him innocent of all crimes of which he stands accused. Dismantle the stake. Semerkhet will return to his position as Royal Valet. And..." He smiled at Semerkhet, chuckling as he wondered how his friend would respond to this next proclamation, something that he should have done a long time ago but would carry more weight in this situation. "Furthermore, we appoint our friend Semerkhet as Sole Companion, the Favorite of the Pharaoh, and Our Unique Friend... Our Attentive, Unique Friend."

Semerkhet stared at him from where he stood beside the bed, eyes slowly filling with tears of awe. Silently Tutankhamun smiled at him, slowly taking off his ring and sliding it onto Semerkhet's finger. Then he took the red sash and placed it over Semerkhet's shoulder, carefully tying it at the opposite hip. These symbols would identify him as Sole Companion and Favorite, titles Tut's father had conferred on Pentu's father Penthu, after whom the young Vizier had been named. No one received the distinction of Unique Friend who hadn't already been named King's Friend... or at least they hadn't until today. The court's eyes got bigger with every word the Pharaoh spoke, as if they wondered if his next act would be to appoint Semerkhet his heir.

Semerkhet slowly knelt down, looking down in awe at his new symbols of office. Tut had never seen his eyes so big. Although he did notice that Semerkhet winced slightly as he bent his knees.

The promotion complete, Tutankhamun took a deep breath and looked out at the members of the court that had come to condemn his friend.

"The Pharaoh has spoken; all depart."

Tut stared down the room. He knew he had powerful, sometimes frightening, eyebrows, and the kohl around his deep, dark eyes did not make them any less intense. Neither did the impressive shiner on the left side. He stared at them with eyes of thunder and lightning, the eyes of a god. Even sitting here in bed with two broken legs and bruises from head to toe, he was the Lord of the Two Lands, the one whose decisions could not be opposed.

The judge, the Viziers, the guards, and Semerkhet all blinked. There was silence. Ringing silence. "I have spoken," Tut repeated. "All depart."

Everyone seemed to shudder slightly, and after the valet stood up, the head guard removed Semerkhet's chains without looking directly at him. Then everyone was on their faces before the Pharaoh, honoring him as the dispenser of true justice. Bowing to the judgment of Pharaoh.

"Hail to thee, Ruler of Truth; all life, prosperity, and health!"

Slowly the guards, the Viziers, and the judge wandered out of the room without a word, as if they didn't know what to think of what had just happened. Ay glanced at the Pharaoh as he went, looking away before they made eye contact. Tut felt like growling like a lion. When he was back on his feet, the Grand Vizier would be the one facing trial.

There was a charge in the air, as if a thunderstorm were approaching. Tut's heart was pounding. He felt powerful. Was that what making major decisions for his country would be like? This was how he had felt after finalizing the budget— lowering taxes, limiting slavery, and building schools. And how he had felt after firing Sennedjem the tomb-robber. And on those brief, shining days when he had been the one conducting the morning meetings, approving shipments of building materials and finalizing trade agreements. It was intoxicating, and he felt like he just might be good at it.

He could not imagine burning at the stake. Hanging, even beheading, but being burned to ash... He shuddered. If you were burned at the stake, you could not be mummified. Osiris would never meet you, and you would be doomed, trapped in limbo, unable even to receive judgment. It was the worst fate.

Tut lay back on the bed, worn out. And chuckling faintly. This was probably the first time in Egyptian history that court proceedings had taken place in the royal bedroom. Silently Semerkhet crept back over to him on his knees, his plain tunic dirty, the marks of his shackles still visible on his wrists and ankles. And a bit of pain on his face as his bandaged knee scraped against the floor.

"My Lord?" he whispered. Tut looked at him and smiled. "I don't know what to say." Slowly Semerkhet bent to kiss the hem of Tut's robe. "Thank you."

Tut held out his hand for a clasp, but found it being kissed as well. Then Semerkhet grasped it, clinging to it as tears of gratitude shone in his eyes. Tut looked down at their entwined hands and saw that the henna on their nails was fading. The red jasper ring seemed to weigh heavily on Semerkhet's hand, and the red sash contrasted brightly against his white tunic. "Thank you." Sem swallowed back a sob. "Five minutes ago... my hope was g-gone... no afterlife... l-lost forever... nothing b-but ash... and now... S-sole C-companion?"

"Get up here!" the Pharaoh choked, pulling at Semerkhet's hand. And the valet rose, perching on the side of the bed. Blinking back tears, Tut threw his arms around his friend, smiling as he felt Semerkhet's warm arms gently wrap around him. They felt one another's heartbeats. They shared a sob. And slowly, gently, Semerkhet let his Pharaoh settle back into bed.

The two shared a heavy sigh. There really was nothing to say. They stared at one another, exhausted, at a loss. Then Tut gave his servant a little smile.

"May I have some grapes?"

The spell was broken. Semerkhet popped up, and with a quick bow and a "yes, Master," he was off to the kitchen to find his King a snack, his wishes for life, health, and prosperity echoing behind him as he went. Tut took off the false beard and circlet and closed his eyes, trying to ignore the rising pain in his legs, the aching of his bruised body. What a big day this had been.

11

The Sole Companion

Tut closed his eyes. The Vizier. The Grand Vizier was behind it all. Now it all made sense; the odd, whispered conversations, the secrecy. Ay, Maya, Horemheb, Nakhtmin were all in on it. This effort to get rid of him. To make themselves Pharaoh, either through one of them gaining supremacy afterا conflict, or one after the other. But they had worked together to send him to his death.

Bastet had been right.

The Vizier was moving in, Tutankhamun could see. Positioning himself as the only available successor to Tut's throne; pulling strings to ensure that Tut predeceased him. Why else would he consider himself authorized to declare the death penalty— unless he already considered himself Pharaoh?

And why would Horemheb have betrayed Tut on the battlefield— unless he had pledged his loyalty to the Vizier whom he hoped to see take the throne? Tutankhamun shook his head as he remembered the letter delivered by the Vizier's secretary that had changed everything; the letter that Tut now realized, biting his lip in pain, had been his death warrant.

A dark, strange future loomed before him; a future he could not divine. And those he had once trusted were now circling him and his loved ones like vultures.

But what could he do? The Vizier had always been his regent. His mother, before she had died, had officially designated the Grand Vizier as Tut's regent in the event that she died before Tutankhaten became a man. The decision of when Tut had stepped into full power had legitimately belonged to Ay, because as far as Nefertiti had known, he was a loyal courtier.

And... The Pharaoh's stomach clenched as the thought hit him. He had chosen his moment so well. The Vizier had offered the thing Tutankhamun had always wanted most, the opportunity to prove himself on the battlefield as a strong warrior King, so soon after stepping back, laying aside his regency and declaring Tut as Pharaoh in his own right.

The decision had been Tutankhamun's. But the Vizier had all but placed it in his lap.

So here was Tut, reigning alone, supposedly mature enough in the eyes of the Vizier to no longer need a regent. He was the Pharaoh, responsible for all the hiring and firing that took place anywhere in the palace, anywhere in the entire government. What was to stop him from removing the traitor from the royal court?

He thought of the web of deception within which he, Ay, Horemheb, Nakhtmin, Maya, and the Queen were tangled together. He thought of what the Vizier had done before. Killed Meritaten. Sent Tut off to die. What would happen if he threw him out?

Somehow, the Pharaoh had a strong sense that if he declared war on the Grand Vizier, Ay would respond by doing something with much more permanent consequences than turning Semerkhet into a scribe. And he thought of what his sister would say— *keep your friends close, and your enemies closer.* Right now, he had to keep the Vizier close; watch his every move. Only then could he keep what was left of his family safe.

Semerkhet stumbled out of his Pharaoh's bedroom, heart pounding, legs shaking, even the one that wasn't hurt. Cleared. Not going to be executed. Royal Favorite. Unique Friend. Sole Companion. Still the Pharaoh's valet. Not guilty. Not going to be burned at the stake. Safe. Alive. He looked down at his ring, his red sash, and could hardly believe all this was real.

He was dizzy, actually dizzy, with joy, excitement, relief. Right now his mind could hardly grasp, hardly process, what was happening. But that was all right. Suddenly he remembered how starvingly hungry he was.

Laughing, Semerkhet ran down the hall, hurt knee or no hurt knee. He was going to go see Meresankh. He was going to get his Master some grapes, and some breakfast for himself. And then he was going to ask if he could go swimming in the Nile.

"What do you suppose the meeting's about?" Ankhesenamun asked her handmaiden. An hour ago, the Pharaoh had very gently asked her to excuse him, as he had an important meeting she didn't need to take part in. Now she sat in her room, waiting for whatever meeting to be over so she could go in and sit with him again. Although she was glad that he was feeling strong enough to have a meeting, whatever it was about. More secrets, she sighed to herself.

Meresankh sighed, closing the box of jewelry she'd been cleaning, using a soft linen cloth to brush away the sandy dust that always accumulated on the Queen's necklaces just through being worn. It looked as though something was bothering her, something even beyond the Pharaoh's injury. Absentmindedly, she stroked the silver necklace she wore.

"Hard to say. But when... when it's done, maybe the Pharaoh can send someone to look for Semerkhet. I haven't seen him all day."

Footsteps sounded in the hall. Ankhesenamun looked through the open door. Grand Vizier Ay, Vizier Usermontu, and the Priest of Ma'at were leaving the Pharaoh's bedroom, along with six spear-bearing guards, marching in sync as if they had an invisible prisoner between them. One had a set of manacles and a set of shackles dangling from his belt.

"What's that about?" Ankh asked, looking at her handmaiden. "Do you suppose that was the meeting? An arrest of some sort?" Strange thoughts moved inside her heart, a hesitant query of if the mystery had been solved, and those who had sent the Pharaoh to Kadesh brought down. If, however, the events were unrelated, and the meeting was still going on, it wouldn't exactly be appropriate for Meresankh, or even the Queen herself, to march into the middle of it. Ankh shook her head. "Go ask the guard!"

Meresankh went out into the hall. And the Queen waited in impatient, intrigued excitement until she saw her return.

There were tears in Meresankh's eyes. And her voice was thick with tears. "Semerkhet was brought to trial for failing to protect the Pharaoh during the battle."

The Queen's eyes widened. "Brought to trial?" So that was what the meeting had been. A royal trial, with the Pharaoh as judge. "So that's where he's been! Oh, poor Semerkhet... But why? Why would they arrest him? He saved the Pharaoh's life!"

Meresankh nodded, eyes glimmering as she reached up to touch her precious necklace again. "Because he wasn't hurt, except for his knee, but the Pharaoh was, they were going to execute him for dereliction of duty."

"Execute him?" Ankh gasped, clapping her hand to her mouth.

Meresankh nodded, a small smile now coming to her face. "But the Pharaoh cleared him of all charges. He's safe."

Ankhesenamun smiled, heart warming with pride. In the midst of all this, her husband was taking his power.

Then a tiny shadow fell across the light of joy. Why hadn't he called her in, for something as important as a trial? Why hadn't he asked for her help, discussed it with her first? She was the one who always answered his questions, guided him with her wisdom. Why would he exclude her?

Then the answer hit her, and she smiled.

Because he knew what to do. Because she had taught him well. Because his good judgment had developed to the point where he could trust himself to make the right decisions. And she was proud of him. And of herself. The day had come when he no longer needed to ask her what to do.

Suddenly, Meresankh gave a tiny, shuddering gasp. The Queen looked at her and smiled. Her face was glowing, eyes shining as she gazed longingly at who was waiting in the hall, heart straining against her dutifully planted feet. Almost out of sight, Semerkhet was standing just outside the door.

They shared a brilliant smile, Queen and servant, both squealing and clapping with joy. Meresankh actually gave a little hop. "Go, go!" Ankh laughed, hands flapping as she playfully shooed her elated handmaiden out of the room. "And tell me how it went!" Meresankh gave her Mistress a breathless grin, half-throwing the jewelry box onto a shelf with fumbling hands. And with a bow, she ran out the door, heart launching her as fast as a gazelle. A moment later came the sound of a man and a woman laughing for sheer joy.

"Semerkhet!"

"Meresankh!"

Semerkhet's heart began to pound as he saw her standing there, face glowing in the happiest smile he had ever seen. Meresankh flew down the hall towards him, and he scooped her up, swinging her around and around as they laughed for joy. Then he held her tight, and she held him too.

Breathlessly, he set her down, and they stood there holding hands, both her tiny little hands cradled in his. "You're not—" she panted.

He shook his head. "No, I'm not. Cleared of all charges. And I'm Royal Favorite and Unique Friend and Sole Companion!"

Meresankh looked at his ring and sash appreciatively. "You deserve it. No one takes care of our Pharaoh like you do." She hugged him again, pressing her face against his chest. "Oh, I'm just so glad you're safe…"

He hugged her too, her soft, warm, little body pressed close to his, wrapped tightly in his arms. "It's all right now... it's all right... I don't even know what to think..." Then he smiled down at her. He did have one idea. "Want to go swimming later?"

Ankh chuckled as Meresankh hurried out of the room to greet Semerkhet. Her baby brother was answering his own questions.

Although... it wasn't as simple as all that. Because, of course, he was stuck in bed with two broken legs because of his own immaturity in self-control. So although she was pleased, and quite impressed, with the wisdom he had shown today, could it be trusted? Would it last?

She sighed. If he could make these good decisions now, hopefully he would remain wise after having gotten some sense knocked into him on the battlefield. And hopefully running off to battle had been a fluke, the last vestige of childish immaturity. But... which decision, she wondered, the wise or the impulsive, was the fluke? What would he choose the next time he was faced with a major decision?

Ankh shook her head. *The trial went well*, she thought. *He did the right thing. Maybe the lessons I've taught him have stuck.* She gave a wry chuckle. *But I'm still going to keep an eye on him. And I'm going to find out what happened!*

But even as her brother's maturity proved to be developing unevenly, Ankhesenamun was proud of him. Because he had handled his most important meeting to date flawlessly.

I've worked myself out of a job, she thought with satisfaction. *That was my goal all along... Now what do I do?* She put her hands on her hips. *I need a hobby...*

Semerkhet ran down to the kitchen, actually ran, despite the jolt of pain his knee gave with every stride he took. Everything looked shiny and new— the bright paintings on the walls, the graceful lotus columns that supported them, the gleaming stone floors. The rooms looked grander; the colors looked brighter. Even the air felt fresher. It was all so beautiful. Now that he was going to continue to live there. Or anywhere at all.

And that was why it was so beautiful. Because he had so very nearly lost it forever. He had stood there clinging to it with the tips of his fingernails as the court tried to pull it away from him, and now... it had been given back to him. And now no words could express the gratitude with which he wanted to wrap his arms around the entire palace.

He took the familiar route to the kitchen, selecting his Master's favorite bowl and filling it with juicy red grapes. He tried one, just to make sure it wasn't poisoned. Somehow it seemed that he had never even really tasted grapes before, or any food. Suddenly something as simple as eating was special again; an hour ago, he had been wondering if he had already eaten his last meal. Now he could wonder what was for dinner, secure in the knowledge that many delicious meals were ahead of him.

Semerkhet looked around the kitchen, wondering what else it would be all right for him to eat. He took an apple, crunching into it and gulping it down in a few sweet bites, then a bit of cheese, a handful of almonds, and a hunk of bread, followed by half a cup of beer. Even a sliver of last night's royal roast beef, which was going to the servants' hall tonight. He was hungry, after all. And nothing had ever tasted so good.

Finally Semerkhet's stomach was satisfied, the hunger pains replaced with comfortable fullness. He sighed. It felt good to eat.

The ceramic bowl now carefully filled with grapes, it was back to the Pharaoh's room to present it to him. Even something as simple as getting his Pharaoh a snack was something to cherish.

Although as he looked down at himself, he felt embarrassed. He was sweaty, disheveled, unshaven, streaked with dirt and dust, and smelled rather bad. And he had presented himself that way to the Pharaoh during the trial.

Then he shrugged. It couldn't have been helped. And that was what friends did, wasn't it— ignored inadvertent little shortcomings like that? The Pharaoh was so gracious that he hadn't been offended. And as soon as Semerkhet had delivered his brother's bowl of grapes, he was going to ask if he could go swimming. Because not only would he look and smell better, he would feel a thousand times better after a bath.

"Thank you, Sem," the Pharaoh said with a tired smile. Semerkhet stood there, bouncing on the balls of his feet, face glowing. Carefully he handed his Master his bowl of grapes. "Now go take a break," Tut continued. "Get some fresh air. Go take an hour or two." He chuckled. "The river looks beautiful today."

"Thank you, Master," Sem said, bobbing his head. And he was off again with a wish for life, prosperity, and health, barely remembering to shut the door behind him.

"How was the trial?" Ankhesenamun asked as she sat down beside her husband. Finally he had invited her back into the room. He looked tired… but satisfied. He'd put on a nice, warm outer robe, and he'd gotten help with shaving. Privately, she thought he looked better.

Tut looked up at her from choosing a grape out of the bowl in front of him. Even moving his bruised arm to pick up a grape hurt. And soon the bruises would be as purple as the grapes.

"How do you—"

"Meresankh told me," she said quickly. "She said Semerkhet was going to be executed for letting you get hurt, but you saved him."

He nodded. No secrets could be kept around such an effective gossip. But not that he really didn't want Ankh to know about the trial. "He saved me first. But I argued that he hadn't done anything wrong, and that through saving his own life, he had been able to save mine. And he's been cleared, and everything's going to go back to normal." He sighed, eyes downcast. "Or… anyway…"

She took his cold hand in both of hers, her tiny fingers tracing the tender bruises on his hand and wrist. Her hands were nice and warm. Then she gave a little smile. "Meresankh sure was happy that you set him free."

He looked up at her. "I'm sure she was." He chuckled. "They sure are cute."

"Where is he right now?" Ankh said, looking around the bedroom, hoping they hadn't been talking about the valet while he'd been listening.

"Taking a break," Tut said. "He needs one."

The Queen nodded. "Yes. He does."

"Maybe he'll go have a swim in the Nile." Tut sighed. "Wish I could." She just squeezed his hand.

Then she smiled. "Meresankh's taking a break, too." The King chuckled. "I'm proud of you," Ankh said, bending to kiss his forehead. Then she snitched a grape, popping it into her mouth. "Holding court in your bedroom. Making sure justice is served, no matter what. Not every Pharaoh could accomplish what you just did with two broken legs."

He smiled, looking proud. "I do feel pretty good about it." Then he sighed, doubt twisting in his gut. "Did I do it right? I don't know— should I— should I have called you first, brought you in so you could tell me how to make my defense— I'm sorry if I should have talked to you before I started the trial—"

She raised one hand, using the other to gently squeeze his shoulder. "No, no. I'm proud of you. You know that you know what to do. You're applying what you've learned, using your knowledge, your experience. You're answering your own questions. And that's exactly what I want to see you doing. And what... what Mother and Father would be so proud to see. I knew the day would come when you wouldn't need my help anymore. And that day... is today."

Tut just gave her a grateful smile, and she gave him another peck on the forehead as she let go of her brother's childhood once and for all.

Then he gave a wry chuckle. "I think I've learned my lesson about thinking twice," he said. She just sighed.

Ankh's mind trailed away, back to other questions, other things she wanted to discuss with him. Then a maidservant came in with lunch on a tray. Time for her husband to eat.

"Is it to do with Pentu? The secret?" Ankhesenamun asked as she stirred a bowl of soup that was too hot to eat yet. Although not too hot for Nuya, who had faithfully eaten a spoonful of the soup and a bite of the bread before letting the Queen offer it to the King. No poison.

Tutankhamun picked at the piece of bread that accompanied the soup and gave a small nod. Mealtime vaguely made him wish he could visit the kitchens again.

"Yes."

She looked closely at him. Just now she was his big sister, trying to divine her baby brother's secrets so she could sweep all his problems away. He wished she could.

"If I get better, the secret won't matter, but knowing it might still put you in danger," he finally said, not looking at her as he took a bite of bread.

Ankh snorted, the blue beads of her wig jingling dismissively. "*If* you get better? Darling, you're getting better every day! So unless you intend to fall out of bed and break your neck, I don't see any question." She sighed. "Another month or two and this will all be behind us, secret or no secret."

The King swallowed. "What I was going to say… is that if I don't get better, then I'll tell you. Because you'll need to know."

His sister sighed, looking down into the bowl of soup. Then she smiled. "Then I suppose I'll never know."

12

Friends

"I couldn't imagine if my husband was hurt," Mutnedjmet said as the four wives sat in the Queen's sitting room. It felt good to take a few minutes for tea, snacks, and chatting after what had just been accomplished in the other room.

Amenia took Mutnedjmet's hand. "But you never know. And we haven't heard anything since… since the Pharaoh got home."

"He's the General," Mutnedjmet said with a confident nod. "He's experienced. If anyone comes home, he will."

"How is the Pharaoh?" Meryt asked the Queen. The Treasurer's wife looked much different than the last time they had met; her time had come, and instead of cradling a large stomach, she had just come from settling a baby in with a newly-hired nanny… a tiny baby girl. Named Tjauenmaya, after her father.

"Tolerable," Ankh said with a little smile. "I really am amazed at how well he's doing. And how he's kept going, with two broken legs, and covered in bruises. I mean, literally, covered in bruises. Just today he conducted a trial, right in his bedroom."

Amenia looked up from sipping her tea from a delicate alabaster cup, red henna gleaming on her finely-manicured nails. She and Mutnedjmet also looked different. Today they were wearing dresses that actually fit; that flattered their shapely bodies rather than flaunting them. And their perfume was tasteful rather than choking.

"A trial?"

Ankhesenamun nodded. "Apparently his charioteer, who's also his valet, jumped when the chariot fell, and since he wasn't hurt when the Pharaoh was, or not nearly as badly, the royal court wanted Semerkhet executed. But the Pharaoh told them that keeping himself alive was the only way that Semerkhet could have saved his life, and he got him cleared. And made a Royal Favorite, Sole Companion, and Unique Friend."

Meryt raised her eyebrows. "That's quite impressive. He must be a special valet."

Ankh smiled. "He is. And he's more than a valet... he's my husband's friend. He's like the only brother he's ever had."

Amenia almost frowned. "But he's a servant."

The Queen shook her head. "That doesn't matter. My handmaiden has become one of my best friends."

Mutnedjmet looked at Amenia and shook her head questioningly, her silver-beaded braids chiming. "What a thought... being able to be friends with your handmaiden."

"You should try it," Ankh said, taking a sip of tea from her delicate cup of blue pottery. "They're people too, you know."

Amenia chuckled and popped a tiger-nut sweet into her mouth. "I think I will. And when our husband gets home, I'm going to start talking to him more. Asking him more questions about what he does." She sighed. "What an idea... that I could actually help him; actually do something alongside him. I think it's time I started taking a real interest in his life. Instead of just..." She giggled. "Entertaining him."

The Queen smiled. "I think that sounds like an excellent idea."

And Amenia smiled back, sweetly but confidently making eye contact with the Queen.

Mutnedjmet laughed too. "And so will I. I'm sure he's quite an interesting person." She winked. "Outside of romance."

Ankh nodded, fighting back her blush. "I'm sure he is." The three smiled at one another, the air full of new ideas.

"What will you do?" Meryt asked out of the brief silence that had fallen.

Ankhesenamun looked at her. "About what?"

Meryt looked down at her post-delivery belly, which represented one more failure to bear her husband a son. "If he doesn't live." She sighed. "You don't have an heir."

The Queen shook her head as the awful thought shivered down her spine. Just what her brother had made her ask. "The doctors are good," she said emphatically. "And he's always pulled through with everything else that has happened." She took a sip of tea, stomach twisting as something told her that Meryt was right... every possibility, good and bad, had to be accounted for; planned for. "We'll talk about it."

Meryt closed her eyes. "Losing a husband... I can't imagine anything worse."

Ankh looked at the Treasurer's wife. "What about losing yourself?"

Meryt looked up. "Hmm?"

Ankh shook her head. "Never mind." She sighed. "Whatever happens, I do know that I'll be there for him every step of the way. And I know that with my knowledge and experience, I could be... a politician in my own right." She gave a little smile. "I already am. Most of the decisions he's recently passed, like the new schools and the minimum wage, were my ideas." She looked at Meryt. "Will you send your daughters to one of the trade schools we're opening?"

Meryt looked down. "My daughters will find just as much meaning in good marriages as they could in a career."

The Queen just nodded.

"We're all praying," Mutnedjmet said. "For the Pharaoh, and for you."

Ankhesenamun smiled at her. "Thank you."

Horemheb's wife gave her a real smile. "And I wanted to say... I don't feel like a failure anymore."

The Queen reached out her hand, gently taking Mutnedjmet's in hers. The other woman looked down in surprise, but didn't resist.

"I'm glad," the Queen said sincerely.

"I can be a good wife… and a good person… whether or not I'm ever a mother."

Ankhesenamun nodded. "Exactly." She swallowed. "And you are a mother…" she said very softly. "And so am I."

Mutnedjmet just squeezed her hand.

Amenia smiled, scooting closer to softly lay her hand over the Queen's. "And whatever happens, it's our honor to be your friends."

"And it's my honor to count you as friends."

Ankh smiled as her friends left. A beautiful thought had just touched her heart. This was it— the next opportunity she had been looking for. Teaching her friends as she had been— leaning in to teaching them would be the hobby that would add meaning to her life as her brother blossomed into the independent Pharaoh she had always known he would become.

More than a hobby, she thought. A mission; a calling. And one she was proud to fulfill.

With a heavy sigh, Tutankhamun found the most comfortable position he could and closed his eyes, pulling his blanket up around himself as the cat lay down against his side. Gratefully he rested his hand on her warm, furry, gray back. He gave a little smile. He'd done some good work today. Time for a nap.

Semerkhet and Meresankh went swimming in the Nile; splashing, jumping, shouting for joy. It felt good to be outside, the birds singing, the breeze blowing, the bright flowers shining in the sun, the water washing away the fear and stress of the previous day. The water was chilly, the air only warm, rather than hot, but it felt good. It felt good to be alive. And it felt good to be with the one he loved. Sem could still see the marks of the heavy chains on his wrists and ankles, but that was all right. He was getting clean, the sweat, dirt, and prison grime washing away in the cool water. He was alive. And he had two hours to spend how he pleased... and with whom he pleased.

Finally refreshed, he and Meresankh laughed their way inside, shivering as their teeth chattered, goosebumps rising on their skin. Semerkhet made his way to his own chambers, where he had barely spent more than a few minutes total since coming home. He felt so light— not only were the heavy chains gone, but so was all the fear. After getting dried off, he smoothed his favorite moisturizer over his elbows and left knee, enjoying the sweet fragrance, the simple comfort of being home. He changed his clothes, putting on a soft, blue outer robe over his tunic, then sat down and made a thorough examination of his knee. To his relief, it looked no worse than yesterday; possibly even a bit better. And there was no evidence of infection. Carefully, he dabbed it with the doctor's ointment, and, satisfied, wrapped it up again in a fresh bandage. Finally, he shaved the stubble that had been growing unchecked since the morning of the battle, on his chin, his cheeks, and his scalp.

Slowly, reflectively, he sipped a cup of licorice tea, which tasted better than any tea he'd ever had before. Then he scribbled a few disjointed thoughts into his journal about his experience, one he had never imagined having. And he spent a few minutes in grateful prayer to Amun-Ra and Horus, so grateful that he practically didn't mind when he felt absolutely no response.

Then he lay down for ten minutes, letting his exhausted mind and body rest after a day and night the likes of which he never wanted to experience again. His bed was so comfortable; the bed he had not been sure if he would ever lie on again. And he was clean, properly, refreshingly clean from head to toe, for the first time in a month. Relief, exhaustion, joy, exhilaration, shock, amazement, gratitude coursed through his mind... and a hundred other emotions that didn't even have names. He was safe. Safe in his own room. Safe in his own bed. Safe.

When he was ready to get up, Semerkhet got a fresh wig and did his makeup, then put his new ring and sash on again. He looked in the mirror and smiled. He looked better. He looked like a Sole Companion.

Meresankh watched Semerkhet disappear into his room with a smile. They were dripping Nile-water on the floor, but they didn't care. He was alive. And they were together again. She had sent up a thousand prayers of gratitude since the first moment she had clapped eyes on him after the trial. And yet even a thousand more could never express what this answer to her prayer meant to her. Living out the joy that had been given back to her; that was what she could do to express her gratitude to I-AM.

She thought of the Pharaoh. And how he had brought her beloved back to her, saving him from the very brink of execution. She had more than respect for him now, the respect due a King that she had always paid him. Now she had gratitude. He was the best friend of the man she hoped to marry, and now he had saved Semerkhet's life just like Semerkhet had saved his.

Her heart warmed as she thought of him— warmed in a completely different way than when she thought of Sem. And she smiled. He was *her* Pharaoh now. And she more than hoped for his smooth recovery because he was the King (and not because he was divine, because he wasn't, not any more than she or Semerkhet was). She hoped and prayed for it because she cared about him as a human being. And she always would.

Shivering, Meresankh squelched back to her own room to change into dry clothes. Then she would draw herself back, see what she could do for the Queen. She was her handmaiden, after all.

"Sole Companion? Royal Favorite? Unique Friend?" Semerkhet said in an awed whisper as he brought the King a cup of tea after having been gone for two whole hours. "I don't even know how to..."

"Thank me?" Tut said, taking the tea with a little wince as he moved his bruised shoulders. They were still very tender, although in general he was feeling a bit better, refreshed by his short nap. He smiled up at his friend, who also looked much better, having shaved, reapplied his makeup, replaced his wig, and put on a warm, blue outer robe. He looked like he might even have had a little swim. Good. He deserved a few hours to himself (or to share with Meresankh) after everything that the past two days had put him through. "This is *me* thanking *you*, dear Sem. I should have given you those titles a long time ago."

"That's really what you think of me?" Semerkhet said, sitting down on the end of the bed and petting the cat, who was curled up in a furry little ball. He looked down at the ring that denoted his new offices, then ran his hand over the red fabric of the sash.

Tut smiled. "Even those titles can't say what I think of you." He reached out and put his hand on Semerkhet's shoulder, trying not to show how painful the movement was. "Brother."

Semerkhet chuckled, reaching out his other hand and putting it on the King's shoulder. "But I'll always be the Washer of Pharaoh."

Oh, it felt good to laugh together.

Then Semerkhet smiled, a wistful little smile. He had just put his hand on the Pharaoh's shoulder, casually, without asking permission. And it had been so natural.

"It was so strange," he said, shaking his head a little, "when you started acknowledging me, right around Tribute Day. I didn't know what to think. I'd always… felt concerned for you, felt compassionate towards you; you were… people in town, the old ladies, anyway, called you the poor orphan, and I was sorry that your parents were gone, and your sisters. And I was sorry that you couldn't run around and play."

Sem shook his head with a soft chuckle. "And then my life turned upside-down when I actually got to come work at the palace and help you every single day. First just fetching things for Hetepheres, and then doing the things she always had. And it was exciting to be able to help. But at the same time, you were the Pharaoh, and I was your servant. You were… called a god… but then… then, you were acting like you wanted to be friends with me. It was almost scary. I knew I wouldn't be struck by lightning if I looked at you; I'd always known we were both human, but it still felt… disrespectful. Took awhile for me to feel like I could really look into your eyes."

"But…" Semerkhet felt tears beginning to fill his eyes as a lump built in his throat, "you saw me as a person. A real person that was worth being friends with. And…" He swallowed. "A brother." He reached out, almost surprised by his own boldness, and took his Master's cold hand in his, gently squeezing it. Tutankhamun squeezed it back. And they smiled.

"That was all I wanted, for so long, to have my brother Nedjes back," Sem said softly. "And then I realized… that I did. Not him, but that you… that you were my brother. And now I get to be a brother again."

"And I always wondered what it would be like to have a brother," Tut said wistfully. He smiled. "And now I know."

Ankhesenamun walked down the hall from her room to her husband's. Her guests were gone, and it was time to come back.

Suddenly, she wasn't alone. The Queen stopped as she saw portly old Vizier Usermontu standing there in the hallway, eyes flickering around nervously as if he had been waiting for her.

"My Lady?" he asked, still looking from this way to that.

"Yes, Vizier?" she asked gently, pausing.

He was twisting his fat hands together, his numerous chins wobbling anxiously as he searched for the right words.

"May I speak with you?" He gulped. "In private?"

The Queen looked at him. He knew something. By Anubis, he knew something.

Ankh nodded at the study. "Of course. Let's sit down."

He followed her into the study, and she locked the door behind them.

"What's going on?" she asked, sitting down. He sank down in a chair across from her.

Usermontu took a deep breath. And suddenly he appeared crushed by sadness, lined old face crumpling as he seemed to fight back tears.

"I want to apologize," he said in a voice that was almost choked. "I should have known something like this would happen. Some of the... others... don't share the Pharaoh's dreams for the future... I knew they were planning something, but I never thought it would go this far. I should have known... and I should have said something." He hung his head. "And now no apology can heal the injuries that are my fault. Because I did nothing."

The Queen reached out and gently touched his rounded hand. "This is bigger than any of us," she said softly, shaking her head. "I don't know if— if someone out there wanted this badly enough, I don't know what any one person could have done to stop them."

He shook his head. "So much strangeness... so many secrets."

She nodded. "The Pharaoh told me... he told me he'd tell me the secret about what happened if... if he thought he might not get better. But not before. Why would he even say something like that?" she murmured half to herself, shivering even in her warm robe.

Ankh frowned at Usermontu. He'd come to her heartbroken because he felt his silence had hurt her brother— if she could trust any of the remaining politicians, it was him. "What can you tell me?"

Usermontu closed his eyes, bowing his head slightly. "That the Pharaoh is right to be suspicious." He swallowed. "That both of you need to be careful." The old man paused, taking a shuddering breath. "And that Vizier Pentu, my dear, dear friend... did not die of ague."

And with a sad little look, he got up, bowed, and left the study.

The Queen watched him go. And she felt that she was getting in very deep.

"I just want to say how sorry I am," the Queen said.

Semerkhet looked up from the endless sorting of dishes and linens that he had returned to; the daily activities that were as easy and familiar as breathing.

"About what, My Lady?"

She shook her head, biting her lip. "That they arrested you," she said simply. "Arrested you for saving the Pharaoh's life. And we— we didn't even know where you were; what had happened. If we'd known why you were missing, we would have tried to help." She shuddered. "I can't imagine being thrown in the dungeon. And I can't imagine… facing execution." Slowly, she extended her hand, and gently, Semerkhet took it, sharing a brief clasp with his Lady. Her hand was tiny, but just like when he touched Meresankh's hand, he could feel her strength. "You're so brave," she continued with a nod. "And you… you deserve to be Sole Companion, and Favorite of the Pharaoh, and Unique Friend. More… more than anyone else who has ever borne those titles. Because you truly are… a unique friend. The friend who brought him home to us."

Semerkhet gave the Queen a gentle smile, looking hesitantly into her wise face for just a moment. She looked like the Pharaoh, but she was as beautiful as Meresankh. And in her bearing, she seemed to carry the legacy of all the Queens who had come before her.

"It's my honor to serve, My Lady," he said, offering a bow. "And my honor… to call the Pharaoh my brother."

"Did you want to see the gifts the people sent, from the different towns we stayed in on the way home?" Semerkhet asked.

Tut opened his eyes and tried to sit up a little, then stopped as the pain in every inch of his body held him back. He just nodded.

"Yeth, pleathe."

Semerkhet crossed the room with a large basket, a smile on his face. And one by one, he began to place a variety of items on the little table they'd set up next to the Pharaoh's bed.

"Some willow-bark tea," he said, "a homemade pillow… these wineskins were full of broth… honey-cakes…"

"Mmm!" Tut said appreciatively—

"—and this blanket…" Sem paused, eyes almost beginning to fill with tears.

Tut looked at him curiously. "What?" he asked.

"This blanket belonged to a six-year-old girl… a six-year-old girl who heard you were hurt and really wanted you to have it."

Tutankhamun took the blanket carefully, holding it gently in his lap. Softly, he ran his hands over it, imagining the tiny little hands that had held it tight, the comfort it had brought to the child who had cuddled with it every night, the big heart that had recognized a need and selflessly given away such a precious object.

And now it was his. Carefully, Tut arranged the gift over his body. He would wear it with pride.

13

Usermontu

The Washer of Pharaoh continued to do his job with a willing smile. That night Semerkhet carefully helped the King wash away the day, gently dabbing a cool, damp cloth over the tender purple bruises. It was starting to get slightly less painful to have them touched. Starting to, anyway. With a few basins of water, Tut could have just as good a bath in bed as he could in the shower room.

"I never would have imagined I could have so many bruises," Tut said, shaking his head as he examined one of his arms. From his shoulder to the tips of his fingers, his skin was blotched with purplish-green. The other one was just as bad, as were what he could see of his legs. He craned his neck with a wince, trying to look behind him. "How's my back?"

Gently Semerkhet ran the cloth down Tut's back. That was rather nice. "Just the same," he said. "You'll be stuck with these for at least a month."

"How about you?" the King asked. "I bet you got bruised up too, having to jump." He shook his head, regret filling his heart; embarrassment at what an inattentive friend he had been. Shame on him. "I saw your bandages. I'm sorry I only asked the one time."

Semerkhet still looked uncomfortable, even though he knew he had done the right thing. "Both my knees are pretty banged up," he admitted again. "Especially the right one. And one of my arms, with the way I rolled when I hit the ground. But the doctor looked at me, too, and he said it's nothing to worry about. The bandages will keep my knee clean until it heals, and the bruises will heal on their own. I have my own jar of that good salve." He shook his head with a little grimace. "Still hurts, though."

Tut nodded. Now Sem was washing his chest and stomach, which were just as bruised as any other part of him. Then with one final dab to the Pharaoh's face, he set the cloth aside and gently dried him off with a soft linen towel.

"There we are," Semerkhet said with one of those smiles that could make any day better. "Now let's get some of that good salve on those bruises."

And the King smiled.

"Don't worry," Semerkhet said with a chuckle. "I locked the door. And I made a sign."

The Pharaoh laughed out loud, eyebrows rising. "You made the sign?"

Sem nodded with a little smile of his own. "It just says 'Do Not Disturb,' since Cranky Crocodile retired. But I think it should be sufficient." He paused. "You ready?"

Tut nodded. "Thank you, Sem."

Sem hadn't asked the usual "May I" before starting in with the bruise ointment. But Tut wasn't offended. If anything, he was glad. Because brothers didn't have to ask.

As Semerkhet tucked him in on that third night home, a question occurred to the King.

"Sem?"

Semerkhet looked up from adjusting his blankets.

"Yes, Master?"

"What was it like… in the dungeon?"

Semerkhet looked down, giving a little shiver, even as he stood there in his warm outer robe. Tut was sorry he'd asked.

Finally he looked up. "Cold. And I felt… alone. More alone than I've ever felt before." The valet gave a sad little smile, and Tut knew there were things, feelings, that he was choosing not to mention. But it was his right, his decision, to answer the question as he chose. "Makes me appreciate what I have a hundred times more, since I know I almost lost it."

The Pharaoh reached out and took his friend's hand. Semerkhet looked the tiniest bit surprised, but accepted the gesture with a smile. "I missed you. And I would have missed you a hundred times more if I'd known where you were." Tut swallowed, heart aching with guilt; guilt a hundred times heavier than the shame he felt at the inattentiveness he'd shown toward his friend's injured knee. "I'm sorry I let it happen."

Sem shook his head. "It's not your fault. I knew it would happen, even before we got home." He sighed, giving another very intentional smile. "But the important thing is that I'm back now."

Tut still had hold of his hand. "I couldn't imagine… Saying that I'm glad you're all right is a grain of sand compared to what I want to say. I don't know what I'd do without you."

Semerkhet gave him another smile, a happier one. "You'll never have to find out."

Semerkhet lay down on the cot beside his Pharaoh's bed, where he slept now. It was their third night home. Tutankhamun was asleep, his chest steadily rising and falling, his brown face at peace. And Semerkhet was clean, warm, and comfortably cuddled up among pillows and blankets for the first time in literally weeks. The valet closed his eyes, going over the past two days in his mind. Getting home… getting arrested… getting cleared… getting promoted… What could possibly be next?

Semerkhet wasn't sure he even wanted to know what might be next. But whatever it would be, he would face it in the morning. After a good night of sleep.

He was almost comfortable, Tut thought with a smile as he drifted off, snuggled up among his blankets. If he was going to be stuck in bed for an extended period of time, he was glad that it was cool, cuddly blanket season.

Ankh closed her eyes, relaxing into the chair she was going to sleep in. Her brother needed her. He needed her much more than she needed to sleep in her own bed.

But before she could drift off, a thought began aching in her heart; a thought so painful that it made her open her eyes again to wipe away the tears. Over the course of this day… she had had three conversations about what would happen if her brother never recovered. Conversations that forced her to ask herself…

What if?

Every once in awhile Tut would find himself shivering, cocking his ear to a haunting sound he couldn't quite make out. Whatever it was, it was outdoors.

"What's that sound, Sem?" he asked the morning of the fourth day they'd been home, the fifth day of Sholiak.

Semerkhet stepped toward him, tucking his blankets in around him. "It's the people crying, Master."

The Pharaoh blinked, forehead crinkling in concern. "Crying?"

"Crying for you, because you're hurt."

Tut shook his head. "Well, have someone go out and tell them I'm not dead."

Semerkhet gave just the ghost of a smile. "I'll see what I can do."

"O Mighty King?"

Tutankhamun opened his eyes as he recognized a voice he had not heard in a long time.

"Usermontu?"

The fat, jolly old man was standing in the doorway of the bedroom. Only he was not jolly now. He stood there looking sad for the King, and... worried about something. Very worried. Nervous. Afraid, even.

"Come in," Tut said, nodding at Semerkhet, who stood aside to welcome the Vizier. "What is it?"

"There's something... I need to tell you," the older man said hoarsely. He looked over his fleshy shoulders, one side, then the other. Then he licked his lips, brushing his fat hands over his tunic as if it was dirty. Slowly he approached, almost sneaking into the Pharaoh's room.

"What? What's going on? Is something wrong?"

"I think so," Usermontu whispered urgently, forehead wrinkling as his gray eyebrows came together in a frown. "How do I... how do I say this?" He paused, eyes darting around the room, wringing his fat hands as he struggled for words. "Remember Pentu," he said abruptly. "I'm being transferred to work in Thebes."

"Vizier?"

Tut looked up, barely noticing Usermontu bite his lip as they heard the voice of Ay calling from out in the hallway. It was strange to hear Ay's voice saying that word, but it was how the Viziers formally addressed one another. "May I speak with you?"

And with a look of fear and pain, Usermontu waddled out to join him, lips forming the wish for life, prosperity, and health.

Usermontu had given him a lot to think about, but after the old Vizier left, it was time for the Pharaoh to turn his mind to his recovery.

"Your Majesty is getting stronger," the doctor announced after checking his bandages. "By your leave, I recommend that you spend some time in your chair today."

Tut's heart leapt. "Get out of bed?" he said with a smile.

The Chief Physician nodded. "The longer Your Majesty stays in bed, the more your strength will deteriorate. With the help of myself and your valet, you should be able to move to your chair."

Tut grinned and sat up, pushing his blankets aside. Oh, what a relief it would be to be out of this bed, even for a few minutes.

"Let's do it!"

Sem pushed the chair against the side of the bed, and slowly and carefully, he and the doctor helped Tut slide into it. Without a leg to stand on, Tut wasn't able to help them, but even despite his great height, together, they were able to move him. The Pharaoh lay back in the chair with a sigh, looking around the room from a new angle. How beautiful it looked from even the slightest new perspective.

"Darling, where— what are you doing out of bed?" Ankhesenamun sped into the room, dropping to her knees beside him and grabbing his hand. She grinned. "I didn't think—"

"Neither did I!" he said with a grin, squeezing her hand. She stood up, then bent to hug him. And there was nothing to do but sit together and enjoy the moment.

Ankh sat in her chair, smiling and smiling as she watched her brother sitting up in his own chair. What a surprise, what an amazingly pleasant surprise, that he was already strong enough to get out of bed. What an answer to prayer. The gods were listening.

There was a knock at the door. Semerkhet answered it, and a moment later, stepped back.

"Presenting Amenmose."

The Pharaoh sat up a little straighter in his chair. "Come in, Amenmose."

"Your Majesty?"

Amenmose stood at the door, a large group of anxious-looking men in military uniform crowding into the hall behind him, their eyes darting under nervous eyebrows, shifting their weight from foot to foot, crossing and uncrossing their arms.

"Yes? What is the nature of this visit?"

"Soldiers from the campaign in Amurru requesting permission to speak to you."

Tut nodded, sitting up straighter in the chair and straightening his wig and sleeping-tunic. Was another trial about to take place in the royal bedroom?

"Show them in."

The soldiers filed in in respectful silence, then prostrated themselves before the Pharaoh. There were about fifteen of them; now the bedroom was even more crowded than it had been during Semerkhet's trial. But that was all right. Tut felt confident; confident that he would be able to address their concerns as a Pharaoh should. He just wished he had had the time to put on an outer robe, and maybe his circlet.

"O Mighty King, we do not deserve to live," the captain announced, speaking almost directly into the floor. "We did this. We abandoned you on the field, leaving you vulnerable. Every one of us is as guilty as if we had shot your horse down ourselves. We blindly followed the orders of General Horemheb, not realizing he wished you harm. Deserting the traitor to escort you home was not enough to blot out what we have done. Now we offer our lives in payment for abandoning our posts and failing to protect you. Say the word, and it will be done."

Every one of the soldiers rose to his knees and drew his dagger, placing the naked bronze blade against his own throat. Tut looked at them, heart aching at their self-destructive loyalty.

The Pharaoh shook his head. "Be still," he said gently. "Put down your daggers. You are not responsible for what has happened. Pharaoh will deal with the ones who are. And do not forget; you did defend me after I fell. You wiped out any trace of wrongdoing when you put your lives at stake to protect me until I could be rescued. And then you deserted the treacherous General, leaving him and his campaign behind to bring me home safely. Now Egypt needs you to defend her, perhaps now more than ever. Your Pharaoh needs you, to keep a close watch on Horemheb and prevent him from doing even greater harm in the future. Your Pharaoh needs you to live. Rise. I hold you innocent."

He didn't want to tell them it had ultimately been Ay; he didn't want them to lynch the Vizier. Justice had to be served in accordance with law.

The soldiers rose, some appearing to tear up with gratitude. Slowly they put away their daggers, far away from their throats. They stood in respectful silence, not daring to make eye contact with the Pharaoh as they waited for what he would say next.

"Thank you, Major," the Pharaoh said, extending his scraped hand. The promoted captain crept over and took it, kissing it gratefully. "You are all dismissed, with my gratitude for your service."

"Hail to thee, Ruler of Truth; all life, prosperity, and health!" they all murmured, heads bowed in reverence. Now that he could see their faces, the Pharaoh noticed that to show their shame and grief at what had happened, the soldiers had stopped shaving. Now all sported short, scraggly, uneven beards and moustaches, a symbol of what they had done wrong. Tut hoped that now, they would feel they had the right to shave and return to a look of guiltless self-confidence.

Slowly the soldiers filed out of the bedroom in moved silence, leaving dusty footprints on the clean floor. At least it was not puddles of blood. Tut lay back in the chair and closed his eyes, worn out. Even like this, he could still save lives.

And then he shook his head. He had just spoken with the brave soldiers who had helped save his life; brave soldiers who had been willing to risk their lives on the battlefield. And who, through their bravery and skill, had come home unscathed.

Tutankhamun looked down at the legs under his blanket. And he felt anger rising in his heart. It wasn't fair; all he had ever wanted to do was become the warrior King that he was supposed to be and prove himself on the battlefield. Prove that he could do it; prove that he was a man. Show the world that he was strong and capable; convince his disobedient courtiers that he was worth listening to. Demonstrate that he truly was a strong Pharaoh.

It was his destiny, his legacy, everything he had ever wanted, the answer to every prayer he had ever prayed. He was the heir of his long-ago grandfather Thutmose, the warrior-king who had made Egypt great. And he should have been making Egypt great in his own way.

Not stuck in bed with two broken legs. What kind of a weakling was he that he could not even get through his first battle without falling out of his chariot?

Everything was pointing toward me being a warrior, he thought bitterly, angry tears coming to his eyes as the hope that had filled his heart at this "great opportunity" flickered like the flame of a lamp. *This was it. And then it wasn't.*

Why had this happened, anyway? What had he ever done wrong? Why had his chance to become a warrior, the strong Pharaoh he'd always dreamed of becoming, been stolen from him on his very first battle? Why had the answer to his fervent prayers ended in epic disaster? And why was he now trapped in bed, less mobile than ever, unlikely to even leave the palace for days, if not weeks? Why?

What had he done, anyway, going into battle? And what was he going to do now?

The Pharaoh gave an angry sigh. It wasn't right. Wasn't fair. But all he could do was wait for his legs to heal. Then… then he could go out and show the world what he was made of. And he would establish a legacy that would make Grandfather Thutmose proud.

His brother needed to rest. So Semerkhet had a little chat with all the servants who had usually filed in and out of the Pharaoh's chambers multiple times a day, cleaning, putting away clothing, assisting the Chief Valet. And he told them to give the king space. Told them not to come into the royal bedroom unless it was strictly necessary. Because he was the Sole Companion, the Royal Favorite. And he had the authority to protect his little brother from any and all disturbances.

"Where is everyone?" Tut asked Semerkhet as his valet brought him a cup of peppermint tea after lunch. With the help of the doctor, Sem had gotten Tut back into bed soon after the soldiers had left. Although he was tired from even the short stint out of bed, the Pharaoh was delighted at how quickly he was recovering. "All the other servants? It's so quiet." Kahotep, or later on, Ptahmose, had generally helped Semerkhet in putting away the King's clothing and jewelry at the end of the day, but his valet had been almost the only servant the King had seen since coming home.

Semerkhet handed him his tea. "Well, they want to let you rest," he said. *Or I wanted to make sure my Pharaoh had all the peace and quiet he needed*, he thought silently. Then he sighed. "But it does seem quiet."

Tutankhamun shrugged. He never would have thought he would miss the bustle of a roomful of servants all looking after him and his clothing.

And here were no meetings. Not anymore. Or not since Semerkhet's trial, or since the suicidally-remorseful soldiers had converged on the royal bedroom. Nothing to sign, authorize with his signet-ring; no questions to answer, decisions to make. There were no lessons either; no hours of listening dutifully as the Vizier droned on and on, reciting fact after fact about the long, glorious history of their country. The lessons he was learning now were taught to him by life itself, as he continued to make the decisions that came to him hour by hour, even trapped in bed with two broken legs.

Tut had just been getting used to his new responsibility as a King without a regent. And now it was gone. He missed it. The Grand Vizier was making the day-to-day political decisions again, going back to what he had been doing for the past nine years.

What would Ay do next?

14

Recovery

"There's something he's not telling me," Ankhesenamun sighed that evening. She was sitting at her dressing-table in her sleeping-tunic, makeup washed off and wig set aside, ready for this long day to end. Of course she was going to sleep in her brother's room, but as much as she loved him, as much as he needed her, there were moments when she needed a little time to herself. Especially after a long day. "Some secret. Even before the battle, there was something, and now…"

She sighed, looking down at her folded hands. "I think someone did this to him. And he knows who, or he thinks he does, but he thinks that if I knew, they might go after me, too." The Queen shook her head. "He said that as soon as he figured it out, he would tell me. But then he said that if he got better, I would never need to know what it had been." She looked at Meresankh. "So do I want to know the secret or not?"

Meresankh shook her head sadly, looking up from arranging the Queen's wigs on their stands. Most of them she kept in her storage room, but a few favorites stood proudly displayed on a shelf.

"You want him to get better, and for life to go back to normal, secret or no secret." Meresankh swallowed, fiddling with a single braid. "But it can't. Even when change is good, it's still change. We can't keep things from changing, and we definitely can't go back in time. Whatever happens, the decisions he's made, the policies he's established, will still be in place. And the politicians who disagree with him will still disagree with him. There will still be battles to be fought."

"But he wanted to be the King of peace," Ankh whispered.

Her handmaiden gave her a sad smile. "Maybe you can talk about it with him in the morning. It's getting late."

Ankh nodded. It was. Her handmaiden finished with the wigs and stepped closer, so their faces were both reflected in the bronze mirror, side-by-side, just like her husband had observed with Semerkhet. A beautiful Light shone from Meresankh's eyes, the Light the Queen always noticed. And like Tutankhamun and Semerkhet, she and Meresankh were very much the same. Was Ankhesenamun really any more equipped to be the Queen than Meresankh was? And who knew but that she was hiding a secret skill at wig-styling that would never be uncovered because she would never be anyone's handmaiden?

The Queen saw a slight movement reflected in the mirror. And she smiled as she felt Meresankh's soft little hand gently come to rest on her shoulder. She felt her handmaiden's strength flowing into her; felt... felt as though the Light in her friend's eyes was touching her.

She still didn't know what it all meant. But she was grateful for her friend, and the caring, reassuring hand on her shoulder.

Meresankh smiled. She had done it. Literally reached out and touched her friend, her Lady, offering the support she knew the Queen needed. And in the mirror, she could see her friend smiling.

And she was glad that she could help the Queen feel better. Glad that she could take care of her friend. Glad that... Meresankh chuckled to herself as it hit her. Glad that she could take care of her sister.

Because that was who her Queen was to her.

Tut thought of Ay, then pushed him away. So much for having had no intention of the Pharaoh being hurt. So much for fond wishes for a grand future. So much for sincerest apologies. So much for trust. And he thought of Horemheb. Of the growing friendship that had suddenly disappeared like the flame of a blown-out candle, leaving only the vaporous, wispy smoke of deceit and betrayal.

He held Bastet tighter in his aching arms, rubbing his face against her soft, warm, gray fur as she purred. At least cats could never betray you.

Tut and Ankh still played *seega*. Even with him stuck in his room, spending a little more time in his chair day by day. And he continued to improve as a player, until it truly was anyone's game; there was no telling until the last move who would win. She had taught him so much. And he would continue to play the game they were in until its final move.

"I never liked *seega*, back when you first taught me," he said.

She made a move, blocking the capture he was setting up. Silently, he chuckled at her excellent strategy.

"No?"

He shook his head with another chuckle, setting up another attempt at capturing one of her pieces. "No. You were always so bossy!"

Again she evaded him, turning his attempt to claim one of her pieces into an apprehension of her own. He winced as she took his piece, groaning as he saw his strategy fail.

"No, I wasn't!" she laughed. "I was never bossy!"

"Oh, yeth, you were!" he countered, finally taking one of her pieces as she gave a little groan of her own at his discovery of the one possibility she hadn't considered. "Telling me every move I made was wrong. But you never told me what I wath doing wrong or helped me fix my strategy."

Slowly, Ankh made another move, neither evading his offense nor setting up her own.

"So that's why you never wanted to play anymore," she said thoughtfully. Then she smiled again, a teasing smile. "I'm glad you grew up enough to see that I was helping you be the best player you could be."

Tut rolled his eyes. "And I'm glad that *you* grew up enough to quit just picking on me and help me figure out how to actually win!"

And as he captured another one of his sister's pieces, they both smiled. They had both come a long way.

Even now, Tut still smiled. Because every few days, his sister brought him flowers. He would wake up to see a fresh bouquet right where he could see it best— bright poppies, cornflowers, late roses. And it warmed his heart to think of her arranging them, making sure they were in the best spot, imagining how much joy they would bring him. And she was right. Because even with everything that was going on, her flowers always brought him joy.

"I heard the Vizier talking to the Treasurer about 'this morning's meeting,'" Semerkhet said as he came into the room with a bowl of sliced melon for the Pharaoh, who was up to spending a whole half-hour in the chair in one go. "He's been running them for you again, hasn't he?"

Tut nodded, accepting the bowl of fruit. Just what he'd been thinking of. "Yes, he has. Thank you, Semerkhet. Keep an eye on him. And if anything raises your suspicions... you know where to find me."

The valet gave a little chuckle. "I'll keep my ears open."

"Those flowers are wilted," Tut heard his sister say. "And we really should have gotten a fresh pot of peppermint tea by now. And where are the clean cloths?"

"It's under control, My Lady," Semerkhet said, and the Pharaoh saw him dip his head respectfully. "We'll get it all taken care of." And Tut winked at his friend as together, they shared in the joys of big sisters.

The Queen found the time for another short visit with Mutnedjmet and Amenia. Her sweet friends were delighted to see her; ready for another session of deep conversation, probing questions, and soul-searching. Over licorice tea, they talked about following in the footsteps of

Great Royal Wives like Tetisheri and Ahhotep, who had supported their husbands through taking incredibly active roles at home, making sure that their warrior Pharaohs had an Egypt to come home to. Nowhere was it written that wives could not be heroines.

The ladies also updated Ankh on their growing personal lives. Amenia had taken an interest in writing poetry, and Mutnedjmet had gotten a flute. Ankh smiled. Maybe they would discover that they were artists. But wherever these skills went, it was wonderful to see her friends expressing themselves, their true, individual selves, not in terms of how they related to others, but pouring out their own hearts through music and words. It made her wonder if she should learn to play the lute.

But with all the joy that she felt to spend time with the General's wives, Ankh regretted that the Treasurer's wife was not there. And the Queen reminded herself that that was Meryt's choice.

Tut smiled, lying there in bed as Semerkhet fussed over him. Yes, it was getting thoroughly tiresome to be stuck in bed, especially considering the fact that he'd been there all week. But it wouldn't last forever. And the way he was recovering, he would be not only out of bed but back on his feet even before his bones were fully healed. Even if he had to use two canes, it would not be long, ultimately, until he was able to return to normal life.

He thought back to all those months ago, back in the days when they had been a Pharaoh and a servant. Sem had never looked directly at him in those days; had kept his head down and his eyes averted as he performed the duties of a valet out of gratitude for the honor of having such a job. He'd been so stiff. So formal. So… frightened of the Morning and Evening Star whom it was his responsibility to take care of.

But after Tut had realized that he and his valet were both human, and changed the way he behaved toward the other boy, the warmth of friendship had slowly cut through the stiffness and the fear. And Semerkhet had started making eye contact with him, accepted a nickname, and found his smile.

And those changes had been good. But then... then had come Kadesh. And then everything had changed. Friendship... friendship had blossomed into brotherhood. And now the touching of a hand or an arm around a shoulder was not only something to be grateful for, but something normal.

So much had changed in the past year.

But some things had not changed. And Semerkhet was taken aback one day when the Pharaoh asked him,

"So, when is your next hockey game? Or your next horse race?"

The valet set aside the empty plate of honey-cakes he'd just served his friend and sighed. "I haven't... haven't thought about hockey for awhile," he said.

Tut gave him a little frown. "Sem," he said, "I want you to go play. I know how much you love it. I'm just sorry I can't be there. Goodness knows I like sitting and chatting with you, but the Queen and I can get along for a few hours. Go on. And tell me all about it when you get back."

Semerkhet looked away, then finally met the Pharaoh's eye with a smile. "My team is playing against Khem today," he said, "but I didn't tell the team captain I'd be there."

"Well, you'd better get going, then," Tut said with a smile, clapping him on the shoulder. "Go win one for me."

They didn't win. But Semerkhet was refreshed by the feeling of the wind in his face, the hockey stick in his hands, the focus and concentration he had to muster as he watched the ball's every move. And he came back to the Pharaoh's room with a smile on his face, a spring in his step, and a story to tell his friend.

Ankh sat on her bed, watching her handmaiden and friend putting away five or six freshly-cleaned wigs. And as she watched, she listened.

"...and Khenut has been having terrible headaches, but if she'd just use some peppermint oil and make sure she's drinking enough water, I'm sure she'd feel much better..."

The Queen just smiled. Her friend cared so much about those around her. And she could never keep from sharing when she had a story to tell.

"So if Hepu can't get his team in top shape before next week, I don't see how they're going to beat the grays from Per-Amun," Semerkhet said. He was updating the Pharaoh on recent wins and losses in the worlds of horse-racing and field hockey.

"How are St—" Tut stopped himself before the words left his mouth. And he bit his lip, wondering what to say instead. Sadly, he sighed. "I'm sorry," he said softly. "About Stormy and Flash."

Semerkhet looked up, then back down at his feet. He swallowed. "Thank you," he said.

"I remember hunting with them," the Pharaoh continued with a sad smile. "They were so beautiful. So strong. And you were so good with them."

Tutankhamun looked at Bastet, curled up on the end of the bed, and felt his heart begin to ache. And in that ache, he thought he caught a glimpse of the grief his friend felt for his beloved horses.

He shook his head. As Pharaoh, he could present Semerkhet with the finest horses in all of Egypt. But would that really ease his friend's pain? Tut sighed. Maybe... even with all his authority, all his power, the best thing he could do was simply to be there for his friend.

The sixth morning home Tut woke with a hiss of pain; the pain in his left leg had grown from a dull roar to a sharp wail.

Ankh was bent over him, eyebrows full of fear, as soon as she heard him gasp. She'd spent the night in her chair, Semerkhet sleeping on his cot on the floor.

"What is it? Where does it hurt?"

"My leg," he gasped, groaning with the sudden pain. "Hurts bad. Need... need to get the doctor."

Semerkhet was up in an instant, throwing on a wig. "I'll get him, Master." A moment later, he was out the door.

Very, very gently, Ankh helped her brother sit up, resting securely against the pillows. "There. Let's get you settled for him... and me presentable." After getting him comfortably positioned, she crossed the room and put her own wig on, then found a simple, green outer robe to cover her sleeping-tunic. Then his sister sat down beside him again, and they waited for the doctor.

"Infection," the Chief Physician said grimly, looking at the gash on the King's leg that had become red and hot. He had shaken his head when he had taken Tut's pulse, and he was shaking it again now. "Sometimes happens when a bone is broken such that the skin also breaks. The wound hasn't been thoroughly cleaned since it was initially treated, has it? And it is quite a wound... You and your charioteer took quite the fall when the General ordered the retreat. I can contend with it, but... everyone responds differently. We will ask the priests to pray."

And he tucked the King in again, hiding the ugly wound from view.

But there was something. Something in his face the Pharaoh didn't like. He was saying the words, treating the situation with the gravity it deserved with his tone of voice and the expression on his face, but still... Tut couldn't help but think that the doctor was trying to *look* concerned, more than he actually *was* concerned. Besides which, he had stated that the wound must not have been cleaned recently, but made no suggestion of cleaning it again himself.

And— that was it. The most important part. *When the General ordered the retreat*, the doctor had just said. But just like Ay, he hadn't been there.

How did he know?

The Pharaoh swallowed down his questions. And he turned to look at the doctor. "You will clean it now, Physician. And the bandages need to be changed. That is an order."

The doctor swallowed, dipping his head almost respectfully. "As you wish, Glorious Lord," he said a little grudgingly. And with a reluctant grimace, he went to gather his materials.

The doctor cleaned the wound. Very thoroughly. The Pharaoh shut his eyes and held tight to Ankh and Sem's hands, practically holding his breath until it was over. But for as painful as it was, it was effective. Such a procedure just might allow the infection to heal.

The Queen walked back to her brother's room, across the narrow hall that separated their suites. The short break she had taken had left her refreshed, and she was ready to come back and continue pouring her love and energy into him.

She almost bumped into the Grand Vizier. "My Lady," Ay said with a deep bow.

"Vizier." She kept walking, continuing on her way toward her brother's door.

"My Lady," he said again, and she paused.

"Yes?"

"My Lady, I can't help but notice how much time you've been spending assisting in the care of the Pharaoh… even sleeping in his chambers."

"That's correct." How did Ay know that?

"And I wish to ask you… is such nursing care befitting the rank of a Queen? Should not a Queen of Egypt leave bandages and soup to the doctors and valets?"

Ankhesenamun smiled up at Ay. "The Queen is also the Great Royal Wife," she said. "And my husband needs me."

And she excused herself, leaving the Vizier standing there.

Infection. Semerkhet sighed as he sat beside his Master, handing him his cup when he was thirsty, trying to fill the emptiness of his endless days with cheerful gossip about life as a member of the palace staff, long-winded accounts of recent horse races and hockey games. And as always, he wished he could do more.

The Queen was restless. She could sit with her husband, bringing him comfort, but what could she *do*; how could she *help?* What could she do for their country while he was unable to leave the palace, leave his room? He was the Pharaoh, but she was the Queen. She had a responsibility to their country just like he did, and if he was busy, she needed to take action.

What can I do, right now? she thought. Then she smiled. *I can be his eyes and ears; go out and see if his policies are being maintained. Then he can take that information and decide what to do next. I'm going to go be effective for my husband, just like Mother's title said.*

Ankhesenamun went to find her cloak.

15

Maya

"I don't think they're keeping their promises," Ankh said to Tut as she sat with him, reaching into a blue ceramic bowl of bright red pomegranate pips, carefully sampled by Semerkhet, and scooping out a handful of ruby-red fruit. Pomegranate season had finally begun, and Tut licked his lips as he imagined the first sweet mouthful of his favorite fruit. It had been a long time since last year.

"What's going on?" he asked, frowning and searching her face.

"Well, I decided to go out earlier, just for a little while, to see how things were going with all your new policies. And there wasn't any work being done on the schools, even though it's a perfectly sunny day, and I couldn't find any of the gardeners we just hired. And even before I got outside the palace, there were definitely some faces missing from the culinary department. And when I got out to the building site, I thought I heard one man say to another that he'd known the minimum wage wasn't going to last."

"Wasn't going to last?" Tut asked, sitting up in bed. "You mean they've canceled it?"

"I don't know," she said, shaking her head sadly. "But it doesn't sound good. You've been… busy… so they're taking power right back.

I even heard..." She swallowed. "I went past Ay's chambers on my way back in, and I know I heard him say 'in the name of the Pharaoh.'"

Tut gave a disgruntled sigh. Sounded like someone wanted to keep his temporary powers. The Pharaoh was going to have to talk to his remaining courtiers.

But then he smiled. Almost to his surprise, he was in the mood for a meeting. And feeling pleasantly confident in his own abilities, trusting in his own knowledge, secure in his growing experience. Tutankhamun would handle his obstinate royal court like the Pharaoh he was.

"Thank you, Ankh," he said. "Could you have the Treasurer sent in, please? And bring me a wig? And maybe my circlet?"

She did. And she brought Semerkhet and Amenmose, who carefully moved Tut from the bed to the chair. He was the Pharaoh, after all.

Maya came in a few minutes later, giving a deep bow.

"Your Majesty summoned me?" he asked in his deep, booming voice.

"Sit down," the King said pleasantly, nodding at the chair across from his. Maya seated himself and looked at the King, waiting to hear whatever this was about. "I got an interesting report earlier today... from my wise wife."

"Was her jewelry not polished properly? Or is her makeup running out?" Maya asked, scornful tone and curling lip showing just how much he respected the King's sister. "What concerns does the dear Queen have?"

Tut shook his head. "The dear Queen has observed that on a beautiful, sunny day, no work is being done on either of the new schools, and that the newly-hired gardeners and cooks seem to have disappeared. She also mentioned something about one man saying to another that he'd known the minimum wage wasn't going to last." He paused, watching the Treasurer's face. It remained perfectly calm, except for a little tightness around the jaw. "I wanted your perspective. Please enlighten me."

"Glorious Lord," Maya began without a hint of doubt in his own decision-making, "the Grand Vizier and I have been reconsidering the budget you approved, and we have determined that we simply don't have the funds to add to our landscaping or culinary departments right now. I'm afraid we had to lay off the new cooks and gardeners. As for the work on the schools, if we were to continue paying the builders for daily work according to your new minimum wage— with taxes at their new rate— we would be cutting into military funding within six months, long before the projects would be complete. As such, we've decided to conduct work only every other day, and to trim the minimum wage according to our current resources."

Tutankhamun looked at him with hard eyes and dark, dangerous eyebrows. And a fierce black eye. Boldly, Maya stared right back, until his eyes finally began to flicker.

"What is your job title, Maya?" Tut asked quietly.

"Overseer of the Treasuries, O Mighty King," he responded, sitting proudly at attention.

"And for whom are you overseeing the treasuries?" the Pharaoh said even more softly.

"For you, Glorious Lord."

"What is my job title, Maya?"

"You are His Majesty the Pharaoh, O Great Morning Star, Lord of the Two Lands."

Tut let his voice drop to a whisper, plastering a sweet, loving smile on his face as he nodded again. "That's correct, Maya. So you continue being the Treasurer, and I'll continue being the Pharaoh… I need you right where you're at." He paused. "Overseeing the treasury is what you're being paid to do. So why don't you do your job, and I'll do mine. Thank you so much."

Maya just looked at him, as if unsure of how to continue the conversation. The Pharaoh continued to bare his teeth. Again they locked eyes. Getting into a staring contest with the Pharaoh was a very bad idea, Tut thought. But Maya seemed determined. Determined to risk immediate dismissal for insubordination, or worse.

But the Pharaoh didn't want to do that. He wanted to make Maya respect him. Make him knuckle under. Master him. Tame him. Bring him to the point of submission. Bring him to heel. But not with threats, not with a raised voice, not with bluster. In a whisper. And with a smile. Today, Maya would learn who was ruling Egypt. Even confined to his chambers with two broken legs.

"Who makes the decisions in Egypt, Maya?" Tut whispered.

"The Pharaoh, My Lord."

"And am I of age, and competent to lead?"

"You are, Great Morning Star."

Tut nodded again. "Yes. I make the decisions, Maya. And I will continue to do so for as long as I live. The minimum wage is to be restored to the figure I approved, and work is to be conducted on the schools on every day without rain. Taxes are to remain at the established figure. Also, all the gardeners and cooks are to be re-hired with my thanks for their work, and my sincere apologies for your oversight. Any deficit can be made up from the military budget or salaries of the Viziers. I need you to do your job, Maya, and let me do mine." He looked at Maya, who was stone-faced. "Any questions?"

"No, Your Majesty," came the answer through clenched teeth. Finally Maya had dropped his eyes, staring at his own knees. A muscle throbbed in his locked jaw.

Tut nodded with the same plastered-on smile. "Then you are dismissed, Maya. Thank you so much for coming to see me."

Maya rose, bowed, murmured, "All life, prosperity, and health!" and turned from the room.

Tut lay back in the chair with a heavy sigh, exhausted by the battle of wills. But glowing in the knowledge that he had won. And Maya would know who was boss, much more effectively than if he had been fired. Tutankhamun had shown him who was master.

Meanwhile, the Queen sat in her room, watching the steam rising from the two cups of peppermint tea on her desk. She had asked Meresankh to pour them so that by the time her brother's meeting was over, they would be cool enough to drink.

As she sat, she thought. Infection. One terrible word that had knocked his recovery sideways, threatened the time-frame of healing in which they had hoped, stolen a portion of the joy she had felt as she had watched him grow stronger with each passing day. Now, instead of wondering what glorious things her brother would go on to do once his recovery was complete, she was forced to wonder how long it would be before he was well again. And she was forced to wonder…

What life would bring them next.

"Darling? Are you busy?" Ankh asked from out in the hall.

"Come in, dear," Tut said, sitting up straighter. She walked in, two cups of peppermint tea in her hands. The Pharaoh reached out with a smile, and carefully, she handed one to him.

"Thank you," he said, sipping it. Somehow the exhilaration of victory had caused his pain to fade into insignificance. "That's good."

"How did it go?" she asked anxiously, searching his face. He could see the worry-lines on her forehead.

"Pretty well, actually," he said, giving her a satisfied smile. She returned it with a sigh of relief, her tense shoulders dropping. "Treasurer Maya knows he's not the Pharaoh. Everything's going back to what we agreed on— the building, the minimum wage, the gardeners, the cooks."

"What did you have to do?" she asked, eyebrows rising in curiosity as she sipped her tea.

"Nothing much," he said, setting his teacup down and taking the cat into his arms, petting her as she purred, congratulating him for his success. Now he was feeling so good about things that moving his arms didn't even hurt. "Really, all I had to do was whisper at him."

"Whisper?" she asked, confusion showing on her face.

He chuckled. "Yes. Real quiet. Real sweet. Gave him this horrible big smile. Asked him—" He affected the same horrible sweetness he'd just used— "'What is your job title?' And he said 'Treasurer,' and then I asked him what my job was. And I told him, 'Then you do your job and let me do mine.' I think he got the message."

Ankh laughed. "I'm sure he did. You got the better of the Treasurer by whispering? This *is* an age of wonders!"

Tut nodded. "I know. It sure is." He smiled. "All thanks to you, actually."

She raised an eyebrow. "Me?"

He smiled. "Remember a few months back when you said I should find a different approach, one that would make them respect me because they could see I deserved it?" She nodded. "Well, I thought about not shouting, and what's a better example of not shouting than whispering? I even practiced it with Semerkhet; he pretended to be Ay and Maya, and I tried shouting at him, and then whispering. And he said that the whispering worked better. And I thought about being sweet and deadly, civil and sneaky, courageous and cunning, getting people under control without threatening them. So I tried it today, and it sure worked!"

Ankh laughed. "What do you know."

He shook his head. "Never would have dreamed I could get control of him, much less like that. But it sure worked." He chuckled and took her hand, pressing it to his lips. "Just like Mother. Effective for her husband. You're the power behind the throne."

"Power *beside* the throne," Ankh said, running her other hand over his wig. "Well, I'm glad it worked. Now you can be sure he'll honor your decisions."

Tut nodded with a satisfied smile, leaning back and folding his hands under his head. "I'm pretty sure he will."

Together they smiled. Despite everything, today they could celebrate a small victory.

But even in his victory, the Pharaoh was exhausted. And with the help of Raherka and Amenmose, he got back into bed.

Semerkhet walked down the hall to the kitchen to get his Master a snack. As he walked, he caught a glimpse of Treasurer Maya walking in the same direction, as if he, too, had just come from the Pharaoh's room.

Sem kept walking with a silent grumble. Why hadn't his friend asked him to keep the Treasurer from bothering him?

She was so proud of her brother, Ankhesenamun thought. Today he had taken a step forward as an adult… as a politician. Although… The Queen sighed. If only she was still friends with Meryt. She wanted to be; of course, she wanted to be. She would always hold the wife of the Treasurer in high regard; always welcome her just the same as Amenia, Mutnedjmet, Meresankh. It was Meryt who had decided to step back from the friendship; from the Queen and her ideas of what a woman could accomplish.

But even as the Queen reminded herself that that was Meryt's choice, she regretted that they no longer seemed to be friends. And she regretted that through her friendship with Meryt, she could not prevail upon the wife of the Treasurer to lovingly encourage her husband to honor the Pharaoh's vision for the future of Egypt.

Semerkhet walked down the hall from the kitchen, a bowl of jujubes in his hand, his bright red sash and ring standing out against the white and blue of most of the staff's uniforms. Like him, most of them had added outer robes of various colors to their uniforms, shelter against the growing chill of the month of Sholiak. His Pharaoh had finished his pomegranate pips, and now he wanted some jujube. This early in the season, the jujubes would be green and crisp, almost like an apple, but as they continued to ripen, their color would deepen to reddish-brown and their smooth skin would begin to wrinkle as the sweet flavor of the fruit deepened. But they were still very good when they were green.

An odd flash of movement caught his eye. He turned his head to see something that almost made his jaw drop with shock...

Someone was bowing to him. Three servants he didn't know personally, although their uniforms indicated that one was a cook, one worked with sandals, and the third was from the laundry department, were bowing before him.

"Hail to thee, Sole Companion, Favorite of the Pharaoh, Unique Friend," they intoned, eyes on the ground.

Semerkhet just stared at them.

"R... rise," he said shakily, beckoning gently with his free hand. Slowly they stood, still not looking directly at him. "H... have a nice day," he said, giving an awkward little wave as he kept walking. They did not respond.

Semerkhet shivered as he made his way back to his Master's room. Other servants continued to pause and whisper as he walked by, a few of them dipping their heads respectfully, most avoiding his eye, all carefully clearing a path for him as he made his way back to the royal suites. Was this what it was like to be a member of the nobility?

The sixth night, it got harder for the King to sleep. His infected leg burned, making him struggle to find a comfortable way to lie.

He was home, many miles from Kadesh, but that didn't mean he wasn't in battle.

The infection got worse. It spread through Tut's leg, making every moment pain. Even the poultice of moldy bread and daubing of honey, both known infection-fighters, did not seem to be helping. Neither did the poultice of onions. On top of the pain he was already in from the broken bones, this was becoming difficult to bear.

"I'm going to get better, Ankh," he told her, swallowing down some sort of foul-tasting medicine the doctor had given him in a tiny clay bowl. He almost chuckled as he remembered a long-ago conversation about whether a particular medicine had crocodile eyeballs in it. "Wait and see."

She only nodded, gazing at him with eyes full of worry and questions he could not answer.

His Master was asleep. Quietly Semerkhet walked back to his own room to get ready for bed before returning to the cot next to the king's bed where he'd been sleeping. The seventh night since they'd gotten home, and he hadn't yet slept in his own bed. After relaxing for a few minutes with a cup of tea, he went to his dressing area, poured a basin of water, and had a wash, washing away the day with a cool, damp cloth. Then he sat down to put on his own bruise salve and put on his sleeping-tunic.

Then it was back to the Pharaoh's room, to lie on his cot and try to sleep, always keeping one ear open in case his Master needed him.

It had been a long day.

Ankhesenamun and Semerkhet kept trying to pray. But "trying" was the only word for it. Because even as they poured out their hearts to the gods and goddesses of their people, all they ever heard were their own words echoing back to them in the silence. Just as they always had. As the silence went on, they grew weary. Weary of not knowing. Not knowing if the gods cared. Not knowing if they were even listening.

And as the silence ached in their hearts, they turned away. Spent less and less time trying to communicate with the unresponsive Divine. And trusted, very simply, that in some way, they were not alone.

The next day, Tut found his appetite somewhat improved and his energy slightly higher. The infection in his leg, although still present, seemed to be dying down, the pain, warmth, and redness all less intense. The Pharaoh felt so good, in fact, that he asked Semerkhet to do his makeup and bring him his favorite wig and one of his lighter necklaces. And of course, he reveled in spending several pleasant hours sitting up in his chair.

He had been home one week.

"I think I've turned a corner," he said with a smile as Ankh cracked open a small pile of pistachios for him. "Actually feel alive today. I'll be out of this bed before you know it."

Ankh popped a pistachio into his mouth and kissed his cheek. Beside the chair, Bastet was chasing a stray nutshell, pouncing on it as if she were hunting a mouse. "I'm so proud of you," the Queen said, reaching out to squeeze his hand.

Tut just smiled.

"Your recovery seems to be going smoothly since your procedure," the Chief Physician said, tying a fresh herbal poultice over the wound on the Pharaoh's left leg. "The Vizier will be delighted to hear how well you are recuperating… and how quickly." Busy with his own smile, Tut barely noticed that instead of joyful like his words, the doctor's face looked a little sour. "At this rate, I would estimate that you can begin putting weight on your legs in about a week, unless there are any… complications."

The fat, waddling Chief Physician gave a little nod as he left the room, the examination complete. But as he left, the Pharaoh couldn't help but notice that he looked a little disgruntled about something. Disappointed. Downright annoyed. And then a twinge of unexpected pain made Tut look down. The bandages had been tied on much too tightly. At that rate, the circulation to his foot would be cut off. And as a strange uncertainty began to tiptoe around his heart, Tut asked Ankh if she could retie the bandages for him.

16

Teamwork

"How's your knee?" Meresankh asked as she and Semerkhet walked through the servants' dining hall with their plates of lunch, looking for a place to sit. It was busy; employees from such diverse departments as sandals and beekeeping chattered and gossiped loudly over their meal of mutton, stewed onions, flatbread, cinnamon-dusted dumplings, and beans.

He shrugged as they sat down at one of the only empty tables. On their left Persenet and Tentamun were talking about babies; on their right, Amenmose and Nuya were discussing horses.

"Getting better," he said. He looked much better than when he'd first gotten home; the bruises and scratches on his limbs were slowly fading, and he had had the chance to shave. He winced. "Starting to, anyway."

"Did the doctor give you anything for it?" she asked, scooping up some beans with her flatbread.

He took a sip of beer. "Mm-hmm. Same salve the King has, actually."

She gave him a little smile. "Well, I hope it works. If it doesn't, I can always take you down to Merneith and she'll mix something up for you."

He looked at her questioningly. "The midwife?"

"She's a lot more than a midwife," Meresankh said. "She's got an herb for everything. Grows them herself in a big herb garden near the staff quarters. And," she said, raising her eyebrows playfully, "none of her remedies have dead mice in them."

Semerkhet took a bite of mutton. "That probably is a good thing."

Meresankh reached out and took his hand, smiling as he blushed at the touch of her warm little fingers. "I hope it's better soon."

He shook his head, the small braids of his wig swinging across his face. "I'll be all right."

Meresankh squeezed his hand. "I know you will." Then she chuckled, gently running her fingers over the red ring on his hand. "Now that you're Sole Companion... do you get your own valet?"

Semerkhet laughed out loud... just as everyone seemed to notice his presence at the same moment. Ten people bowed with the words, "Hail to thee, Sole Companion, Favorite of the Pharaoh, Unique Friend."

And he tried to hide his embarrassment.

"The funniest thing happened the other day," Semerkhet said, giving a little chuckle as he sampled the beef the Pharaoh was going to have for lunch. Nothing raised his suspicions, so he handed the plate to his Master, who began to eat.

"Hmm?" Tut said with his mouth full. He was grateful that today he had the strength to have lunch sitting up in his chair.

His friend shook his head. And with an incredulous chuckle, he described being bowed to and honored with "Hail to Thee's" twice in the past two days.

"It was so weird!" he finished, shaking his head again.

Tut smiled, reaching out to pat his friend's hand, nodding at the red jasper ring of the Sole Companion. "Well, it comes with the territory."

"How do you get used to it?" Semerkhet asked.

His Master shook his head. "You don't."

The Queen bled on the ninth of Sholiak. But seeing it come didn't bring the same heartache that it had so often in the past. They had not come together recently, so she should expect nothing else. And right now, she had so many other things to think about. But it reminded her that her body was healthy. And despite everything that was going on, it gave her hope. Hope for their uncertain future.

Meresankh continued doing her best. She worked hard, keeping the Queen's chambers neat and tidy, helping her Mistress get arranged in the mornings and settled at night. It felt good to be of help. Felt good to bring joy. And it felt good to know that she and the Queen were friends... best friends.

It had occasionally occurred to her to wonder what it would be like to have a sister. And for a long time, she had not known. But now... she knew. Because she had found one in the Queen.

Meresankh shook her head as she realized what she had not yet told Semerkhet since his arrival home.

"I was so sorry," she said one day as he stopped by her chambers for a cup of tea, "about Stormy and Flash."

Sem looked down into his teacup, biting his lip. "Thank you," he said softly. Slowly, he looked up at her. "So am I."

Even bathing had become more difficult. Every time that Semerkhet gave the Pharaoh a bed bath, Tut found himself contracting in cold, wracked by shivers that made every inch of his body shake. Over the past week of bedrest, he had lost muscle mass, and with it, his body's ability to keep itself warm. Sem was working so quickly that he broke a sweat, but Tut was colder than he had ever been.

They were both surprised that his body had changed so much in such a short time. But there was little they could do about it. So Tut winced with the cold as his teeth chattered and Sem tsk'd encouragingly, wrapping him warmly in a towel before getting the Pharaoh a fresh loincloth and sleeping-tunic. And every time, Tut was glad when it was over.

The valet's knee still gave a twinge of pain now and then, but it no longer kept him from getting outside to pour his heart into the athletics he loved so much. Semerkhet always checked in with the Pharaoh before he went, but he made it a point to race his chariot, with the new team of horses that didn't handle as well as his old friends but were fast and sure. One black and one white, they were named Thunder and Lightning, and he raced them to victory as often as he had the two chestnuts. As residents of the Royal Stables, they lived at the palace, the same as Stormy and Flash had, and the same as his old friends, he didn't own them. At this point in his life, owning a horse would have been more of an expense than a benefit. But he loved the royal horses he tentatively thought of as his own.

And Semerkhet played hockey with all his heart, letting go of all other thoughts as he focused his mind and body on the task of keeping the opposing team from getting the ball into his net. And he spent that time with his teammates, who may not have been bosom friends, but were cheerful and fun to be with. Their laughter and gossip about their simple, happy lives took his mind off of the darkness and complexity that had entered his own life. Win or lose, he came home from his games tired, sweaty, and refreshed, ready to face the next few hours solicitously watching over his friend in the same room where they had both been trapped for the past week.

Somehow, those hours in the bright sun and the bracing wind made the hours in the cool shadows of the palace a little easier.

Tut missed being able to go to Semerkhet's hockey games and horse races. He imagined his friend saving goal after goal and leading the Stallions to victory; pictured him swinging around a curve in the racetrack on two wheels as his horses pulled ahead of the other teams. Semerkhet always told him about the games, about the races, when he came home. But the Pharaoh was sorry he could not see them himself.

He thought of the hockey games he had gotten to see. And he thought of all the moments that had brought them to this very day. Thought of all the time he had spent with Semerkhet over the past months. And how much this friendship had helped him to grow. Surrounded by sisters, he had never really spent a lot of time doing "boys'" activities; never had a role model. But Semerkhet... as the older brother Tut had never had, he had taught him to be a boy, a young man. He had opened his eyes to a whole world of teamwork and excitement that he had never participated in. And even if it was weeks before Tut got to go to another one of Sem's hockey games, he was glad for everything that this friendship, this brotherly bond, had taught him.

Meresankh went to as many of Semerkhet's races and games as she could. She wasn't into athletics herself; although the energy of the crowd quickened her heart and brightened her eyes, all the sweat and dirt didn't appeal to her for its own sake.

But even from the stands, she could see Semerkhet's smile as he saved goal after goal; guided his horses past competitor after competitor. And her beloved's smile was all she wanted to see.

"You're looking better today," Meresankh said as she arranged the delicate braids of the Queen's wig that afternoon.

Ankhesenamun nodded. "The Pharaoh's doing better. The infection's going away, and the doctor says it's only one more week before he can start putting weight on his legs." She sighed, giving Meresankh a satisfied little smile. "I think he's going to make it."

Her handmaiden smiled and set Ankh's necklace over her shoulders. Her own was in place, the tiny silver figurine that represented Semerkhet's love for her. "What a Pharaoh... overseeing a trial with two broken legs."

Ankh grinned, smile reflecting in the copper mirror. "I am awfully proud of him. And just imagine what he'll do once he's better. Just imagine."

Meresankh sighed, rounded little hand moving up to stroke the silver necklace, the joyful Light gleaming from her bright eyes. "Semerkhet's doing better too," she said, the dimple in her cheek deepening as she smiled. "His knees were really banged up, especially the right one, but they're starting to get better."

The Queen nodded. "Oh, good. He was pretty brave, wasn't he, taking care of our Pharaoh all the way home?"

Meresankh nodded with another sigh, looking off into the middle distance. Ankh tried not to giggle. "Yes, he was."

Tut was quite pleased to spend a fair proportion of that day in his chair rather than in the bed. It was refreshing to be out of bed, to get a new view, see his room from a different perspective. Even such a small change felt good. And being upright would make him a little more imposing as he conducted the meeting he'd called today.

It actually felt good to have a meeting. Even if it was going to be with Ay.

"I'm sure you're wondering why I've summoned you," Tutankhamun said, looking up at his Vizier, who stood just inside the doorway of the bedroom, as far from the King as he could get. The scarab pendant of the Vizier gleamed on the old man's chest, as cold and hard as his murderous heart.

"I was curious, O Great Morning Star," Ay admitted. He appeared to be avoiding the King's eye. Eyes that shone darkly, outlined by black kohl, peering out from under his favorite wig and the icy gaze of the *uraeus* on his circlet. And the one on the left was accentuated with an impressive shiner. The bruises on his limbs and body were concealed by the warm, blue outer robe in which he was comfortably wrapped, protecting him from the chill of the day.

"Something interesting that the Queen told me the other day," Tut said lightly, as if whatever he was going to reveal really wasn't all that important. "She went out for a little walk in Memphis, just to see how the implementation of all our new policies was going…" Ay gave the tiniest flinch, lips tightening— "and she said that when she was coming back inside, she was going past your office, and she heard the words 'in the name of the Pharaoh.'" Tut looked up at his Vizier calmly. "I suppose we haven't had a chance to talk about it since I've been home, but I'm officially withdrawing the temporary decision-making powers I granted you for the period of time I was in Kadesh. Thank you for handling things while I was gone, but since I'm home now, I'll be resuming my duties. And you can resume yours."

Ay suddenly became very interested in a loose thread on the sleeve of his fine, white linen tunic. "I merely thought, Glorious Lord, that in your... confined condition... your healing might be better served through you being allowed to continue your... hiatus... from political responsibilities," he said, glancing up at the King as if to judge his reaction. Tut kept his face unreadable.

"I appreciate your concern," the Pharaoh said gently, plastering on the same honeyed smile with which he had defeated the Treasurer. "But I believe that as Pharaoh, and being that I am of age, standing alone in full power, my decisions about my health and my activities are mine to make. As are all governmental decisions, including the decision of how long temporary appointments may last. As Pharaoh, I want to use this time of healing to its greatest effect... even in terms of politics. I will continue fulfilling my responsibilities as Pharaoh of my country as long as I live."

He paused, scribbling a few sentences on a stray piece of papyrus, nodding at Semerkhet to apply a drop of wax, and finally stamping it with his signet-ring. "So again, thank you for your concern, but it is our royal decree—" He nodded at the document he'd just signed— "that our Viziers will no longer make decisions for us in our name, no matter how many broken bones we have. I know that you and the Treasurer decided to reverse my minimum wage and tax cuts, slow the work on my schools, and lay off my cooks and gardeners, but I've already taken care of that." Ay blinked, but Tut went on. "I want you to continue conducting the morning audiences in my stead, as I commanded you before I traveled to Kadesh, but you will bring me a report of each request, and I will decide what is to be done."

The Grand Vizier did not respond. He just swallowed, Adam's apple jumping in his skinny old throat.

The Pharaoh looked up at Ay. He didn't need to put the thunder and lightning into his gaze; he just looked calmly at his Vizier, a sweet, loving smile on his face, the same sweet smile with which he had defeated Maya.

"Any questions?"

Ay looked down his nose at the Pharaoh, searching for a solution where none existed.

"No, O Great Morning Star." He gave a deep bow. "All life, prosperity, and health." And he was gone.

Tutankhamun lay back wearily, and sensing his exhaustion, Bastet jumped up into the chair, curling up against his side with an encouraging purr. He petted her gratefully, giving a deep sigh. He had brought his Grand Vizier to heel, just as he had Treasurer Maya. And with a soft voice and a sweet smile. He was quite proud of everything he could accomplish with two broken legs.

Although... just as he had found when he had brought Treasurer Maya to heel, the victory seemed to have caused the pain to fade, pushing it into the background.

What a relief.

"You are a highly effective Queen, my dear," Tut said. He was back in bed. The change of position had done him good, but it couldn't last forever.

Ankh looked up from stroking the cat. "What did I do?" she asked with a smile.

"Told me about Ay going back to making decisions in my name. I just took care of it; he won't be doing it again."

She bent and squeezed his hand, golden beads chiming happily under her diadem. "You see what you can do?"

He smiled, raising his face for a kiss. "All because you opened my eyes."

"I know that you haven't had a chance to clean our Pharaoh's room since he's been home," Semerkhet said to the three anxious maids who stood just outside the Pharaoh's door that evening, "but he's not going to be able to leave his room for... quite some time."

"What do you recommend we do, Your Excellency?" one asked. Semerkhet chuckled. This was much the same work as he had always done, directing other staff members and administration, and as a high-ranking servant, he had sometimes been addressed as "sir." By the other servants, anyway. But to be called Your Excellency... that was something new.

"I think the best solution is to clean while he's napping," he said. "The Pharaoh sometimes sleeps for an hour in the afternoons, so that might be the best time. When I sense a good opportunity, I'll summon you."

"Yes, Your Excellency." All three of the maids gave little bows and filed away. He just shook his head.

"Khenut and Persenet are fighting," Meresankh reported as she helped the Queen get ready for bed, putting away her wig, having a quick rinse in the shower, and changing into her sleeping-tunic.

"Oh?" Ankhesenamun yawned, trying to keep her face friendly. It had been a long day, and she didn't really want to listen to a story. But that was one of the joys of having Meresankh as a handmaiden.

"Mm-hmm. Menhet started some story about Ptahmose liking Beket, and of course, they're both sweet on him, Persenet and Khenut, so now they're competing worse than ever. Falling all over one another trying to meet him in the hall, giggling and fanning themselves and being ridiculous. They're getting his attention, of course, but I don't think it's working. Everyone knows it's Ashait he likes. I just wish for their sakes that they'd quit wasting their time."

"Mm-hmm." The Queen let the story wash over her like the cool water Meresankh had just poured for her as she had washed away the day in the shower. "Well... I'm sure you can do something. You're an excellent communicator."

With a chuckle, Meresankh paused. And she and the Queen shared a smile. The handmaiden knew what her Mistress was saying.

17

Healing

The next morning, Ay came in to visit the Pharaoh again as he spent a little while sitting up in his chair. The moment the Vizier entered the room, Bastet awoke from the nap she had been taking in Tut's lap, launching into attack posture, back arched and ridged with raised fur, ears flat against her skull, the gray fur on her tail standing out like a brush, hissing and spitting like a cobra about to strike.

"And how is the Lord of the Two Lands today?" Ay asked with an affectation of caring, as if he were hoping to mend fences. He ignored the cat, which accepted Tut's reassuring pat and slunk off with one last angry hiss.

"Much better, actually," Tut said, taking a sip of fresh milk out of his favorite cup, one of delicately curved blue pottery that evoked the lotuses in the reflecting pools outside the palace. "The infection is going away, and the doctor says I'll be able to start putting weight on both legs next week." He smiled. "I'm starting to think I might survive."

"I cannot even begin to express the joy that fills my heart to hear you say that," Ay responded, with an expression on his face as if each word tasted like the dead mouse a mother sometimes ate to cure her sick baby. "I've brought you a report on yesterday's meetings."

Tut reached out to accept the papyrus. "Thank you, Vizier."

"Of course, Glorious Lord."

Then the Vizier excused himself with an obsequious wish for life, prosperity, and health, the exact things he had stolen from the King.

Tut looked over at Bastet, who sat in the corner of the room, licking herself huffily as if the Vizier's visit had dirtied the entire room. Somehow, in her cat way, she knew the truth.

Ankh shivered. Meresankh looked up from sorting through her Lady's library of historical papyri, then went into the Queen's storage room and got down one of her chests of warm robes and shawls.

"Here you are, My Lady," she said, offering the shawl that looked softest and coziest.

But instead of accepting it, Ankhesenamun froze. And as tears slowly filled her Lady's eyes, Meresankh began to understand what she had done wrong. Silently, she put the shawl away.

"Not that one. That was the only one that fit when I was going to have Senebhenas," the Queen said in a hoarse whisper. All Meresankh could do was reach out and squeeze her hand.

Their routine had not changed much, despite everything that had. Every morning Semerkhet got the Pharaoh up, helping him get dressed and adorned for the day. Just the same as he always had. And just the same as he always would. And each afternoon, Tut looked over the list of decisions that needed approved or denied and made them official with his signet-ring.

Semerkhet watched the door. And he let in the maids who absolutely needed to come in and gather up dirty linens or dishes or bring back clean ones. He watched his Pharaoh, and he determined the best times for different staff members to flit in and out of the royal chambers. And he kept them quiet.

The King's bruises were slowly getting better. Very slowly. Semerkhet thought of his own bruises. He applied his own salve every day, and he, too, could see that the bruises on his body were slowly healing. His were actually healing faster than his Master's. And his knee was much better. It hardly hurt him to walk on it.

But was that a good thing? Even as he smiled to see himself getting better, Semerkhet had to work hard not to feel guilty for recovering before his Master.

Where did the Queen want her favorite necklace to be put away, Meresankh wondered. She would have to find her and ask. She set out from her Lady's bedroom, heading down the hall. Not out there.

She heard voices from the Pharaoh's room, across the hall from the Queen's. And she heard her Lady's voice.

The usual bodyguard, Minnefer, wasn't standing in the hall like he normally was, so she couldn't ask him to go in for her and deliver her message. She would have to do it herself, if she dared.

Meresankh stood in the hallway just outside the Pharaoh's room, standing at such an angle that she could peek inside the half-open door. Semerkhet was sitting by the King, quietly reading while the King petted the cat. The Queen was in her chair, snacking on a bowl of grapes.

Then the King looked up. And looked at her.

Meresankh froze, heart pounding. For so many years none of the servants had looked at him; wouldn't you go blind or get struck by lightning if the Pharaoh's eyes met yours? Even after his royal proclamation (which she had spread) that servants were welcome, in fact, encouraged, to look straight at him, it still felt odd. Uncomfortable. Disrespectful. Almost... still a bit frightening.

She waited, gaze dropping to her own feet. Waited to see if he would say anything, if he would be upset that she was looking into his room, if he would tell her to move along or if he would have her punished.

But even as she kept looking at her feet, she saw his face move into a smile. And she saw his hand gently beckon to her.

"Come in, Meresankh," he said graciously. Slowly she raised her head, looking up at his friendly, welcoming smile. And she returned it.

"Really?" she asked, swallowing. "I'm allowed?"

He nodded. "You are allowed. And you are invited."

Invited. Not ordered. So she didn't have to go in if she didn't want to. But she decided that she did. Besides, it was only polite.

Meresankh stepped into her Pharaoh's bedroom, one foot, then the other. She stopped. She was standing in his room. In his royal room. It was almost frightening. She had been there twice before, when he had given her the mission of spreading the news that the staff could look at him, and then later on when Semerkhet had told them about the battle, but that only made three times. Her heart was still pounding, and her hands were sweating. Subtly, she wiped them on her skirt.

She looked around. Gold-plated bed, jewel-encrusted chair, another chair inlaid with ebony and ivory, wooden desk, sword and shield hanging on the wall, an open doorway into a storage area much like the Queen's. Beautiful romantic pictures adorned the walls between graceful columns painted like lotuses— the King and Queen together, in poses of love that would last forever.

Her Pharaoh sat in the bed, his little gray cat in his arms. Semerkhet had mentioned that he had a cat, but she had never seen it. Both of his legs were splinted and wrapped in linen bandages, and there were purple bruises on his face and arms, along with a number of scratches. The black eye he had on the left side was impressive. He was much worse off than Semerkhet.

But their prayers, her prayers, had been answered. Because he had come home alive.

Meresankh realized she had forgotten herself in all her wide-eyed staring. Even the self-professed chattiest member of the entire staff had been struck silent by the unexpected honor of being invited into the Pharaoh's room. So she bowed. But she didn't grovel on the floor; just showed all the respect she wanted to offer to her Pharaoh, respect without fear.

"What a beautiful room," she said finally, giving a nervous smile as she raised her head.

The Pharaoh smiled, as if her compliment really meant something to him. There was a dimple in his cheek; she had never realized. Of course she had never realized; she had never looked at his face to see if he might have a dimple. So she had never before really seen how beautiful his smile was... and she had never seen the prominent front teeth that were something of a whispered legend among the staff. The legend was true.

He looked like the Queen, his older sister. Same nose, same eyes. The Queen just had a bit more of a chin.

This was a bit like when she had first started making eye contact with the Queen. Meresankh thought back to those moments, the first time she had really smiled at her Lady, looking her in the eye. Back when they had first become friends. Could she and the Pharaoh become friends, in some way?

Meresankh looked at her Mistress, who was smiling gently at her just like her Pharaoh was. But there was something else in her smile. Something subtle. Something that said, "Did you need something, Meresankh? Because the Pharaoh needs to rest."

Meresankh gave another quick bow. "I was just wondering where you wanted me to put your necklace, My Lady." She turned to the King. "And I wanted to see how you were. And... see your beautiful room again. Your guard wasn't out there, or I would have asked him."

He returned the nod, still with that same pleasant smile. "You're welcome to come in," he said. Then he winked. "Just knock."

"Of course, Your Majesty. Thank you." Slowly she looked up at him again, and she smiled at him. They really were just two human beings. What a strange thought.

"You can put the necklace on the stand on my dressing-table," the Queen said. "Thank you."

They kept looking at her. Meresankh felt her face growing hot and gave another little bow. "H-hail to thee, Lord of the Two Lands. All life, prosperity, and health. And yes, My Lady."

And with her legs shaking slightly, heart still pounding, she turned and walked away. Time to find some other work to get done.

"Why isn't Minnefer out there?" Tut asked, sitting up in bed and craning his neck as if he could see out into the hallway.

His sister shrugged, shaking. "Strange. Semerkhet?"

"Yes, My Lady?" With a quick bow, he came back into the room from his latest errand.

"See if you can find Minnefer, will you? He's not at his post."

The valet nodded. "Yes, My Lady. I was wondering myself what had happened to him." And with a wish for life, prosperity, and health, Semerkhet was gone again.

When he returned, it was with a slightly confused frown. "Your Majesties," he said, "I found him."

"Where was he?" Tut asked.

"Apparently the Grand Vizier had summoned him. Wanted to speak with him. And he made the foolish decision of attending to that summons without asking to be dismissed."

Ankhesenamun looked at her brother and sighed. This was not sounding good.

"Have him relieved," she said. "For the rest of the day. It sounds as though he needs some time to decide on his priorities."

Ankh watched her brother healing. And she found herself almost setting aside the fact that someone had done this to him. Maybe he was simply going to get better and none of this was going to matter.

Life had changed so much. Tut had always needed help; limited independence had always been part of his life. But now... now, if he wanted a cup of tea, he had to ask for it. If he wanted a bowl of grapes, he had to get someone's attention. If he wanted another blanket, he had to interrupt Ankh or Sem as they went about their days; days that were occupied mainly with the activities of looking after him. Frustratingly enough, it seemed that he would always need something just as one of them sat down after accomplishing the latest errand he'd sent them on.

And as he sat helplessly in bed, unable to fetch or accomplish anything for himself, he felt bad. Grateful, but bad. He felt guilty for being a burden; for having turned into so much more of an inconvenience than he had been already. And he hated to bother them with his constant whining; keep them running back and forth for tea, snacks, reading materials, the cat. So when he wanted something, he made himself wait. And once he'd thought of two or three things he needed, and at least half an hour had passed since the last time he'd asked for something, he would send them on a mission down this or that corridor for what he wanted. And he would thank them, over and over.

But even though he felt guilty, he wouldn't apologize. Because he knew he hadn't done anything wrong, and he knew he was being the best patient he could. And he would remind himself that life was full of things you could change… and things that you couldn't.

"Where's my bracelet?" the Queen asked, walking into her room for a break.

Meresankh paused in arranging a stack of historical papyri. Her Lady could be referring to any of several dozen bracelets.

"Ah, which one, My Lady?" she asked.

"You know, you know," Ankh said, waving her hand. "The gold one with the blue scarab and the little falcon on it. I just had it yesterday."

Meresankh shook her head. "Well, let me have a look."

"He's getting better," Sem said to Meresankh at lunch, as they sat down together with their plates of second-day roast beef and crisp, green jujubes. They weren't quite as green as they had been, the color warming toward yellow, but they were still fresh and crisp.

Meresankh took a bite of beef and washed it down with a sip of peppermint tea. And she smiled at her friend.

"Oh, I'm so glad," she said, reaching out to squeeze his hand. He let her, blushing as her hand touched his. "We've been praying, Granny and I."

He nodded. "Thank you." He sighed again, then smiled wistfully, looking off into the middle distance.

Meresankh chuckled. "What?" she asked.

"I still can hardly believe I'm back," Semerkhet said.

Meresankh took another sip of tea. "Hmm?"

The valet shook his head with a chuckle. "I mean it. I mean, everything's the same as it ever was… or at least most things are. Our routines are the same. Mornings, evenings, all the usual day-to-day things. But it's…"

Semerkhet paused, eating another jujube. "It's all so… *meaningful* now. Every bit of it. Even the small things, things I… didn't even always enjoy doing. Because I…" He paused, brushing at his nose as he fought against choking up. "I almost lost it forever. If the Pharaoh hadn't saved me at the trial, not only would I be dead, I wouldn't even have an afterlife if I was burned. So he… he saved me from a fate worse than death."

Meresankh just looked at him. And in her face he saw the echoes of joy that they were together again, but at the same time, something uncomfortable. As if what he had said about the afterlife had offended her.

He let it go and went on. "So I'm glad I'm here… glad I'm with all of you. And I'm glad that I get to go back to all those good old routines. Just like always."

"Our prayers have been answered," Meresankh said.

Semerkhet nodded. "Yes. They have been. Even…" He looked down. "Even my prayer for Nedjes. That I would get to keep him. I know he's gone, but somehow, I feel… like I'm still a big brother. And that part of me doesn't feel empty anymore."

Meresankh put her arm around him. She didn't have to say anything.

Semerkhet looked at her, biting his lip. "Nedjes died a year ago in Paophi, and it's been… it's been like a hole in my heart. No one to take care of, give advice to, cheer up, all the things you do for a baby brother… or a baby sister, I'm sure. It was all gone… gone in a heartbeat. But now…"

Sem's eyes shone with tears, which Meresankh tried not to notice. "Now… I have that back again. A couple of months ago, the Pharaoh started talking to me, acting like we were both people. And… before I knew it, I was thinking of him as a friend, not just the person I work for. Now... now, I enjoy caring for him. It means something to me now, not just the wages I earn, or the sense of duty. And I feel like I have some of it back. A little brother. And I'm just... glad." He brushed his nose with the back of his hand, and Meresankh smiled.

"I'm happy for you," she said with a little nod. And she smiled. "Me, too... As the Queen's handmaiden, I've seen... that over the past year, things have changed a lot. And it's like you said. It's not just a job anymore. It's a friendship. Even... even the sister I never had." Then she chuckled, taking Semerkhet's hand again as her other hand rose to touch her little silver necklace. "And of course, working here... I get to see you every day."

Semerkhet just grinned.

Ankh still visited with Mutnedjmet and Amenia. When she had the chance to slip away for half an hour, they would have tea, just like they had in the days before all this. And they would talk. About womanhood. About history, the legacy of the Queens of the past. And about life.

And Ankh was grateful to have her friends.

And she was grateful to have Meresankh, the friend she saw all through the day, every day. There was something about her... something about the way they worked together so smoothly. Something familiar. She wondered what it was.

He was counting the days. And, bored as he was becoming, trapped in his room, the Pharaoh had also taken to counting the tiles on the floor, the flowers in the paintings on the walls. Tutankhamun's heart beat faster when he imagined actually getting out of bed or his chair, walking around his bedroom, however slowly he had to move. Looking out the window at the flowers, the birds, the lotus-pools in the distance. Walking into his storage room to look at all his things; into his private sitting room to enjoy his favorite papyrus scrolls. Someday... He smiled. Someday, going out into the hall outside his room, making his way down to the royal feasting hall for a meal. And someday...

Tut chuckled with delight at the very idea. Someday... he would be able to go outside.

18

The Other General

That afternoon, there was a knock at the door. A knock that somehow sounded lazy. Without even having seen, Tutankhamun knew General Nakhtmin was at the door.

"Come in," he said, sitting up and pulling his blankets up to his chest, wrapping his warm, red outer robe closer. As he moved, he winced. The bruises on his chest and back still ached when he sat up or lay down, and moving his arms hurt, too. If he had known to expect a visitor, he would have been sitting up in his chair, but oh, well.

Tut had been alone in the room, for the moment. His sister was taking a walk, and Semerkhet was on an errand. But no one would get past Kamose, who was on bodyguard duty instead of Minnefer. Somehow… knowing that he was there made Tut feel even safer than he did when Minnefer was standing guard. That man needed to work on his priorities.

The young General sauntered in, his hooded eyes sweeping in their under-awed way around the Pharaoh's bedroom. Tut almost expected him to flick out his tongue like a lazy cobra.

Nakhtmin sat down in Tut's favorite chair without being asked, popping one foot up on his knee as he brushed a speck of something off his finely-pleated tunic onto the floor. The cat snorted at the impertinence and jumped lightly onto the bed next to the King, curling up beside him protectively. She truly did personify the lioness goddess that was her namesake.

A second snort turned into a sneeze. Silently Tut agreed with her. The General was wearing too much perfume.

"I just wanted to ask how things were going," Nakhtmin said in his lazy drawl, leaning back in the chair. His eyes flickered to Tut's bandages and splints. "Is your, ah, leg any better? Father says it is."

Tutankhamun tried his best to give Nakhtmin a grateful smile. "It is, thank you. They both are. Your father was just in to visit me, actually, earlier this morning."

"Really…" Nakhtmin was looking out the window, eyes following the path of a bird that had just flown by. Then he blinked, eyes moving back to the person he was talking to. "Well, sorry to hear you were hurt and all that. So… have you decided, what we were talking about earlier, about me going to Nubia?"

"General Horemheb already went to Nubia," Tutankhamun said. "Things are going quite well in our territories there."

Nakhtmin shook his head as though the context of his question had been obvious. "No, I mean to move the border. We need land in the south, Your Majesty, beyond what we've already brought under our control. Southern Nubia has resources we don't. Particularly gold." He stroked the front of his finely-pleated tunic, the gold ring on his finger shining in the sunlight streaming through the window.

"I have no plans to campaign in Nubia this year, General," Tut said straightforwardly. "We are at peace, and our limited resources necessitate that we should postpone any territorial expansion for at least the next several years."

Nakhtmin gave a scornful frown. "So, can I speak plainly, or what?"

"Proceed," the Pharaoh said, inclining his head graciously.

"Our resources wouldn't be so limited if you'd just bring in slaves again," Nakhtmin pouted, folding his skinny arms over his chest. "I don't understand why you're so opposed to it. It's not as if they're people."

Tut raised an eyebrow. Talk about plain speaking.

"Well, General, that's an area where you and I... and your father and I... have a major philosophical difference," Tut replied. "I believe that people who may be in a position of slavery are human beings just like the people in mastery over them. And as such, even enslaved people should have the same rights as the free... and ultimately, no one should be enslaved. Everyone deserves to receive a fair wage for the work that they do, and a safe environment in which to do it. It may seem that providing servants with a good wage is a waste of resources, but remember the impact on Egypt's economy when all the Hebrew slaves suddenly left?"

Nakhtmin swallowed.

"We're still recovering," Tut said. "If the Hebrews working in Egypt had received fare wages and decent working conditions— without abuses such as beatings— they might never have left, and we wouldn't have been left to pick up the pieces and rebuild the economy from the ground up. We've had to replace the workforce that disappeared, first with more slaves, and now, with a workforce that will receive a fair wage. My grandfather's policies resulted in rather a lot of hard work for our generation. So you see, General, slavery is bad for the economy."

"Only if they get away," Nakhtmin grumbled.

"I beg your pardon?"

"I mean... I see your point," Nakhtmin said, collecting his thoughts. He paused. "Well... what about next year?"

Tut raised an eyebrow, letting it just begin to get dark and dangerous. "In terms of taking over the rest of Nubia? The only land I am concerned with bringing under Egyptian control is the land my father lost in Amurru, territory that General Horemheb is reclaiming as we speak." He paused, a surprising thought suddenly popping into his mind. "General..." he asked. "Why didn't you join us on our campaign in Kadesh?"

"My father didn't want me to go," Nakhtmin said with another hint of pouting. "Said he wanted to keep me safe... for my next opportunity."

Tutankhamun nodded, mind working a mile a minute. "Well, thank you for coming to see me, General. I'll see you again soon."

Nakhtmin stayed in his chair, raising a hand to scratch at his wig.

"General," Tutankhamun said again. "You're dismissed."

Nakhtmin blinked. "Oh. Goodbye, Your Majesty. Good health and all that." And he got up and strode out the door. Without closing it behind him.

Tutankhamun picked up Bastet and petted her with a bruised hand as he let his conversation with bratty little General Nakhtmin replay in his mind. *Father didn't want me to go... wanted to keep me safe, for my next opportunity...*

What opportunity would that be? If Ay took the throne as he intended, would he make Nakhtmin his heir? And was the little General already in on it; already considering himself Crown Prince? The King tsk'd to himself. That was going to be a problem. Because from what he had seen, Nakhtmin would be a disaster of a Pharaoh.

"Was that General Nakhtmin?" Ankhesenamun asked as she came in from a refreshing ten-minute walk in the garden, golden beads jingling cheerfully as she rubbed her cold hands together, the sleeves of her warm, red outer robe fluttering. Tut could smell the fresh air on her. Her bright eyes and springing step made him wish he could get outside, even if he had to be carried. As he got stronger, though... maybe he could. Outside in the hall, he could hear the guard walking away, Hannu, who accompanied either of them whenever they left the palace.

"Yes," Tut said, rolling his eyes. It felt good. "Cocky little brat. Mind like an empty room."

Ankh gave an embarrassed little chuckle, eyebrows rising. "Really?"

Tut nodded, nostrils flaring as he released his frustration with a heavy sigh. "Really. You think Ay is greedy... his son's a jackal. Wants to completely re-institute slavery; take over all of Nubia for the gold..."

"Take over Nubia?" Ankh asked incredulously. This time her eyebrows nearly disappeared into the bangs of her wig.

"Yes," Tut said just as incredulously. He sighed, the secret he hoped he would never have to tell, of the Vizier and his betrayal, aching inside his heart. "And I know what he's hoping for. He's hoping I won't get better, and that somehow, the Vizier will elbow his way onto the throne. As Ay's son, Nakhtmin will be the heir."

"But Horemheb is your heir," Ankh said with a little frown. She paused. "For now."

Tut nodded with a little smile. "Yes. For now."

She took his hand in her little one. Her hand was cold, as was the other one, which she gently rested on his cheek. "You'll get better," she said with a confident nod. The tinkling golden beads of her braids echoed her certainty. "And someday we'll have an heir of our own. Don't even worry about Nakhtmin."

Tut smiled, raising his face for a kiss. "Yes, dear."

Ankh felt it again, that twinge, that question. Even having no use of his legs at all, her brother was still just as good of a Pharaoh as he had been before he had ever gone to Amurru. And she was proud of him.

But she still wondered. What was the purpose? The purpose behind all his pain?

"Why was Nakhtmin in here?" Semerkhet asked as he came back into the Pharaoh's room, his errand complete.

For an instant Tut wondered how Sem could possibly have known, then sniffed. Of course. Semerkhet had smelled the little General's perfume.

"Oh, he just had some questions," Tut said lightly. "Silly ones, really. But it's all taken care of."

Semerkhet gave a curt nod, then a bit of a frustrated sigh. "Why didn't you call me?" he asked with a frown. "I would have gotten rid of him."

Tut smiled. There was that loving big brother. "It's all right," he said, shaking his head slightly. "I can deal with him. You know I wouldn't have let him in if it wasn't safe. And you're not the guard, anyway."

Semerkhet chuckled. He couldn't argue with that. "Maybe not. But still…" And as he went to stack some dirty dishes to be taken back to the kitchen, Tut knew that Semerkhet wished he'd been called to save his little brother from the annoyance that was General Nakhtmin. And probably wished he could be appointed Royal Bodyguard to boot.

"These dishes can go down to the kitchens, and we need a basket of fresh linens," Semerkhet whispered to the maids. The Pharaoh was drowsing, and their opportunity to do some tidying had arrived. "And these flower arrangements are starting to droop. How about some fresh roses from the garden?"

"Yes, Your Excellency," one whispered back, taking the wilting bouquet.

He chuckled. Still so strange to be called "Your Excellency."

Tut woke up from his nap feeling even a little better… and desperately bored. He sat up, lay back down, stretched his stiff arms and back as well as he could, tried as hard as he could to see out the window. Gave a groan of restless annoyance. Grabbed whatever medical papyrus was within reach and scanned half a page, putting it away in amused embarrassment when he got to the chapter on enemas. Not what he wanted to read about just now.

Having put the papyrus away again, the Pharaoh reached for Bastet, who was curled up at the end of the bed. She purred in his arms, but even holding his beloved kitty wasn't going to make him stop being bored. So he let her go, watching her hop lightly to the floor and go after an almond someone had dropped.

And he rolled over again, unable to get comfortable. He was too fidgety. Too restless. Too maddeningly bored.

This… was… not… fun. He was starting to feel like he had just before going on that chariot joyride they'd taken long ago in Epiphi. About ready to do something reckless.

"Sem," he moaned. His valet came out of the storage room, where he'd been sorting clothing and jewelry the Pharaoh had not worn in weeks.

"Yes, Master?" he said with that friendly smile.

"I want to go on a chariot ride," the Pharaoh said, putting just enough playfulness into his voice so his friend would know he wasn't raving with fever.

Sem raised his eyebrows. "Which chariot ride? The fun adventure we had... or the one that got you here?"

Tut rolled his eyes. "Heh, heh. The fun one..."

Semerkhet chuckled and shook his head. "I know. That sounds fun, doesn't it." He sighed. "Well... what can we do instead?"

"Read, I suppose," Tut said, folding his arms with a heavy, frustrated sigh. He loved reading, but too much of a good thing... still got annoying.

Semerkhet gave a mysterious little smile. "Well, there is something I could show you... if you want," he said.

Tutankhamun looked up, curious. Whatever Sem wanted to show him, he was sure it would help cure this fatal boredom.

His friend produced a long-necked lute. "I've decided to move from poetry into music," he said. "Set some of my poems to melodies." Semerkhet swallowed. "I'm writing one for Meresankh."

The Pharaoh smiled. "Can I hear it?"

"If you want." And Semerkhet sat down in the chair by the bed and began to play.

My one, the sister without peer,
Most beautiful of all
Her face is like the rising morning star
At the start of a happy year

Tut grinned. "That's beautiful, Sem."

His friend almost blushed. "You think she'll like it?"

"I know she'll like it." The Pharaoh paused. "Sem... will you teach me to play the lute?"

Semerkhet chuckled. "I'm just learning myself."

Tut shook his head. "We'll learn together. And I've got all the time in the world."

The Pharaoh sat in his chair and spent a surprisingly interesting afternoon learning a few chords on the lute. Soon he could stumble his way through the sweet song Sem was writing for Meresankh. Sometime, he would have to play it for Ankh.

"Well, I have something I could teach you," Tut said when his fingers were sore from the strings of the lute. "Although you probably know. Do you play *seega?*"

"I know how it goes, but I haven't played very much," his valet replied. "I'd love to play."

"The Queen has been helping me with my strategy," the Pharaoh said. "Maybe we can hone our skills together."

Together, they spent a happy hour playing game after game. And Tut smiled as, with the Pharaoh's mediation, Semerkhet even beat him once. It was rather enjoyable to be the teacher for once.

19

One Perfect Day

Ankh was glad that Mutnedjmet and Amenia wanted to visit her every week. And she was honored that they wanted to learn from her; excited that they wanted to know what it meant to be a Queen, how to become the Queens of their own lives.

But as they left her sitting room that day, smiles on their faces and new knowledge swirling around in their minds, she had to close the door before they saw her begin to cry. Quietly, she sat down again, wiping her eyes.

Because she could see them. Her tiny precious ones, the two Princesses whose names she whispered inside her heart. She could see them in her imagination, climbing up onto her lap as she and her own sisters had climbed into their mother's lap, ready to learn from the wise Queen. She was the wise Queen now, ready to pass on her wisdom to her daughters. Only, they were not there to teach. There in her heart, in her mind— but she could not hold them in her arms, bounce them on her knees, answer their deep questions and teach them everything she had learned.

She could not hear their little voices, pass on the writing palettes their aunties had used when they had been little girls, raise them into the Queens of the next generation. She could not remind them to sit up straight, teach them how to spot a lie or tell an advantageous truth, train them to become sweet and deadly, courageous and cunning, civil and sneaky when the situation required.

She could teach her brother, her friends. The knowledge she possessed would be passed on; would not be lost. But the direct line of mother to daughter was broken.

"Tell me a story, Ankh," Tut said that night at dinner, looking up from the hot vegetable soup Semerkhet had just declared free of poison. She looked up at him over her plate of roast beef and smiled.

"All right," she said. "Let's see… Do you remember Shadow, Mother's favorite horse? I remember the time he jumped clear over the palace wall at Akhetaten and the guards had to chase him through the city…"

Tut nodded and gave his sister a vague smile at the funny story, but his stomach was clenching. Because he was remembering another story about their mother and a horse. A story that had ended with her lying in the dust, not moving.

Tut shivered as he remembered the way that Ay had drawn him and Ankh to his heart as a group of weeping servants had carried their dead mother away as the crowd began to panic. "No one ever means for these things to happen," he had said softly. But now… now Tutankhamun felt sick.

Because he was not sure if the Vizier had been telling the truth.

"…and that was how Shadow came home covered in flour from the baker and with ten apples in his stomach from the fruit-seller," Ankh finished merrily.

Tut looked up with another polite smile, setting aside his disturbing thought for the moment.

"What a horse," he said, shaking his head. "What a horse."

Ankhesenamun looked at her brother strangely for a moment, then bent and kissed his forehead. "You look tired, love," she said softly.

Again, he gave her a little smile. "Well," he said sarcastically, "it has been rather a big day."

She just kissed him again.

They were laughing together, Ankhesenamun and Meresankh. Over something simple, silly, and utterly hilarious. Later on, the Queen would not remember what they had been laughing about, but she would remember this moment. Because as they reached for one another's hands, struggling to catch their breath as their bodies shook with laughter, Ankh realized what she had caught a glimpse of, just the other day, as well as so many days ago, putting those sticky masks on their faces together.

Sisterhood. As they laughed together, the Queen felt it filling her heart, the same fun and joy she remembered from the good old days she had spent with her sisters. Somehow, with Meresankh... the sister-shaped hole in her heart was healing.

His body was feeling better. But his mind was not. Tut tossed and turned that night, chased by thoughts of his mother, thoughts of the Vizier who had mourned her like everyone else had but whose reaction to her death... suddenly didn't feel right. And the same bitter feeling filled the pit of Tut's stomach as when Ankh had realized that Meritaten's death had been no mere case of the ague.

No one ever means for these things to happen... it was never my intention that your first battle should actually result in injury... Why had those two phrases spoken by the Vizier connected themselves in Tut's mind? There was something... something he couldn't quite catch; couldn't quite remember. Something still missing. But something... something was very wrong.

Tomorrow. He could get out of bed tomorrow. Tut smiled the next morning, the twelfth day of Sholiak, as Semerkhet got him dressed and brought him his breakfast. He could see the Sun shining through the window, even hear the wind blowing in the trees, see the delicate linen curtains rippling in the cool Sholiak breeze. Just one hour outside... just one.

Could he? Today?

"Semerkhet?" he called.

"Yes, Master?" Semerkhet hurried to the royal bedside with the smile his Master always loved to see. On such a cool day, he had on a warm green outer robe.

"I need your help."

Semerkhet nodded. "What is it?"

Tutankhamun looked out the window and smiled up at Sem.

"I want to go outside. Just for a few minutes. The doctor says I can get out of bed tomorrow, but... just for a few minutes? If you and Amenmose help me, I'm sure I can get out to the pavilion... see the Sun... listen to the birds..."

Semerkhet smiled. "I think we can make that happen. But first... It's kind of chilly outside." The Pharaoh smiled to see Semerkhet open one of his chests of clothing and pull out a soft, cozy, blue outer robe. And his friend wrapped it around him, slipping in one arm, then the other, getting ready for the glorious cool day.

Tut sat and waited while his valet found another servant. "Good morning, O Great Morning Star," Amenmose greeted him with a bow. He was also warmly dressed on a chilly day like this.

Tut smiled at him. "Hello, Amenmose."

The servant rose. "How are you this morning?"

"Better," the King said. "You think you can help Semerkhet get me out into the pavilion?"

Amenmose smiled. "As you wish. We have the stretcher all ready, and we'll bring your couch out for you."

"Excellent."

Semerkhet nodded, and a small crowd of servants walked in, two carrying an empty stretcher between them with a pillow at the head end. Tut gave a little sigh, then smiled again. How else was he going to get outside, into the beautiful sunshine?

With Semerkhet's help, Tutankhamun transferred himself into the stretcher, which two of the assistants Amenmose had brought in were holding at an accessible height.

He smiled and lay back. He was out of bed.

"And off we go," Semerkhet said with a grin. The Pharaoh and his entourage began the journey to the outside world.

Ankh looked up from her cup of tea as she heard laughter in the hallway. What shenanigans were the servants getting up to? She set her cup down and went to check.

"Darling! What are you—"

"We're going outside! Come join us!" her brother laughed from where he sat on a stretcher borne by two servants. Four other servants were carrying the couch from his sitting room. "It's so beautiful outside... I can't wait for tomorrow."

Ankh grinned, wrapping her red outer robe closer around herself. "It is a beautiful day."

Slowly, carefully, they made their way down the corridor, toward the royal feasting hall, just past the office. The servants' sandals echoed on the polished floors; echoed in the largeness of the hall. Tut looked around in delight; it was so big out here, the air was so fresh, the paintings and carvings all around them were so bright and beautiful... and they weren't even outside yet.

"Great Morning Star!" Three or four servants bowed in surprise, offering stammered wishes for life, prosperity, and health. The Pharaoh just smiled graciously. Life, prosperity, and health aside, this was going to be a glorious adventure.

The front door was just ahead. The door that led to the outside world. Tut's heart was actually pounding; he couldn't help smiling. He was going outside.

"And here we are," Semerkhet said with a grin, opening the door wide. They were through. The Pharaoh was outside.

Tut took a deep breath of fresh air, blinking as the bright Sun touched his face for the first time in weeks. The birds were singing, the lotus-pools lapping gently, the fish begging like puppies. Softly the breeze touched his face, blowing the braids of his wig and bringing him the fragrances of the flowers. The flowers were so bright, so much brighter than he had remembered, the fruit and shade trees were taller, the grand garden even grander. The cool of the month of Sholiak, the end of the Season of Inundation, was welcome after the stuffy palace, a relief after the sticky heat of the Season of the Harvest. But the Sun was so warm. He closed his eyes, breathing it all in.

Ankh smiled as her brother took in the beauty of the garden he had not seen for so many days. Stuck inside for so long, what a simple joy to be able to feel the Sun and the breeze on his face, smell the flowers, watch the birds… She wiped away a tear at the very thought.

The servants carried the stretcher to the pavilion, and carefully, they transferred the Pharaoh to the couch they'd brought out, padded with a few extra cushions, with his legs comfortably supported and a blanket around his shoulders against the cool Sholiak breeze. He sat back with a sigh, looking and looking at everything around him as if he had never seen it before. He had been so hungry, he realized. Hungry for air. Hungry for color. Hungry for light. Hungry for bird-songs and the fragrances of the flowers borne on the breeze. Hungry for the loving touch of the Sun on his face. The Sun his father had loved so much. The Sun that felt real, felt warm, felt true, not cold and silent like the image of Amun-Ra at the temple. Its gentle rays made him feel as warm and safe as he had as a child, back when his Father was Pharaoh, and he and Mother had worshiped the Aten in the bright, sunny temple courtyards…

Tut shook his head. Was he thinking blasphemy? Still… whoever was right, whoever was wrong, the Sun seemed to touch something deep within him, and its warmth made him feel… so very loved.

He and Ankhesenamun played *seega* together, out in the garden. And they smiled as they shared their favorite game; the game that neither of them had even thought to wonder when they would be able to play again.

And the Pharaoh won.

Semerkhet stood watching his Master and his Mistress playing *seega* in their pavilion. Just like old times. They laughed and teased together, just as though it was six months ago, before all of this. Even Hannu, who stood ready to protect them, was smiling, delighted to watch them sitting there together just like they always used to.

There was no telling what would happen next, Sem thought. How long it would be before his Master was better; even how his health would continue to fluctuate throughout his adult life. But right here, right now, they could enjoy a beautiful day together.

There was something... special about just being outside. Feeling the bright, warm Sun on his face. Somehow... Semerkhet didn't understand, but somehow, feeling the Sun on his face made him feel the way he always wished he would feel while praying. Loved... and heard. Someone was up there. Whatever Their name was.

Meresankh slowly walked out of the palace, into the sunshine. She had heard laughter... familiar laughter. Laughter she had not expected to be coming from outdoors.

And now she stood with Semerkhet, smiling and smiling as she watched the King and Queen playing *seega* in their pavilion. It was a beautiful sight.

She raised her face to the warm Light of Aten's sun, the Light of the World that I-AM poured out, and breathed a prayer of thanks.

He was tired in an hour. Tut yawned, leaning against Ankh's shoulder as they sat side-by-side, her chair pulled up beside his couch.

"What a beautiful day," he whispered.

She nodded, reaching up to stroke his wig, brushing a few stray braids out of his tired eyes. "It is," she whispered back.

"Wish it could... last forever," he yawned.

She smiled. "So do I."

But it was time to go in. Slowly Semerkhet helped Tutankhamun into his stretcher, and the other servants carried him inside. The sun was getting low, and mosquitoes were beginning to bite... odd though that was. But they were all smiling. Because it had been a beautiful day. One perfect day.

Only one more night, the King told himself as Semerkhet tucked him in on that eleventh night home, the smell of fresh air still clinging to him. He could get out of bed in the morning. He held Bastet close and chuckled himself to sleep. In the morning, he could get out of bed.

He looked forward to the next time he could get outside.

Then he wondered if his sister had let him win the game. And he laughed again.

20

Mosquitoes

A warm spell began abruptly overnight, right in the middle of the month of Sholiak. And in the morning, the mosquitoes returned. They came through the windows, filling every room with their annoying, shrill buzzing, covering everyone's skin with red, swollen bites that itched and itched. The fine linen netting that the servants hung at the windows and draped around the Pharaoh's bed helped a little, but couldn't really keep them out. Tut was soon covered with bites, and Ankh, though she tried, couldn't get rid of every one of them. But he wasn't about to appoint some sort of Royal Mosquito-Shoo-er or some such nonsense, so he was just going to have to deal with it.

His sister was with him every moment, holding his hand, stroking his head, trying to get rid of the mosquitoes. Now every part of him that didn't hurt itched all the time, and it was the least difficult to rest when he was nestled in her lap. Of course, she didn't have a problem with that, but he hated to keep her sitting on the bed all day. All day.

Tut didn't feel right. His head ached; to his surprise, he felt himself shivering even as he wiped sweat from his face. And he was so tired… so much more tired than he would have expected, even after yesterday's adventure.

Was something wrong? He felt so strange. And his thoughts... did not seem to be flowing properly. He could never get up; he couldn't go outside like he had yesterday, to where the Aten was... Now he was really confused; he knew his father's old religion was a bunch of bunk, the priests had said so when he died, but still, there were times when Tut wondered if the Aten really was real...

Was he sick?

Ugh. He shivered with a nasty chill, and he felt sweat on his forehead; it was so cold in here, though the sunlight blasted through the windows and made his head throb... He tried to sit up, then fell back as his head began to swim. And he struggled to speak.

"I don't feel good," he mumbled. His sister looked down at him where he lay in her arms, cuddled against her.

Softly she reached up to brush the braids of Tut's wig out of his face, gently touching his hot head with a soft, little hand that felt surprisingly cold. And fuzzily, he saw her frown.

"Darling, you're burning up," he heard her say, but her voice seemed strange and faraway.

Now his teeth were chattering. "Blanket... please? So cold..."

Ankh frowned again, pressing her hand to her brother's forehead, then his cheeks. "But you have a fever. You're not cold."

"I know," he whispered through the strange swimming in his head. "All these mosquitoes... could it be... ague?"

She frowned, her face betraying more fear than she meant to show him. "I'll get the doctor."

He nodded. "Thank you." Carefully, she settled him back into bed, safe until she got back. Wrapping her warm robe close, she hurried out of the room, and this time, the clinking of her braids sounded like fear.

The Chief Physician was in only a few minutes later, puffing under his heavy wig. He paused for an instant, supporting himself on one of the graceful pillars at the edges of the room, then bent from the waist in a deep bow.

"Unfortunately, it's not unlikely that the Pharaoh has the ague," he said, hurrying over to the bed. He took the King's wrist and felt his pulse, then touched his sweaty forehead. "You have a fever," he said solemnly. Although somehow, not quite as solemnly as when Tut had gotten the ague after that hunting trip.

"But... so cold," Tut said, shivering again.

"I know," the doctor said. "It's like the last time you had the ague; that's how it feels— you have a fever, but you feel cold. And every third day, the fever gets worse. No one knows why, but that's just... the way it is." He sighed. "I can... contend with it. And I shall. For as long... as necessary."

The King closed his eyes. Just the way it is. No one knows why. Everything had been that way in Tut's life.

Although the phrase "as long as necessary" had piqued the Pharaoh's blurry interest... and a hint of fuzzy suspicion. What did the Physician mean by that? And what did the expression on his face, the tone of his voice, mean? Because to Tut's hazy perception... the doctor did not seem as upset about him having the ague as the King would have expected.

He almost looked like he had an idea.

The Chief Physician talked to Ankh while Tutankhamun drowsed off with the warm cat curled up beside him, trying to let his body rest and fight this illness that no one understood.

Semerkhet came back from his break and started at what he saw, his heart beginning to pound. "What's wrong?" he gasped, running to the bed, where his Master lay in the Queen's lap, sleeping fitfully, quite obviously burning with fever. Sem dropped to his knees, gently taking his Pharaoh's hot hand, pressing his other hand to his brother's burning forehead. Tutankhamun didn't respond. Just kept sleeping. Although as Sem watched, he kept tensing, head and shoulders tossing and turning in his sister's lap as though he was having a bad dream.

The Queen shook her head sadly. "Ague," she whispered.

Semerkhet closed his eyes. *Again.*

And all he could say was, "Tell me what to do."

His Lady smiled at him, a sad, grateful little smile. And she reached out her free hand, her fingertips brushing the valet's wrist. "Just what you've been doing. Just being the best brother anyone ever had."

Semerkhet was surprised to feel himself smiling, heart warming at the compliment, at the encouragement. Just keep being a good brother. He could do that.

Ankhesenamun closed her eyes, feeling her sleeping husband weighing her down as he lay in her lap late that night, the twelfth night since he had come home, the end of the thirteenth of Sholiak. Ague. Again. She thought back to the last time he had had it; the two weeks of gradual recovery, the long, hard nights of fever and chills. But he had been strong then; strong enough to fight it off and make a full recovery. Now he was weak. Weak from his injury; weak from infection. Would he be able to fight it off this time?

The doctor had given him more medicine, but it hadn't been the medicine that had cured him last time; it had been time.

She sighed. They couldn't do anything about it right now. All they could do was rest. Ankh closed her eyes and tried to sleep.

The next morning, he was worse. Although the fever had gone down, Tut was so weak and dizzy that he could not sit up; he could just lie in Ankhesenamun's lap and let her care for him, feeding him like a small child. Bastet was always near, ready to be petted, ready to curl up beside him for a proverbial catnap, the soothing warmth of her body helping him relax. The pain in his legs was worse; the infection had returned with a vengeance, leaving the left one hot, red, and swollen, pus seeping out onto the bandages. This time there was no painful deep-cleaning. This time… the doctor didn't even change the nasty bandages. Not until the Queen had ordered him very clearly to do so. And then he did it, as before, with bitterness on his face. With grudging, contrary reluctance. And not very carefully. He didn't even apologize when his slightly haphazard wiping of the wound and zealous tightening of the bandages made the King wince.

But why? What was his problem?

Ague. On top of everything else. For the first time, Semerkhet wondered, a shudder running down his spine. Would his Master get through this?

The week had come and gone. And he was still stuck in bed, now worse than ever. Tut felt himself blinking back tears of disappointment as he remembered the doctor telling him that there was only one more week until he could get out of bed; one more week until he could begin putting weight on his legs. Now he couldn't even be moved to spend two minutes in his chair. He was trapped.

He hugged the cat to his heart, feeling her purr as she rubbed her face against him. She sounded almost like she wanted to console him. He sighed. Now how much longer would it be?

Would he ever be out of this bed? Ever?

The mosquitoes were gone. The brief warm spell had ended, cool days and crisp nights returning. As quickly as they had come, the biting insects had disappeared, back to wherever they hid during the coldest parts of the year.

Had they taken his hope for recovery with them?

"Thought... I was getting better," Tut whispered sadly as Ankh sat with him that afternoon, gently stroking his head. Bastet scurried around across the room, playing with a jeweled ring that had been missing for two days.

The Queen tried to smile as she took his hand, holding it tight in her little one. "Give it time. Your body has to fight on another front now. Allocate its resources. You're working hard."

He tried to smile back. "Suppose I am."

Tut fell asleep in her lap. Ankh watched him sleep, continuing to stroke his head as he breathed slowly, warm brown face at peace as he rested, momentarily free from his pain. He was working hard. He was going to have to work very hard to get better.

Ankh held her husband in her lap for most of the day, doing everything she could for him. But she wasn't sure if it would be enough. She could have gone out into town again to bring him more information on how their new policies were being applied, but that wasn't the greatest help she felt like she could be right now. Right now, politics were the least of their worries.

Semerkhet stayed near, fetching things, switching places with the Queen when she needed a break. He was honored to help, honored to do everything he was doing, but his heart ached that he couldn't do more. Because ultimately... he couldn't fix any of it.

Now there wasn't time to visit with Mutnedjmet and Amenia and Meryt. Wasn't even time to update them on how things were going. The Queen would stay where she was needed.

Meresankh saw everyone less and less. The Queen was always in her husband's room, looking after him; Semerkhet was in there too, helping. Because now, on top of everything else, their Pharaoh had ague. She kept at her own work, making sure all her Lady's things were properly arranged, but there wasn't much to do. Only wait for when she was needed. And hope and pray for the best.

She wished she could see them more. Wished she could make them smile; make them laugh. She thought back through the years, back to the days long before she had been the Queen's handmaiden. Granny had always called her her happy little birdie, and she had carried that with her, finding her greatest joy in bringing joy. As a teenager, she had served as Granny's assistant, entertaining laboring women with stories, songs, jokes, and cheerful gossip as they waited through the pain to welcome their child into the world. Everywhere she went, she had always found a way to bring joy.

And she wished she could bring her friends joy now.

Semerkhet and the Queen prayed for the Pharaoh every day, to Horus, Isis, Thoth. Maybe... maybe this was the way it was supposed to feel. Maybe it was unreasonable to expect a direct response, even that warm, loving feeling of having been heard. Maybe their cries were being listened to.

They could only hope.

The Chief Physician gave Tut all kinds of bad-tasting medicines and applied several strange preparations to his leg. This included more chamomile poultices applied amid elaborate prayers to Ra, to whom the herb was considered to belong. But though the latter soothed the feverish heat a bit, they didn't do much. The only medicine that didn't turn his stomach was the cups and cups of chamomile tea the doctor made him drink to help lower his fever. He usually drank it for colds, but maybe it would help him fight off the ague.

The next time the doctor came to change the bandages, the poultice, this one of mustard-seed, had stuck to the wound, which was more irritated than ever. More and more of Tut's leg was becoming hot, red, and inflamed... and there was a great deal of pus. The doctor changed the bandages then, of course, at the emphatic, authoritative command of the Pharaoh's sister, and wiped the wound out, but there was still something in his manner... that the Pharaoh didn't like.

It looked like disappointment.

"What is this?" Tutankhamun asked the fourth morning of his illness, as he sipped a terracotta cup of wine made bitter with some sort of powdered medicine. Raherka had just brought it in on a tray, announcing that it was from the doctor. It was his favorite white wine, from a cask he'd received on Tribute Day from far away, and they were wasting it, contaminating it with disgusting medicine. He was feeling a tiny bit better now, compared with the first hour he'd been sick, but if the doctor said he needed medicine, he should probably take it.

This was the sixteenth day of Sholiak. He had been home two weeks.

"A new medicine, Glorious Lord," Raherka said, not meeting the Pharaoh's eye— and in a way that was different from the nervousness with which servants usually avoided his gaze. Different from the fear with which Raherka himself had refused to make eye contact on the day he'd helped keep the King from falling after tripping over the cat. Different from the fear Tut had seen in the servant's eyes when he had been the first to reach the King's side after the chariot had fallen on him. This was uneasy, like something was carefully not being mentioned. "An emetic. To… help cleanse your system of bad humors."

Now there was a hint of guilt in the servant's voice. And an attitude of regret as he looked down at his feet.

Semerkhet frowned as the King brought the cup to his lips. "Don't you want me to test it?" he asked, putting out a restraining hand, whole body going tense as if he was preparing to knock the cup out of his Pharaoh's hand like he would backhand an attacking cobra.

Tutankhamun shook his head with a little shrug. "It's medicine. I wouldn't take medicine made for you. I'm sure it's all right."

Raherka nodded a little enthusiastically. "It's not necessary for your wine-taster to try it. The doctor prepared it with great care. He has only the best interests of Egypt at heart."

Tut smiled at his friend. "You see? It's all right."

Semerkhet shrugged uncomfortably. "As you wish."

Semerkhet watched the King sip the wine with a strange, uneasy shudder. Something was up. He felt miffed— the Pharaoh had rejected his usual testing of the wine, the way Sem always protected him. The way he did his job. Something about this… was making the valet very uncomfortable.

The King took the wine. An hour later he was vomiting, and sitting up made him dizzy and lightheaded. His throat burned with thirst as a headache pounded between his temples. The doctor said the medicine was working.

"Something's not right," Ankhesenamun said as she stroked her husband's bald head. Semerkhet was holding a basin steady in his lap, and Tut was sitting up to vomit, bringing up the small lunch of broth and bread he had managed to eat.

"You think?" Tut panted, turning his face away as the vomiting finally ceased. Semerkhet took the basin away.

"I don't know why the doctor thinks you need an emetic," she said, handing him a cup of water and another basin. He rinsed his mouth out, then sat back sipping the water. "What is that medicine, anyway?"

"Something doesn't seem right," Semerkhet agreed, coming back into the room after leaving the basin in the hallway for a lower-ranking servant to dispose of.

Tut just shook his head. Fears and suspicions were growing inside his heart, but he wasn't ready to share them. He hoped he was wrong.

His wife kept a close eye on him, even closer than before. Because something was wrong.

His Master had thrown up after taking the wine. Semerkhet took the cup away, feeling very uncomfortable indeed. The broth wasn't the problem; Semerkhet had tasted it like he tasted every meal. And the medicine had been described as an emetic. So it made sense that the Pharaoh would be ill. Only...

He shook his head. Why was the doctor giving Tut an emetic in the first place? The Pharaoh had two broken legs, an infection, and the ague. But Semerkhet could think of no way that an emetic could help with any of those. It simply did not make sense.

He wouldn't do anything yet; wouldn't ask his Master whether he trusted that taking the medicine was really in his best interest. Maybe this was just a fluke. Or maybe the wine was just doing what it was supposed to— cleaning out the Pharaoh's system. Maybe tomorrow his brother would be back to normal.

Then the Chief Physician came in again, a stack of fresh cloths over his arm and a bowl of what looked like yellow gruel in his hand. The mustard-seed he had been using on the Pharaoh's wound.

He unwrapped the current bandage and bent to examine the wound, which was redder and hotter than ever, almost as though it had been burned. The inflammation had been getting worse since the new poultices had been introduced. Tut hissed in his breath with pain when the doctor touched it.

"The treatment appears to be working," the Chief Physician said with what looked like a satisfied smile.

"It's supposed to be getting more inflamed?" Tut asked, raising an eyebrow. The Queen, sitting beside him, silently echoed his expression.

The doctor applied another stinging mustard poultice and re-bandaged the Pharaoh's leg.

"I know it hurts… but it's part of the healing. The Lord of the Two Lands must trust me. I did graduate from the House of Life, after all. And I have only the best interests of Egypt at heart."

Tutankhamun and his sister just looked at one another.

Ankh went to the royal library. Returning with a medical text, she sat down again with her brother.

"Mustard-seed," she read. "Draws out infection by attracting heat to the afflicted area and helping the body eliminate it. Particularly effective in easing chest congestion by serving as an expectorant. May be used in a poultice for this purpose… but must not be used on broken skin, for fear of increasing inflammation."

Tutankhamun looked down at his leg, the poultice that even now was resting against very broken skin; broken skin that was getting more and more inflamed by the day.

Carefully, the King's sister removed the poultice, replacing it with a folded cloth containing no herbs at all. When the doctor asked why it was gone, Tut would simply say it had been uncomfortable.

"Your recovery is coming along... better than expected," the Chief Physician said as he bent to check Tut's pulse with his fat, clammy hand. He looked at the Pharaoh, and his smile was warm, but his eyes... his eyes were not lit with the joy he seemed almost to be affecting rather than feeling. "You must be taking your medicine."

21

Fever

Then the Vizier showed up for a visit. "I was so sorry to hear of your illness, O King for Whom the Sun Shines," he said sadly, offering a deep bow and kissing the Pharaoh's hand. Tut took his hand back, not impressed. "A thousand, thousand good wishes for your recovery. Don't forget to take your medicine," he said warmly, pressing a cup of wine into Tut's hand even though he had just taken a dose a few minutes ago. "It'll soon set you to rights. After all, we have the good of the future of Egypt to think about."

With a sweet smile, the Pharaoh accepted the cup. And he raised it to his lips without drinking.

Then the doctors burned a painkilling incense for the Pharaoh that was made with hemp, but it made him feel like he had had too much wine, dried out his mouth, and made his heart start pounding, and his stomach growled even though he had just eaten. The bizarre sensations distracted him from his pain, but he did not like the way they made him feel. Besides which, the fumes made Bastet sneeze.

They also gave him a mixture containing poppy, and a preparation of mandrakes. Tut lay in a trance-like drowse in Ankh's arms, feeling almost as though he were floating; the pain had faded, but his thoughts were fuzzy and hard to form. His legs did not hurt, precisely, but they were difficult to move... even difficult to find with his mind. He could no longer tell if he was awake or asleep, and found himself dreaming of his parents. Were they coming to get him?

Then his fuzzy mind remembered that outside of surgery, or, of course, for those wounded in battle, mandrake and poppy were not usually given to someone who wasn't dying. He looked at the cat, lying quietly beside him.

"Am I dying?" he whispered too softly for Ankh to hear. The cat did not respond. She only kept looking at him.

Tut lay in his wife's arms, gazing blankly at the ceiling. He wasn't quite asleep, but he seemed barely to hear her when she tried to talk to him.

Ankh shook her head. If there was any other way to control the pain, that poppy medicine might not be something to continue using.

He could not think. There was only the pain, and the fever, consuming Tut with fire and then contracting him in excruciating shivers that sent agony wracking through his legs. But his legs were never cold. They always burned.

Every two hours, Raherka came in. And Sem would help his Pharaoh sit up slightly so he could take a sip of that new medicine.

Every single time, he was vomiting fifteen minutes later. Some patients responded like that, the doctor said, although just like with Raherka, there seemed to be a bit of discomfort in his voice... or was it just Tut's mind playing tricks on him? But strangely, it was after throwing up that he could think for a few minutes.

Twice, the Vizier came back into the Pharaoh's room, and each time he encouraged the King, in a voice like honey, to continue taking the medicine that would protect the future of Egypt.

"You've got to stop taking this, Master," Semerkhet said the morning of the second day Tut had been taking the medicine, the fourth day he'd been sick. Sem shook his head. Or at least Tut thought he did; his fuzzy vision detected the movement of his friend's head. "It's hurting you. At least let me taste it and figure out what it is."

"But it's doing its job," came Ankh's voice from Tutankhamun's other side. Her words echoed strangely; she sounded like Mother. "Cleaning out your system, like Raherka said. The doctor knows what he's doing." She paused. "And maybe... maybe it *is* just the ague. Ague can act like this. Granted, you've never had it this bad..."

Tut just closed his eyes against the pounding headache that was rising between his temples. He didn't have the mind-power to ponder this right now.

And once and for all, he was plunged deeply into a world where he could not think, not act, only exist, floating in pain, all-encompassing darkness, scorching heat, and waking nightmares, a world where he could no longer distinguish between what was real and what was happening within his feverish mind.

Ankh and Sem sat with him all through the day, helping him lift his head to take a sip of water or tea, holding a basin as he vomited, gently washing his sweaty face with a cool, damp cloth. He couldn't say anything intelligent to them, could hardly even remember their names, but in the moments that he was able to recognize their presence, he knew he was safe.

He existed in a haze, rousing occasionally with a moan of "drink," "wash," "barf," "hot," "cold," "pee." They helped him through his tasks, but he couldn't attend to them. Could only accept the help that they offered and then drift off again. It frightened him when his stomach contracted in nausea, and he groped for whoever was near, clinging to their hands as someone helped him sit up so he could get rid of whatever was left in his stomach. And it frightened him when a hand would suddenly touch him from out of the darkness, even if it held a cup of cold water or a cool cloth for his head. Nothing made sense. He knew the people who were looking after him, but he couldn't say from where.

His lips, his mouth, were so dry. But whenever he took a drink, he only threw up again.

Suddenly something moved beside him, something small and covered in fur, and he gasped in fear, thrusting his hand out to push it away. There was an animal in his room.

"Darling, that's Bastet!" he heard a woman's voice say reproachfully. Bastet? Who was Bastet?

"Who there?" he murmured into the fuzzy, wavering darkness around him. "Mommy? Hetty?" A soft, cool little hand touched his, and he flinched in surprise, then took hold of it.

"Ankh," he heard her say. Right. His sister. His sister would take care of him.

"Sem's here too," a boy's voice said from his other side. The Pharaoh blinked. Sem? Did he have a brother he didn't remember? But the voice was familiar. He would figure out who it was and how they were related later on.

Then came another voice. Many voices, it seemed. Five voices, birdlike and sweet, mostly from somewhere around where his elbow would have been had he been standing. And he reached for his sisters, for Setepenre, Rure, Tasherit, Meketaten, and for Meritaten, who towered above them all.

"Stay here," they said gently, their soft hands brushing his, then stroking his face, his head. "Wait for us. Be strong. Don't be afraid." And finally, "Find the Light."

And as the afternoon sun slanted blindingly through the window, they were gone.

There was nothing Tut could do but press his face into the pillow and cry.

Every two hours, Raherka brought the poppy medicine. And with a smile, he would encourage the Pharaoh to take it; remind him warmly that it was from the doctor, and it would help him. "Doctor's orders," he would say cheerfully, although once the Queen caught him biting his lip, tripping over his words as he began a word that almost sounded like it began with "v."

She did not acknowledge his blunder. But as the servant smiled, the Queen shivered.

Because it reminded her of something… something she couldn't put her finger on, but frightened her nonetheless.

The haziness in Tut's mind came and went with the doses of medicine that Raherka offered. And it always seemed to decrease, at least a little, after he would throw up and get it out of his system. Whether that meant it was working, or…

By the end of the afternoon, Tut was turning his face away when Raherka offered the medicine. Somewhere in his fuzzy mind, a connection was forming.

He was drowning, it seemed. Drowning in fever; in a strange fuzziness that clouded his mind. The Queen bit back tears as she helped her brother take a sip of tea. As he turned his face away, mumbling, "No more chamomile," she saw no recognition in his eyes.

Her baby brother did not know who she was.

He had collapsed. Completely collapsed. And so suddenly, four days after the ague had come, the same hour that he had started taking that new medicine. Now he lay there in bed, flinching every time someone touched him, rolling back and forth, muttering as if in a dream. He didn't even seem to hear them when they spoke to him. He couldn't eat the porridge they tried to spoon down him, hardly ever accepted the water and tea they tried to offer him in the hopes that this time he wouldn't throw it up— and when he did take a sip, it was without recognition.

He only lay there, mumbling, flinching, gasping in apparent fear and surprise every time someone spoke or touched him. Going stiff, arms reflexively thrust out, when they tried to help him raise his head to take a sip of water; protecting his face with his hands whenever a sound or movement startled him. Occasionally, very occasionally, giving a demanding grunt of "drink" or "wash." Occasionally shuddering, eyes opening in childlike fear as his hands grasped for whoever was near him, struggling into a half-sit as whatever was left in his stomach made its way back up. Occasionally lying there quietly crying inconsolable tears.

A thought touched Ankhesenamun's heart, gentle but cold, as cold as the sharp edge of a knife resting lightly against her throat.

He was going to die.

They… needed a plan.

The Pharaoh was dying.

Thoughts of politics floated through the Queen's mind, disparate elements slowly swimming toward one another as if they were about to connect in an epiphany. Memories, ideas, questions from the past months. She watched them make their way toward one another, waiting to see what they would tell her.

Suddenly, they came together like an explosion, an explosion that nearly knocked her sideways.

And she could see the whole thing clearly.

The Vizier's statement on Tut's birthday that he was no longer regent. His slippery promises. And the way that he had wrapped her little brother around his finger, convincing him that going off to war was a good idea.

The wounds with which Tut had returned. And the attitude of the doctor. The doctor who now was nowhere to be found. The medicine that seemed to be making her brother worse rather than better; the medicine that Ay himself had reminded the Pharaoh to take, just as, years ago, he had urged Ankh's ailing father to take his medicine. And the secret that Tut was not willing to tell her unless and until he had no hope of survival.

Ankhesenamun's heart filled with pain as she took her little brother's limp hand and pressed it to her lips.

He was being murdered.

Semerkhet bit his lip as he watched his Master lying there in the bed, sweat running down his grayish-pale face, muttering incomprehensibly, flinching and gasping when the valet offered him water; adjusted his pillows or blankets to try to make him more comfortable. Tutankhamun's eyes moved restlessly under half-shut lids; his mouth hung half-open, pale, cracked lips growing drier by the hour. And as the hours went by, his cheeks became hollow, his sightless eyes sunken like a skull.

Nedjes had gotten the ague once. Mother and Father had stayed up with him through the nights, and Semerkhet had barely slept either. He had lain awake praying to every god and goddess he could think of, begging them to preserve his baby brother. And eventually, Nedjes had recovered.

But the brother who now lay stricken with ague was not recovering.

Something had to be wrong with that medicine. And Semerkhet had to figure it out, whether he had permission to or not. His Master's life depended on it.

His... brother's life depended on it.

As she peeled a bedsheet, damp with sweat, off her brother to replace it with a fresh one, Ankh paused. And she looked at his legs. On the left side, the tightly-wrapped bandage, which had not been changed since the fever had risen so sharply, appeared to be stained yellow, even though they had removed the mustard-seed poultice. Gently she probed it, stopping as he winced, giving a painful gasp. It was very warm.

His infection was getting worse.

She was afraid. And Ankh wiped away tears as she dabbed a cool cloth over her baby brother's face, whispering prayers even as she barely noticed to Whom she was addressing them.

"He's burning up," she whispered. "He's never been like this. Never." She bit her lip, looking at Semerkhet. "We have to do something."

"Yes, we do," Semerkhet agreed, reaching out to gently touch his brother's hand. Tut twitched at the contact, then latched on to Semerkhet's hand like it was the only real thing in the world. And Semerkhet sat down beside him. "The doctor?" the valet asked a moment later.

The Queen shook her head with a jingle of beads. "How long since he's been here?"

"All day," Sem replied. And he shook his head. "We can't trust him, can we?"

"We can't trust anyone," the politician responded. Again, she stroked her brother's sweaty face. "The poppy and mandrake have to stop," she said decisively. "They're only making him worse."

"And the wine?" Semerkhet asked.

"Especially the wine," Ankh said emphatically. "I don't know what's in it… but it's not helping."

There was a loud gasp, and both Ankh and Sem turned to stare at the Pharaoh. Disturbed by something outside of their sight and hearing, he suddenly went so rigid that for a heart-stopping moment, the Queen was afraid he was going to go into convulsions. But he only gave rather a miserable moan and relaxed again, returning to his feverish muttering. All she could do was fight back her tears and moisten another damp cloth to lay on his neck.

"The doctor," Semerkhet whispered. "Poisoning him? Why?"

"Politics," Ankh said sadly. She swallowed back the lump in her throat. And she looked up at the valet. "The Pharaoh is being murdered, Semerkhet. It started on his birthday."

"The Vizier?" Semerkhet said in a horrified whisper.

The Queen just nodded.

"But why?" Semerkhet asked again.

The Queen shook her head, feeling the terrible truth filling her heart just as surely as if it were written on one of her beloved historical papyri. Maybe one day, it would be. But she could see the Vizier's plan clearly. And every terrible piece of political reasoning that had gone into it.

She swallowed. And she began to explain the Vizier's plot to her brother's valet. "Because he hates our politics; the fact that we love our people more than we love gold. And because he's decided to make sure that the Pharaoh predeceases him... now, before he has a son of his own, and while General Horemheb, the real heir, is out of the country." Ankhesenamun sighed. "The Vizier wants the throne, Semerkhet. And he's willing to commit murder to get it."

Semerkhet shuddered. "What can we do?" he asked finally.

Ankhesenamun gave him the ghost of a confident smile. "Not let the Pharaoh die," she said. She looked down at her brother. "We won't."

There was a hand. And Tut held onto it, through the pain, through the heat, through the fear and confusion. It was one real thing, the only real thing in the world. And it would pull him through to whatever was on the other side of this nightmare.

"Get that doctor," Ankh said hoarsely as her brother tossed and turned in the bed, sweat standing on his gray face. And with a bow, the valet was gone.

"You have a concern, My Lady?" the doctor said, offering his own bow as he entered the room.

Ankhesenamun looked up from dabbing a cloth over her brother's face and hands as he twitched and moaned.

"Many concerns," she said coldly. "What are you giving the Pharaoh?"

The Chief Physician's eyes flickered as he folded his fat hands, digging the toe of one sandal into the floor.

"A simple emetic, Your Majesty," he said with a little smile. "To... cleanse his system."

"And do what else?" Ankh asked in a harsh, clipped voice. "No emetic does this. And I don't know why you think he needs an emetic in the first place."

The doctor looked down at the Pharaoh in apparent concern, reaching out a pudgy hand to check his pulse. "It is true that the Pharaoh has an abnormally severe case of ague," he conceded. "But the dizziness, lightheadedness, thirst, vomiting, and headache are all symptoms."

"And why haven't you been in here, taking care of him?" Semerkhet asked the doctor. "Just sending Raherka to bring that wine. And why should the Pharaoh be taking both poppy and mandrake, if he's not dying?"

The Chief Physician swallowed, eyes flickering to the half-full cup of "medicinal" wine that sat on a nearby table.

"The Pharaoh needs no care that his valet and the Queen are unable to provide," he said warmly. "I thought to offer privacy."

"Really," Ankh said, raising an eyebrow.

"As for the poppy and mandrake, my only concern is keeping the Lord of the Two Lands as comfortable as possible," the doctor continued. He glanced at the wine again, then crossed to the table and picked it up, approaching the bed as if he was about to offer it to the Pharaoh, who lay tossing and turning, moaning as he dreamed.

"No more of that," the Queen said simply. As her eyes flashed, the doctor set the cup back down with a little splash and stepped back. "Ever. Whatever you've been giving him, he doesn't need it."

"And why aren't you changing his bandages?" Semerkhet asked.

"The Pharaoh needs to rest," the doctor said simply. "I will change them when he is ready to be disturbed."

"Be that as it may," the Queen said. She stood up, looking up at the Physician with her own eyes of thunder and lightning. "As the Great Royal Wife, I hereby decree that my husband is no longer to be subjected to mind-altering painkillers that seem to be delaying his recovery, rather than supporting it. And I further declare," she said, stepping forward so that the doctor had no choice but to take a step backward, "that he will no longer be given this 'emetic.' Not until the first fever has passed, and even then, only if he chooses to receive it." She stared up into his face, eyes flashing. "You are dismissed." The Queen swallowed, knowing that her next words would have consequences. "And you are not to return until you are called for."

Seeing no other choice, the doctor bowed and left the room.

"How did he know?" Semerkhet whispered as the doctor left. "About the dizziness and headache? He hasn't been here."

The Queen sighed. "Because they're being caused by the poison, not the ague, that's why." Then she felt herself give a little smile. Whatever he had been given, her brother was safe from here on in. By order of the Queen, that poison would never pass his lips again.

The Queen shuddered as power seemed to course through her. She had used her authority as Great Royal Wife, put her foot down, refused to take *no* for an answer. And through wielding that power, she would be able to protect her little brother from further harm.

Now she knew what Tut had felt like, bringing Maya under his control, reclaiming the power Ay had tried to steal back in making decisions in his name, saving Semerkhet from execution, passing the laws they had developed together, even firing Sennedjem the tomb-robber. It was exhausting. But exhilarating.

And she knew that if she needed to do it again, she could.

Meresankh had not seen her Lady, her friend, her sister, for a surprisingly long time. Not Semerkhet, either. When had they both gone so long without a break?

Their Pharaoh must be getting worse. With a deep sigh, the handmaiden bowed her head to pray.

There was no shock. The Queen had known since her brother's birthday that something was happening; the Vizier was positioning himself for attack. This... this was the heartbreaking fulfillment of what she had predicted... but had hoped would never go this far.

So there was no shock. But there was sadness. Sadness that the elder statesman who had seen them grow from children into young adults, whom their own mother had trusted with their safety, had seen fit to betray them. Had seen fit to kill Meritaten. And had seen fit to try to kill Tut. All to try to steal their family's throne and warp Egypt to his own selfish design.

It was clear as day. Something was wrong with that medicine. And if they didn't figure out what, the Queen's brother was probably going to die tomorrow.

22

Investigations

Semerkhet walked out of the King's room at dinnertime, the half-empty cup in his hand. He looked down into the cup, at the medicine that made his skin crawl. The medicine that he wasn't allowed to taste like he had always tasted his Pharaoh's wine ever since he had become his valet, protecting him, claiming any harm that might have been intended for him. It was still half-full; the Pharaoh had not been able to get down much of the last dose he'd taken. What was left shone like blood.

Semerkhet dipped his finger into the wine and licked it. And choked. Bitter. So bitter. That was not normal wine. And even medicine should not taste like that.

He didn't want to leave, with his Master still lying there moaning and muttering. But he had to. Strange as it was, this was the way he could best do his duty. "I'm going to find some answers," he had said, leaving the room with a whispered wish for the Pharaoh's life, prosperity, and health.

It was his dinner break; the Queen wouldn't expect him back for an hour. That was good. He needed this time. And if the Pharaoh woke up hungry before he got back, he could eat the beef stew the valet had already tested for him.

Semerkhet walked through the palace, down a dozen hallways to the servant quarters. On the way, two or three people bowed to the Sole Companion. He tried to acknowledge every bow with a gracious nod.

He knocked at Meresankh's door, and there she was, smiling up at him with that adorable dimple.

"Hello, there," she said shyly. Her tiny little hand jumped up to stroke the necklace he had given her. It looked beautiful on her. Like him, she was wearing a soft outer robe, hers yellow, offering warmth against the chill of the Sholiak day. His was green.

"Hello, Meresankh," he said. "C... can I come in?"

She stepped back, opening the door the rest of the way. "Sure. Is something wrong?"

"I think so..." Semerkhet stepped into the room, finding himself smiling as he looked around. Her suite was exactly like her; soft pillows, warm fabrics, a basket of her favorite honey-cakes on the table. All around, he saw her favorite colors; flowery pinks, warm reds, in the fabrics on the bed, the curtains draping the windows. He sat down in a chair, giving her a grateful smile as she poured both of them a cup of water before sitting down across from him. Then he noticed how low he was sitting, and how his knees seemed to be slightly bent up. Meresankh was so tiny that her custom-made furniture was distinctly smaller than the furniture he was used to.

He handed her the wine-cup. "Can you ask your Granny what's in this?"

Meresankh sniffed the cup, then grimaced. "Smells bitter," she said. "What's it supposed to be?"

"The doctor says it's an emetic, but our Pharaoh's been so much worse, so much worse, since he started taking it, and I just... feel really uncomfortable, since they won't let me try the wine. It's my job; I've always done it. And now that they won't let me try it... I'm just worried."

Meresankh shuddered. "That doesn't sound right. Why would he need an emetic, anyway? And why would it be so bitter? If he really needed an emetic, the doctor could give him mustard-seed."

"They've been putting mustard-seed on his leg," Semerkhet said, remembering the irritating poultices the Chief Physician kept tying onto the Pharaoh's leg.

Meresankh looked up. "They *what?* On— on his *leg?*" She shuddered. "Doesn't the Chief Physician know anything? You never put mustard-seed on broken skin; it draws heat and helps the body eliminate things, like when you use a mustard-plaster for a chest cold, but you'd never put it on an open wound… What in the Ten Plagues is he trying to do, kill him?" Meresankh shook her head. "Oy, vavoy. Now you've got me worried." Again, she looked down into the wine-cup. "Well, whatever's in that wine, it's certainly not mustard-seed, or castor oil, or bitter cucumber. And if they won't let you try it…"

Semerkhet shuddered. "That tells us there's something in it that the doctor doesn't want me exposed to… because then I'd know… whatever's actually going on. The Queen thinks so too," he said. "The doctor… the Vizier. Trying to hurt the Pharaoh." He sighed. "I keep hoping and hoping that I'm imagining things; that I'm wrong. Even that the Queen's wrong. But I want to be sure."

Meresankh put her tiny, warm little hand over his. Semerkhet smiled as a warm feeling stole over him, ten times the thrill he got whenever he saw her. And the wish… someday… to kiss her.

But for now, she just looked up at him solemnly. She got up, gripping the cup carefully in her other hand. "Come on. Let's go talk to Merneith."

The old midwife lived even further from the royal suites than Semerkhet and Meresankh did, inside her own little workshop not too far from the offices of the male physicians. She was the one people usually saw first, who could administer a strange old cure and a bit of timeless wisdom that often worked better than the treatments offered by the pompous doctors who had graduated from the House of Life. And she had delivered more babies than she could count.

As they walked, Meresankh told Semerkhet about her Granny. The midwife's grandmother had worked alongside Shiprah and Puah, the two Hebrew midwives who had disobeyed Pharaoh's order that all baby boys born to the Hebrews should be killed; the order that had never been recorded, but only whispered of. But Merneith was proud that her grandmother had followed Shiprah and Puah in refusing to hurt an innocent child.

If anyone would know what this strange "medicine" was, and whether it was meant for good or for ill, she would.

"Right in here," Meresankh was saying. It was darker in this part of the palace, and the halls were narrower, their walls plain and undecorated. No one of any rank ever walked around down here, so it didn't have to look quite as fancy. Meresankh stopped at the second door along the hallway, giving a firm knock.

"Who is it?" a creaky old voice asked.

"Meresankh, Granny," she said rather loudly, pressing her mouth to the door.

"You're drunk? Can't help you, dear," the old voice said dismissively. "Don't overdo it next time."

"No, it's Me-re-sankh," she said even more loudly.

"Oh, Meresankh!" The door opened to reveal the tiniest little grandmother Semerkhet had ever seen. Her hunched old back carried her head at about the level of his elbow, even shorter than Meresankh. Silently, Semerkhet chuckled to himself— he could probably lift her with one arm.

"Come in, dearie."

"Thank you, Granny." With a smile, Meresankh led Semerkhet into the old woman's chambers.

He immediately started coughing. At least three types of incense were burning in little recesses on the walls; pots of water bubbled over a fire, steeping more herbs. The fireplace was the only source of light; most of the room was shrouded in shadow. Bunches and bunches of dried herbs hung from the low ceiling, brushing the top of his head as he walked by. Pairs of bricks decorated with painted scenes of mothers and babies were stacked in a corner, ready for a laboring mother to stand on while she pushed, along with a number of stools. Charts and graphs were tacked to the walls— lists of herbs, diagrams of acupressure points, complicated recipes for herbal remedies. And a very old, very fat black cat with a gray muzzle snoozed on the table between stacks of papyrus documents, bundles of dried herbs, and jars of prepared medicines.

Meresankh bent to hug the little old lady, then bent even further to accept a loud, squeaky kiss on each cheek. Then the granny looked up, squinting at the second guest.

"Who's this hunk?" she asked matter-of-factly.

Even in the dim firelight, Semerkhet could see Meresankh blushing as her tiny fingers stroked her silver necklace. His heart warmed every time he saw her touch it.

"This is Semerkhet," she said loudly and clearly. "He's my…" She glanced up at Semerkhet with a slightly embarrassed smile, unsure of how to go on.

"Beau," Merneith finished for her. Meresankh just smiled. And didn't correct her. "Sole Companion," the midwife commented, nodding at Semerkhet's ring. "What did you do for the Pharaoh?"

"Saved his life on the battlefield," Meresankh said proudly. "Brought him home safely."

Merneith nodded, eyes almost disappearing under a multitude of smile wrinkles. "He's a good one," she said with a wink. Semerkhet tried not to blush.

"We have something we need you to identify for us," Meresankh said, producing the blue lotus cup. She was also trying not to blush. "There's a bit of red wine mixed with some sort of medicine that the Chief Physician made for the Pharaoh, but Semerkhet is suspicious about the medicine. Can you analyze it for us?"

Merneith took the cup in her gnarled, wrinkled old hands. She was so old that her joints were all crooked, fingertips pointing this way and that. She squinted into the cup, then sniffed it.

"Bitter," she said, shaking her head and frowning. "Oy, vavoy. Not any medicine I would give anyone."

Semerkhet shook his head. "The doctor said it was an emetic to get rid of bad humors, whatever that's supposed to mean, but the Pharaoh doesn't just throw up every time he takes it; he's gotten so dizzy he can't sit up, and he's got an awful headache," the valet summed up. "He has two broken legs, and now the ague, but I can't think of a single reason to induce vomiting."

"We all know about his broken legs, my dear boy," the old woman said gently. "And his ague. But inducing vomiting certainly won't help a person with ague. And vomiting should only be induced to reverse poisoning; not to adjust humors. Our bodies were not created so that our health would be controlled by how much blood or bile we have."

"But even the wine isn't the only thing we're worried about," Meresankh added. "Semerkhet said the Chief Physician has been putting mustard-seed poultices on the Pharaoh's leg."

Merneith looked up, eyes widening in horror. "He what?" she whispered. Meresankh just shook her head sadly, and Semerkhet said,

"The past few days, the doctor has been putting them on the Pharaoh's leg. I don't think the Pharaoh has one on now, but his leg is still really irritated."

The old woman shuddered. "I think the Pharaoh may need to consider the loyalty of his inner circle," she said softly.

"Can you identify what's in the wine, specifically?" Meresankh asked. "See if it really is medicine?"

"We haven't even gotten started yet, dearie," Merneith said with a smile. The little old herbalist hobbled over to the table, where she pulled up a stool, climbing up onto it before Semerkhet could offer to help. He could easily have put his hands under her arms and lifted her up to the high stool, but she was too fast for him.

Then Merneith began mixing. Semerkhet didn't know the names of any of the herbs she was combining, but she ground five or ten of them into a fine powder with a stone mortar and pestle, then mixed the powder with water. Then she spooned half of the resulting paste into a bowl, and the other half into another bowl. She poured what was left of the wine into one of the bowls.

"Now for the test," she said. She got down from the stool, hobbled over to one of a dozen shelves full of bottles, boxes, and bags of ingredients, scurried up a ladder before Semerkhet could offer to help, opened a bag, and brought her hand out full of what looked like almonds. Then she climbed back down, brought the nuts to the table, clambered back up onto the stool, and began grinding them up.

"What are those?" Sem asked as he watched Merneith grinding up the nuts. "Is that what you think they gave him? Are they poison?"

"These are peach-pits," Granny said as she pounded the seeds with the pestle. "Or rather, the kernels found inside peach-pits. After the peach-pits are dried, they can be broken open with a hammer, and inside each pit is one of these kernels. This is where the poison is found."

"Why… why do you have them, if they're poison?" Semerkhet asked carefully.

Granny smiled up at him. "The poison is neutralized by heat," she said. "When they're cooked, they become harmless. And then, they're quite good for you."

Semerkhet nodded, his vague fears that this wise old midwife would turn out to be a wicked witch blowing away like dust in the wind. And he continued to watch Merneith grind up the little kernels. When there was nothing left but a fine brown powder, that went into the second bowl.

Merneith stirred both bowls carefully, then placed two small pieces of plain linen cloth on the table, pushing the cat aside to make room. It sniffed in annoyance and waddled off to find another place to nap. The herbalist dabbed a small spoonful of each of the mixtures onto the linen. And she examined them carefully.

"A match," she said, looking up. "This wine has been laced with raw peach-pits." She looked at Semerkhet. "And they are not medicine. They are poison. The same poison as bitter almonds." She shook her head. "And a terribly perfect choice for a murderer who wishes to kill someone already suffering from ague, as their symptoms overlap a great deal. The only differences are that with peach-pit poisoning, the headache and dizziness can be even more pronounced than with ague."

Semerkhet closed his eyes, feeling the terrible truth crashing over him. His Master was being poisoned. And it was all his fault. The words he always said when he tasted the King's drink echoed through his mind... *I taste your drink, Son of Ra... and if there be harm in it, let the harm fall upon me...* and he had to fight back the tears. He had failed. He had been presenting the harm to his Master, rather than taking it upon himself.

Meresankh was looking up at him, frowning in worry as she saw his reaction.

"Is there..." he finally asked, swallowing away the sudden dryness in his throat, "...is there anything we can do? Any antidote you can make? Counteract it?" He looked around her workshop, casting about him for some magical herb, some strange nut or seed, that would stop the poison in its tracks.

Merneith shook her head. "Time," she said simply. "If he's stopped taking it, it should be out of his system in a few hours, and the symptoms should pass... if it's not already too late. After that, it will be nothing more than giving him all the water he'll take, and within a few more hours, offering him broth or porridge."

Semerkhet just closed his eyes.

Meresankh sighed. "Thank you, Granny," she said, hugging the old woman goodbye. "Now we know what it is. And now we know what to do."

"Any time, dearie, any time," she said, waving as they went.

23

Suspicion

Semerkhet stumbled out of the workshop, squinting in the comparative brightness of the hallway. And searching for a bench. He had to sit down.

Finally he found one and collapsed onto it, holding his head in his hand. Meresankh sat down next to him, putting her tiny little hand on his back.

"I knew it," he whispered in a broken voice, clutching the stem of the empty blue lotus cup until his knuckles went white. "I knew it. Knew they were doing something. Knew something wasn't right." Now he couldn't help but cry, tears running silently down his face as Meresankh's little hand rubbed soothing circles over his back. "What have I done to my brother?"

Meresankh put her arm around Semerkhet. Bad news. Their Pharaoh had been getting worse… because he had been poisoned.

For the hundred-thousandth time she began to pray. For their Pharaoh… and for Semerkhet.

Semerkhet had gone to find some answers, he had said. Ankhesenamun sat with her brother, watching him continue to shudder, rolling his head to one side, then the other as sweat beaded on his gray face; the face that was now nothing but skin and bones. He hadn't eaten, and had barely even been able to keep down water, for hours. She sat there beside him, listening to him continue to mumble.

He had been poisoned. And if Semerkhet didn't find answers… Tut was going to die.

The Queen got up and walked across the room, creating the tiniest space between her and her brother. Space to think. She closed her eyes, trying to pray. All she heard was the silence, just as she had expected. But at the same time… there was a tiny ray of hope. She knew she had been heard. But by Whom was the question.

Then Ankh looked up. What had changed? She retraced her steps, returning to her place beside her brother. He wasn't muttering anymore, or twitching. Now he seemed to be sleeping very quietly. He looked… peaceful.

His sister continued to watch him very carefully. Was that a good sign… or not?

Slowly, the fires began to cool, the storm of confusion to ebb. When Tut felt a hand gently touch him, he didn't flinch with fear. And for the first time in hours, his stomach was calm. Gently, he felt himself drifting into a peaceful sleep, the first peaceful sleep he might have had in years.

Gently he dreamed. His Mother and Father stood in a bright courtyard, smiling at him as they stood hand-in-hand. The Sun was shining, but it seemed to be coming from everywhere, rather than from a single Solar Disc.

"Be strong," Mother said, reaching out to take his hand.

His Father took his other hand. Because somehow, in this dream, Tutankhamun was able to stand without his cane. "Find the Light."

Suddenly, Tutankhamun felt himself waking up. Where was he? He looked around, feeling that he hadn't been able to for days. Or was it weeks? He was in bed, and Ankh was sitting there beside him.

Why was he so weak? Was he sick? Slowly he remembered— ague. And... some sort of poison. Or had it been medicine? He wasn't quite sure. But somehow... he was starting to come out of whatever haze he had been trapped in. It felt good to know where he was. Who he was. Now he felt safe, for what felt like the first time in weeks. He closed his eyes, giving a deep sigh. He needed to rest.

"Ankh?" he asked a little while later. She looked up from the bowl of water she was moistening a cloth in, ready to dab it gently over his hot forehead. He was safe now, safe from the effect the fever had had on his mind, and whatever else had been hurting him, but he was still so hot.

She smiled, giving a deep sigh of relief as they made eye contact— eye contact full of recognition and joy. "Yes, love?"

He smiled back. "I'm feeling better."

His sister set the cloth aside and wrapped her arms around him, giving him a gentle hug. "Oh, I'm so glad."

Ankh closed her eyes as she hugged him and kissed his forehead, praising all the gods she could think of. Her brother was talking again. He could think; could look at her and know who she was. Maybe... maybe he wasn't dying. It was a miracle. An answer to every prayer that had seemed to echo back in empty silence.

And she sighed as she thought about that medicine.

Tut hadn't had a dose of the new medicine in four hours. And to his relief, his mind was starting to become clearer, his headache improving. And he hadn't thrown up since shortly after his last dose. All the water and tea and broth he wanted, taken in little sips as his sister held a cup or spoon to his lips, stayed exactly where it was supposed to. He could even sit up a little without getting dizzy or lightheaded. Just being free of those new symptoms felt like a miracle.

The Queen asked Meresankh to go to the Royal Library and bring her the papyrus that described the properties of every herb used in

Egyptian medicine. She sat by her brother as he slowly continued to improve, scanning the document for a reference to a remedy that would exacerbate the symptoms of ague. She had to find the treatment the doctor had given him.

As she scanned, Ankh paused over snippets of the listings she was glancing through. *Nettles, used in infusions to treat joint pain; not to be used in patients with weak hearts... peppermint, tea made from its leaves treats nausea and its oil treats headaches... bitter cucumber, makes an effective laxative... chamomile, relieves nervous tension and insomnia and lowers fevers... spikenard, calms the mind and promotes sleep...*

But none of the herbs in the compendium was listed with a warning that it should not be given to ague patients, for fear of worsening their symptoms. And she found no references to an emetic whose side effects included dizziness and headaches.

She shook her head. Whatever Tut was being given wasn't in the papyrus. Therefore, it followed... that it was not real medicine.

Quietly Semerkhet knocked at his Pharaoh's bedroom door, entering when he heard the Queen's soft "Come in." What would he find when he came in, he wondered, his heart beginning to pound.

"Hello, Sem," a soft, familiar voice said. And Semerkhet felt himself melting with relief. His Master was sitting up in bed, the Queen carefully helping him sip a cup of tea.

Tears of gratitude springing to his eyes, Semerkhet ran over and dropped to his left knee beside his Master, heart exploding with joy. He wanted to throw his arms around his brother, but restrained himself to taking his hand and squeezing it.

"Glory be," he whispered, smiling up at his healing friend. And although he was not sure he knew the name of the One Who had saved his brother, he meant it.

The Pharaoh reached out and patted Semerkhet on the shoulder. "Fank you," he whispered.

Semerkhet crossed the room to where the Queen stood, urgent words on his lips. Maybe it wasn't his place, but he had to tell her— had to tell her that the Pharaoh's very life depended on his never taking that peach-pit wine again. Tut was his brother too, after all.

"The medicine—" he began, but Ankhesenamun cut him off with a glowing smile.

"I know," she said. "I know. Whatever that was, it was only making him worse, but he won't take it again." She pointed at Tut, lying quietly awake in the bed, and blinked back happy tears. "Just look at him. He's so much better. Doesn't it feel like he's back; like he's really here again? Come on. Let's change his sheets and clean him up and make him feel better."

Semerkhet turned his attention to tidying up his Pharaoh's room; tidying up the Pharaoh himself with a gentle bed-bath, sponging away the sweat of the fever and helping him into a fresh loincloth and sleeping-tunic, then replacing the rather nasty bedsheets with fresh ones and making a pile of dirty laundry for the Handlers of Royal Linen to deal with. Once the King was settled fresh and clean into a fresh, clean bed, Semerkhet set about arranging containers of medicine, stacking medical papyri, organizing dirty dishes. And pouring out his gratitude in a thousand prayers of thanks, to every god and goddess he could think of. Because his brother had stood there at death's door... and turned back around.

Finally... finally, the gods he loved were answering his prayers.

Tut was better. The fever had broken, and Semerkhet had cleaned him up and changed his sheets. And Ankh would bring him a bit of water or tea whenever he wanted it, replenishing him after so long without being able to keep anything down. Tut lay there in bed as exhausted as if he had swum from one end of the Nile to the other, upstream. But happy. And so very, very grateful. Because whatever recovery still lay ahead of him, he was alive. The gods were listening.

The valet kept checking on the Pharaoh as the evening went on, marking his progress as he continued to return from what might have been his deathbed. His Master really did seem... a little better. He was still pale, but his eyes and cheeks were no longer so sunken, his face no longer so gray, his lips no longer so pale, so dry and cracked. And free from the mustard-seed poultice, his leg was free to begin to heal.

Semerkhet was overjoyed, to be sure, to see his Pharaoh free of that terrible haze, able to talk, able even to think, able to eat and drink, but this sudden improvement... only proved what he had just found out from Meresankh's granny.

Sem closed his eyes with a deep sigh.

There was something else... something else that kept prodding at the Queen's mind like Bastet trying to climb into her lap. Something important.

On a hunch, she leafed through the medical papyrus again, which lay on a table in the Pharaoh's bedroom. Chamomile, peppermint...

Nettle. *Used in infusions to treat joint pain. Not to be used in patients with weak hearts.*

Ankh closed her eyes, bowing her head. Father had had a weak heart. And she remembered, plain as day, the Grand Vizier urging him every day to take his nettle tea. Urging him with the same kind, friendly attitude with which he had pressed the doctor's new medicine on her brother.

Her stomach clenched, nausea rising in her throat. It couldn't... couldn't be. It couldn't. The Vizier... He couldn't have had her Father killed; he wouldn't have. Not the loyal old Grand Vizier.

The loyal old Grand Vizier who had killed Meritaten in the first year of their reign; killed Pentu only a few short months ago. The Grand Vizier... who had seemed altogether too enthusiastic about the Queen's baby brother going to Kadesh.

And now her stomach clenched until she bowed over, curling into herself as the truth hit her, finally hit her, with no more room for any doubts or questions.

The Vizier who had murdered Meritaten, Akhenaten, and the loyal young Pentu was killing Tutankhamun as well. That was her brother's secret.

Ankh sat down in her room that evening, releasing a deep sigh. He was getting better. Her brother had turned around at death's door. Glory be.

She saw Meresankh come into the room from the storage area, an assortment of freshly-cleaned wigs in her arms, ready to be arranged on her Lady's shelves. And she smiled.

"He's getting better," Ankh whispered, face glowing.

Meresankh set the wigs aside and hurried to the Queen's side, taking her hand. "Oh, glory to I-AM!" she cried. Then she paused. The Queen only smiled. Whatever god had saved the Pharaoh was greatly to be praised.

"As soon... as soon as he stopped taking that medicine, it turned around," Ankhesenamun continued. Slowly, the sun-bright bubble of joy in her heart was beginning to deflate, go dim. Because of that medicine, and what it meant.

And it hit her. Slowly, the Queen felt tears begin trickling down her cheeks, the face that only seconds ago had been glowing with joy. Because of what the turnaround meant.

Ankh sat down on her bed. A moment later, she heard a little purr, and felt Bastet jump up beside her. Gently, the Queen picked her up.

Rocking the cat in her lap, she sobbed. Poison. The doctor, the Vizier, had been giving him poisoned wine. Even as he healed, it meant that they were trying to kill him.

"My Lady?" Meresankh asked gently.

"It was the wine," Ankh sobbed, wiping away her tears.

"I know," Meresankh whispered, sitting down beside her on the bed and putting her arm around the Queen. It still felt strange to touch her, hug her, as if they were both humans. Although, of course, they were. A pair of humans, a pair of friends, a pair of sisters. "Semerkhet had his suspicions, and we took one of the cups down to the midwife. She told us it was peach-pit poison." Meresankh swallowed. "Sem feels awful. He is the wine-taster, after all."

Ankhesenamun shook her head as the news that the Vizier had tried to kill her brother with the same poison that was used to execute criminals broke her heart. "He wasn't tasting it because it was medicine. H... how could they?" she moaned, eye-makeup beginning to run down her face. "Why do they hate the Pharaoh so much?"

Meresankh held her tighter, rocking her slightly. "Because he loves his people more than he loves gold."

"And why hasn't he told us, if he knows?" the Queen whispered, her voice broken.

Meresankh shook her head. "Because he doesn't want it to be true either."

Ankh sat up, wiping her eyes. "Actually," she said, "we need your help. I told the Chief Physician not to come back, so that means we need a replacement. And I know... I know that you know your herbs. Will you... will you help us take care of him?"

Meresankh looked up at her with a proud little smile. "Yes, My Lady. And so will my Granny."

Semerkhet didn't sleep that night. He tossed and turned, going over the past week in his mind; every time that Raherka or the doctor had brought that "medicine;" the medicine that he, Cup-Bearer to the Pharaoh and royal wine-taster, had let through. Medicine that had not been medicine at all, but poison. Poison that Semerkhet should have taken.

Sem rolled over on his cot, pressing the heels of his hands into his eyes. He should be the one who now lay ill; he should be dead, struck down by the poison intended for the Pharaoh, the same poison used to execute criminals. That was why he did his job. So that if anyone ever tried to poison the Pharaoh, Semerkhet would be the one who died.

I failed, he thought. *By not dying of the poison myself, I failed to do my job and save his life at the expense of my own.* That was what the Priest of

Ma'at had said at the trial, and Semerkhet remembered how the words had pricked his heart.

An image of Nedjes' funeral rose in his imagination; carefully placed in his coffin, the damage done by the hippopotamus, which had nearly torn his leg off, repaired by the embalmers as well as they could manage. And Semerkhet's heart filled with wretchedness that right here, right now, he again stood helplessly by, unable to protect a beloved little brother from death.

It was a long, sleepless night of guilt. Self-loathing filled the pit of Semerkhet's stomach as his shame at failing to protect the Pharaoh, his guilt at not having done his job as cupbearer, regret at having been the one who had survived, burned inside his mind.

I don't deserve to be the one who survived, he told himself. *My life was not worth saving. But I saved it anyway.*

But— Semerkhet sighed, unexpectedly finding himself almost smiling as a sudden thought touched his heart. He had survived at Kadesh— survived to continue protecting his Pharaoh; stayed alive to keep protecting his little brother. Maybe that was his job now. Just as before, through surviving now, could he protect his brother from whatever harm yet loomed in their future?

Father. Ankhesenamun tossed and turned that night, closing her eyes against the tears. And she thought of her father; the father she had not seen since her tenth year. Memories of her first ten years of life filled her heart like a wineskin about to burst; happy, sad, confusing, proud. He had turned Egypt inside-out for the sake of the Truth he believed he had found. And he... Silently Ankh wiped her eyes. He had died for it. She thought of the nettle medicine he had taken, trusting in the Vizier's wishes for his long life, prosperity, and health. The nettle medicine... with which he had been murdered. Just as the Vizier had later murdered Meritaten, then Pentu, and now had made his move against Tut.

The Queen rolled over in bed. And she wondered if even she could protect their future from the Vizier and his murderous treachery.

She wasn't looking at him as much, Tut noticed the next day. His sister brought him tea and snacks, held his hand, did everything she always did, but she looked uncomfortable, looked… almost angry. At him.

The Pharaoh closed his eyes. He knew why she was angry. Because she had figured it out.

His fever was better today. But his strength was gone. He was no longer as wiped out as he had been in the grip of the fever, but he felt nearly as weak as he had been when he had first come home. And he had no strength to sit in his chair.

24

Trying

"Where's the Chief Physician?" Tut asked as quite unexpectedly, Meresankh bent over his leg to examine it.

His sister shook her head. "I told him not to come back unless we called for him. Because clearly... clearly, he was not taking very good care of you." She bit back her fears, her doubts, hoping against hope that things could still turn around.

Slowly, Tut nodded. And he, too, bit back his fears and doubts. He knew she was right. But he knew there was still a chance that he would recover, and that life could go on.

"Thank you," he said. He shook his head. "Thank you for making that call."

She bent over him to kiss his forehead. "We're a team. Just like Mother and Father."

"When was this last checked?" Meresankh asked as she carefully undid the ties of his splint and set it aside. Her tiny fingers were very gentle.

"Two dayth ago," he said, then hissed in pain as she began unwrapping the bandage. Trying to, anyway. The day he had been taking that wine, his wound had been neglected. The linen bandage had stuck to his wound, and even though it was no longer in place, the mustard-seed poultices the Chief Physician had used on his leg seemed to have literally burned what was left of his skin. More and more of his leg was becoming hot, red, and inflamed... and there was a great deal of pus.

"Who in the Ten Plagues puts a mustard-seed poultice on an open wound?" Meresankh asked, gently waving her hand over the area. Tut let out his breath. The tiny breeze she was creating felt so good. Free of the tight linen bandage, his leg felt so much cooler.

Someone who wants to kill their patient, Tut thought about saying. But he just shook his head sadly. Because he didn't want to give up hope.

Meresankh cleaned up the Pharaoh's leg as well as she could, touching the painful wound as gently as possible. As she worked, she shook her head. Because she could hardly believe that she was being entrusted with the Pharaoh's health. And as she worked, she prayed. Prayed for a miracle.

The Pharaoh took a sip of the wine Semerkhet had brought him; his favorite white wine from Tribute Day, carefully checked for poison.

And he almost spat it out. With a shaking hand, Tut put aside his cup, closing his eyes as a terrible realization hit him.

That wine. The wine he had been given during the first days of his ague; the strange new "medicine" Raherka had faithfully brought. The medicine he had not taken since yesterday afternoon.

Tut thought back to what he could remember of his day of fever. He remembered the Chief Physician offering him a cup of wine made bitter with the new medicine, remembered Raherka bringing it again, even remembered the Grand Vizier himself stopping by to make sure he was taking it. Remembered Semerkhet offering to taste it; Raherka claiming that there was no reason for him to test it. And that was when... that was when Tut had gotten worse, wasn't it? When he had first started taking the wine?

And that was when he had started feeling better. When he had stopped taking the wine.

Tutankhamun lay back down in bed and pulled the blankets over his head. He had been poisoned.

But even with his focus being so concentrated on his Master's well-being, Sem found himself thinking about other elements of life; the things he had turned away from over the past days of spending every waking hour looking after his friend. Coming to and from meals, he would sometimes run into other members of his hockey team, other chariot racers. And they would update him on recent wins and losses; the twisted ankles, sprained shoulders, strained deltoids, and torn ligaments that would change the trajectory of what was left of the season.

He missed running with his teammates in the bright sunlight; missed guiding his horses around the track as the chariot rumbled beneath his feet. He would remain where he was needed. But the things that he loved were never far from his heart.

Ay and the others had sent him off to die in Kadesh. And they had poisoned him with this fake "medicine." Ay was the mastermind, but he had clearly gotten Horemheb and Maya on his side. The Chief Physician, too, was involved; Tut shook his head as he remembered the doctor speaking absentmindedly of the retreat Horemheb had ordered, the retreat he could only have known about if he had been in on the plan all along. There was no longer the slightest doubt that Tutankhamun's loyal courtiers wanted him dead.

What— what if he did die? Tut closed his eyes as the thought hit him; hit him in the gut like a kick from a horse. What if, despite the care provided by Ankh and Sem, despite how desperately hard he was working to get better, he didn't recover?

He shuddered. And for the first time, he was truly forced to wonder if he would ever get out of bed again.

Semerkhet brought the King a cup of his favorite white wine. He was doing it quite selfishly, though. Because how could he call himself cup-bearer, wine-taster, if he didn't actually taste his Pharaoh's wine before offering it to him?

"I taste your drink, Son of Ra… and if there be harm in it, let the harm fall upon me." He sipped it conspicuously, tasting the good, clean, unadulterated wine. "It's good." With a self-satisfied nod, he handed it to the King. Today he had done the right thing, done his job, lived up to his title.

Tutankhamun took the cup. "Thank you, Sem." He looked up at him, the expression on his face. And as he took his own sip of the wine, he saw that Semerkhet already knew.

But he still didn't want to tell them. Because there was still a chance that he would get better. Tut kept clinging to that chance. He would cling to it until the last possible moment.

Why had Horemheb betrayed him? Why had the Vizier and the Physician worked together to poison him? Why were the gods doing this to him?

The wind was changing, Meresankh felt. The days were getting colder, darker. And inside the palace… it also felt colder, darker. Because in her Pharaoh's room, a change was also taking place.

One that made her shudder. Because even now that he was no longer taking either the peach-pit wine or the painkillers, he was still getting worse.

"How are your legs today?" Ankh asked out of the silence of the quiet afternoon. Tut looked up with a slight start from wistfully petting Bastet, who lay curled in a pool of sunshine on the edge of the bed. And quickly, he arranged his features into a smile.

"Tolerable," he said, and that was true. His legs didn't hurt so badly at the moment, even the infected one. It was the weakness that was wearing him down.

He sighed without meaning to. And his sister bent toward him, forehead creasing as she studied his face. Gently, she reached out a hand

and brushed the tiny braids of his wig out of his eyes. Thankfully his fever was lower today.

"When are you going to tell me?" she asked softly.

His eyes flickered for an instant. But he tried to smile at her. "Tell you what?" he asked innocently.

Ankh got up, turning away and hiding her face. "I think you know," she said in a choked voice.

"What is there to tell?" he asked lightly, shrugging even though she wasn't looking at him. "I'm doing better than I was."

Slowly she turned back, giving him a wan flicker of her own smile. And she squeezed his hand.

But he could tell she didn't believe him.

If he listened hard enough, Tut could hear the sounds of the town blowing in on the breeze that blew the bedroom curtains; the laughter, the bustle of the marketplace. But from his bed, he couldn't see it. Tut lay with his eyes closed, remembering the one day he'd spent out in Memphis, taking in the sights and sounds. If he could only go into town one more time… he wouldn't ask for much more.

He thought back to the perfect day just before the mosquitoes had come, the day he had spent in the pavilion, playing *seega* with Ankhesenamun out in the sunshine. He remembered the warmth of the Sun on his face, the cool brush of the breeze, the sweet fragrances of the flowers, the twittering of the birds. He had spent the days since wondering when his next opportunity to go outside would come. But now he was no longer sure it would ever come.

Then he gazed out just at his own room; the room that had become his whole world. Most of the things in his room were exactly as they had been a year or two ago, but a few things had changed. A new table had been brought in, for example, to hold all the extra things he had come to need. It was a place to set a stack of fresh linen bandages or a jar of medicine, a place for Ankh to prepare tea, a place to set a pitcher of water so it was handy. It was useful, but whenever Tut looked at it, he thought it looked out of place. So many things in his life were out of place now.

Tut looked in another direction, into what he could see of his private sitting room. He hadn't been in there for months, after two weeks spent traveling to Amurru, a day spent on the battlefield, three days gathering his strength, another week spent traveling home, and the past nearly three weeks being spent in bed or in his chair, except for the one wonderful, beautiful, perfect, shining day he had spent out in the garden.

He could see the archway that led into the storage room where most of his clothing lived, and his shoes, and all his walking-sticks, the walking-sticks that, shocked as he was at the thought, he missed. Because they represented the ability to get out of bed.

He never would have thought he would miss his walking-sticks.

Tut gave a heavy sigh. He could only sit and look at all his beautiful things. He could not even get out of bed and touch them. He swallowed back a tear. He could not help but think that he was never, ever going to get out of bed again.

But still he kept waiting. Kept his secret hidden inside his breaking heart. Because he didn't want it to be true.

Patiently Ankh and Sem cared for him, bringing him his meals, helping him wash, helping him rest as well as he could. Something was wrong, they both knew. Someone very powerful was trying to hurt him, beyond the ways in which he had already been hurt. And something had changed in his face. He was more solemn. Looked... older.

The bruises and scrapes on his face had healed, but what he'd lived through these past weeks had stripped away whatever was left of his baby face, the child that the Boy-King had been. Now his face looked thin, careworn, serious, wise. The face of someone who had seen battle; the face of a politician with some experience under his belt. He truly had become a man.

And not just a man who was no longer a boy. Aged by care, weary with pain, he looked like an old man.

And he was quieter. Didn't talk about the battle; didn't talk about how he was feeling or what he would do when he got better. When he did talk, it was to chat about unimportant things, even joke, but his smiles never reached his eyes. They could tell that this cheeriness was false, put-on. Could tell that he was trying very hard to hide how he really felt.

He knew what was going on. But he wasn't ready to tell them.

So they waited. Loved him, cared for him, and waited.

As he lay there in bed, wishing he was not dying, the Pharaoh felt his mind itch as the wrongness of the Vizier's response to his mother's death; the creepiness in his reaction to Tut's injury, followed one another around his heart.

Tears prickled in his eyes as he remembered his mother's funeral; remembered watching Ay perform the Opening of the Mouth ceremony that would allow her to eat, drink, and speak in the afterlife, even though only the previous day, Nefertiti had reminded her children that although a loving Pharaoh allowed his or her subjects to worship as they chose, the Aten, the Lord of Light, was the One in Whom she trusted. He remembered standing arm-in-arm with Ankh as the funeral went on, Meritaten towering above them as she sheltered them like a mother hen with her chicks, the big sister who would protect them against all that was evil in the world as she nurtured and guided them as both Mother and Father, the only sister they had left. He remembered all the days since; all the days in which he had continued to learn, grow, and mature without his Mother there to guide him. And he remembered... all the moments in which he had wished so painfully that she was still with him.

The Pharaoh thought of Meritaten... whom the Vizier had murdered in the first year of Tut's reign. Pentu, killed only a few short months ago.

He thought of his Mother again, who had died when Tut had been nine years old. Died so suddenly; torn from their lives when they needed her the most. And the truth slapped him in the face.

His mother had been murdered.

Tut curled up as tightly as he could, holding Bastet to his heart. Murdered. It couldn't be. And the Vizier, the loyal old Vizier... he couldn't have. And yet, looking back, it was the only explanation for the suddenness of her death, the response of the Vizier. Tutankhamun clenched his hands into fists as anger burned in his heart. He had killed her, the Vizier who had killed so many of those whom Tut loved and cared about. Ay had planned it out; ensured that the horse would be spooked, Nefertiti's fall fatal. And he had calmly accepted the authority that had then come to him, becoming regent for a Pharaoh too young to rule even though he was the murderer of the Pharaoh who had gone before. And then... Tut sighed. Sent him off to battle. Poisoned him. Ensured that his festering leg would be neglected until the worsening infection rendered any recovery truly impossible.

The flame of anger that made one small part of the Pharaoh want to arrest the Vizier for high treason that very night melted into sadness. And he wept for his mother's death.

Was it physical pain? Depression stemming from guilt about the battle? The burden the ague and his worsening infection were placing on his body? What was it that was making him so quiet, had brought the chill and stillness of the dark month of Meshir to rest inside his heart? What was it that was sapping his strength, his energy, his joy, his fight, his heart, his spirit, his very will to go on? What was it that was slowly pulling him away from them?

What was it... that was killing him?

The Pharaoh looked down at his leg. He could separate the pain of the infection from the pain of the broken bone; feel the itching and the heat that continued to worsen even as Meresankh faithfully tended the wound.

He wiggled his foot. And bit back a yelp of pain as his stomach did a somersault. Sweating, he lay back.

His leg was getting worse. And his hopes for a full recovery were dying.

Night had fallen. But Tut still lay awake, staring into the blackness of the long, chilly night. And in that darkness, he prayed.

Make me better, he begged, even as he wondered Who it really was Who was listening. *Let me live. Please. I'll do anything... give You anything. I'll build a hundred temples... open a hundred schools... anything. Please. Just don't let me die.*

And the words *don't let me die* echoed through his heart until morning came.

The morning of the nineteenth of Sholiak, Semerkhet helped his Pharaoh get ready for the day as usual. And despite all the fear, all the worries, all the unknowns, there was one thing that made him smile. The mustard-seed poultice was no longer strapped to Tut's leg. Whatever happened in the future, those poultices were no longer going to be making his leg worse.

"Why don't you try sitting in your chair today?" Ankh asked him after lunch. Tut was curled up with the cat, staring into space.

Slowly, he sat up, releasing Bastet, who hopped to the floor to search for marauding insects or stray nutshells. And he shook his head.

"Not today," he said softly. "I'd like to; I'd really like to, but... I don't think I can."

Her brother looked tired. He looked resigned. He looked... old. Like there was less life left in him than before. Like he was waiting for the bitter end of a story he could not control. Only endure.

A story she could not control either.

And she turned away before he could see her sadness.

Ankh sat in her room, fighting with the lump in her throat. Her brother seemed to be a bit better; the fever was down and his mind was clear. And the p… the peach-pit poison was out of his system. So why was he so weak? And why wouldn't he even try to get out of bed?

She put her arms around herself, closing her eyes. And a question slid down her spine like a cold raindrop.

What if this really was the illness from which he never recovered?

She reached for the Queens List. And she found Ahmose-Nefertari, who had served as regent for her son earlier in their own dynasty. By her guidance, Egypt had remained solid and stable until Prince Amenhotep had become Pharaoh Amenhotep the First.

And then Ankhesenamun found Sobekneferu, the final Pharaoh of the Twelfth Dynasty. And she sighed as she looked down at the familiar page. Because Sobekneferu had become Pharaoh when there had been no one else to take the throne… no one left. She had been the last one standing in her family.

Gently, Ankh stroked the papyrus. And she swallowed as the legacy of Sobekneferu filled her heart with a strength that was both as warm as the Sun on her face and as cold as the depths of the longest night. If, somehow, she found herself the last one standing… could she do the same?

25

Possibilities

"If the worst happens, what can I do?" the Queen asked her handmaiden as she got ready for bed. Night was falling, another long, hard day ending.

"What do you mean, My Lady?" Meresankh asked, setting aside the sleeping-tunic she was about to offer her.

Her Mistress clenched her hands, knuckles showing white as she fought to hold onto the precious past as the coldhearted future stole it away piece by piece. Crossing the room, she locked the door as if what she was about to say was meant for no ears but Meresankh's.

"It would be best to rule alone," Ankhesenamun said, turning back around to face her friend. "I know I could. Could take the throne after my brother."

Meresankh frowned up at her in confusion. "What do you mean?" she asked again, voice a horrified whisper. "He's not taking the wine anymore— isn't he starting to get better yet? Why are you..." She bit her lip. "Why are you making plans for after he's gone?"

The Queen bowed her head. And she gave a heavy sigh. "The poison's out of his system now; he's not in any danger from it anymore. But he..." Ankh bit her knuckle, fighting back tears. "It's like the last time he had the ague, back in Epiphi. He got better then, but he never has been… quite the same. And I'm afraid… I'm just afraid. That this could be it. Because he… he's not improving. He just lies there with the cat, taking nap after nap, and when he's awake, he's so quiet and sad, and he just sits there frowning, like he *knows* something…" She shook her head as the truth ached within her heart. She knew what it was that he knew; knew what he was concealing.

She looked up, swallowing. "Maybe I'm wrong. Maybe all this will turn around, and a month from now, he'll be back on his feet, and everything will go back to normal. But I… I have to be prepared for… everything to change."

Meresankh just looked at her. "Are you sure?" she whispered.

Ankh shook her head. "I'm not sure about anything. And that's why I have to be prepared for everything. They did this on purpose, Meresankh," the Queen continued. "The doctor, the Vizier. They worked together to poison the Pharaoh."

"But why?" Meresankh asked.

"Politics," Ankhesenamun said simply. "Because the Vizier hates the way that we value the well-being of Egypt's citizens more highly than the number of gold pieces and sacks of grain in the treasury. And because he's decided to make sure that he outlives the Pharaoh… and that the Pharaoh doesn't leave behind a son to succeed him… and he's timed it all so that he can grab the throne while General Horemheb, the real heir, is out of the country." Ankhesenamun sighed. "The Vizier wants the throne, Meresankh. And he's willing to commit murder to get it."

Meresankh shook her head. The details she had just received filled in everything she had not yet known. But all they did was solidify the terrible truth she had already learned from her Granny. And turned her vague wariness of the Vizier into a burning ember of righteous anger.

The Queen swallowed. "I know I could take the throne. My Mother did, and I truly believe that I have enough experience, enough knowledge, to see me through as Pharaoh." Meresankh looked up at her Lady, standing tall and strong and noble, shoulders wide, head up, wise eyes wide open as she faced the unknown future. And she had no doubt that the Queen could become an excellent Pharaoh.

"But they won't let me," the Queen continued, face falling, shoulders sinking as she almost seemed to shrink under the weight of so much pain, so much struggle. "One of them will try to marry me. The Vizier will try, I'm sure. Maybe even…" She gave a harsh laugh, even as Meresankh saw a flicker of nauseated revulsion cross her face. "Maybe even General Nakhtmin."

"That would be awful!" Meresankh cried with a little laugh, sensing that in this moment, they needed to connect over a chuckle, even at something horrible. And the Queen gave her a smile.

"So," Ankh continued, still with a disgusted smile, "I could become Nakhtmin's wife… or his stepmother."

Now Meresankh held her stomach as if she were about to vomit.

"He's not an option," she said, shaking her head emphatically.

The Queen chuckled again. "No. He's not." Then she sighed. "Or the Treasurer might try, or even General Horemheb. Even though they're both already married. I'm sure either of them would be happy to claim me as a stepping-stone to the throne."

"We won't let them," Meresankh said, shaking her head again.

Ankhesenamun also shook her head, beaded braids swinging. "No. We won't." She looked away, out the window, where the birds were singing in the mid-Sholiak garden, a chilly breeze blowing in the trees. And she shuddered at the thought of what Ay would do with Egypt if he became Pharaoh. "The moment the Vizier took the throne, we would lose everything we've worked for… more, even. He would close the schools, raise the taxes higher than we ever had them, cancel the minimum wage, start importing slaves again…" An image rose in the Queen's heart, of that little girl she and her husband had seen on that day in town. And she clenched her fists as the pain rose. "I have to stop him," she said, "for that little girl out in the city. And for all the little girls like her."

Her handmaiden nodded. And she invited the Queen to go on.

"Horemheb is technically the Pharaoh's Crown Prince, in the… in the event that…" She trailed off, and Meresankh continued watching her in silent, tender concern. "But he's not here right now, and if he's going to be in Amurru for— I don't know; it could be weeks, or even months, then he might not be here when…." A sob choked her, and she covered her face in her hand, shoulders shaking. Taking a shuddering breath, she gulped, wiping her eyes. "I should be the one," she said.

Her handmaiden just looked at her. And listened.

"My Mother reigned as Pharaoh, after my Father died," Ankhesenamun said again wistfully, still looking out the window. Meresankh nodded. She knew the stories, and she herself remembered glimpses of the reign of Pharaoh Smenkhkare from her own childhood. "But that was different," Ankh continued. "They had a long co-regency, eased the citizens in, showed them that she was a good Pharaoh in her own right, that she would be able to rule them herself after Father was gone." She looked down, folding her hands. "But now… there isn't really time for a co-regency between Tutankhamun and myself, to make things easier now and to establish me as the next Pharaoh.

"Things would be so different if there was an heir," she said, touching her flat belly. "Or if…" She sighed, looking back into the past, into the future that had never been. "If Meritaten had had a son. The Pharaoh would have a nephew. And he could be the heir. And that would change everything."

Then another thought touched her heart; a thought that made it ache. "If the Pharaoh had another wife… he might have a son by now. And then I could be like Hatshepsut, acting as regent for my little nephew-stepson." She bit her lip. If only, if only her brother had not been so naïve; had not loved her so much that he felt that selecting a secondary wife would be an act of betrayal. If only he could have been a politician too. Now, with no son and with widowhood creeping up behind her, Ankh was the one who was having to plan a second marriage for the sake of their country's future.

Meresankh saw more tears glimmering in her Lady's eyes. And shyly, she extended her hand, letting the Queen grasp it gratefully, squeezing it as she might a sister's. "But we don't have an heir. So I have to do it myself. The only ones who would have backed me up as Pharaoh, Pentu, Usermontu, Mother, Father, Meritaten, are halfway across the country… or gone." Her eyes cleared. "I could rule alone, in principle. But in politics, I can't. To remain leader of Egypt, I have to have a husband."

"Who, then?" Meresankh asked softly.

Ankh shrugged, then gave another sad smile. "I remember Pentu… such a nice man. Sweet, kind, generous, noble. I never felt even the least bit attracted to him, but as a person… under these… these circumstances… that's a match I could imagine not regretting. If he was still here."

Meresankh sighed. Of course, the whole discussion was entirely theoretical. The point was moot. Pentu was not an option.

"Usermontu…" The Queen chuckled. "Very wise. Very sweet. Very kind. Very noble. And old enough to be my grandfather. Again, not really a consideration."

Meresankh looked up at her. "Who, then? Who could you make some sort of future with?"

The Queen thought of the battle where Tutankhamun had fallen. Against the Hittites, for possession of Kadesh. And an astonishing thought… a strange thought, a wild thought, a shocking thought, a perfectly outrageous thought, touched her heart.

What if in the middle of this war, they reached out to the Hittites in the most intimate way possible, with a proposal of marriage?

Her heart began to pound as she suddenly felt lightheaded. Could… could that work? Through wielding her authority as Queen, could she save her country through marrying Egypt to Hattusa?

"King Suppiluliuma has several sons," she said slowly, "and Prince Zannanza isn't married."

Meresankh's eyes grew as round as apples. "The Hittites?" she asked in a choked whisper.

The Queen nodded, the tears in her eyes beginning to roll down her cheeks. "Even… even if not for love, an intermarriage could end this war, and turn two enemies into allies. Or even one country."

Her handmaiden just stared.

"That's what I'll do," the Queen continued with a courageous nod. "I will... offer myself to the Hittites, my hand in marriage. And I will offer the throne of Egypt to the Prince I marry." Meresankh gasped again, but Ankh kept going, even as tears choked her voice. "This is Egypt's only hope, Meresankh. Anything... literally anything... would be better than letting Ay become Pharaoh. Even if it means surrendering ourselves, giving ourselves up to our enemy and becoming their territory; the Hittite-Egyptian Empire." She swallowed. In her mind, she could see the choices that she... and others... were making, like *seega* pieces moving on the gameboard of history. She was about to make the boldest, craziest, most shocking move in all of history. "The Pharaoh's family never marries a Princess or Queen to a foreigner. But it's the only move that is daring enough that it might just work."

Meresankh shuddered. "Are you sure it's the only way?"

Her Mistress nodded. "Yes. It's the only way I can maintain my power without an heir."

Meresankh just nodded, squeezing her friend's hand again. And she let the Queen keep talking.

Ankh sighed. "I should be King," she summed up. "But if I stay Queen, Ay and the others won't fight me. And, if we surrender ourselves to the Hittites, the war will end. And I will continue leading Egypt. From beside the throne."

She gave her friend a sad smile as she seemed to feel power coursing through her. By her authority as Queen, maybe she could write the letter, enter the marriage, forge the alliance, that would save Egypt.

"But, My Lady," Meresankh said, looking down at the Queen's flat stomach, "what if there *is* an heir?"

Ankhesenamun smiled, resting her hand on her belly as her handmaiden had seen her do so many times before. Then she sighed again.

"Even if I get pregnant before our time together ends, there will be a power vacuum while Horemheb and Ay fight me for the next throne before the baby is born, even if it's a boy. Remarrying and consolidating my power through remaining Queen will allow for a smoother transition for Egypt. I..." She chuckled as the thought came to her. "I am going to wield the new Pharaoh, and he will enact all the decisions I'm making. Since he'll be standing in front of me, no one will suspect." Ankh made her voice deeper, threatening an imaginary foe. "I have a Pharaoh, and I'm not afraid to use him! And he'll be my weapon, my disguise, as I continue to lead our country."

She took a deep breath. Her decision was made.

And now there was nothing for it but for Meresankh to open her arms and for Ankhesenamun to fall into them, hugging her friend as hard as she could as the shorter woman's soft, strong little arms embraced her.

"Thank you for keeping my secret," the Queen said softly. "Thank you for being someone I can trust."

"We'll get through this," Meresankh whispered to Ankh as they stood there, held tightly in one another's arms. "I promise."

Ankh just squeezed her tighter.

Only friends stood like that in one another's arms, whispering to one another that everything would be all right. Only sisters. And Meresankh felt her heart glow with Light as she stood there, hugging the Queen as she hugged her back.

Whatever happened, they would get through it together. And history would unfold according to I-AM's perfect plan.

Ankhesenamun felt safe, standing there with her arms around Meresankh. If she closed her eyes, she could make believe she was hugging Meritaten or Meketaten, the two older sisters she had not seen in so long. Because this hug felt the same as the ones she had shared with her big sisters.

But Meresankh was not Meritaten or Meketaten. She was herself. And as much as she longed for the sisters she had grown up with, Ankh was glad. Because Meresankh was the person, the friend, the sister, she needed.

Her smile, her support, and her faithful prayers would see them through whatever came.

And so the Queen picked up a pen, took a deep breath, and began.

And her heart bled with every word she wrote, tears staining the papyrus.

Because the first words under the salutation were "my husband has died."

26

Waiting

Ankhesenamun kissed her brother goodnight, but she couldn't be as warm as she always was. And she knew he had noticed. But the secret lay in her heart like a lump of ice on a faraway mountain. And she had no smiles to give him.

Tut seemed to sleep well. But Ankhesenamun never fell asleep. She sat there in her chair, fearful questions, heavy doubts, and anxious thoughts chasing one another around her heart and mind.

Was this the right thing to do? Was it? She asked Isis, asked Thoth, asked Osiris himself, but none of them answered. So finally... she begged the Divine Whose name she was no longer entirely sure she knew for a sign as to whether she should send it.

The image of that little girl rose in her mind. And Ankh shut her eyes against the pain. She had her answer. For that little girl... she had to fight. That little girl, and every little girl just like her, had to be protected from what Ay would do if he became Pharaoh. She had to stop him, no matter what it took.

And she would.

And after so many heavy hours of doubt and worry, she felt peace touch her heart. Much remained unclear. But to send the letter... was the right decision.

Tut felt awful all night. What with the pain and the fever, he barely slept, spending another night desperately whispering prayers, beseeching the gods to heal him, to spare his life. But he was quiet; didn't make even a peep.

Because he didn't want to tell his sister that he was dying.

The next morning, as Meresankh tidied up the Queen's room, where her Lady had hardly spent any time in over a week, she saw a letter on the Queen's desk.

"My husband has died and there is no one I can trust," it began. Or she thought it did, because the tear-stains on the papyrus had blurred some of the words.

Meresankh nodded. The overture to the Hittites was being prepared.

The Pharaoh and the Queen looked tired. And sad. But they didn't say much. It made Semerkhet feel restless as he went back and forth, tidying, arranging, bringing bowls of almonds or plates of fruit back and forth from the kitchen. They both knew something, Sem could tell. Something neither of them was ready to talk about.

He listened. He waited. And the songs he played on his lute to while away the long, lonely hours grew sadder and sadder.

Something was bothering his sister. Tut thought that the Queen seemed distant, seemed worried. Like... like he was, hanging on to the last faint hope that his life was not ending. He was almost sure that she knew his secret, but this was something more than that. Like she had a secret of her own.

Her face had changed, her tired eyes filled with a greater pain, and yet, even greater wisdom, than they had held a week before, her weary face slightly older, almost lined by care. And as mature as she had always been, now she looked as wise and formidable as Grandmother Tiye, as strong and powerful as Mother, as Meritaten.

She was strong. So strong. But he could see in her eyes, her face, her posture, her tired smiles that didn't quite reach her eyes; hear in her sighs and long silences, that her secret, whatever it was, was a heavy burden. He wondered what it was. But just like he would not tell his secret until he had no other choice, he knew that his sister would not tell hers until she was sure that it was time.

He would wait until she was ready.

Meresankh kept trying. Kept smiling, even through the sadness. Kept telling stories; kept trying to bring light, life, and joy to her Lady's day. Sometimes it worked, and sometimes it didn't. But she knew that the Queen needed her. And she knew she would always do everything she could.

Semerkhet didn't ask his Pharaoh what was going on. And he didn't tell the story of going with Meresankh to ask the midwife what was in the wine. Because he already knew the answer. And he knew his friend would tell them eventually. When he did, Semerkhet would tell him his side of the story. And until then, Semerkhet and Meresankh would share silent sighs as they passed in the hallway, sad smiles at lunch, brief hand-clasps as they shared a cup of tea during a break. Because they both knew the Pharaoh's secret.

He was worn out from praying. Tut never stopped begging the gods that he would be spared, pleading in a thousand different phrasings that the ague would be taken away, that his legs would be healed, that he would go on to live the life of a strong Pharaoh, make Grandfather Thutmose proud, find the legacy he was meant to establish. Making grand promises; offering to build a hundred— no, a thousand— temples; build a school in every city in Egypt, if only he would be healed. His country needed him, he said. His sister needed him. His brother needed him. There was still so much he could accomplish. Still so much to do. Still so much life to live.

If only the gods would listen, and would have mercy. If only his prayers would be answered.

And if only he knew... Who it truly was Who was listening. The Pharaoh was praying so hard, pouring out his petitions with such intensity, that he found himself hardly attending to the Name of the One to Whom he was directing his prayers. And yet, as he prayed, he almost smiled as he once again felt the peace of being heard, like the warmth of the Sun on his face.

Someone was listening.

Sem did his best to keep it together; keep being the one who made sure all the little things of life went smoothly even as the bigger things were falling apart. But he was so... so... painfully restless. Outside the sun was bright and the birds were singing, and inside it was dim and silent and sad.

But inside was where his Pharaoh was. Inside was where he was needed, and where the loyal valet would faithfully remain.

He met Meresankh out in the hall as he took a moment, just a moment, to at least stretch his legs. And she smiled at him.

"That kind of day, isn't it?" she asked gently, reaching out to squeeze his hand.

He let her take his hand, even as locusts seemed to be jumping around inside his stomach.

"What kind of day?" he said.

"A restless one," she said, raising her eyebrows. He chuckled, then shrugged, trying to laugh it off and leave it at that. But she pressed on. "Go practice," she urged him. "Go burn off some of your energy. Go see your team."

Semerkhet's heart was pulling him out the door, out into the sunshine, but his mind held him back.

"I can't," he said, shaking his head. "He needs me here."

Meresankh popped up onto her tiptoes to peck him on the cheek. "Can't you at least ask?"

And she was gone.

Slowly, Sem wandered back into his Pharaoh's room, to sit down again in the dark and the quiet and help his friend while away the next few hours.

But when he got to his familiar chair, the Queen was standing there, a little smile on her face. The Pharaoh, meanwhile, was drowsing in the bed, unaware of the proceedings around him.

"Go on," the Queen said gently. "Go take an hour."

"You mean it?" Semerkhet started to ask, then realized he didn't need telling twice. And with a bow and a breathless wish for life, prosperity and health, he was off, racing down the halls out into the sunshine, ready to fill the next beautiful hour with horses and hockey.

Politics seemed to have stopped. They hadn't seen the Vizier in days; only received his daily reports of the morning audiences he'd been conducting. Hemmed in by the directives that Tutankhamun had signed into law, he held the reins of the palace, and indeed, of the entire country; hiring, firing, keeping day-to-day matters on an even course. The King and Queen decided they could let him get on with it for the time being. At the moment, what additional harm could he do?

"How are you?" Ankh asked gently. Tut jumped slightly, startled out of the prayers he had been whispering inside his heart; the pleas for his survival that he didn't want anyone else to hear.

Softly, he smiled at her.

"The same," he said quietly. And that was true.

There was still a chance, the Queen kept telling herself. Still a chance that everything would turn around and she would never even have to tell her husband about the emergency plan she had developed, back when he'd been nineteen, during the roughest part of his recovery after that awful time when he had been wounded. There was still a chance that this was nothing more than the most dramatic event of the first independent year of his long, glorious reign.

She would wait as long as she could. Until she had no other choice, but before it was too late. As a politician, she would know when the time had come.

As Ankh took care of him, and the desperate prayers he never stopped whispering inside his heart began to weary him, Tut began to wonder. What would happen to her if he did not survive? They had no heir... the two precious, precious baby girls who waited to join him in his tomb were their legacy. Would Ankh take power, rule her country as Pharaoh like her ancestress Hatshepsut, who had ushered Egypt into an era of unprecedented peace and prosperity? Like their mother, Queen Nefertiti, who had ruled Egypt as Pharaoh Smenkhkare after Akhenaten's death? Or would duty require her to become the wife of another?

There was no son who could take the throne after him, no brother, no nephew born to another of their sisters. Who, then, would become his heir? Horemheb, who was technically Tutankhamun's heir until the day the Pharaoh had a son of his own? Tut shook his head as he thought of the one man who had a legitimate claim to the next throne. Horemheb had betrayed him, and anyway, he was far away in Kadesh, finishing up the war against the Hittites. Who else? Creepy old murdering Ay, whose lust for the throne had landed Tut in what might very well be his deathbed? Tut shuddered at the thought of that old mummy holding Ankh in his arms, kissing her, making her his Queen. If not him, if not Horemheb, then who?

"I'll try to get up for a bit," Tutankhamun said one afternoon. If he never tried to get out of bed, he would never know if he could do it. And the longer he lay here, the weaker he would get, and the harder it would be when he got around to trying again. So today was as good a day as any.

He smiled wistfully. Maybe... maybe if he managed to get up today, that would mean that today was the turnaround he had been praying for, proof that his secret was meaningless because there was no secret to keep. Maybe, being able to get up would be his sign that he was not dying after all. Just maybe.

His sister got up from her chair with a smile, bending to kiss him, then hurrying to get Semerkhet and Amenmose.

Amenmose pulled the Pharaoh's chair close to the bed, and Semerkhet helped him sit up, then slide to the side of the bed.

And he did it. With a heavy sigh, Tut collapsed into the chair, returning his sister's proud smile. And he lay back, exhausted.

He had done it. And he was glad that he had. But somehow... he wondered if he would be doing it again.

He didn't last ten minutes in the chair. And as Ankhesenamun watched Semerkhet and Amenmose tenderly, laboriously assist the Pharaoh back into bed, she felt her heart break. And she knew... without a doubt... that the letter had to be sent.

All day she thought about it. The letter weighed on the Queen's heart, making her feel almost guilty that she had this secret, that she was hiding her plans from her little brother. And yet, the pain... the pain they would both feel when she revealed her secret.

But she had to do it. She had to send the letter... and she had to tell him about it first. Her heart was broken. But she could feel the broken pieces joining back together, bonded by a will of iron, her promise to do what was best for Egypt. To be... to be the Pharaoh her country needed.

The Queen took a deep breath. She was ready.

The next day, she would tell him.

Finally came the morning, nearly three weeks after coming home, that Tutankhamun's broken legs felt like they were on fire, his fever and chills came back with a vengeance, his aching body gave him no rest, and a migraine kept him from keeping down his food. Curled up in bed with the cat in his arms as silent tears ran down his face, Tut reflected on his life. Today, he knew, marked an irrevocable turn for the worse. The faint hope for recovery had disappeared like the flame of a blown-out lamp. His days were numbered. The moment he had been putting off had finally come.

It was time to tell his secret. Even if everyone already knew.

27

The Secret

"I'm ready to tell you the secret," Tut told his wife as she sat with him, bathing his head with a cool cloth. Semerkhet sat across the room, cleaning dusty pieces of heavy jewelry the King had not worn for a long time, while Bastet chased dust motes in a ray of sunshine streaming through the window.

"Yes?" She looked earnestly into his face, ready to hear. And yet not ready. Because if he was ready to tell her, he was preparing for death.

Semerkhet stood up. "Did you want me to go?" he asked the King. "If it's not for me to hear?"

Tutankhamun shook his head. "Stay. It is for you to hear." He paused. "But lock the door first."

Semerkhet hurried across the room to lock the door, then joined the Queen at the Pharaoh's bedside.

Tut swallowed, steeling himself to tell Ankh and Sem. It was time for them to know. He licked his lips, taking a deep breath.

And he said the words he had been hiding in his heart for so long. "Ay has murdered me."

Ankh gasped, pulling away. Even though she already knew, it ripped her heart out to hear him say the words.

"Murdered you?" Semerkhet clenched his fists, seeming to shrink as the words hit him. The cat jumped onto the bed with a self-satisfied snort, as if to say, *I told you so.*

Tut nodded as their eyes widened in horror, fixed on him as they waited for him to tell them what he knew. One hand flying up to cover her mouth, Ankh grabbed his hand, henna-dyed nails digging into his skin, and forgetting himself, Semerkhet grabbed his other hand.

The Pharaoh continued. "He suggested that I go to Amurru, and he arranged to have everyone pull back so I could be wounded. And whatever the Physician gave me, the 'emetic' Ay made sure I kept taking, it wasn't real medicine. He's killing me."

His sister just looked at him, pain in her eyes.

"I know," she whispered.

Semerkhet just nodded. His face said it all.

The Pharaoh shook his head. "The Vizier intends to be the next Pharaoh. Not drinking the wine might buy me some time, but I'm really starting to wonder… and I'm genuinely afraid… that this time… I might not get through." He swallowed, the ache in his heart intensifying as he felt himself choking up. "It just feels… different from anything I've been through before." Tut looked at them. "And I don't know."

"There has to be something we can do," Ankh said, trying to smile encouragingly as she squeezed his hand. "You've gotten over the ague five or six times already. We'll get you a different doctor; we'll get you ten doctors. Even if they have to come from as far as Babylon." She sniffled back a tear. "Don't give up hope. You'll get through this too—you're not going anywhere."

He just looked at her. And the hope in her eyes faded. But it was replaced by determination; a resolve to stand by his side no matter what happened. Even if he was right.

"I'll have failed you if I can't keep you from this," Semerkhet said in a choked voice, shaking his head as tears shone in his eyes. His heart ached as he looked down at the King, lying in the bed with dwindling hope of reaching the future. "Poisoned wine? That's exactly why I always taste it for you. If you die of poison, I've killed you myself. I'm the one who should have died."

"No," said the King, taking his hand again. "You're the one who saved my life when Ay first tried to take it."

"Then General Horemheb is responsible too," Semerkhet said, looking down at their entwined hands. "I remember him blowing the trumpet, just before everyone pulled back. And he saw you looking at him."

Tut nodded, remembering the message the General had received from the Vizier's secretary; the message that the Pharaoh now knew to have been his own death warrant. "I know. I'll deal with him when he gets back."

"And Maya," Ankh said. "He hates your new policies."

He nodded again. "Yes. I'll deal with him too."

"But why in the name of Anubis don't you just fire the Vizier?" Ankh asked, throwing her hands into the air. "Banish him for treason— even execute him, if you have to? You have the authority as Pharaoh, and you can demonstrate that he's trying to kill you and steal your throne. Use your authority and get rid of him!"

"I'd like to," Tutankhamun said sadly. "I really would. But Mother made him my regent, and he has the paperwork to prove it."

"But he's not your regent anymore!" she objected. "He hasn't been since your birthday!"

"No," Tut said, shaking his head sadly, "but think... think of what he's done. Killed Meritaten; convinced Horemheb to help him kill me. If I throw him out, what will he do? Remember when he made Semerkhet into a scribe—" Sem smiled sadly for half a moment as he remembered along with them— "and you said that that was the least the Vizier could do, and that next time it wouldn't be reversible?"

She just nodded. "So," he went on, "I'm trying— trying to do what you would advise me to. Keep my friends and family close... and my enemies closer. Keep him where I can see him, and hopefully keep him under control. If I got rid of him, he would only become more dangerous. And then all of us would be in trouble. And it's the same with Maya. Maybe he deserves to be fired, but if I sent him away, he would just plead his case to the Vizier, and everything would get worse. If I do that, the Vizier might see no reason to keep me alive at all. Or even you."

The Queen just gave a sad, proud smile as she ceded to her little brother's political reasoning.

Semerkhet's eyes cleared as he looked at the King. "So, what do we do?"

Tutankhamun gave his loved ones half a smile and gently shook his head. His sister, his wife, and his almost-brother. And he remembered what his sister had told him to do when his suspicions had first been raised by Ay's statement about getting rid of him.

"Nothing yet. We can't make any sudden moves. I'll watch, and wait, and if it becomes strategic for us for him to know that we know, I'll tell him."

They both sighed, giving him solemn little nods. They would keep the secret until he told them otherwise.

"I think you're right," Ankhesenamun agreed in a hollow whisper. Sadly, the politician smiled, approving his decision.

Tut gave her the tiniest, tiniest little ghost of a smile. "How long have you known?" he asked two of the only people he could still trust.

"Since the day I was gone at dinner," Semerkhet said. "Meresankh and I took your cup down to the midwife and she told us it was poisoned."

"What was the poison?" Tutankhamun asked softly. He shook his head. Somehow, his friend knew more than he did.

"Peach-pits," Semerkhet said sadly. "Like they use in executions. The midwife told us its symptoms are similar to ague."

The Pharaoh shuddered. He knew of the terrible sentence known as the Penalty of the Peach. He shook his head to think that that awful medicine he'd been given… had been meant to kill him like a convicted criminal. And that it had been so cleverly selected, escaping detection by all but the wisest, most experienced healer.

Semerkhet shook his head as he continued. "But I suspected when the new 'medicine' made you sick." He swallowed. "And when I wasn't allowed to test it for you." He gave Ankhesenamun half a sad smile. "That was what I was going to say, My Lady, when I mentioned the medicine, just as the Pharaoh was starting to feel better. I was going to tell you... what Meresankh and I had found out."

The Queen bit her lip. And she, too, confessed how long she had known that the King was being poisoned. "I knew something was wrong when you got so much worse right when you started that new 'medicine.' And Meresankh told me," she said, looking up at Semerkhet, "after you found out the wine was poisoned."

The King sighed, closing his eyes. They had been following all this so carefully, laboring to solve this mystery. His heart ached with how much he was loved. And the secret he had kept for so long.

Gulping, Semerkhet stood up, wiping his eyes. And Tut let him go; let him make his way to the other end of the room to clean something and think.

Then Tut looked at Ankh, a wave of guilt suddenly crashing over him. "You were right. Ay couldn't be trusted." He paused, trying not to choke up. "I... I'm sorry I didn't listen to you." He swallowed. "Sorry I didn't let you keep me safe."

She shook her head, taking his other hand again. "No. If he was determined, he would have found another way of going after you. I don't know if we ever could have won." She bowed her head, voice breaking. "I don't know if I could have kept you safe this time."

"The game's not over yet," he said, trying to give a little chuckle. "Time will tell what we can still accomplish." He swallowed. "And maybe... maybe I am wrong."

"Watch... wait... don't make any sudden moves," the Queen said with half a sad smile. "And not everything is reversible. Sounds familiar."

He smiled back. "Advice from the wisest politician in Egypt." Then he sighed again. "What about Horemheb?"

His sister shook her head. "Even I don't know yet. We're just going to have to see what choices he makes when he comes home."

Tut nodded, giving another heavy sigh. "But it's more than what the Vizier might do," he said. "I'm not the only one he's murdered."

"Meritaten," his sister said solemnly, bowing her head. "Pentu."

He nodded. "And..." He paused, biting his lip and fighting back tears. "I didn't want to believe it, but... Ankh... I think... think he killed..."

"Father," she said at the same moment as he said "Mother."

They stared at one another. "Mother?" she said in a horrified whisper as he echoed, "Father?"

"The medicine Father was taking... Nettle isn't good for weak hearts, but Ay always made sure he took it," Ankh whispered.

Tut gave a shuddering sigh. "And the parade... He had Mother's horse spooked. He had it all planned out."

It was too deep for tears. Brother and sister stared at one another, shock echoing into grief as they realized that Grand Vizier Ay had murdered both their parents. All they could do was fall into one another's arms and try to breathe as they held one another as tight as they could.

"So what do we do now?" Tut whispered.

Ankh shook her head. "I don't know yet." She wiped away her tears and lay down beside him, taking him in her arms again. "All I know is that I'd fight Anubis himself to keep you with me."

Tutankhamun gave a little smile and nestled closer. "I know."

The Queen walked into her room and slowly lay down on her bed. Her mind was blank. He was dying. Really dying. And Ay had been the one who had orchestrated it. Horemheb, too. She had known, but hearing him say it made it official. And his face had told her that even if they got another doctor, ten more doctors, a hundred more doctors, there was little they could do. It was too late for that.

How did this fit in with the hope she had carried in her heart for so many years, the secure hope that one day, they would find the purpose for which he had been placed on this Earth with feet that didn't match, legs that struggled to carry him? If he... if he didn't get through this, how would he fulfill the unknown destiny that she had been searching for for as long as he had been on the throne? Would she ever find it? And would this still-unknown purpose ever be fulfilled?

If the gods loved them, why had they done this? Why had he been wounded; why was he now struggling with the ague and worsening infection? Why had the other politicians tried to poison him? What was the purpose?

And why were the gods not answering? Why were they so silent?

She had told him not to give up... but now she could see that he hadn't. He had hung onto his secret even longer than she had held tight to the one she was still waiting to reveal; had surely gotten up every morning hoping that today things would be different. Like her, he had waited until the last possible moment to tell his secret. Waited until he was absolutely sure that there was no hope.

He had not given up. He had accepted reality. As nightmarish as it was. He had accepted the things that they could change... and the things that they could not.

But it wasn't... it wasn't even only his coming death that was breaking her heart. It was the deaths... no, the *murders,* of their older sister Meritaten, of their mother, of their father, and of Pentu. Grand Vizier Ay had killed them all. And if they made a move to get rid of him, they would be the next to die.

Her heart was as full of pain as a wineskin overfilled to bursting. Almost too full of pain for her to be proud of her baby brother for the nuanced grasp of politics that was now guiding his decisions. Almost.

She closed her eyes, trying to breathe. She barely heard Meresankh come into the room and sit down beside her; barely realized her handmaiden had entered the room until she felt her warm, reassuring presence. And her heart burst, her pain overflowing as she poured out her anguish in an explosion of tears.

And with Meresankh sitting quietly beside her, the Queen cried until she had no more tears, wailing in helpless grief.

The Queen had excused herself. The Pharaoh had seen it in her eyes; she was about to cry. She needed to cry. And he needed to give her space.

"Sem," he said, beckoning to his friend. Semerkhet set down the pile of documents he'd been sorting through and approached the bed, sitting down by the King. Tut put his hand over his valet's, and Semerkhet looked down at them, his eyes full of sadness.

"Yes, Master?" he asked after a few moments of silence had passed. Companionable silence, but silence spent in wondering what the Pharaoh wanted to say.

Tutankhamun looked up at his friend with a sigh. This was not easy.

"Sem," he said again, "I have another secret to tell you."

Semerkhet's eyebrows drew together in a worried frown.

"What is it?" he whispered as if he wasn't sure he wanted to know. He scooted a tiny bit closer to the Pharaoh, taking his hand and holding it tightly.

Tut sighed again. "Semerkhet..." he said, "Ay didn't just send me to Amurru to be hurt. You remember, a long time ago, when Princess Meritaten died?"

"Of course," Semerkhet said, bowing his head respectfully. "That was terrible. She died so young, so suddenly. Just like..." He looked up at his Master, a questioning frown spreading over his forehead, a realization growing. "Just like Vizier Pentu," he finished in a horrified whisper.

Tut nodded with a heavy sigh. "We don't know how he did it, but the Queen and I believe the Vizier killed our sister. And..." Tut looked steadily at his friend as Semerkhet's eyes continued to widen, "our parents."

Semerkhet's grip on Tutankhamun's hand tightened, the valet's knuckles whitening as the red jasper ring gleamed on his finger. "You know I would go after him if you told me to," he said in a harsh whisper through clenched teeth, staring down at their entwined hands under dark, deadly eyebrows. Did *he* look like that when he was angry, Tut wondered. If so, he must be truly terrifying. "I'm quiet. And I can lie.

He's old; he's not strong. He wouldn't even have time to yell. Old people have fatal accidents all the time."

Tutankhamun looked at his friend and gently shook his head, braids softly swinging. "No, dear Sem," he said gently. "That's not how I want to handle this." He swallowed. "I know you'd do anything for me, even something that could only end in you being executed. And I'll never be able to tell you how grateful I am for everything you've done. But if you will do anything for me…" He paused, giving his valet a little smile. "Will you trust me?"

Semerkhet heaved a heavy sigh, releasing the anger, the homicidal thoughts. Slowly his shoulders dropped. And he gave his Pharaoh a smile.

"Yes, Master," he said softly.

Tutankhamun smiled at his friend, giving his hand one more squeeze before letting it go. "Thank you, Brother." He chuckled. "Thank you, Sole Companion, Royal Favorite, Unique, Attentive Friend." And with one more smile, Semerkhet got up and went back to tidying.

They heard the Queen weeping, Tut, Sem, Meresankh. Semerkhet's heart ached as he imagined the loss she was facing, the loss of a beloved baby brother. Tutankhamun's heart broke to think that his was the death that she was mourning, and that he could do nothing. And Meresankh sat with her, silently praying as her Mistress wept for the loss that was to come, one loss of many.

What did the future hold, she wondered. He wasn't her husband, wasn't her brother, but Meresankh was about to lose her Pharaoh as well. It hurt already. She shuddered to think of the pain they would feel on the day it finally happened. And she shuddered as she thought of the heartless Vizier who had orchestrated it all. Who had, in fact, been orchestrating it since before Tutankhamun had taken the throne. Because, as the Queen had choked out, their Pharaoh was not the only person that Grand Vizier Ay had gotten out of the way. First the Queen's father, Akhenaten, then her Pharaoh mother, her wise big sister, and finally Vizier Pentu, had fallen to the murderous schemes of the Vizier.

All Meresankh could do was pray. She closed her eyes. She would pray now, to I-AM, the true Lord of Light, even as she continued to rest her hand reassuringly on the Queen's shaking back.

She would pray that their Pharaoh would be healed. She would pray that they would be strong. And she would pray that all of them would find the Light before the end came.

28

Sorrow

The valet sat silently bathing his Master's face with a cool cloth, watching him try to rest as he fought the pain. And fighting the pain inside his own heart. He'd known already. Known since that "medicinal wine" first showed up that something was wrong; known since Merneith had analyzed it that the wine had been poisoned. But now the King himself had told them. Now it was real. And he might not make it through this time.

Sem watched his Pharaoh's face as he dabbed his forehead with the cloth, patted it over his neck, his jawline. And he wished this day could last forever.

The day had become cloudy. And the Sun had gone in, hiding itself from their view. Then, as evening fell, it began to grow dark.

Tut shivered. He could feel the darkness in his spirit. It was… it was the opposite of the loving warmth he had felt out in the garden. Now, that same loving warmth seemed to be withheld.

But why? And by Whom?

As evening fell, shadows lengthening, the Pharaoh felt that he could not find the Light.

Semerkhet came out of the bedroom for just a moment. Meresankh had been waiting for him in the hallway. Slowly he came into view, moving slowly, almost weakened by grief. He walked toward her, and she opened her arms. And she held him.

"I know," she murmured as she felt her friend leaning into her strength, weighed down by sorrow. And he began to shake with sobs. "I know."

The secret was out. Free. No longer hidden in his aching heart. Tut sighed as he tried to rest early that evening, stomach comfortably full of the simple lentil stew Semerkhet had helped him eat.

There was... there was relief in telling the secret. Now he no longer had to hide it from his loved ones. And he no longer had to carry it alone.

Softly they talked, Semerkhet, Meresankh. And the handmaiden and the valet told one another what the Queen had told each of them—that the hardhearted Grand Vizier had destroyed the Pharaoh's future in order to steal the throne and bend Egypt to his own selfish will. Together they spoke of the terrible truth that the deaths of Akhenaten and Nefertiti had been no mere illness; no mere accident. Together they sighed. Together they grieved. And together, each in their own way, they prayed for the future of Egypt.

Again, Meresankh examined the Pharaoh's leg. Again, she tidied it up, silently shaking her head as she saw it continuing to grow worse.

"You know..." she said softly, "I know my herbs, but it's my Granny Merneith who's the expert. I would like to recommend that you make her your new doctor. She..." Meresankh smiled as warmth rose in her heart. "She's the one who did the test; proved that the Chief Physician was giving you peach-pits."

Tut smiled. "Then she's already saved my life." He sighed. "And so have you. I never got to thank you for your part in the investigation."

The Pharaoh nodded. "I would be glad to have her. Would you ask her for me?"

Meresankh nodded with a little smile of her own. "Of course. But I already know what she'll say."

"They betrayed him," Meresankh told her Granny.

Merneith let the cat she'd been holding hop down onto one of the chairs in her workshop and took Meresankh's hands.

"What do you mean, dearie?" she whispered.

Meresankh shook her head, biting her lip as tears came to her eyes. And freed by the permission she'd sought from the Queen to tell Merneith what had happened, she told her Granny everything.

"The Pharaoh. The Vizier and the General betrayed him. It's their fault he got hurt… and then they poisoned him with peach-pits. They… they're trying to get rid of him because he's not selfish like them."

Merneith gave a heavy sigh, wise old eyes filling with pain. And she opened her arms. Meresankh stepped into them, and her Granny held her close, seeming to pass on some of her boundless strength through her embrace.

The old woman did not need to say anything. In her embrace, there was a promise. A promise to do everything in her power to help the Pharaoh.

As she got ready for bed, eyes dry but red, throat raw, mind, body, and heart exhausted, Ankhesenamun thought of the ladies, Meryt, Mutnedjmet, Amenia. Their husbands were in on it; the plot to kill her husband. She probably wouldn't see them again until this was over, but she wondered… would it be productive for her to tell them what their husbands had done?

And, as always, she thought of the purpose she still searched for; thought of her endless prayers. Prayers… that she had thought were being answered. Until today. With a sigh, she wrapped up what was left of her hopes, placing them carefully on a shelf within her heart. She would not discard them. But she would set them aside. Because waiting for the answers that had never come was too painful to sustain. If the answers came someday, they would come. And if they did not... they would not. Right now, there was no way to know which it would be. Silently, she let go of the outcomes.

The Queen sighed. Would she be able to sleep tonight? Would she be able to sleep ever again, knowing that each day, each night, brought them closer to the end?

And knowing that tomorrow, she had to tell her brother her own secret?

Tutankhamun was tired. The day was over, the day he had hoped would never come. And it was time to let it end. See what tomorrow would bring.

Tut was safe. He was surrounded by loved ones. And they would take care of him, walk beside him, no matter what. Until the end.

Semerkhet sat at his Pharaoh's side that night, watching him sleep. He'd gone to sleep easily tonight, after a nice cup of chamomile tea and a silly old story. Semerkhet was only two years older than his Master, but right now Tut looked so much younger, lying there asleep; so innocent, so vulnerable. So... mortal. With a sigh, Semerkhet tucked Tutankhamun's blankets closer around him. Only time would tell how everything would play out.

The gods hadn't answered, he realized, confusion aching in his heart. Or had they? He had rejoiced when the Pharaoh had seemed to improve after he'd stopped taking the poisoned medicine, convinced that the gods and goddesses he loved loved them enough to save the friend he had begged them to spare. So much joy had filled his heart as he had felt that finally— finally— they had responded. But now... Semerkhet shook his head. Mere hours after feeling that the weeks of doubt were finally resolved, he was not even sure if the deliverance of his best friend from death's very door was an answer to his prayers or not.

Should he even keep praying, Semerkhet wondered. Was there any point? He shook his head, remembering the peace he longed to rediscover. Where... where was the Light?

Eventually, Ankhesenamun did fall asleep. And she dreamed.

She was in Memphis again, not in her palanquin, but walking through the streets. Streets that were narrow and dirty, littered with broken boxes and discarded fishbones.
And there she was. The same little girl the Queen had given her new shawl to that one day, clad in dirty rags, thin face smudged, hair tangled, eyes... large, catlike eyes wide and brave and cautious of the world she had to navigate alone. Ankh smiled at her, holding out her hands. The child looked up at her.
And she disappeared into thin air.

The Queen awoke, haunted. Haunted by the child; by the future she and all the little girls like her were facing. The future that would become ten times more grim if Ay became the next Pharaoh.

Silently they wondered, the four of them. Wondered how many months, how many weeks, how many days the Pharaoh had left in this world. But whatever their number, they would spend those days together.
They would draw closer, Ankhesenamun, Semerkhet, and Meresankh thought to themselves. To Tut, and to one another, as friends, and, in a strange and unexpected way, almost like family. Together the four of them would move toward the unknown future... and they would hope and pray it was not the future the Pharaoh feared.

29

The Gift

The days were passing. Today was the twenty-second day of the month of Sholiak, and the days were getting cooler and shorter, the Season of Emergence beginning. His wife looked sad, Tutankhamun thought. But at the same time... she looked... *determined* about something.

"I'm ready to tell you *my* secret," Ankhesenamun whispered that night after dinner, gazing into his face and stroking his cheek. Her hands were so soft.

"Tell me," he whispered back. They were alone in the room; Semerkhet was taking a break, a little walk around the garden on this cool, breezy evening that Tut was sure would amount to almost chilly. Tonight he expected that he would want an extra blanket. Outside the bedroom window, the light was beginning to fade, the sky darkening into a deeper, dimmer blue as the pink sunset splashed across the west, just out of sight.

"I've written a letter to the King of the Hittites, explaining what's happened. When... when the day comes, I'll send it to him, and he will send me Prince Zannanza. I will marry the Prince, and we will make him Pharaoh."

Tut looked up at her in shock, his heart beginning to pound as light-headedness seized him, even sitting there in bed.

"What?" he gasped. The Hittites, against whom they were currently at war, whose arrow had toppled Tut into the sickbed he was now never to leave? "I don't understand—" His breath came faster, his hands clenching. "There has to be something else— anything else— I'll nominate you; I'll nominate you a hundred times; I'll make them see that you—"

His sister was looking at him with tears in her eyes, face and body full of pain. And he stopped, bowing his head. Slowly, his heart and breathing calmed, and his hands uncurled. With a deep breath, Tut swallowed, preparing himself to listen. Calmly, he looked up at her.

"Tell me more," he said finally.

Ankh took a deep, shuddering breath and closed her eyes for a moment. But when she opened them, they were clear.

"Well, I was thinking about our... about our options," she said softly, taking his hand. "I have to remarry. I could be Pharaoh on my own, I know I could, but they'll never let me if I don't have a husband. And maybe... maybe the war will end if we unite our countries in marriage. Even... even if we're only a state of the Hittite-Egyptian Empire, that would be better than..."

Ankhesenamun squeezed his hand, bowing her head as more tears came to her eyes. "That would be better than seeing my husband's murderer on the throne." She sighed. "I'd be your successor if I could," she whispered. "And I could. But at the same time... I can't. So this will have to do. I would... would never do something like this if we had any other options." Then she gave him a sad smile. "Like we always say... things we can change... and things we can't."

The Pharaoh sighed. What an idea. What a bold move his wife was planning. And yet, for all its boldness... she had clearly been thinking about this for a long time. Agonizing, he was sure, about whether it was really the right thing to do. Searching for any other options, the painful secret hidden in her heart. And she, in her experience and wisdom, had realized that there was nothing else that could be done. This was the only way forward.

Ankhesenamun looked at him again. "I know Horemheb is your Crown Prince, but we've seen what he has done. And I would never marry Ay, that old mummy. I wish…" She paused. "I don't wish, but with what… we're facing… I would have married Pentu, but…" She swallowed, biting her lip. "I suppose the Hittites will have to do."

Ankh shook her head. "It doesn't… doesn't matter what the country is called. I would rather be part of something that is not even called *Egypt* that upholds human rights than watch Ay bring people back to their knees in slavery and poverty and hunger. This is too important. We can't go back on what we started. We can't let him win. Then all the little girls in Egypt would be just like the one we saw. So this… this is for all the children." The Queen sighed. "I'll marry Zannanza, and I'll make him Pharaoh, but I won't love him like I've loved you. It's just… it's just politics."

The Pharaoh's sister looked at him quietly, inviting him to offer a reply.

Tut shook his head. What was there to say? Slowly, he gave her a sad little smile of his own, a nod of approval. "You're right. It would be better to unite Egypt with the Kingdom of Hattusa than to leave it in the care of either of those snakes." Tut sighed again. "You had a secret too," he whispered, squeezing her hand. She just nodded.

"Thank you for trusting me," Ankh said softly, running her hand gently over his head. "You can… you can trust me to put our country first in every decision I make." She looked down. "Even… even in my choice of a second husband." The Queen gave a little sob, covering her face in one hand as she groped for his with the other one. Tut clasped her hand in both of his, showing her that he was still alive, he was still with her, trying to comfort her as she comforted him.

"I don't want you to go," Ankhesenamun sobbed, her body bending low. "Nine years, that's all we've had… This should be just the beginning... And those snakes, trying to kill you in Kadesh and then giving you poisoned medicine..."

Ankh's heart began to pound, and she felt a rushing in her head as a red haze came over her vision. Every muscle went taut; she felt her hands clenching into fists as her body seemed to shake. She had to stop them. Now. Stop them. Hurt them. Hurt them like they had hurt Tut.

There was a knife on a shelf on the wall within arms' length of the bed, just below Tut's ceremonial shield, throbbing through the red haze that clouded the Queen's vision. Ankh dove for it— she would march into Ay's chambers right now and kill him; that was what she would do. Kill that lying jackal for sending her brother to his death.

"I'll kill them myself!" she shrieked.

"Darling, do you want them to kill you too?" Ankh wailed as someone caught her skirt, dragging her back to the bed. Before she knew what was happening, Tut had spun her around, and he was holding her, holding her tight, his strong arms around her waist. "This is the lot we have been cast. And now... now, all we can do is treasure every moment we have left. With the things we can change... and the things we can't."

Somehow his gentle whisper cut through the pulsing in her head. And she knew he was right.

The strange fog that had seemed to cloud the Queen's mind began to dissipate, her pounding heart slowing, the red haze before her eyes fading as she began to see clearly again. What... had she done? Hearing herself begin to sob, she let the dagger fall from her hand, hitting the floor with a clatter. Slowly she lay down on the bed beside Tut, confused thoughts flooding her mind as hot tears ran down her face and her body shook with wracking sobs. She was the Queen. How could she pick up a weapon and try to race out the door to murder the Grand Vizier, whatever he had done? She knew it made no sense. It would not take away any of the tragedy they were facing. It would only add to it.

She was back in control. Now that she was thinking clearly again, rage and confusion giving way to tears, she wondered how she could even think that way, even for a moment. And she was suddenly ashamed, so ashamed, that she would pick up a knife and try to hurt someone. How could someone like her do something like that?

It was because she loved her husband, she decided. Loved him so much that for a moment, she had thought that ending the life of the person who had hurt him would be worth it. She loved him. And in that there was no shame. And that he had stopped her... showed how much of a team they were. And always would be.

She closed her eyes as he held her tight, feeling his warmth, his strength. Slowly she stopped shaking, her sobs stilling. Slowly the rushing in her head faded, her teeth stopped chattering, her heart stopped pounding. It was over now. They were safe... even Ay was safe. It was time to do the next right thing.

He kissed her cheek, her forehead; then their lips met, meeting over and over, tasting one another's tears. "One more time?" he whispered.

She looked at him. "Can you?"

He smiled sadly. "We can try." He swallowed back his own tears. "And if we are blessed... I may have a gift for you from beyond." Then he chuckled. "Where's that 'Do Not Disturb' sign?"

They could feel it. The rightness they had been waiting so long to sense. Their hearts were calling to them. The time was right.

They had spent so much time together since his injury, but so little of it had been spent *with* one another. And if time was growing short... they needed that time.

They had shared so much over the course of their life together. Shared so much pain, so much grief, so much sorrow, so much loss, so much hardship. Things that were coming for them again.

So if they could share joy tonight... if they could share laughter... that would be their greatest gift to one another.

And they did. Hearts entwining, they were united. They were together. And they were one.

Semerkhet came back from his evening jaunt rubbing his cold hands together, ready to give his customary knock at his Pharaoh's door and stroll right in. But when he got to the door, he stopped short at what he saw. His own "Do Not Disturb" sign was staring him in the face.

And from inside the bedroom, he could hear a husband and a wife giggling together.

Quickly, he turned away, hiding his blush. He would come back later.

Ankh lay silently holding her sleeping husband, feeling his warm body resting against hers, his slow, steady breathing, his heart beating in time with hers. Thinking about the beautiful experience, the complete and perfect closeness, that they had just shared for the last time. And wondering.

Wondering, yes. They both wondered. But they knew that in sharing this union of body and soul for the last time, they had found what they needed. They had been blessed. Because heir or no heir, the gift that the Pharaoh would give to the Queen, even from beyond, was that of precious memory.

He was in her heart. And she was in his. And they would carry one another with them… forever.

And in memory… distance and time would not matter. Every time she thought of him, he would be with her.

Forever.

An hour later, later in the evening than he usually started his "evening shift," Semerkhet returned to the door. The sign was gone. Carefully, he knocked. And waited, in slight embarrassment, for one of them to verbally extend permission for him to enter.

"Come in," he heard his Master say. Slowly, he opened the door. The Pharaoh was sitting up in bed, the Queen just about to hand him a cup of tea. At some point, the two of them had changed into their sleeping-tunics.

They looked up at him. And they just smiled.

Twenty-second day of the month of Sholiak, Ankhesenamun wrote down in her journal. That would be her starting place. And now she would begin to count.

The Hittites, Tut thought as he lay there in bed the next morning. His wife had written to the Hittites, the very enemies responsible for his impending death. With a proposal of marriage, her marriage, to their Prince; the union of their countries with Hattusa as master.

It was a horrible thing to have to consider. Handing themselves over, probably losing their independence, possibly even relinquishing the divine line of succession. Would this decision make him the Pharaoh who lost Egypt to the Hittites— *gave* Egypt to the Hittites prepared like a gift?

But she was right. He knew she was right. This marriage was the only thing that could save the future of Egypt.

He knew it was the right thing to do. But he would have given anything for it not to be necessary.

Tutankhamun shook his head. Now that he had told Ankh and Sem the secret, revealed that the Vizier had poisoned him, that Horemheb had abandoned him on the battlefield, he was free to truly think about it. And he let the pain fill his heart, blinking back angry tears as he thought of the two men he had thought he could trust most in the world, the wise old Vizier and the faithful General. Both had betrayed him. And not in open disagreements; straightforward declarations of war against him and his ideas. With secrecy and deceit, taking advantage of the trust he had still placed in them, believing them to be faithful to him. They had stabbed him in the back almost without him noticing, ensnaring him with subtlety and lies. And now, they had left him to bleed.

There was a smile on her face, Meresankh saw. A smile on her Lady's face the next morning as she quietly crept from their Pharaoh's bedroom to her own to change from her sleeping-tunic into the day's outfit.

The Queen closed the door behind her as she entered the room, face glowing with some sort of joyful secret. And Meresankh found herself gasping in shock as the Queen of Egypt lifted her off her feet and began to dance around the room with her.

"Wh— what—" Meresankh gasped, gently trying to extricate herself from her dancing partner, who was swinging her around with almost as much strength as Semerkhet. "What happened?"

Ankhesenamun set her down, then threw her arms around her again, holding Meresankh tight as she whispered into her ear. "There might be an heir after all," she said softly, and all the hopes and dreams of a hundred dynasties echoed through her voice.

Meresankh laughed, stepping back to admire the Queen's still-flat belly.

"When—" she asked.

"Last night," the Queen whispered. "It was... it was... beautiful," she said softly, tears sparkling in her eyes as she cradled her belly in her arms. "Even if we never... even if this was the last time, it was... it was beautiful. And now... now there's hope for our dynasty."

Even the self-professed chattiest member of the palace staff had no more to say. So she just hugged her friend again.

"I won't tell anyone," she said finally.

The Queen shook her head. "We'll tell you when we're ready to share the news. Thank you. I know... I know I can trust you to keep our secret." She swallowed, face glowing as she smiled at her friend. "You might be an auntie, Meresankh."

And tears in her eyes, Meresankh stepped back again and smiled at the Queen's belly and the hope that lay within.

A baby. Her Mistress might be having a baby. Meresankh sent up a hundred thousand prayers of thanks to I-AM; a hundred thousand prayers for her Lady and for the child. If only. If only, amid all this sadness, they could know the joy of welcoming a baby into the palace. In that baby might lie the hope for the future of Egypt.

There was relief in having told her secret. Later that morning, Ankhesenamun stepped outside, taking a short walk around the garden. The Sun shone warmly on her face as she pulled her green outer robe closer against the chilly breeze, and the first chrysanthemums were just beginning to bloom.

And her heart… it was not light. But it felt free.

"My Lady?"

Coming back inside the palace after her walk, Ankh stopped when she heard the gravelly old voice of the Grand Vizier.

"Yes, Vizier?" She kept her voice cold, formal. She was speaking with her husband's murderer, after all. She looked up at him haughtily, with the eyes of a Queen, the eyes of Isis.

He looked at the floor for an instant, then back up. There was something in his old eyes; something she didn't like. Something in his smile. "My Lady," he said again, "I want to urge you… to consider your options." Ever so slightly, he held out his hand. "It's a lonely life when one's spouse is gone."

The Queen felt her gut tighten. Had he just proposed? She tried not to show the nausea that rose in her throat at the very idea. But it was just as she had expected.

"I am considering them," she said coldly. That was true. He didn't know about the letter. But she wasn't going to tell him without discussing it with her husband first. "The situation… is under control." Unconsciously, she raised her arm, the hanging sleeve of her outer robe hiding her flat stomach.

He looked at her questioningly, not sure what she could possibly mean. She held his gaze, imagining grabbing his cold, gnarled old claw and twisting his wrist; twisting it until he pulled back in pain. She would not back down.

Finally he dropped his gaze, looking away to examine one of his fine golden rings.

"My husband and I will inform you of any decisions we make at the appropriate time," she said shortly, then turned on her heel and walked away, leaving him to his confusion.

Ankh walked back into Tut's bedroom, heart pounding, a rushing in her head. She had beaten the Vizier. For a moment, she wanted to do it again. For a moment, she could almost feel the crook and flail in her hands. And for a moment… she truly, truly wondered what kind of Pharaoh she would make.

"You know when you asked me awhile back, a long time ago, if I played *seega* with Ay, who would win?" she said as she sat down on the side of the bed, warm outer robe flapping.

Tut looked up from petting Bastet. "Mm-hmm."

She gave a weary sigh. "I would," she said. "I just did."

Her brother raised his eyebrow. "You just played *seega* with him?"

She shook her head. "I played politics with him." And the Queen described the unpleasant conversation she had just had; the marriage proposal she had just deflected.

The King chuckled, shaking his head as he took her hand and kissed it. "You're the politician, not me."

Ankh stroked his head, brushing the delicate braids of his wig out of his eyes. "You're doing just fine."

Then he sighed. "But what if we do have a child? Will you still send the letter?"

Ankh closed her eyes sadly. "If I don't, then Ay will have time to push me out before it's born. If we'd had a co-regency like Mother and Father, it would have been different, but now, there's no time. The only way I can stay in charge is by staying Queen. The only way I can finish what we started… so one day, no one will have to live in a little mud hut. And everyone will have the opportunity to go to school." She swallowed. "I have to. For Egypt."

Tutankhamun sighed and gave his sister a little nod. What a brave choice she was making for the good of their country.

Then he swallowed. If she married Zannanza, even if at this very moment Tut's child was growing in her belly… that meant that their baby would grow up with a father.

30

Power Play

Early that afternoon, Ay came in; stood by the foot of the bed. "My Lord," he said softly, inclining his head.

"Vizier," Tut said. He knew deep in his heart that Ay had engineered all this, sent him on campaign, just so this would happen, so he could see the King lying before him on his deathbed.

"I want you to know that your country is in good hands. Egypt will flourish no matter what happens."

Tut nodded. Ay had all but admitted to his murder, the murder that would be complete when these broken bones, infection, ague, and nineteen years of divinely-ordained infirmity finally carried him into the west as the sun set on his life. And yet, from the Vizier's perspective, he spoke the truth.

"I know."

"Your grand tomb is not ready," Ay continued. He picked up a terracotta cup of wine (a generic red wine, not the special, imported kind they'd wasted last week) and sprinkled some of the peach-pit powder into it from the tiny linen bag the Physician had left behind, then handed it to the King with his gnarled old claw of a hand. Tut took it and looked into it, as if he were considering whether to drink it. It gleamed in the cup like blood.

Ay slowly began to walk around the bed, steadily circling the King. The man was like a vulture, skinny and bald and wrinkly, his long, billowing robes falling to his sides like heavy wings, circling and waiting for his prey to collapse before devouring it. The scarab pendant on his chest gleamed in the lamplight, as cold and hard as the heart within.

The Vizier went on, his gravelly voice calm and quiet, a mockery of respect. "We had looked forward to honoring your rule for many years, and had not yet begun preparations. I am an old man, and my tomb is finished. A decision has been made that my tomb will be made available, although it is admittedly smaller than the Pharaoh deserves, and that when the time comes, I will make use of the tomb that had been intended for Your Majesty."

Tut nodded. He could picture Ay's tomb in the Valley of the Kings. So that was where he would be buried.

Ay nodded at the cup waiting in Tut's hand and smiled warmly, the wrinkles around his mouth deepening. "You haven't been taking your medicine."

Tut looked up at him. "I know it all," he whispered. It was too late for anything now; he had nothing left to lose. Even if Ay cut his throat right now, his illness and injury would have carried him off before long anyway. "I know you sent me to Amurru to die. I know you convinced Horemheb to order my men to abandon me on the battlefield. I know you had Vizier Pentu killed. I know you're colluding with Maya to undermine my decisions. And I know that you poisoned me."

He dropped the cup of wine on the floor, where it spilled in a great red splash like a bloodstain. Flecks of wine arced through the air, splattering Ay's white robes until it looked like he was the one who had been murdered. The Grand Vizier stood in silence as wine dripped from his clothing, waiting for whatever was coming next.

"Peach-pits," the Pharaoh said calmly. "The same poison as bitter almonds. Am I a convicted criminal, to be executed by the Penalty of the Peach? I know you gave the order. 'Medicine' to cleanse my system. Or kill me. To protect the future of Egypt."

Ay looked at him bitterly, nostrils flaring. His face had gone livid, mouth twisting in ugly fury as he listened to the Pharaoh recite his plan. With a sneer, he dropped all pretense; made no attempt to deny anything Tutankhamun had said. "Then you know that your time is running out, Glorious Lord, and I will be the next Pharaoh of Egypt."

"What makes you think the General will wait for you?" Tut asked. "When I thought I could trust him, I appointed him as my successor in the event that I had no heir."

"The General will wait his turn because he has no choice," Ay said silkily. "He is still in Amurru, cleaning up the mess you made."

"The mess I made?" Tut interjected, raising a dark, dangerous eyebrow. "As I remember it, you were the one encouraging me to go wipe the Hittites off the face of the earth."

Ay cleared his throat. "By the time Horemheb is finished, they will be but a memory, an unfortunate inkblot on the papyrus of history. And by the time he returns, I will have taken the throne. Unless he wishes to take the throne by force and risk plunging Egypt into civil war in a coup, he will have to wait for me." He swallowed, and made a face Tutankhamun did not like. "Not to mention other bargaining pawns through which I can help him... understand my perspective. I know, my dear Pharaoh, that when he returns after the campaign, he will find me on the throne."

Ay sneered. "Although, why should Horemheb not wait for me? When we began discussing what would be best for the future of Egypt, I promised him the throne after mine in exchange for his loyalty... to me and to the good of Egypt."

"You almost tricked me," the Pharaoh said softly, "when Vizier Pentu died. Ague was almost plausible. Until you said he had been disfigured, and I realized it was the wrong season. What did you do, slit his throat, run a horse over him?"

Ay just looked at him.

"And you know what else I know," Tutankhamun continued. He stared at Ay, kohl-lined eyes hard and deadly, full of thunder. Ay looked at him with a faint glimmer of fear in his eyes, as if wondering what secret the Pharaoh was about to reveal he knew. "I know you killed our sister. I know you killed Meritaten the year I took the throne. We always believed you when you said she died of ague, but after you said the same thing about Pentu... we realized they were both lies. Well done, Vizier. You murdered a member of the royal family. One so far, anyway. And you got away with it." He scoffed. "Did your murder our father, too? And what about our mother?"

Ay closed his eyes. "What I do, I do for Egypt, My Lord."

The Pharaoh raised a dark eyebrow. "Really. Like putting yourself on the throne and then giving it to the General. How did you twist him around your finger, anyway? How did you convince him that my naïve generosity made me worthy of death? And how much did you pay the doctor to poison me?"

Ay sighed, looking down at his stained robe as if he was considering the laundry that Khenut and her washerwomen were going to have to do. "There are different kinds of strength, indeed," he said softly. "Strengths of inspiring one's people by defying the odds... and strengths of expanding Egypt's influence. I proved to the General that I intend to stretch the borders of our glorious nation from sea to sea, rather than avoiding war at all costs, threatening our struggling economy with wasteful minimum wages and dangerously low taxes, and expending massive amounts of time, resources, and effort on schools intended to fix problems that don't exist. We also discussed the fact that through attempting to remove peasants from the role they have always played in our great society and turn them into scribes, teachers, doctors, and business-owners, you were threatening not only the social structures we have relied upon for millennia, but *ma'at* itself. And I reminded him that although I was preparing to take the throne, in order to continue leading the country in the direction we agreed was right, he was your original heir. He agreed that upon your death, it would be best that you not yet have a son of your own to succeed you. My, but that would have complicated the royal succession." The Vizier brushed a speck of dust from the heavy necklace he wore. "As for the Chief Physician... he agrees with my vision for the economy of Egypt, and his son will be honored to become my Vizier when I take my place as your successor."

The Pharaoh took a breath as he prepared to respond, but the Vizier went on. "It's questionable whether Horemheb will ever take the throne. Nakhtmin outranks even him in the army, and although I have promised the throne to Horemheb, I know that my son could… pose a formidable challenge. After I myself pass into the west, I know that I shall watch with interest to see who will prevail."

Tut nodded. And he decided that it was no longer time to keep their plan hidden. "Who indeed? The Queen is preparing a letter to the King of the Hittites to ask for the hand of Prince Zannanza in marriage. We would rather give Egypt to the Hittites and give up everything we just fought for on the battlefield than give it to you or to Horemheb and give up everything we just fought for in the conference room. And not just put ourselves at risk of takeover, but actively hand ourselves over."

The Pharaoh shook his head, continuing before the Vizier could register his shock. And keeping one secret inside, the revelation that there might be an heir after all. That piece of news would wait for the proper time.

"You failed to drive a wedge between me and my sister, my wife. I need her at my side. We're a team, just like our Mother and Father. And that will never change." He chuckled wryly. "The Queen could rule without a consort; she is wiser than I am. When you first suggested I go to Amurru, she asked me if I was quite sure you were not trying to kill me. How sad that she should divine the truth."

"I could kill you now, Glorious Lord," Ay whispered, resting his fingertips on the bronze dagger at his side.

Tut raised an eyebrow. Silently taking a deep breath, he kept the rest of his face perfectly calm, even as his heart began to pound at the sight of the Vizier's gnarled old hand resting on the hilt of his dagger.

"Ah, but if you do, you will truly have murdered the Pharaoh. And then you will never get your chance. You will be burned at the stake, just like you tried to burn my friend Semerkhet. Which you never had the right to do, by the way. But," he continued, "your attempting to do so gave me a clue that you coveted my throne— that you in fact saw yourself as Pharaoh already."

He looked steadily at his Vizier, thunder rumbling softly in his eyes and his words as he let his voice drop to a murmur.

"I could have *you* killed with a single word, a snap of my fingers. Loyal guards are everywhere… there are three just outside the door. All it would take is a word. I could force you to drink your own peach-pit wine in execution for treason." He paused. "But I won't," he whispered, shaking his head. "Because that's not who I am. I value life too much to take it like that. Even yours. You're a person, just like me. Whatever I think of you… or whatever you've done. I think of your son and wonder what sort of Egypt you'll leave him one day… I can only hope that his son, and *his* son, have something to rule. I'm sorry for Nakhtmin, really. I see the way you've raised him to be just like you. But maybe, if he learns, he will be a good Pharaoh."

The Vizier was staring at him, listening silently, squirming in the Pharaoh's grip. Tutankhamun chuckled as he went on, heart calming as he saw Ay remove his hand from the hilt of his dagger.

"Maybe that will be your legacy. To rule between two good Pharaohs. So that's why I won't kill you. Because maybe, if you do succeed me, your reign will be a stepping-stone to a new era. Maybe." He smiled again, a smile full of irony. "And in a way, I have you to thank. Because it was your dismissiveness, your abuse, even, of the people who work for us, and your disregard of the poverty suffered by the citizens of the royal city, that got me thinking, and helped me realize that we are all people. And because you are a person, I will show you mercy. Because I am the Pharaoh. And I can show mercy to whom I choose… whether or not they deserve it. And because I can see that we are all people, I will not let you take control of my country and plunge the populace back into the darkness of poverty and fear." And he smiled at his Vizier. "How ironic. You were the one who awakened my mind with your cruelty; inspired me to change things. And now you've killed me for it. That was your last move in this game. And marrying Egypt to Hattusa is ours."

Tut chuckled. He had the Vizier cornered.

Ay looked at him, an ugly questioning expression spreading over his face. Tut looked back calmly, lying helpless on the bed with two broken legs, his face as placid as the golden mask the craftsmen were even now forging for his mummy. Was this their final battle, a battle of wills?

"What may happen remains to be seen, My Lord," Ay said shortly, and spun on his heel, stalking from the room with his wine-stained robes billowing behind him. Where the traditional farewell wish should have been, there was only silence. The moment he left, Bastet padded in, suddenly sneezing as if she had smelled something vile.

Tut sighed and lay back in the bed. There was some hope for Egypt yet.

"Your Excellency?"

Semerkhet looked around from his journey to the kitchen for a nice bowl of almonds for his Master.

It was the Grand Vizier.

"Yes, Vizier?" he said coldly. He was talking to the man who had murdered his Master, after all.

Ay looked tired, Semerkhet thought. As though he'd just had an argument with someone. And Sem wasn't sure if he'd won.

"Change is coming, Your Excellency," Ay said. "No matter how hard some of us may try to fight it… no matter what secrets may be uncovered. A time when all of us must choose a side."

Semerkhet stood straighter, shoulders back. And he looked steadily at the Grand Vizier. "I know where my loyalty lies… and so do you." He nodded. "Good day." And he kept walking.

He barely noticed that the Vizier actually inclined his head as he walked away. He barely even cared. The respect of Ay was not of any value. And he barely noticed that there was no real respect in Ay's gesture. Only empty formality.

Tut rested, thinking about his conversation with the Vizier. And how he had defeated him. For the time being, at least. He smiled, almost in spite of himself. Because he was proud of how he had handled it.

He had fought that battle of wills like a Pharaoh. Even if his heart was still pounding, his palms still sweating, his stomach still twisting.

But he wouldn't mention it to Ankh, to Semerkhet. He didn't need to. Or at least, not yet. He could keep his proud secret to himself until it became relevant.

He had been home three weeks as of today. And he wondered... how many were left.

The Queen thought about what Ay had said, in that horrible moment when he had proposed to her. *It's a lonely life when one's spouse is gone...* She thought back over all those years she and Tut had spent together, side-by-side. Brother and sister, united against the world. There hadn't been romance. But there had always been love.

And suddenly, Ankh realized that in this one thing, one statement in all his cold-hearted, treacherous, deceitful life, the Grand Vizier was right.

Without Tut at her side, she would be alone. So alone. Whether or not he had ever truly, truly been her husband, he had always been her brother. And he had been the Pharaoh to her Queen. Just as they had told one another so many times... they only had each other.

But now, she wouldn't have him any longer. Only the precious memories of him; memories she would struggle to touch, struggle to hold in her arms.

Closing her eyes, Ankh put her arms around herself. She would try to prepare herself. But she knew she couldn't. How could anyone prepare themselves for that?

Who would she turn to? Meresankh, of course. Her sister would comfort her; walk with her on this hard road. But who... would hold her? Whose strong arms would enfold her as she listened to his heartbeat, knowing that he would protect her as she protected him? That wasn't a sister. Wasn't even... quite... a brother. That was a husband.

Somehow Ankh knew that as she mourned her brother, he would be the one she wanted with her the most to comfort her.

The Pharaoh still looked like he was holding a secret inside; a secret that bothered him. Alongside the sadness he now showed them, the heartbreak of preparing to face what might be the end of his life, there was something else. And the valet wondered what else his Master had not told him.

Semerkhet stopped going out to play hockey, race his horses. Because there was no longer any time. And any moment spent away from his friend, his brother, was a moment wasted.

Every hour the Queen wondered. Had they conceived; was a tiny, precious baby even now curled inside her belly, waiting to rule Egypt? She focused her mind, listening to every detail of how her body felt, straining to recognize those first early signs. And she held her stomach, remembering those terrible days. Trying not to cry as the pain of those days cut like a knife, even after so many months. The joy, the waiting… and now the silence. Emptiness.
But now… She hugged her stomach again, hoping. Now there was a chance. There was hope.

31

Plans

"I don't want any," the King said as Raherka came in with a blue cup of red wine on a tray.

"Doctor's orders," the servant said cheerfully, trying to hand it to Tut. He didn't move his hands.

Gently he shook his head. "No. Ay's orders."

Raherka flinched, eyes darting, lips tightening. The wine sloshed in the cup he held out, a tiny bit spilling and staining the white linen bedsheet with red drops as bright as blood.

"I know, Raherka," Tut said softly, looking up at him. Raherka didn't meet his eye, but looked down, biting his lip, brow wrinkled in internal conflict, knuckles going white as he gripped the stem of the cup. He took the cup back and set it on the tray again, then put the tray down on the desk.

"I'm sorry," Raherka whispered, shaking his head. A glimmer of tears shone in his eyes. "I… I'll… I'm sorry. I won't… I just…"

Tutankhamun held out his hand, gently brushing Raherka's wrist. The servant shuddered at even the slightest, most casual touch from the Pharaoh. "It's all right," Tut said with a gentle smile. "It's not your fault."

"I won't bring any more," Raherka said emphatically, shaking his head so the braids of his wig swung across his face. "Never. I'll dump it out; bring you a clean cup. He... he paid me to do it; said he'd give me a promotion, too. But I can't... I can't hurt you anymore." He bit his lip. "And I'm sorry I ever said *yes*."

Tut smiled at him again. "But you're the one who helped me in Kadesh; called the others to get the chariot off me. You helped save my life." He raised his eyebrow. "Besides which, I'm the one who pays you."

The servant gave a watery chuckle and a sniffle. He knelt down by the bed, taking the Pharaoh's hand and kissing it. "And you are my Pharaoh. And I am your loyal servant. Hail to thee, Ruler of Truth; all life, prosperity, and health!"

"Sem?" Tut said shortly after his sister had gone for a quick walk around the garden. The valet set aside the pile of clean linens he was arranging on an end table and reported to the royal bedside.

"Yes, Master?" he asked, his eyes as bright and his smile as sweet and willing as ever.

But the Pharaoh didn't smile back. He had some serious news to share with his friend.

"Sit down," he said, gesturing at the chair. Semerkhet took a seat, looking earnestly at his Master.

"What's going on?" he asked.

Tutankhamun sighed, looking down. How to say it? Then he looked up again. No way to say it other than to say it.

"We've been talking... the Queen and I... about the future," he said slowly. Semerkhet nodded, forehead creasing in concern. He knew that the future was not looking promising.

He listened in silence, eyes growing wider by the second, as the Pharaoh outlined the Queen's plan to marry Zannanza of Hattusa, and how such an alliance would both stop the war and keep Ay from ever taking the throne.

"It's not... not something we ever... ever would have imagined..." the Pharaoh finished, "or wanted to imagine... but if we have to... that's what the Queen will do."

Sem just bowed his head. Was there really anything to say?

Then he looked up. "And you're all right with that? Really and truly?" he whispered.

Tut shook his head slightly, tears shining in his eyes. "What else can we do? I never... never wanted something like this, but... she's right. If *she* can't take the throne after me; if we don't..." He paused, his facial expression changing for half an instant, then looked at Sem again. "If our line ends with us," he said after a moment's pause, "she will do everything she can to continue our dynasty through marriage to the Hittites. And that... that will be better than letting them annihilate us, or letting the Vizier take the throne."

Semerkhet released a deep sigh. And he looked at his Master. And he smiled.

"If she remains Queen... Egypt is in good hands."

Tut gave the tiniest ghost of a chuckle. "I think so."

Sem looked away, letting all this new information begin to settle. Then he looked at the Pharaoh again.

"May I tell Meresankh?" he asked.

Tutankhamun nodded, giving his friend a small smile. "I think she already knows."

Semerkhet sighed to himself as he went on with his day. So that was what was still bothering his friend. That was why the Pharaoh looked bowed down with worry, aged by care, his young face almost lined by anxious thoughts; why dark circles ringed his eyes. And that was why the Queen looked worn and weary and preoccupied. That was why.

The Queen took her time out in the garden. She drank it in; the bright, warm Sun, the cool breeze that made her pull her warm robe closer, the birds singing in the trees, the flowers whose bright colors seemed to glow in the sunlight. Carefully she bent, selecting a few chrysanthemums of red and yellow, bright white daisies, and delicate cornflowers, forming them into a bright bouquet. And she smiled to think how much her brother would love them.

She went back inside, her feet finding their way down the familiar hallways that led back to his room. He was drowsing, so she tiptoed in, bending over him and dropping a kiss on his forehead.

Slowly he woke up with a sleepy smile. "Hello, Ankh," he whispered.

"I brought you something," she whispered back, holding the flowers close enough for him to see. His smile grew wider, showing his prominent front teeth.

"Oh, I love them," he said softly, reaching out a hand to stroke the delicate petals. "Tho pretty. Fank you, Ankh."

"You're welcome, love. I'll just put them over here." The Queen turned away to place the bouquet in one of the vases on her brother's dressing-table. "How… how are you feeling today?" she asked gently.

There was no answer. Settling the flowers into place, Ankh turned back around to see why. And she sighed as her heart began to ache.

He was asleep again.

Semerkhet had a look on his face, Meresankh noticed at dinner. And within moments, she figured it out.

"Did the Pharaoh tell you about the letter?" she whispered over her plate of beans and mutton.

Semerkhet set down his beer and nodded slowly, head bowing solemnly. "Yes," he whispered back.

And all she could do was reach across the table and take his hand. That was all she needed to do.

In two thousand years, such a thing had never happened. But now, it might be the only thing that could save them from destruction.

Semerkhet sighed as another thought rose in his heart. Something else they needed to discuss.

Slowly, Sem reached out to take Meresankh's other hand. And she looked at him questioningly, without smiling.

"It's only a matter of time," he whispered through the lump in his throat.

Meresankh bowed her head. And she got up, joined him on his side of the table, and put her arm around his shoulders.

"I know," she whispered back. "The Queen told me."

As he held Meresankh's hand, felt her small strength as her arm encircled him, Semerkhet closed his eyes and tried to pray for the future of Egypt. But there was only silence.

Faithfully, Meresankh supported the Queen. Ankhesenamun would walk into her room for a break worn and sad, and the handmaiden would tell her a funny story. And eventually, the Queen would smile. And Meresankh would be glad.

That night, the night of the twenty-third, the Pharaoh couldn't sleep. Tutankhamun rolled back and forth in bed, partway, at least, struggling to find a comfortable way to lie. It was chilly tonight, but he had plenty of blankets. Being cold wasn't the problem. It was the pain.

Even when he lay perfectly motionless, both legs still throbbed, especially his left one, where the infection was. And when he tried to move, it got so much worse. It had been difficult to fall asleep at night since his injury. But tonight it felt like it would be impossible.

How long had he been lying here? One hour, two, three? He opened his eyes, squinting around the room. Bastet was asleep beside him; Semerkhet was on his cot, presumably asleep. Ankh, too, was sleeping in her chair.

The King hated to wake his valet. But there was only one thing he could think of that just might get him to sleep.

"Sem," he whispered, sitting up slightly. Two seconds later his valet was hopping up from his cot, hurrying to Tut's bedside and dropping onto his left knee. He looked funny without his wig on; just his bald head. The cat woke up as Semerkhet approached, curling up again at the foot of the bed.

"Yes, Master?" he whispered back, looking earnestly at the Pharaoh as if meeting this need, whatever it was, was all he wanted to do.

Tutankhamun looked at him a little plaintively, almost not wanting to ask. But how else could he ever get to sleep?

"Would... would you rub my back?" he finally asked, trying not to feel bad. He was the Morning and the Evening Star. He could have anything he wanted, day or night... except for a brand-new pair of legs. Or an unbroken pair of the legs he had always had.

Semerkhet gave that smile Tut loved to see. His friend wasn't annoyed. He was delighted that there was something he could do to help. "Of course, Master. Just get comfortable on your stomach."

Slowly and painfully, Tut rolled himself over, finally settling himself on his front. And just as he had on the evening after Tribute Day, he had to chuckle at the words "get comfortable." Then he felt those gentle, familiar hands touch his back, softly beginning to rub slow circles. Slowly, the pain in his legs began to fade as his mind focused on this new sensation. An incredibly pleasant one.

And to top it off, Semerkhet began to sing under his breath. Tut chuckled as he recognized the lullaby that had gotten him home from Amurru. It was one that Hetty had always sung to him; almost more of an incantation than a lullaby, warning any evil spirits that the singer would not allow any harm to come to the child.

Away, away, o ghost of night
My baby do not harm
Your face turned back, your nose behind
You'll wither at my charm
Have you come to kiss him, or sing him to sleep?
Have you come to harm him, or steal him as I weep?
I will not let you kiss him, or in the window creep
I will not let you harm him
And I'll sing him to sleep

The King smiled as he heard the familiar words of the ghost lullaby. It brought the same feeling of safety as it had when he had been a toddler. He was safe under Semerkhet's care; the attentive watch of his faithful friend. No ghosts would trouble him tonight.

The Queen slept, cuddled up in blankets in her chair, where she had slept for the past three weeks. And she dreamed.

"He's so beautiful," a voice said. A warm voice, as sweet as honey, from over her shoulder.

The Queen smiled down at the baby in her arms. Little Tutsenmut, the healthy son who would carry her dynasty, her brother's dynasty, into the future. And she turned to smile up at her husband.

"Yes, he is," she whispered to Zannanza. She stepped into his arms, pressing herself close to him. And he wrapped his strong arms around her and their child, holding them to his heart. He smelled good. She felt him touch her chin, gently raising her face, and they were kissing, kissing...

Ankhesenamun awoke with a start, covered in cold sweat. She was in the chair in her brother's room, and it was the middle of the night. Zannanza was nowhere in sight. And the baby... if, glory be, there was one, was safe inside her belly.

She tried to get the image out of her mind; the image of the strong, handsome Hittite Prince kissing her. She could still feel the soft scratchiness of his curly, brown beard; still feel the warmth of his broad hand on her cheek. She shook her head, pressing her hands into her eyes. *What are you doing?* she asked herself.

And as she lay back down to try to get back to sleep as conflicted thoughts and feelings swirled inside her heart, she realized that she did not know the answer.

"It's not a secret anymore," Tut announced the next day as he lay on his side with the cat in his arms. He was halfheartedly trying to solve the riddles Semerkhet was reciting while Ankh gently bathed his hot head with a cool cloth, occasionally offering him a sip of cooled peppermint tea out of a shallow bowl that wouldn't spill. Over three long weeks had passed since his return home. They were nearing the end of the month of Sholiak, each night growing longer and colder than the last.

"What happened?" Ankh asked, frowning anxiously, jingling red beads echoing her question. Semerkhet looked up with his own frown, waiting for the King's explanation.

"I told the Vizier yesterday," Tut said simply, shaking his head, then wincing as his legs gave a sudden jab of pain. "Foolish, I know. But I figured it was too late for anything. And now his hands are tied. I have him cornered. He has to wait for me to die, because if he does anything dramatic, it'll look suspicious. You'll be safe too. He... in a way he's won, but he can't do us any more harm. Because I told him about Meritaten, too— how we know she and Pentu didn't die of ague. Even told him what we know about Mother and Father. And... when the Hittite Prince gets here, you can marry him and keep that vulture off the throne forever."

Ankhesenamun just nodded, her eyes filling with tears. Neither she nor Semerkhet had anything to say. They just nodded, bowing to the decision the Pharaoh had made.

The secret was out. The secret of the proposal to the Hittite Prince. There was nothing to say, nothing to do, nothing to think. So the Queen put the thought away. History would unfold the way it would unfold.

Whether or not the gods cared. Whether or not they heard a single one of the prayers she sent up every day.

"So you told him."

Tut sat propped up on pillows, trying to stay awake as Semerkhet prepared to feed him some soup for dinner on the evening of the twenty-fourth; soup that, just like always, the valet had sampled for poison before offering to the King. None today. Tut had been feeling weaker today, though. It was subtle, but every day, he could feel himself... fading slightly. And today, sitting up, staying awake, and feeding himself soup would be too much to do at once.

Tut nodded. "Yes." He paused. "I thought... I thought I could corner him by telling him. At least protect us for as long as it matters. And even..." He sighed, looking down and watching Semerkhet stir the hot soup, the ring of the Sole Companion gleaming on his finger, the sleeve of his blue outer robe swaying. Tut's stomach rumbled as he smelled the chicken and garlic. "Even if he does become Pharaoh someday, he's an old man. If you lie low, I don't think he'll go after you. And what does he have left; three, four, five years?"

Tut paused with a little sigh, pulling his warm blankets closer. The fever was low today, but rather than feeling relief, he had been freezing all day. "That is, if you even want to stay here. With your skill set, you could make it any number of places. And I don't want you to feel like you're bound here after I'm gone. Or even..." He swallowed. "Even now."

Semerkhet had just spooned up a bite of soup, but now he set the bowl aside. The valet dropped onto his left knee, looking into the Pharaoh's face. "Even now?" he asked. He gave half a sarcastic smile. "Are you firing your Sole Companion?"

Tut chuckled, recognizing the sarcasm. And smiling as Semerkhet's eyes locked with his own. "No... but I want you to know that you're free; free to make all your own choices, work where you want. I want what's best for you, even if that means not working here anymore. And I want you to be thafe."

Semerkhet returned to perching on the side of the bed, and finally, he fed the King a bite of soup. Tut smiled as he tasted the rich, warm chicken, the zing of garlic and onion, the little bit of spice that added just enough zest. That was good soup. For an instant he wondered about the life stories of the people who had prepared it, from the farmer who had raised the chicken to the gardener who had grown the garlic to the cooks who had transformed the ingredients into this amazing soup. Even the lives of the chicken and the vegetables. Did chickens have thoughts, he wondered. And did onions have thoughts?

The Pharaoh shook his head, letting go of his philosophical questions about the consciousness of vegetables. He was getting sleepy. "The point is, whether I'm right or wrong, whether or not it makes any difference, I told him to keep him from doing any more harm. Now he knowth I could have him ekthecuted if I reveal that he sent me off to die, and so he won't do anything more to me, and he won't hurt you or Ankh or Meresankh, either. He won't do anything suspicious until I'm gone, or until… if we get a miracle… I get better. But even if I don't have much longer, and even if something falls through with the Hittites and he becometh the next Pharaoh, he still won't go after the three of you, because ath Pharaoh, he won't want to do anything suspicious. The fact that he'th Pharaoh will be suspicious enough. So whatever happenth, you should be safe."

"I'm honored that my safety is such a high priority," Semerkhet said softly, offering another bite of soup.

Tut smiled as he felt the warm soup slowly filling his stomach. "You are my Unique Friend."

"I am in a bit of high demand, actually," Semerkhet said a moment later, a small smile playing about his mouth.

"Hmm?"

"Nakhtmin knows… that I might be moving toward a… career change," he said, "and he wants me to be *his* valet."

Tutankhamun almost spat out his soup.

"Nakhtmin?" He stared up at his friend in horror.

Semerkhet laughed. "I know. Ridiculous, isn't he? And he has *no* awareness of when he's not wanted. Proposing to the Queen; trying to hire me. But… well, I'll start at the beginning. I was taking some laundry down to Khenut, and then I heard him yell at me, 'Hey, valet!' And I thought to myself, that's not really the proper way of addressing the Sole Companion— I probably outrank him now— but I turned around to listen. And he told me that he doesn't feel like his valet Neferkare really likes him…"

"Understandable," the King said with a nod.

"...and that Neferkare isn't a massage therapist. And that he had a kink in his neck, and did I have a minute?"

The Pharaoh facepalmed.

"And he said that if... if he was Pharaoh one day, and I worked for him, that would make me Valet of Pharaoh again. But I told him that the Sole Companion hadn't yet decided upon his next career move, and I kept walking."

Tutankhamun shook his head. "The little jackal. Mind like an empty room. Well done getting rid of him." He sighed. Then he looked up and smiled. "Did you tell him to go jump in the Nile?"

"I wanted to," Semerkhet said with a laugh, "but I thought it would be beneath my station as Sole Companion. I also restrained myself from throwing my laundry basket at his head."

Tut patted his hand. "Very true. Very true. I'm very proud of you." He paused, biting his lip. "I can only imagine how difficult that was."

Semerkhet wrinkled his nose. "He wears too much perfume for me to want to get that close to him, anyway. And his stiff neck is his own fault; his posture is horrible. And of course, the whole time he was talking to me, he was gnawing on this plum, and getting juice down his chin, and at one point he had to stop and try to get it out from between his teeth with his finger."

The Pharaoh shuddered. "Disgusting!"

Sem chuckled. "I know! So I finally sort of got away, and I thought he at least understood that I was done talking. Then I heard him say, 'aren't you going to throw this away for me?' and he was trying to hand me his sticky plum pit." Semerkhet gave an incredulous little chuckle.

Tut shook his head again. "Promise me you won't let him become Pharaoh."

Sem chuckled again. And there was silence. Companionable silence. Tutankhamun smiled and waited quietly for another bite of soup, feeling warm and safe as his best friend took care of him.

32

Treason

"What are you going to do about the doctor?" the Queen asked her brother the day after his announcement that the secret was no longer a secret, the twenty-fifth day of Sholiak. "Now that the Vizier knows you know he's behind it all?"

He held the cat tighter and rubbed his face against her soft, warm, gray fur, hearing her purr.

"I could have him executed," he said thoughtfully. "Even though I know it's Ay's orders he's following."

She just nodded. She knew he could, but she knew he wouldn't.

"I think I'll scare him," he said with a smile and a little nod of his own. "Can you help me gather a few things together?"

Giving a little bow to the Queen, Meresankh hurried down to the midwife's workshop. Their Pharaoh needed Granny.

He also needed Semerkhet and Kamose, the tall, strong soldier who had joined the mission to bring the Pharaoh home safely. Throwing an arm around each of their shoulders, Tut let them transfer him from his bed to his chair. And he realized with a sigh that he had not sat in his chair since that one time during the painful days after the first fever of his ague had broken but before he had told his secret. It was exhausting to be moved. And each time he made the effort of getting into his chair, he knew it might be the last. But it was worth it. He had an impression to make.

"You called for me, Glorious Lord?" the Chief Physician asked, bowing to the floor.

The King raised a dark, stern eyebrow as the doctor slowly rose, keeping his gaze respectfully lowered. How disappointing. Staring at the floor, he wouldn't see the false beard of magnificence that the Pharaoh had had Semerkhet drag out, quite possibly for the last time, the eye makeup and wig he had on, or the circlet, which he also was not sure he would ever wear again. Although it was interesting to hear "Glorious Lord" again. No one had called him that in days. Except for the Vizier. And neither one of them were being in any way sincere.

"Yes, Physician." Tutankhamun held up the two small pieces of linen that Meresankh had brought from Merneith's workshop. "I would like you to have a look at these."

The Physician stepped closer, squinting at the stained cloths. "What are they, Your Majesty?"

"A test, Doctor. Proof of a hypothesis. And proof of your betrayal."

Sweat began to bead on the doctor's forehead, and he wiped his hands nervously on the front of his fine linen robe. He looked down at his own sandals again.

"This sample is the 'medicinal' wine you've been giving me," Tut continued, pointing it out, "and this is ground peach-pits. They are a perfect match."

"I'm not sure I understand the significance, O King for Whom the Sun Rises," the doctor said carefully, still not meeting the Pharaoh's eye. "We told you the medicine was an emetic, to cleanse your system. And that is what it has been doing."

"We have a different theory." Tutankhamun nodded at his wife, and she handed him a papyrus they'd been studying earlier— not a medical document, but rather, a legal one, discussing trial procedures and the execution of convicted criminals. Tut squinted at it; it was getting harder for him to read.

"The Penalty of the Peach. A drink containing crushed peach-pits is given to the accused. If he lives, he is innocent. If he dies, he is guilty. The poison contained within these seeds is believed to be the same as that found in bitter almonds. In the guilty, ingestion of the peach-pits produces vomiting, dizziness, lightheadedness, thirst, and headache before causing death."

Tut rolled up the papyrus and handed it back to his wife. Silently, she set it aside, the green beads of her wig clinking threateningly.

"I've been suffering those exact symptoms, Physician," Tut said. "At least I was until I stopped taking the wine."

"What makes you suppose that I wish you harm, Lord of Truth?" the doctor asked, twisting his fat hands together. He still wouldn't look directly at the Pharaoh.

"The fact that in this entire medical papyrus," Tut nodded at another scroll, "no medical application for peach-pits is mentioned. If you wished to help cleanse my system, you could have given me bitter cucumber, mustard-seed, castor bean oil, or simply large portions of dates and figs, none of which would cause the harmful side-effects I've been suffering. Instead you gave me a known poison."

"I... thought that the flavor of the peach-pits would be more palatable mixed with wine than any of the other remedies you mention, O K-king for Whom the S-sun Shines," the doctor stammered. He was still examining his sandals, eyes darting nervously back and forth between his two fat feet.

"Well, you were wrong, if that's true," Tut said, raising a dark, dangerous eyebrow. "It was disgusting. Most bitter thing I've ever tasted." He shook his head. "No, Doctor. There is no reason for you to give me peach-pits except to weaken me and hasten my death. You tried to poison me. Although you very cleverly gave me multiple low doses rather than one large one— you wanted me to die slowly and realistically rather than suddenly and suspiciously."

"But My Lord also has the ague," the Chief Physician said heavily, as though he were trying to sound sad. "Which can produce dizziness, thirst, headache, and alterations of one's perceptions. And which goes through three-day cycles of intensity. What concerns remain that cannot be explained by the ague and the use of a legitimate emetic?" His eyes, still trained at his feet, had changed. Now they looked a little desperate.

"The timing," the Pharaoh replied. "And the very cleverness of the fact that the symptoms of peach-pit poisoning align closely with those of ague. For a little while there, the Queen and I were attributing all my new suffering to the ague. You almost tricked us. Only when I stopped taking the wine and my symptoms magically disappeared too quickly to be explained by the three-day cycle of ague did we confirm the truth. Although you were very careful to start me on the wine on a day when my fever was high." He shook his head. "There was also no clear reason for you to even prescribe an emetic. My unfortunate trust in your having my best interests at heart was the only reason I accepted it in the first place."

Then the Pharaoh looked down at his legs. Which were feeling slightly better, thanks to Meresankh's expert care.

"You're also neglecting my wound," he said to the Physician. "Letting the infection get worse by leaving the old bandages on, tying the bandages too tightly and cutting off my circulation, never giving it a chance to air out, not cleaning the wound thoroughly when you do clean it. It's a subtle trick… but if you take just poor care enough of it, the infection just might kill me… without arousing suspicion. It would be easy to explain my death as resulting from an infection that you simply had not been able to treat… because you let it get incurably bad. Besides the fact that using mustard-seed on an open wound will only worsen inflammation." Tut turned to the Queen again. "My dear?"

Ankhesenamun unrolled the medical papyrus. This time she took a turn to read out loud.

"Mustard-seed. Draws out infection by attracting heat to the afflicted area and helping the body eliminate it. Particularly effective in easing chest congestion by serving as an expectorant. May be used in a poultice for this purpose... but must not be used on broken skin, for fear of increasing inflammation."

Tutankhamun glanced down at his leg, red and burning. "That, Doctor, is broken skin. And some pretty terrible inflammation. It still hasn't entirely cleared up, even with the Queen's handmaiden, who's a doctor in her own right, looking after it.

"You slipped up earlier, too, you know. When I first got home. You told me that my valet and I had taken quite the fall when the General ordered the retreat. But you weren't there. You can't have known that unless all of this was planned, and you were part of the plan all along. You and... others."

"And," the Queen cut in, and the Pharaoh looked at her, curious as to what she was about to add, "you told us that the Pharaoh's dizziness and headache could be attributed to the ague, but you had not been present to see that he was experiencing those symptoms. It was as if you were describing the symptoms you expected to see arising from the poison you were giving him."

"So," Tut said to the Chief Physician, "now you know the reason behind my partial recovery. I stopped taking the wine."

The Pharaoh looked carefully at the doctor. He had closed his eyes, gray eyebrows furrowed, a heavy sigh shuddering through him as he clenched his fat hands. He did not say a word.

"Do you know the punishment for attempted assassination of the Pharaoh?" Tutankhamun asked softly. "I could have you beheaded, I could have you drowned, I could have you burned alive. And there are worse options as well, oh, yes. Not to mention what awaits you after death finally takes you. I don't imagine the heart of one who had conspired to murder the Pharaoh would balance very well with the Feather of Ma'at. I hope Ammut is hungry."

The doctor just stood there stiffly with his eyes shut, sweat rolling down his round face, which was growing pale. Convulsively, he wiped his sweaty palms on his tunic again.

"Or maybe I won't kill you," the King said, tapping his chin thoughtfully. "Maybe I'll send you to Nubia to work in the gold mines... or to Amurru to help General Horemheb finish up his campaign against the Hittites." He looked the doctor up and down. "Although I don't imagine you'd last very long." He sighed. "Hmm... What else could I do with him, Ankh?"

She glanced sideways at him, tapping her own chin, "Hmm... I suppose we could sentence him to five years' hard labor replacing Hemetre as Mayamenti and Tjauenmaya's nanny. You'd have endless fun in Treasurer Maya's household."

The King shook his head. "Mmm... that one's too cruel."

She paused, then nodded. "You're right. That is going a bit far. But what shall we do with him?"

The fat Chief Physician was snorting like a hippo in labor as he struggled to breathe, sweat rolling off his fat face, staining his white linen robe.

"I confess!" he moaned. "Before Your Majesty went to Amurru, the Grand Vizier summoned me. He convinced me that your generous economic proposals would propel us toward ruin; the changes you were making would upend *ma'at* itself. I agreed that if you returned wounded, according to his plan with General Horemheb, I would give you peach-pit wine as 'medicine.' At the same time, I would treat your injuries, but not with my full attention, and, yes, with poultices that would irritate your wound rather than healing it. That way, if... you were not... to survive... it would not seem... suspicious. He said that if I followed his plan, he would make my son Vizier when he became Pharaoh."

The Physician gulped, his eyes still on his feet. He had just told them everything. "If you will have mercy on me," he whispered, "I'll do anything. I'll resign my post immediately, leave the palace, leave Memphis itself if you wish. But I beg of you... not the children."

Tutankhamun looked at him. "I was going to fire you anyway, but it seems only appropriate that you should also be banished from Memphis. Thank you for the suggestion. Meet your replacement. My dear?"

He nodded to the Queen, and she opened the bedroom door to admit the tiniest little grandmother the King had ever seen— Merneith, the midwife whose analysis of the poisoned wine he had just shown off to the doctor.

She bowed gracefully, even though her tiny body was already bent by age. "My King."

"Lady Merneith has been a loyal member of the palace staff since before I was born," the Pharaoh said with a pleasant little smile. "I have no doubts as to her skill… or as to her trustworthiness. She conducted the test we showed you, providing us with the information that allowed us to ascertain your guilt. I suspect she has saved my life."

The Chief Physician just swallowed.

Tut paused. For an instant he considered mentioning the fact that Semerkhet and Meresankh had initiated the investigation into the harmful "medicine," praising them for their loyalty. But he decided to leave that truth where it was, inside his heart. Some things were better left unsaid; better not spread around. Especially when it came to politics.

The Pharaoh heaved a deep sigh. He was starting to get tired from all this royal sentencing, along with the effort of sitting up in the chair. "Well, I suppose that takes care of that, then," he said to the doctor. He narrowly avoided lisping, and swallowed, willing his lips and tongue to obey him for the rest of the meeting. "My dear?" Again, the Queen stepped forward, presenting a document to her husband. Tut showed it to the doctor. "A royal edict," he said, "officially firing…" Taking the pen his sister offered, he added a few words— "and banishing you, and officially appointing Lady Merneith as your replacement." With a smile of satisfaction, he stamped the wax seal with his signet-ring.

"Semerkhet, could you find some guards, please?" His valet bowed and left the room. The Pharaoh turned back to the traitor. "Doctor, I'm ashamed of you, and I never want to see your face in Memphis again. I would have hoped that the loyalty you've always shown me would have lasted, but apparently you care more about what the Vizier thinks than about my life. Although, as you yourself said, perhaps you felt that getting rid of me was in… Egypt's best interests."

Tut looked up as Semerkhet led four uniformed guards with long spears into the room. "Gentlemen, please arrest the doctor for high treason," he said pleasantly. In an instant, the fat Physician was quaking with a large hand clamped on each arm.

"Take him to his house, give him an hour to get his things together, and then escort him to the edge of town and see that he keeps walking. And put out a notice that if he ever does come back, he's to be executed. Or possibly sentenced to babysitting. Off you go."

The guards looked a little confused at the last proclamation, but they led the doctor away, never to set foot in the palace again.

At a nod from the Pharaoh, Semerkhet and Kamose stepped forward to move the tired King back to his bed. It had been worth the work to issue this royal proclamation from his chair. But it was definitely time to get back in bed.

Settled once again, Tut lay back with a weary sigh. Politics never ended, did it? He smiled up at Ankh, and she bent to kiss his forehead. Then he looked up at Semerkhet. "May I have some tea?"

After his tea, he was going to need a nap.

So this was the formidable person named Merneith. The Queen watched the tiny midwife work, looking at her wise, lined face, her gentle, nimble, wrinkled hands, bent and twisted by age. Who would have expected that this tiny old lady would be named after the second woman to rule Egypt?

And yet, as Ankh watched her, she could see that the name was not misplaced. Inside this old woman, the Queen could sense a well of infinite strength, boundless wisdom, measureless courage. And she wondered where they came from.

Merneith turned to smile at her as she mixed some medicine, and Ankh smiled back. But suddenly she felt her smile melting like a scented wax cone as a shock hit her, shining from the old woman's eyes. In her eyes was the same mysterious Light that Meresankh possessed, the same Light the Queen remembered seeing in her parents' faces, a Light full of love and truth that made her heart ache with its beauty; yearn to truly understand what it all meant.

And the Queen of Egypt turned away in confusion.

Semerkhet shook his head. That doctor. Hearing the list of symptoms associated with execution by peach-pit poisoning, the same symptoms his Master had been suffering, kindled a flame of anger inside his heart. And he was glad that that traitor had lost his job. And that he had been replaced by the very person who had helped them solve this mystery of attempted murder.

But before the King's nap, there was work to be done. Because his new doctor had to examine his wound.

She examined it in silence. Tut waited for a moment, before finally asking, "How is it?"

Merneith just looked at it. And she sighed. There was a question in her eyes, of whether even her extensive medical skills would be able to save him. But there was also a promise. That she would not stop trying.

The midwife cleaned his wound again, while Semerkhet had the Pharaoh squeeze his hands as hard as he could and Ankhesenamun kept him from looking. It was not quite as bad as the other time. But there was pus, and there was flesh that would never heal, and the redness and the heat had taken over even more of his leg than before.

Merneith got his wound clean, the pus wiped away and the hole in his leg as immaculate as possible. Then she applied another poultice of her own making, of cooling lavender and rosemary, wrapped his leg in fresh, clean bandages, and placed it back in its splint. And the exam was over.

Tut knew he could trust her to check on it every day. Whether… whether or not she could save him.

"Your Majesty," she said gently, "this leg cannot be saved. The break, the infection, the mustard-seed, and the neglect have injured it beyond repair." She swallowed. "I think we should consider amputation. It may be possible to save your life by sacrificing your leg."

"Amputation?" he asked with a shudder. "Even if it kept me alive longer, I'd be hopping around the afterlife on one leg. And it'th been hard enough for me to get around on two legs."

"That depends on your point of view," she said gently. He just shrugged. What she believed was her choice. "And it is your decision." Merneith sighed. "But based on all my years of experience... I do not see you getting out of bed and walking on that leg." She swallowed. "But I can contend with it. And I will. I promise to do my best... no matter what."

Tut sighed. He knew that she and all her years of experience were right. His leg was never going to heal.

33

Offers

The Queen walked down the hall to lunch on the twenty-sixth day of Sholiak, past the study she and Tut shared; past the grand painting of Grandfather Thutmose the First. Semerkhet was sitting with the Pharaoh, and after a long, quiet morning of faithfully tending to the one she loved, Ankh needed a little space.

She sat alone in the royal feasting hall, watching the torches in the walls flickering. Lunch was good; beef with a salad of fresh radishes, which had finally come into season with the arrival of the coldest quarter of the year, a few sweet, yellow-green jujubes that she ate with her fingers like a tiny apple, eating carefully around the large pit in the middle, and a nice cup of hot peppermint tea. It felt good to sit alone for a few moments.

Then she wasn't alone.

"My Lady?"

A familiar drawling voice made her scalp prickle as out of the corner of her eye, she saw someone sit down beside her. She coughed at the sudden odor of a heavy perfume.

"What do you want, General?" She didn't bother trying to be polite; Nakhtmin didn't deserve politeness. If he ever became Pharaoh, it was only because his father had murdered her husband.

"Just to talk," he said in the smooth voice he had inherited from his father; the smooth voice that meant trouble. "How is our dear Pharaoh today?" he asked unctuously. As usual, slightly too much jewelry gleamed on his neck and hands; a heavy golden necklace and a blue-and-gold scarab ring she knew he hadn't earned. He was just rich.

"Not so bad," she said stiffly. "Thank you for asking."

"That is good to hear," he said in a voice that made it clear he felt the exact opposite. He took an ostentatious sip of his wine, white wine the Queen knew she recognized from among the gifts her husband had received back on Tribute Day. "You know, I've been thinking about something…"

"Have you," Ankh snorted, raising her cup to her lips. She tried to focus her senses on the refreshing flavor and soothing warmth of the tea in the interest of remaining civil.

"Yes, My Lady. I've been thinking… about marriage."

Ankh's stomach twisted; she gripped the cup until her knuckles went white. Now a second member of the inner circle was descending upon her like a vulture. Just as she had expected.

"I'm advancing in my career," Nakhtmin continued, "and I've been thinking that it's time to settle down. Find myself a beautiful wife." He glanced at her under half-lowered eyelids; lids that hooded his eyes just like the hood of a cobra that was considering whether it wanted to bite you or not.

"Well, I wish you luck," she said, standing up and preparing to leave her mostly-full plate and cup. "I recommend you try Memphis, just downhill from the palace. You can't miss it. Good day."

"Wait, Your Majesty," he said in the same drawl, holding out a gold-ringed hand, pleated linen sleeve billowing. "I just want to say… if I found a woman like you… strong, wise…" He chuckled. "Feisty… I'd consider myself lucky."

"I hope you find one," she said in a clipped voice. "I'm not comfortable discussing this with you. Excuse me, General." And she began striding down the hall, long yellow robe rippling behind her, the red beads of her wig jangling angrily as the *uraeus* on her diadem almost seemed to give an audible hiss.

"So does that mean you won't marry me?" Nakhtmin asked from where he was still sitting at the table.

She just kept walking.

"Careful, Your Majesty." Ankh pulled up short just as her nose was about to collide with the white, pleated tunic of a Treasurer's robes.

"Pardon me, Treasurer," she said, lowering her head and preparing to continue on her way. Not the person she wanted to talk to just now.

"Wait, Your Majesty," Maya said, putting out a hand. She stopped, looking up at him with a set jaw.

"Yes, Treasurer?"

Maya looked down at her, a strange look on his face. A hungry look. "How is the Pharaoh today?" he asked.

"Not so bad," she said, just as she had told Nakhtmin.

"Good," he said genially. "I'm glad to hear it."

But there was something in his tone... something else.

"He is still leading our country," she continued firmly. "That hasn't changed one bit."

"Of course, Your Majesty," Maya said, inclining his head. The braids of his heavy wig threw his face into shadow. "I meant no offense." He swallowed. "I merely meant... Your Majesty," he said, a little too warmly, "I wonder... I wonder if the Chief Physician has truly explained to you just how much danger the Pharaoh is in."

"We understand that his condition is quite serious," she said curtly through clenched teeth. And she elected not to tell the Treasurer that the Chief Physician had been fired and banished from Memphis.

"He's never been strong," Maya said sadly, shaking his head. "And now two broken legs... and infection, and ague, on top of all that... Sometimes I wonder how much longer his body can take the strain." He sighed wistfully, kohl-lined eyes gazing off into the middle distance.

"I wonder that, too," she said, looking down. And it was true; she did.

"Another thing I wonder…" Maya said quietly. "Who will succeed him one day." He bowed his head almost respectfully. "Without an heir of your own."

"My husband and I have a plan," she said briskly. "Thank you."

"And that's good," Maya said, nodding, "but I just want to say… you have options."

She nodded. "Yes, I do."

Maya held out his hand, just slightly. Ankhesenamun looked down at it and took a step back. There it was. A third member of the court, trying to get her into his clutches. And the Pharaoh wasn't even dead yet.

"Marrying a member of the royal court would enable you to remain Queen; possibly one day deliver an heir of your grandfather's blood," Maya said softly.

"That is true," Ankhesenamun whispered, subtly resting her hand on her stomach. Inside, she chuckled. He had no idea.

She looked up at him. And he smiled complacently. Inside, she shuddered. But she smiled. Smiled up at Maya. Almost coyly. Above her, she could see him getting drawn in, thinking she was about to accept. She stepped closer to him, gazing up at him through half-lowered eyelashes. "If I married you, I could remain Queen, remain secure… make you Pharaoh."

"That's right, Your Majesty," he said with a haughty smile. And her stomach went sour as she imagined him wearing her brother's crown.

She took Maya's hand in both of her; his large, powerful, domineering hand.

And she dug her nails into it. He grimaced and gasped in pain, pulling his hand away. She let it go, letting him almost lose his balance.

"But you're already married, Maya," she said. "And I don't want to share. Goodbye."

And she turned on her heel and walked down the hall, leaving him nursing his hand. Her white dress and warm, yellow outer robe fluttered behind her and her red beads jangled, "No, no, no…" while her empty stomach growled like a lioness.

Unlike Nakhtmin, Maya at least knew not to yell after her about whether or not she was in fact going to marry him. He knew when he had been rejected.

As she walked, Ankhesenamun kept an eye out for Horemheb. He was probably next. She geared up, preparing to deliver the same clipped refusal. And then she remembered that he was still in Amurru. Good. One person she wouldn't have to contend with today.

Again, she felt the thrill of victory pounding in her heart, coursing through her veins, buzzing in her head. In her full authority as Queen, she had defeated those who challenged her right to rule alone.

Meresankh stood in her Lady's room, trying to get back to the endless stream of small tasks that filled her days. But her heart was aching. Because she had just spoken with her Granny… her Granny, who had shared some news with her. The Pharaoh's leg, she said, was never going to heal. And unless they amputated it immediately, he was going to die. Even the greatest doctor in Egypt could no longer contend with the wound that was killing Tutankhamun.

Time was running out.

Ankhesenamun sat down in her private sitting room, lying back in her chair and resting her tired head. She had just refused two marriage proposals, and her husband wasn't even dead yet.

"Are you all right, My Lady?" a gentle voice asked. Ankh opened her eyes and sat up. Meresankh stood in front of her, a cup of tea in her hand.

"I'm all right," she said, smiling at her handmaiden and accepting the tea. The warm cup felt good in her cold hands. "Thank you. The boys are just a little… eager."

Meresankh gave a concerned frown. "What happened?"

Ankh chuckled. "Oh, Nakhtmin and Maya both proposed to me in the same ten minutes."

The handmaiden shook her head. "Oy, vavoy."

"And Ay did yesterday."

Now Meresankh's eyebrows rose into her wig. "The Vizier?"

Ankh nodded. "Yes. Awful, isn't it?"

Meresankh shuddered. "I would not want to be married to him."

"Neither would I." Ankhesenamun chuckled again as she shook her head, taking a sip of the good, hot tea. "But I told all three of them *no*, in no uncertain terms, and that's that. Thought for a minute that Horemheb would be next, and then I remembered that he's still in Amurru. Thankfully. And I restrained myself from telling any of them to go jump in the Nile." The Queen sighed, resting her head on the back of the chair again.

"Did he..." Meresankh paused, tapping her chin. "I know the Vizier," she dropped her voice, "sent our Pharaoh to get hurt, but what about Horemheb? Did he have something to do with it? I keep hearing something about a trumpet— and that's what they said when they first got back; that a trumpet sounded just before the retreat. Did the General... did he betray our Pharaoh too? Is he working with the Vizier? And what does he want? The Vizier hates the new policies, but how would General Horemheb benefit from hurting our Pharaoh? I thought he..." She paused again, biting her lip as if deciding how to phrase what she was going to say next. "I thought he was technically the Crown Prince," she whispered sadly. Then she tried to smile. "Until and unless."

Ankhesenamun shook her head softly with a jingle of beads and half a smile of her own. "We're not quite sure about Horemheb," she admitted to her friend. Then she gave a heavy sigh. "But we do know that it was his trumpet that called the retreat. We know... we know that the Vizier got to him; convinced him that betraying our Pharaoh was a risk worth taking. But," Ankh said, sitting up a little straighter, "we also know that Horemheb has proven himself faithful to us in the past. And we don't know what he'll do when he comes home after the campaign. If we could get him to listen... if we could get him to repent... we could get him back on our side, and that could change everything."

The handmaiden sighed, shaking her head and rolling her eyes. "Men," she said sadly. "Oy, vavoy. All this betrayal; all these murders.

Why they can't just have a good old *argument* and figure it all out is beyond me. Why they can't..." She smiled at the Queen almost shyly, remembering when Ankh had lovingly corrected her for gossiping. "Why they can't just figure out who was wrong and why, apologize to one another, and move on."

Ankhesenamun shrugged with another little half a smile. "I wish I knew. But things would be a lot better if they could."

"How is... our Pharaoh?" Meresankh asked softly a moment later. A terrible future was aching inside her heart; the future Granny had revealed to her. The heartbreaking secret Meresankh had spoken of with Semerkhet. The reason, of course, for her Lady's letter to the Hittites. And a reason why the Vizier, the Vizier's son, and the Treasurer, delusional though they might be, would consider it in any way reasonable to try to court the Queen.

The Queen sat up straight, looking solemnly at her friend with a heavy sigh. And she shook her head.

"It's only a matter of time now," the Queen replied, shaking her head again. "It's probably... weeks." Her face crumpled, and she pressed the back of her hand to her mouth. Meresankh reached out and took her other hand, and the Queen squeezed it gratefully. Mastering herself, she put her grief away, swallowing it back down for later. And she looked at Meresankh again with clear eyes. "You remember our plan, though. We will just have to see how the Hittites respond."

Her handmaiden just bowed her head.

"I won't tell anyone," she promised. "Not until you give the word."

The Queen looked up at her with half a smile. "I know you won't. Thank you." She swallowed. "We'll tell you... tell you when."

Ankhesenamun finished her tea and got up. "Well, I'd better go check on him. He'll be worried I fell down the stairs or something." She chuckled. "Wonder what he'll think when I tell him what I've been up to."

Their Pharaoh wasn't getting better. Meresankh sighed and closed her eyes. And for the hundred-thousandth time, she prayed for a miracle.

"There you are," Tut said with a relieved smile, sitting up in bed as Ankh came into the room.

"Sorry I took so long," she said, bending over the bed and hugging him— very gently. "I just had some… interesting conversations."

He looked at her. "Is everything all right?"

Gathering her yellow outer robe closer, she sat down in the jeweled chair next to the bed and took the bowl of almonds and pistachios he'd been snacking on and now offered her. Her stomach was growling from having practically missed lunch. Under the bed Bastet was chasing a stray pistachio shell.

"Everything's great," Ankhesenamun said with a smile. She popped an almond into her mouth and crunched it. It tasted like victory. "And I'm not going to marry Nakhtmin or Maya. Ever."

Her husband's dark eyebrows disappeared into his wig. "What?"

"It's just politics," she said with a smile. He chuckled as he waited for her to tell him the whole story. But even before she did, the phrase still made him feel warm and safe and loved, just like it always had. His big sister would always take care of him, no matter what.

She recounted the story, telling him of how she had rebuffed Nakhtmin and Maya's awkward proposals. How she had sent them packing, defeating each of them in the single combat of a verbal battle. And how they would not come asking again.

Tut looked up at his wife, chuckling at how wise she was, how brave, how cool under pressure. "Are you sure you want to marry Prince Zannanza?" he asked. "Because you're doing just fine on your own."

Ankhesenamun shook her head. "We'll need a figurehead," she said. Then she smiled. "Even if I am managing all the politics."

Her brother took her hand and kissed it. "You will be." He chuckled. "Come here, you." And gently, he drew her down onto the bed next to him, wrapping his arms around her, her strong little body, her wise heart. The brother and sister cuddled up together like the children they had once been, facing their future side by side.

And then they had to make room for Bastet, who had no understanding or appreciation for the politics that had just occurred, but wanted to snuggle too.

The General. Meresankh shook her head. She'd never spoken to Horemheb, but he was famously big, strong, and handsome, and she'd always thought of him as being "on their side." But now… now only I-AM knew what he would do when he got home from Kadesh.

The Pharaoh was proud of the way in which he'd defeated the Vizier in the verbal combat of deadly politics. But when he thought back on it… it made his mind itch; itch just as it had before he had solved the mystery of Mother's horse. And he wondered what the bargaining pawns Ay had referred to could possibly be.

His friend was smiling, Semerkhet noticed. Even amid all their pain and grief, Meresankh seemed excited about something, some piece of news, some happy secret glowing in her face even alongside the mysterious Light that shone there. Semerkhet didn't know what it was. But he wondered.

She kept the secret. Even as she smiled, the news shining from her face. Meresankh didn't tell anyone what the Queen had revealed to her; not even Semerkhet, not even Granny. She had a secret to keep. And a promise.

34

Love

Ankh hadn't seen Mutnedjmet and Amenia in days; Meryt in even longer. And she missed them, missed having tea with them, sharing stories of the heroic women of generations past, watching them come into their own as human beings.

But now... now she had Meresankh to spend her days with. And they found themselves sharing tea when Semerkhet was sitting with Tut; found themselves talking earnestly about what it meant to be a woman, studying history together. And that felt good.

What was her name? Suddenly a thought hit the Queen like a charging hippopotamus; a thought that she was mystified and ashamed that she had never considered before.

The little girl in town. What was her name?

She had a name. Of course she did. She and every other child in Memphis, in Thebes, in Egypt, rich or poor, had a name.

But what was it? What beautiful, graceful name could possibly describe the precious little soul they had met that day? As the day went on, Ankh shook her head to think of it. And she desperately wanted to know what her name was.

"So… now he knows," Ankh sighed, sitting down on the edge of the bed beside her brother. They and Semerkhet were safe behind a locked door, the words they would say concealed from those who were faithful to the Vizier and his twisted plans for the future of Egypt.

Tut nodded, reaching up a hand and putting an arm around her. She scooted closer, taking his free hand in hers.

"He does," he said. Then he smiled up at his sister. "It's done… but I did want to hear your perspective."

The Queen chuckled. And she ran her hand over his wig. "I think you made a bold move," she said. "And I think you have limited his options, because he knows that we'll be watching his every move, more so than ever." She sighed. "I think we're both gambling on the future. With this… and with my letter. And all we can do is continue playing our best politics, and pray that our strategies work.

"Interesting, though," she said, her voice growing bitter as she remembered how her brother had recounted the Vizier's confession of his deadly plot, "to get some more insight on the inside of Horemheb's heart. I'm just sorry," she said, squeezing her brother's hand, "that he couldn't see the wisdom that was right in front of him."

Tut just smiled. And pride filled his heart as he realized she was right. "I do wonder, though," he said a moment later, "what he meant about having… bargaining pawns that he could somehow use to influence Horemheb once he gets home."

A horrible possibility twinged inside the Queen's heart, but she pushed it back down. That couldn't be it. Even the Vizier could never be so heartless as to threaten Horemheb's wives… could he?

Gently, she kissed her brother's forehead. "I'm proud of you," she whispered with a smile.

"I'm proud of me," he said, returning the smile.

She chuckled. "Good." And very carefully, she lay down beside him, pulling his blanket up to her shoulder.

Ankh took a turn around the garden. And she thought. About the future. The terrible, awful, cold, dark, empty future that was coming for her.

And she thought about the past. About her sweet sisters, Meketaten, Tasherit, Rure, Setepenre. And how much it had hurt to lose them. She had only been ten years old. But she remembered how much it had hurt. And she remembered how much it had hurt when in her fourteenth year, she had lost Meritaten.

She let the pain fill her heart again until the trees and flowers around her melted into a blur of unshed tears. And as she let them fall, she tried to let the memories of that pain, those losses, prepare her for the loss that was ahead.

"I hope Kamose feels better," Meresankh commented.

"Oh, what's wrong?" The Queen set aside the papyrus she was scanning during a five-minute break and looked up at her friend.

"Well, Semerkhet hasn't been playing hockey lately, but he's been keeping up with his team, and poor Kamose wrenched his shoulder during practice the other day. He might not even be able to play in the next game." Meresankh picked up an empty teacup to be taken back to the kitchen, then sighed. "He should get some comfrey ointment for it. That would put him to rights."

Ankh smiled. Her friend was well on her way to becoming the wise herbalist of her generation.

Semerkhet began visiting Meresankh's suite for ten minutes here, fifteen minutes there, when he was on break. It was good to see her smiling face, feel her tiny hand on his, share a cup of tea or beer and a few minutes of pleasant conversation, about anything other than their daily lives. Even if she was just as wrapped up in all of it as he was, supporting the Queen as he looked after the Pharaoh, it was good to spend a few minutes with his friend.

Merneith was an excellent replacement for the treacherous Chief Physician. And more than an adequate one— her skill made the Pharaoh wish she had been his first and only doctor. Her gnarled, wrinkled old hands softly patting him, her gravelly old voice explaining so gently what she was about to do, made him miss Grandmother Tiye, and dear Hetepheres, all over again.

But she was different. Different from the other doctors; different from any other Egyptian Tut had met. She mixed herbal preparations for him, but she didn't apply them with elaborate prayers to Ra or any other of the gods his people worshiped. If faith and medicine intersected for her at all, it was in a quiet moment, a brief bowing of her old gray head as if in simple gratitude for the existence of herbs with such healing properties. He wondered what she believed.

Semerkhet watched Merneith carefully. But her hands were gentle as she touched his Master and friend, and her smile was warm. And of course, she had already saved his life, by identifying the peach-pit poison the doctor had been giving the Pharaoh. Not to mention the fact that she had raised Meresankh. All in all, she seemed perfectly sweet; perfectly trustworthy.

And the valet let out his breath and let her help.

Ankhesenamun blinked as she heard a knock on the door that afternoon. Tutankhamun was sitting up in bed, perusing a papyrus on the history of Egypt's economic relationship with Mycenae. Semerkhet set the cat on the bed and went to answer the door.

"Presenting Rekhetre and Beket, handmaidens of Mutnedjmet and Amenia," he said, welcoming them with a bow.

Two neatly-dressed handmaidens in matching uniforms of flowing white dresses with elbow-length sleeves, simple green belts, and identical collar-necklaces of alternating rows of blue and white beads slowly stepped into the room. Silently, they looked around very appreciatively, staying at the very edge of the room, barely inside the door. Then they remembered to bow, bending deeply from the waist in perfect synchrony. They were twin sisters, after all.

"Hail to thee, Lord of the Two Lands; all life, prosperity, and health," they said at once. "We have brought gifts from our mistresses." They brought out a few baskets they had carried in, opening them to reveal a variety of treats. "Homemade honey-cakes," Rekhetre said, setting them on the bedside table, "tea," Beket said, setting a small linen bag beside the plate, "and some pillows." Two large, fluffy pillows found their way to an empty chair.

"They send their best wishes, these gifts, and these letters," Rekhetre said, handing Ankhesenamun two sheets of papyrus. She accepted them with a smile.

"Please thank your mistresses for their kind gifts," Tutankhamun said with a grateful nod. "Thank you for bringing them."

The handmaidens bowed again, the braids of their identical shoulder-length wigs falling in front of their faces, then stood quietly with their hands folded, waiting to be dismissed. Only occasionally did they allow their eyes to flicker to the face of either the King or the Queen.

"We're so grateful to know we're being thought of," the Queen said with a smile. She also nodded at them, putting a very gentle invitation for them to be on their way into her smile.

They got it. The sisters bowed for a third time, then chorused, "All life, prosperity, and health," and saw themselves out.

Ankh smiled, her heart warming as she thought of Mutnedjmet and Amenia packing those baskets, thinking of her and Tut. How nice to know that even though they hadn't seen one another in weeks, the ladies were thinking of them.

But then her heart sank slightly. Meryt had not sent anything. Not that she demanded that the Treasurer's wife should send a gift, but it was sad to think why Meryt had not chosen to reach out to her. Sad to think that the Queen's consciousness-raising had not opened her heart the same way it had opened Amenia's and Mutnedjmet's. Sad to think that Meryt was still trapped in her self-imposed prison of seeing herself as an extension of her husband, holding a disappointing baby girl while watching a disappointing five-year-old daughter struggling to play in a starched dress. Repeating to herself that she was a failure for not bearing her husband sons; that it was her fault that she had not given her husband a reason to pay attention to her.

But the Queen had done her best; had provided Meryt with exactly the same information and encouragement as she had given to Amenia and Mutnedjmet. It was up to Meryt to decide what to do with it. What she did with the rest of her life was her choice.

Tutankhamun was appreciatively examining the gifts; squeezing the soft pillows and smelling the honey-cakes and the tea.

"Those look good," he said with a smile. "I think I might actually be hungry."

Ankh put her arm around his shoulders and kissed his head. "I think that was the point. You have as many as you like."

Semerkhet took one, pinching off a tiny crumb, tasting it, and declaring the gift free of poison. And Ankh sat back and smiled as her brother polished them off, saving one each for her and Semerkhet.

The Queen read the sweet notes from her friends and smiled. They said they missed her and wanted her to know that they were thinking of her, praying for her. Whatever harm their husbands may have done, they were true friends.

As he thought about Raherka's interrupted betrayal, a question occurred to the Pharaoh.

"Sem," he said, "Do you suppose the average servants know that Ay doesn't support me… is working against me? Do they even know they have a choice as to who to be loyal to?"

Semerkhet shrugged. "Most of them are born into their jobs, and whether or not the palace is a 'fun' place to work, and even if they're afraid of running into you, they're proud to be honoring you through the work they do. And they're very grateful to have a safe place to work, and to have room, board, and meals. Even… even on a rough day, they can still think to themselves, 'I could be a fisherman!'"

"I don't think they really think about you a lot, and sometimes they might kind of forget about the impact of their job, but it's the best place they could possibly ask to work, even if it is sometimes a little scary. Because like I said... oh, a long time ago now, it's like the magic fountain that flows up instead of down. Everyone contributes to everything. But I would imagine that for most of them, they see you and the Vizier as the same, and they just keep their heads down and do everything they can to look after you and him."

Semerkhet sighed. "So, all that to say, no, I wouldn't think more than a handful of them know what... what happened, and I doubt many of them even know you and the Vizier are at odds. They're... just doing their jobs, like they always have, always will. Whatever happens up at the top. And they're just glad to be part of it."

Tut shook his head. What a simple life. And yet, what a way to live, never questioning anything.

He would have taken his personal involvement in Kadesh back in a heartbeat. But he was glad beyond measure for everything he had learned over the past few months.

When Semerkhet took an hour to sit with the Pharaoh, sometimes the Queen would invite Meresankh into her private sitting room. And they would continue studying history together.

Meresankh knew of Pharaoh Smenkhkare, of course; her Lady's own mother, and of Queen Meritaten, Ankhesenamun's eldest sister, who had served as Queen during her mother's reign as Pharaoh. And she knew about Hatshepsut. She had a vague idea of the accomplishments of Ahmose-Nefertari, and she had heard of Sobekneferu. But the others were new to her; Khentkaus the First and Second, Iput, Nimaathap.

Meresankh sat up a little straighter as Ankhesenamun told their stories to her; shared the legacy of all the women who had gone before. Inspiration was stirring in her heart; thoughts of what she could do with her life one day. Of course... of course, she was happy here, and she would truly be happy to stay here, working for the Queen who was now her best friend, for as long as she was needed. But her heart told her that that would not be forever. And that an unknown future lay ahead of them.

And yet, at the same time, these old stories of powerful Regent-Queens and female Pharaohs told her that that future was hers.

Sem no longer had his horse races, his hockey games, to sustain him. He had turned away from all of that— everything that wasn't necessary; that kept him away from his Pharaoh. It made his heart ache to leave those things behind. But it ached even worse to imagine wasting even one moment by spending it apart from his friend.

"I'm sorry for Rekhetre, really," Meresankh said as she put away the jewelry she'd been cleaning.

Ankh looked up from the historical papyrus she'd been reading. "Hmm?"

Meresankh shook her head sadly. "She's had the worst indigestion the past day or two. She really should take some cumin."

"Is that right?" the Queen said. "You'll have to give her some advice. I know you've learned a lot from Merneith."

"I love it," Meresankh said. "Herbs. I haven't…" She paused, then went on with a little smile. "I haven't followed her as a midwife, but she has taught me my herbs. And I…" She chuckled. "I look at my friends, their sniffles or aches and pains, and I know what herbs they need."

Ankhesenamun smiled. "Well, maybe you should write them some prescriptions… my dear physician."

Meresankh just grinned.

There were always flowers. Every day or two, Tut's sister brought him a bouquet, brightening up the room and making him smile. They were just a gesture, really. But the flowers his sister brought him always made Tut feel a little better… made him feel loved.

And Semerkhet played his lute. Every now and then, he would get it out, and Tut would close his eyes and listen as his friend played music, rambling medleys of folk songs, marching songs, love ballads, lullabies, and wistful improvisation. It was beautiful. And it truly, truly helped to pass the time.

The Queen thought of the letter she had prepared; the letter that might change history. It was waiting among her things, waiting to be fired into the future like an arrow from a bow. But for everything that remained to be seen, she had peace. To send the letter was the right thing to do. And she would know when the time was right to send it.

Semerkhet sighed as he watched the King pet his cat that evening, cooing over her like a father with his baby. His own knee was almost better, a rather impressive scar forming where the injury had been, and his bruises faded more every day. But his Master was still bedridden with two broken legs, infection, and ague... and getting worse every day. Sem tried not to feel guilty for getting better. Just as he had tried not to feel guilty for not dying in Kadesh; not being killed by the poisoned wine. And he tried to pray. Whether or not it would make any difference.

Was Anyone up there at all? Sometimes he would wonder for a moment, if maybe they were alone in the cosmos, no Divine there at all to love them and listen to their prayers. Maybe they really were alone.

But then he would remember the way the Sun had felt on his face out in the courtyard on that one beautiful day, and he would know that they were not.

Tut slept at odd times. Slept when he could. He might nap through the morning, and drift off again at dinnertime, only to spend the dark watches of the night staring into space, struggling to get comfortable amid broken bones, a rising fever, and aches and pains. Although the nights were getting colder week by week, he was not finding that how many blankets he needed consistently corresponded with the dropping temperatures— the fever threw heat and cold into a havoc. Two or three days and nights out of each week were spent in the pure torture of raging fever and agonizing chills; the rest of the week was merely unpleasant.

He fought with his blankets as he alternated between being too hot and too cold, sometimes weeping to himself as the weight of the world threatened to crush him, tempted to wake one of them up and ask them to sit up with him but trying to be strong, wait it out, give himself a chance to fall asleep himself. It did not always work.

Better were the nights when he'd had a tiny bit of energy during the day, avoided napping, and gotten himself genuinely tired, when Ankh or Sem would see to his dressings and fix him a nice cup of chamomile tea right after dinner, early enough that it had a chance to work. And one of them would hum a lullaby or whisper a bedtime story, slowly soothing him to sleep. Those were the nights when the King knew that he would sleep at least for a few solid hours.

He was so loved.

The Pharaoh looked down at the piece of papyrus Ay's secretary had delivered to him earlier that morning, the morning of the twenty-seventh of Sholiak.

Approved shipment of limestone for school, it said. *Approved hiring of fifty laborers for school.*

He smiled as he stamped it with his signet-ring, putting it into motion. And yet, he wondered. Because he knew Ay could not be trusted.

"My Lady?"

Ankhesenamun looked up from her cup of tea. She was spending a quiet moment in her room, and now Meresankh stood in the doorway, a question on her face.

"Yes?"

The handmaiden sighed, some sort of trouble darkening her face. "I was out in town early this morning," she said a little sadly, "and I heard something."

The Queen took a sip of tea. "What did you hear?"

"I was walking by the building site, of one of the new schools, and I heard someone say that the latest shipment of limestone for the building had been indefinitely delayed, so the whole project might have to be put on hold. Someone even mentioned layoffs."

Ankh sighed. Ay had struck again.

"Thank you," she said with a sad, but grateful, little smile. "We'll take care of it."

35

Possibilities

"I have some questions about your latest report," Tut was saying a few minutes later, handing the Vizier's handwritten papyrus back to him, stamped with the royal seal.

"What questions, Glorious Lord?" Ay asked, looking genuinely curious, actually concerned. What a good actor he was.

"I understand that you approved the delivery of a shipment of limestone for the building, but that it has been indefinitely delayed, and that layoffs might be coming," the Pharaoh said. "Although there's no mention of any of that in the report you prepared. Do you know anything about the delay?"

The Vizier swallowed, looking down at his old hands, folded in front of him.

"The... days are getting colder, O King for Whom the Sun Shines, and I feared that sending the necessary teams of men and oxen to transport the stone would endanger their health," he said, not meeting the Pharaoh's eye.

"Hmm," Tut said. He let the thunder rumble behind his eyes, dark eyebrows growing stern. And he became quite frank. "Stop falsifying your reports, Vizier," he said. "I have eyes and ears all over the palace, and I see what decisions you make, whatever you put in your reports to me. And with my signet-ring, I am the only one who can approve them, anyway. Don't try to trick the Morning and the Evening Star."

The Vizier swallowed. And, after seeming to cast about him for something to say, he completely changed the subject.

"Your leg looks better today, Lord of Perfect Laws," he said, glancing at the Pharaoh's freshly-rebandaged leg. He looked at it again, pausing in what might have been confusion.

Tut smiled. Ay had noticed the fresh, clean bandages that Merneith had wrapped around what remained of his leg after gently cleaning it and applying a soothing poultice of lavender and rosemary.

Should he do it? It was only fair; Ay had to find out at some point that he had lost a battle. He looked up at his Vizier. "That was the other thing I wanted to let you know... I've made some... adjustments to the royal medical team. I've fired the Chief Physician and banished him from Memphis. He's been officially replaced by Lady Merneith the midwife, who's been taking much better care of my leg." The Pharaoh nodded at the fresh bandages. Then, with a sweet smile, he showed Ay the document proclaiming the latest royal decision. "I just couldn't keep him around after he'd betrayed me by poisoning me and then trying to let the infection kill me... on your orders. I suppose now, his son will never have the chance to become your Vizier, but that's just too bad, isn't it?" He shook his head. "Too bad that you apparently think that trying to kill me is in the best interests of the future of Egypt."

The Vizier had no answer. But his eyes lingered on the Pharaoh's signet-ring for a moment. Then, with a bow and an insincere wish for Tut's life, prosperity, and health, he was gone.

"What would happen," Ankhesenamun asked her brother, "if I don't marry the Prince?"

Tut looked up at her from his cup of tea. "What do you mean?" he asked. He knew he could speak freely; before sitting down beside him, his sister had carefully locked the door.

Ankh sighed, looking out the window. "I mean, what would happen? Could I... could I become Pharaoh?"

Tut smiled. "You'd be a good one."

The Queen nodded, heart warming at the compliment. And she continued to think.

Again, she nodded toward the window and the bustling city outside it. "What happens… what happens to a regular citizen who loses her husband? What are her options? Widows in Memphis and Thebes can buy and sell property, and many of them live independently, make their own choices, run their own lives, even without a husband. And I know…" She looked down at her hands, folded in her lap. "I know I could do the same. I have the ability."

Her brother nodded. "Yes, you do."

Ankh sighed. "But would I be allowed to? As Queen, do I have less freedom than the women of Thebes and Memphis; less right to live my life as an independent person?"

Tut just shook his head.

The Queen nodded. "It's like I was telling Meresankh. The only hope for the future of Egypt is for me to remarry."

The Pharaoh sighed, reaching out to take his sister's hand. And Ankh looked down at their hands.

"I love you so much," Ankh continued. "I always have. I always will. It's been… it's been so strange, this 'marriage' we've shared. But I love you," she said, "and you love me, and we've made it work. But we never…" She paused. "We never had the chance to meet anyone else. Never had the chance to 'fall in love' like Meresankh and Semerkhet. From the moment you were born, we were going to be married. For our dynasty. It was our… destiny."

Tut coughed. And Ankh refilled his cup with peppermint tea and helped him drink it. And as he sipped it, she continued to think.

Real romance, like she had once dreamed of, had never been part of their relationship. Even in their union… the complete and perfect closeness they found in one another's arms, the connection of body and soul, part of her was still telling her baby brother that it would be all right, because she would take care of him. Something was still missing. They were the Pharaoh and the Great Royal Wife, but was what they had, laughing and crying together as the siblings they had always been, really a marriage?

And their daughters... What would it have been like, watching them grow up? She bit her lip. How would they all have related to one another? How easy would it have been to set aside the fact that while they were Mother and Father to their little girls, they were also Aunt and Uncle?

"Mother and Father made it work," Ankh continued after Tut had finished the tea and she had set the cup aside for him. "And they were cousins. How... how do you suppose they felt about it?"

Tut shook his head. "I never thought about it. But I know they loved one another. And they loved us. We... we were a family."

"We were," Ankhesenamun said. She sighed. "We still are. And if they could do it, so can we. And they did. And so have we.

"I know you love me," Ankh whispered. Her heart ached as the words she was about to speak formed in her heart, but she continued to speak them. "And do you know how I know?"

Her brother smiled up at her, a sweet, tired little smile. A smile she was about to turn into a frown. "How?" he asked.

She took a deep breath. "You never took a second wife." Her voice broke, but she went on. "You loved me too much to take a second wife. You thought... you thought you would be betraying me. So you didn't do it. You had the freedom to do it... but you didn't. You put me... us... our relationship... first. And I know... I know that means... that you love me."

But even with the love, the Queen felt anger rising in her heart. "You loved me too much," she said again, a little more loudly.

He blinked. "How can anyone love too much?"

She shook her head. "You're so sweet... so young... so naïve."

Her brother was looking at her in confusion, wondering why she was insulting him. And she went on.

"Yes, you're naïve," she said, fighting to force the words past the lump that was growing in her throat. "Too naïve to even consider my suggestion to bring in new blood to make sure that Egypt had an heir.

Too... too focused on one person, me, your wife, your sister, your... your mother, half the time, to do what was right for Egypt. And you were so desperate to prove yourself as some sort of strong Pharaoh, so bent on making Egypt the rescuer of the known world, that you'd throw away everything and march off to Kadesh without thinking twice to fight the Mitanni's war for them. If you... if you were a politician, what would things look like now?"

He was staring at her in horror, but she didn't stop. She continued pouring out the angry words that filled her heart; that had been crammed inside it for far too long.

"We've always— we've always been a team. So what changed? I told you not to go! But you didn't listen. And I told you to take a second wife. If you had a son, maybe you would have stayed home to be with him; raise the heir you could have right now if you weren't so selfish. And maybe we could have saved your life if you'd agreed when Merneith told you to have your leg amputated." She shook her head, angry tears shining in her eyes. "None of this is what I wanted. I'm sorry, but I just have to tell you how I feel. It just makes me so angry. Why didn't you listen? All this happened because you didn't listen."

She sighed, feeling the anger slowly beginning to dissipate. "But it all did happen. And now... now we have to figure out what we *can* control. Keep taking care of you; keep managing all the politics that comes our way. And face the future that comes."

Ankh stopped, looking at him to see how her words had landed. He was gazing up at her silently, one tear running down each cheek.

"You're all I have," he whispered simply.

The Queen gave a heavy sigh, shaking her head. "We couldn't have known what was coming. We couldn't. We were both young... both naïve. And I... I love that you love me. And I'm so... so honored that you would put me first. And you... you're all I have, too."

"All I have," Tut said, squeezing her hand, "and all I need."

"But as Queen," Ankh continued, "I couldn't have taken a secondary husband, like you could have taken a secondary wife. And now..." She bit her lip. "Now I'm the one making that choice. Now I'm the one who has to take another spouse for the sake of carrying on the dynasty."

Her brother sighed. And she knew that he understood that it was because of his choices that she was being forced into this decision.

She shook her head, beads jingling. "If we had been older... if we had been looking... if we had known what to look for... could we have read the signs? All the way back to when Father and Mother died, with the nettles and the horse, then Meritaten of ague in the wrong season, and later on, Pentu dying the same way as Meritaten, all the way to the Vizier telling you that you could fight, taking what he knew you wanted most and using it to hurt you. Could we have read those signs? And could things have gone differently?"

Tut closed his eyes with a heavy sigh. And two more tears trickled down his cheeks. "It's my fault," he whispered, his voice breaking this time. "This whole thing. All my fault."

And as he began to cry properly, Ankh felt her remaining anger melt away. She got up from her chair, climbing up onto the bed to sit beside her brother and gently wipe away his tears. And as she wiped them away, she continued to speak.

"But you... you have so many good qualities. So many noble qualities. And those are the qualities that have always guided your decisions. You're young, yes, and innocent, and no one can be born wise, but you're... you're idealistic and altruistic and generous and hopeful... you're compassionate and courageous and wise, and you have the biggest heart of anyone I've ever known. You're not selfish. And you *are* a politician. You lowered taxes, built schools, saved your best friend from certain death. And you..."

Again, Ankh blinked back tears, fighting back the lump in her throat. "You are so loving. And you... you cared about the Mitanni so much that you risked your life for them. And you..." She looked down at the stick-thin legs, lying broken and feverish under the blankets. "You gave your life for them. They're safe now, thanks to you. Whatev... whatever you do, you do it out of a loving heart."

She sighed. "And of course you wanted to prove yourself... they'd hammered into you that the only way to be a strong Pharaoh was to be a warrior. And I suppose..." Now she chuckled, and Tut's eyes brightened as he saw the end of this heavy conversation shining in the distance, "I suppose I can forgive you for loving me so much that you never wanted to marry anyone else."

He shrugged, returning the chuckle. "Why would I?" he asked, as he had so many times. "You're the perfect Queen."

She just scooted closer, wrapping him in a gentle hug and kissing him on the forehead.

"And I... I didn't think it was a decision that had to be made right away," Tut continued, wiping his eyes. "I thought we had all the time in the world."

The Queen sighed with half a sad smile. "So did I. So did I."

He didn't say any more. Just closed his eyes and cuddled closer.

Ankh went for a walk. And Tut lay there in bed, pressing his hands into his eyes, then rolling over as best he could to find a hanky. And he wiped away the tears that were still there. Her words had stung his heart. But they had been true. Good and bad, they had all been true.

He swallowed back what was left of the lump in his throat, then put his arm around Bastet, who had sensed that she was needed. Had he really been such a terrible husband? Such a naïve Pharaoh? Had he really hurt his sister so much? He clutched the hanky, fighting back more tears. Was this succession crisis really his fault? Was the war? And was the fact that Ankh had missed out on so much in her life his fault?

Tut blinked. No, that one wasn't his fault. As she had reminded him, it was the Pharaoh who had the opportunity to enter into as many marriages as he wanted to all at once, not the Queen. So, thanks to age-old traditions, that had not been among his sister's options, whatever he had done right or wrong. Maybe it wasn't fair, but it wasn't his doing.

He was the one who had chosen not to select a second wife. So that was on him. But... but as she had reminded him, he had made that decision, just like his decision to help the Mitanni at whatever cost, out of love.

And it was not wrong to be loving.

36

Hope

"What will your first act as Pharaoh be?" Tutankhamun asked his sister as he sat in his chair that long, weary afternoon, playing *seega* with her. The air had cleared between them, and they were ready to return to the easy familiarity of brother and sister. And again, Tut had gotten Kamose and Sem to move him to his chair.

Ankh shook her head, considering her next move... in the game, and in her own life. She bit her lip. Not something she really, truly wanted for herself. But something that needed to be considered.

"Well..." she said, pondering, "I think we've made excellent progress with taxes, and with the budget in general. And the schools are underway..." She sighed, looking off into the future. A future where she would be able to make Egypt a better and better place to live... but a future she would be walking through without her brother by her side. "More jobs," she said finally. "I'll make it a point to encourage women to open small businesses and hire other women. And as people start to see the impact of education being available to everyone, we... I... will be able to open more and more schools."

She swallowed, looking at her brother's thin face, his bony hands. How much weight had he lost since his injury, she wondered. He had never been heavy, but now, he was definitely too thin. "And Egypt's trade with Hattusa will get stronger and stronger, and we'll send people to study at one another's schools, send doctors to one another to share knowledge... after all, we'll be one country. And no... and no little girl will have to wander around town in rags with nothing but a doll for company. Every child will go to bed with a full belly and know that their dreams of what they want to be when they grow up can come true."

She swallowed again, her hand pausing over the gameboard. What a glorious future... but one they were only discussing in such detail because the current Pharaoh would not be around to lead them much longer. Then she gave a little smile, choosing her move. "Poverty will continue to drop as education continues to rise. And before we know it, no one will have to live in a little mud hut."

Tut smiled, sitting there playing a game with his sister as she told him her plans. When she became Pharaoh, even if it was technically from beside the throne, she would lead Egypt into its greatest Golden Age yet.

But in the meantime, they would share this moment of simple fun... playing *seega*.

He trusted her, Ankhesenamun thought as she watched her brother win a game of *seega*. Trusted that she would take good care of their country after he... was gone. She sighed, carefully setting the board up for another game. She had no doubts as to her abilities... but she hoped that politics... and other politicians... would not prevent her from her fulfilling her goals. Their goals.

But that was in the future. This was right now. And right now... they were having together time, sharing laughter, sharing fun. The future would be here soon enough.

Ankhesenamun closed her eyes as her handmaiden gently traced her eyes with kohl, touching up her look. Even with everything that had happened, everything that had changed, it was important; important to look the part, important to feel like a Queen. And as she sat, feeling the tiny tool accentuating her best feature, she listened.

"And so, little old Hori was carrying this big basket of fruit from the kitchens to the royal feasting hall, and you know how old he is, and he almost tripped over Nuya, 'cause Nuya wasn't looking where he was going, and Semerkhet jumped in and caught Hori's arm before he could go flying. And Nuya was really sorry, of course, and he said he'd be more careful, but everybody was fine, and that's what's important, but Sem was the one who saved Hori; just think what would have happened if he hadn't been there; somebody might have gotten a broken bone!"

The Queen just nodded with a little smile. Her sweet chatterbox of a friend was most certainly in love. And it was beautiful to watch.

It was time for his friend to know. Even if they themselves weren't sure, it was time for the Pharaoh to tell his valet that one day soon, he might be an uncle. The Queen had told her handmaiden, after all, so it was only fair for Tut to tell his valet.

"Sem," he said quietly. Semerkhet looked up from arranging a fresh bouquet of flowers on one of the tables in the bedroom.

"Yes, Master?" he asked, approaching the bed.

"Sit down," Tut said, nodding at the chair. Sem settled into it, looking earnestly at his Pharaoh.

"What is it?" he asked at his Master's obvious excitement.

"Semerkhet..." Tut began with a little chuckle. How to tell him? "How many nieces and nephews do you have?"

Sem glanced at the Pharaoh's face, silently assessing his mood; how cautious he needed to be. He swallowed. And then, because his friend had been the one to raise the subject, he answered. "Just one little nephew, my sister's baby," he said with a smile. "Little Ahmose."

"And are you a... a good uncle?" Tut asked.

Semerkhet shrugged. "Well, I haven't seen him very many times, but I do my best." He chuckled. "I'm sure that as he gets bigger, we can spend more time together; do more things together. Little kids do tend to get more interesting once they're old enough to play catch."

Tutankhamun chuckled. "How would you like another little niece or nephew?"

The valet's eyes grew wide as what the Pharaoh was saying hit him. He gave a breathy laugh of sheer surprise. "You mean—"

"We're not sure yet," Tut said with a toothy grin, "but we... we hope so. Our... our dynasty might not be over yet."

"When?" Semerkhet asked with a chuckle, then bit his lip as he blushed. "The day with the Do Not Disturb sign?"

Tut elbowed him playfully with a wink. "We're very glad you made that sign."

And the two of them just looked at one another in silent excitement.

Now Tutankhamun swallowed, a hint of sadness creeping into his face. "I'm going to need you to be a good uncle. Because I won't be here."

Semerkhet bowed his head. He knew his friend spoke the truth. Even if, glory be to the Light Whose warmth he had felt in his heart on the way home from Kadesh, it was true, his Pharaoh would be gone and buried before those nine months were complete.

He looked up and nodded. "I promise. I... We'll tell your story every day. Meresankh and I. We'll... we'll be a good aunt and uncle. No matter what happens. And I'll... I'll make sure it knows everything— our hunting trip, Tribute Day, playing *seega*, everything. Everything."

Tutankhamun reached out and squeezed his friend's hand, looking up at him earnestly. "Thank you, Sem. We haven't told the world... but we will soon. The Queen told Meresankh, and she'll tell the midwife."

"I won't say anything," Semerkhet promised, shaking his head so his braids swung. "So..." he asked, tapping his chin, "how long does it take to be sure, anyway? My sister didn't tell us until she had started to show and we were all wondering."

"And the Queen," Tut said, and Semerkhet bowed his head again as the Pharaoh spoke of the infant Princesses, "I remember that it was several weeks between her first saying that she thought she might be and saying that she definitely was. But I'll admit that I don't know exactly how long it takes to know. I'll have to ask her."

Semerkhet nodded, reaching out to briefly pat the Pharaoh's arm. Then he smiled again. "Another niece or nephew."

And there was nothing to do but smile together.

The Queen smiled to think of Meresankh checking up on her fellow staff members, diagnosing the source of their aches or pains and skillfully preparing a remedy that would fix them up. She had so much love to give. And the effects of her expert care would ripple out into the universe.

Ankh watched her brother sleep, dozing with the cat curled up at his side. And she remembered. Remembered how much he had grown up over the past year.

She closed her eyes. She was proud of him. And so much of his growth made her smile. But there were things... that had been hard. Like... like letting him have a friend. That sounded terrible, even inside her mind, but she let the thought play out. Semerkhet had come into her brother's life nearly a year ago, and had been Tut's first true friend of his own age. And she was happy that her brother had a friend. Except... Ankhesenamun shook her head, chuckling as she remembered things that had bothered her all those weeks and months ago; things she would welcome now.

She remembered how Tut's earnest chattering about his friend, "Sem says this; Sem says that," had made her grit her teeth in aggravation; remembered how the sudden arrival of someone else with whom she had to share her brother's time and affection; someone else who was stepping up to teach her brother— when she was his teacher; she always had been— had rankled her. And she remembered the disapproval with which she had told Tut, when he had staggered dirty and sweaty back into the palace after taking a chariot joyride with Sem, that while he'd been out "playing boy sports," she had been inside taking care of palace duties.

She remembered. And she wished, how she wished, that she could have those days back.

Semerkhet saw Meresankh that night at dinner, making up a plate of mutton, lentils, and a little pile of pomegranate pips. And he beckoned to her.

"What?" she whispered as he took her by the hand, leading her to a quiet corner of the dining hall, away from the merry gossip of the other servants.

He smiled down at her. "Now I know what you're so excited about. The Pharaoh... the Pharaoh told me."

Meresankh grinned up at him. She knew what he meant. "It wasn't my secret to tell," she whispered back. Setting her plate down on a nearby table, she put her arms around him. "I'm so excited for them! And I'm praying... praying so hard."

Semerkhet held her close. "So am I."

The Queen watched Semerkhet test Tutankhamun's dinner of flatbread and lentil soup. "I taste your food, Son of Ra, and if there be harm in it, let the harm fall upon me." Sem took a bite of soup, then tasted the bread. And when he had confirmed that they were safe, he handed them to the Pharaoh, who, today, was feeling strong enough to feed himself.

Ankh looked down at her own meal, which was the same as her brother's. Semerkhet had brought them both at the same time, so there was no reason to worry. But still... She took a bite, knowing that this time, she was safe. But as the vultures circled her, trying to snatch her up in their claws and claim her as their bride, she wondered. If she refused them all, this powerful Queen who made those courtiers shake with fear as they imagined what she would do standing alone, would marriage proposals become threats on her life?

She put her hand on her stomach, fighting back panic. If her prayers had been answered, a threat on... *their lives.* A double murder would remove both a powerful Queen and the heir to the throne from the scenario.

But it wasn't something to talk to Tut about. He was tired, and he needed to save his strength. And he wouldn't want to even consider the fact that she might be right; he would only tell her not to worry, because that would never happen. She took a deep breath, imagining the nausea, dizziness, and lightheadedness of peach-pit poisoning. She wouldn't mention it to him. After all, it was... just politics. She knew what she needed to do.

"Meresankh," the Queen said as she headed into her room for a short early-evening break.

"Yes, My Lady?" she asked. There was so little to do these days, tidying up the Queen's practically unused room. So to pass the time, she had been arranging and rearranging the many pairs of shoes in her Lady's storage room.

"I'm thinking... about politics," Ankh said slowly.

Meresankh looked up. "What's going on?" she asked with a little frown.

"I'm worried," the Queen said with a heavy sigh, "about... poison."

Her handmaiden gasped, rushing to the Queen's side and taking her pulse with one hand, the other flying up to gently touch her forehead. "What symptoms are you having? I'll go get Granny—"

"No, I don't think I've *been* poisoned," Ankh said, taking Meresankh's hand to stop her from flying out the door. "I'm just worried... that if I refuse to marry any of these traitors, they might see no way to get me under control other than to..." She looked down at her hands.

Meresankh gave a deep sigh, panic fading. No one was going to die today. She straightened her shoulders, looking bravely up at the Queen.

"I'll test your food," she said softly. "Like Sem tests our Pharaoh's."

Ankhesenamun shook her head with a grateful little smile, blue beads of her wig tinkling. "No, no. I wouldn't ask you to do that. Actually, I was wondering... if you could cook for me."

Meresankh's eyebrows rose. "Cook for you, My Lady?"

"Yes. Then I would know the food was clean. You're one of the only ones I can still trust. So if you're making my meals, or bringing me food from the staff meals, then I'll know... I'm safe." She patted her belly. "I'll know... *we're* safe."

Meresankh stood thinking. Then a little smile came to her face, and she looked up at her Queen. "Granny did teach me a really good recipe for spicy chicken."

Ankh stepped forward and opened her arms, giving her handmaiden a gentle hug. "Thank you, sister."

37

The Last Game

The Pharaoh thought of Prince Zannanza as the warm light of the sunset filtered through the linen curtains of his bedroom window. Was he tall, was he short, was he muscular, was he weedy? Did he have a finely-styled beard that he looked after with all the attention that Tut had always paid to his wigs?

The Pharaoh sighed, imagining a generic Hittite, whose peach-pale face he couldn't see clearly but whose brown beard was quite magnificent. And he thought of what he would say to him.

You'd better take care of my sister, you barbarian. You'd better take care of my beloved wife. Don't you dare let her down. And you'd better respect her. She's the politician; not you. All you are is the figurehead. The only reason she's marrying you is to stay in charge as Queen. So you'd best understand that she's going to be making the decisions, not you. Let her run. Believe me, it works best that way. And you'd better...

Tut gave a heavy sigh. Because... in his imagination, seeing her standing beside the vague image of the Hittite, Tutankhamun saw that his sister's belly was gently, sweetly curved, a young life growing strong inside her. That was the other reason she had to choose a second husband.

"What should we call the child?" he whispered as his sister sat down with him again. Night had fallen, and the dim room was lit with the cozy glow of oil-lamps.

"If it's a girl, *Meritsenmut*," Ankh whispered. *"Beloved of her mother's brother.* Or if it's a boy, *Tutsenmut. Image of his mother's brother."*

Tut closed his eyes with a little smile. If the Queen had another child, whether of his seed or Zannanza's, even though it would be raised by the Hittite Prince and call him *Father*, it would be named after him.

Then he bit his lip, feeling angry tears springing to his eyes and a painful lump building in his throat. "I don't... don't want you to marry him," he moaned, clenching his fists so his fingernails bit into his palms. "I remember when you said that if I chose a second wife you would try not to be jealous... now you're the one who's getting married again... I don't want to let you go..."

Ankh lay down beside him, helping him roll onto his side to rest his head on her heart, holding him tight. His big sister. His wife. The only woman he had ever loved.

She held him tight as he sniffled, fighting back tears. Could she tell him, truly, that she didn't want to marry Zannanza? She didn't know yet. But she knew she didn't want her brother to die.

"What can we change?" she whispered, stroking his head, his shaking back. "And what do we have to go through?"

Tut nestled into her heart, feeling her warm arms encircling him, her soft, small strength, her wisdom. Her braids tickled him as she bent her head, whispering into his ear. "You're my husband, my brother, my friend, my Pharaoh, my sun, my moon." He tried to smile as her words warmed his heart. "And I'll tell your story every day."

The Pharaoh looked up at his sister, holding him close. "I want you to be happy," he whispered. "But I don't want to lose you."

"You never will," she whispered, and he heard her heart beating. "You will always be in my heart."

He sighed with a sad little smile. "And you will always be in mine." He shook his head. "If I can let you go... there's nothing I can't do."

Ankh returned the smile. "You are the strongest person I know."

Tutankhamun closed his eyes, feeling warm and safe and loved, just like he always did in his sister's arms. Even if the day would come when he was no longer there for her to hold. Even if the day would come when she would be the one lying in the arms of the Prince who would allow her to remain in power and continue her dynasty. And he knew that even if she and Zannanza never had children, Ankh was strong enough to get through. Whatever happened, she would devise a way of dealing with it. Like she always did, always had. And even if Zannanza was distant, and not the husband he should be, Tut knew that she would be all right. She was the strongest person he knew.

And even if she and Zannanza were happy together, and had ten strong, beautiful children, Ankh would never forget him. And their love would last forever.

Ankhesenamun got up to look out the window; to pet Bastet, who was wondering where all the ants had gone. And as he lay there in bed, Tutankhamun thought of the one whose betrayal had landed him in this bed of death.

"I trusted him," he whispered bitterly.

"Ay?" the Queen asked as she sat down in the chair beside the bed. He meant either the Vizier or the General.

"Ay," he spat. "If there was one person in the world I should have been able to trust, it was him. And look what happened. Betrayed me; sent me off to die. He was... he was family. Only grandparent, only parent I had left. Thought I could depend on him. Thought he would protect me. Thought... thought he loved me. And I thought Horemheb did, too. Taught me so much; made me a soldier. And I thought he was my friend." He shook his head. "So much for trust."

Ankh just shook her head, eyes downcast. She knew the political game all too well.

"Really," he continued, his voice becoming choked and his lisp taking over as the words rushed out. "How could he? Ay promithed Mother and Father he'd keep uth thafe. And he... I mean, he taught me tho much; we thpent all thothe hourth thtudying hithtory... the two of you made me what I am. He taught me the information, and you taught me how to apply it. But then everything changed... my birthday... Kadesh... the doctor... And he... You're the politician; tell me why he did it! And Horemheb— how could he? How could he?"

The Queen took her brother's hand, holding it tightly. And she bowed her head as she thought.

"Greed," she said finally. "And fear. A greed that makes the Vizier hate our policies; want to go back to slavery, poor wages, no education. And fear... fear of us, and of what we might accomplish. It was fear..." His sister paused, looking down at their entwined hands. "He killed Meritaten because he was afraid. And he killed Mother and Father because he was afraid. Afraid of what kind of Pharaoh you would grow up to be with them guiding you." She swallowed. "And Horemheb... he's a leader... but he's not a Pharaoh. And the Vizier convinced him that you... were not a Pharaoh whose priorities were in line with his. Convinced him... that your dedication to peace was a sign of weakness. And Horemheb was afraid... of what kind of Pharaoh you would become. And he thought... thought the Vizier was a better option."

"Fear," Tut said. And he sighed, wiping away the angry tears that had gathered in his eyes. "I never thought of it that way. But I see what you mean. We are..." He gave a wry chuckle. "We are pretty terrifying, you and I."

Ankh bent to kiss his forehead, beads clinking. "Yes, we are, my love. Yes, we are."

Semerkhet tried to pray as he lay down to sleep that night. He prayed for his Pharaoh; prayed for his Queen. Prayed for himself, that he would continue easing their burdens as well as he possibly could. And he prayed, with a smile in his heart, for the baby that even now might be growing big and strong inside the Queen's belly.

Another little niece or nephew. What a wonderful thought.

There was a footstep. Tut glanced over his shoulder, then grabbed a random papyrus, hiding his tearstained face behind it, holding his breath so his sobs would not be audible. He didn't want Semerkhet to hear him crying.

"I'm reading," he choked out.

He heard Semerkhet pause, shuffling through a stack of papyri on a table, then adjourn to another part of the suite. And hidden behind a document on the history of the war chariot, Tut let the tears flow.

Every day, he made himself get up. Even as he grew weaker with each passing day, Tut would laboriously sit up, getting an arm around Semerkhet's shoulders and an arm around Kamose or Raherka or Hannu or Amenmose's, letting them slowly, carefully pull him out of bed and lovingly manhandle him into his chair. It was hard. It was painful. Some might argue that it was a poor use of his failing strength. And others might argue that the risk that those moving him might drop him was not worth it.

But he wanted to prove he could still do it. He wanted to see his room from a different angle. He wanted to breathe a little easier; be able to play *seega* without the board being on his stomach. Wanted the sheer hard work of sitting up, the exhaustion of laboriously being moved, to help him get a good night's sleep. He wanted… wanted to know that he had left this world having gotten out of bed every day until he no longer could. Like the strong Pharaoh that he was.

So every day… he sat in his chair.

Even if it was only for a few minutes.

Tut was never very hungry anymore. Not really. He would always eat a bit of what Ankhesenamun or Semerkhet brought him, but not usually more than a few bites. Mostly he subsisted on broth and tea. Nothing, not even his favorites, really tempted his appetite.

It was tiring to take care of him, every day, every night. But what else were they supposed to do?

It felt good to have things they could do; felt good to work. By working hard, working constantly to keep their brother feeling as well as possible, they could fend it off, that unknown future that loomed closer with every day. Like a strong, brick wall, busyness and hard work protected them; protected them from the pain, protected them from thinking about it too much. Because they had a lot to do. And they would do it well.

The future, for good or for ill, would be here soon enough. And until that day, they would keep working hard.

Meresankh could support the Queen; could support Semerkhet. She wasn't directly caring for their Pharaoh, so she wasn't as tired. So that meant she could take care of them; bring them a cup of tea, rub their tired shoulders, listen while they told her about how much harder things were today even as compared with last week. Help them feel better for just a few minutes; get a few minutes of precious rest. Help bear just a little bit of the load that sometimes seemed like it was threatening to crush them. Make them smile for a moment; bring them joy on a bleak day.

Through being a good friend, she could keep them strong so they could keep taking care of their Pharaoh— if she was keeping them strong so they could take care of him, that meant she was contributing to his care, taking care of him herself. And she would walk beside them on this hard road, her sister and her beloved, wherever it would lead them. Maybe she couldn't fix things, but she could be a good friend. And she was proud to be there for them.

The most important thing she could do, of course, was pray. That I-AM would heal their Pharaoh, and that his heart, and the Queen's heart, and Semerkhet's heart, would be opened to the Light. And that I-AM would bless the heir of Egypt with health and strength. And all through the day, each and every day, she did.

Ankhesenamun sighed as she sat in her chair that night, watching her little brother try to sleep, fighting the pain. It was late, but she wasn't drowsy. She had thinking to do.

What an experience they had shared in this "marriage;" this partnership of politics, forged by centuries of tradition. How different from how it might have been.

She thought of Meresankh, laughing, face shining in the breathless glow of finding her first love, her true love. Running merrily through the newness of it; the excitement, the thrill, the mystery. Falling in love with someone who had not been placed at her side in childhood, for reasons of duty, honor, and tradition as old as time. The spark that the Queen and the Pharaoh had never felt.

And she longed for what her handmaiden had found. All the luxury and convenience in the world, and while she was happy for Meresankh, she craved the same love that her handmaiden shared with Sem. Romance was fun for her. So simple. So pure. So… free.

That was what it was. Meresankh was free to love the one her heart chose. The Queen of Egypt was not. She was not even free to meet, free to see, any man who was not the Pharaoh, an already-married member of the royal court, or a palace employee whom she was not expected to view as a real person. Ankh's cage was made of gold, but it was still a cage. But around Meresankh's heart, and around her options, there was no cage. The Queen's handmaiden was free.

And as much as she loved her brother, Ankh wanted that. Wanted to be swept off her feet by someone with different, complementary strengths, rather than yoked alongside someone whose strengths were comfortably familiar, because, as siblings, they matched her own. Wanted to not know what was going to happen next, not know if the object of her affections loved her back; wanted to lie awake nights dreaming of him, treasure every little thing he gave her. To really want to kiss him, more than a peck on the cheek or the forehead. To give her heart without the reason she knew he would take good care of it being the fact that he was her brother.

Wanted passion, not the responsibility to continue their dynasty... partnership, not the partnership of essentially sharing the role of Pharaoh with her figurehead baby brother, but the partnership of husband and wife.

She had a brother. But she did not have a husband. Her whole marriage to Tut had been... just politics.

What if... she wondered, almost feeling guilty for having the thought. What if... she loved Zannanza? What if with him, she found the romantic love she had always dreamed of, but had always been denied? What if with him she found a marriage, rather than a symbolic standing side-by-side with the brother she had known since he was born? And what if... She touched her belly, feeling it ache as she wondered. What if with the Hittite Prince, she had an heir?

What if in losing a brother, she gained a husband? What if she gained the husband with whom she would raise children and watch them grow; the husband with whom she would share the ups and downs of life; the husband with whom she would grow old?

The Queen shook her head, pulling her blanket closer and laying her head back. It was late, and time to set aside those thoughts and sleep. What would happen in her future, and in her heart, remained to be seen.

"How'th your team?" the Pharaoh asked softly one morning.

Semerkhet looked over with a wistful smile, setting aside the papyrus he'd been perusing.

"All right, I imagine," he sighed. "Haven't seen them in awhile." He gave another reflective smile. "There's another big game coming up. Against Per-Bast." He chuckled. "Our big rival."

Tut tried to sit up a little, and Sem perched on the side of the bed so they could have a conversation.

"I want..." Tut began, feeling his heart warming. "I want you to go," he said. Semerkhet gave a little frown, but the Pharaoh continued. "You have to go. Go play, and win. Win for me. And tell me all about it when you get back."

Tutankhamun fell silent, letting his words hang in the air. Semerkhet bit his lip, forehead crinkling in thought. For a moment the Pharaoh's heart sank; of course Sem was going to say *no*. But finally, his friend looked up. And he smiled.

He took Tut's hand for a moment and squeezed it. And he stood up. "I'll win for you, Morning Star," he said.

An hour later, Semerkhet was on his way down to the hockey pitch, uniform on, stick in hand. His team gathered, facing down the yellow-clad team from Per-Bast. And with a shout from the referee, the game was on.

Trapped in his bed, Tutankhamun closed his eyes and listened. He could… could he hear the crowd roaring in the distance? Or was it only his heart cheering for his brother?

Sem played his heart out. Every save, every leap, every dive, every swerve, every move his brother would never see, was dedicated to his friend. Even as he felt a lump building in his throat, and moisture on his face that was not sweat, he played on.

He would make his friend proud.

How were they doing, out there on the field? Tut tried to picture his friend saving goals, leaping, diving, swerving, making it impossible for the team from Per-Bast to beat the Stallions. He closed his eyes again. Yes…he could hear the crowd roaring. He was sure of it.

And it was over. The stands erupted in cheering as the Royal Stallions stood in triumph, blue collars of victory hanging on their necks. Meresankh was out there; Sem could see her in the stands. He was glad that she had seen him win.

His friend who waited back at the palace would be so proud.

"I'm back."

Tut sat up straight as he heard the footstep; heard the familiar voice. And he grinned as a sweaty, dirty, jubilant young man came running into the room, adorned in a shining blue collar-necklace.

Tut opened his arms, and, perching on the edge of the bed, Sem hugged him, dirty as he was, mashing the cold beads of his new necklace into the Pharaoh's collarbone. Letting him go, he sat back, glowing.

"We won," he announced in a triumphant whisper.

Tutankhamun just smiled back, blinking back tears of pride. "Tell me all about it," he whispered. "Every single moment. I want to hear it all."

And as he closed his eyes and listened, Sem told him.

38

Philosophical Differences

The other General came to see the King after the game, just before lunch on the twenty-eighth day of Sholiak. Semerkhet was cleaning up after the game, and Ankh had slipped away to her own room for a few minutes, leaving Hannu standing guard in the hallway. As usual, the son of the Vizier, who posed an annoyance but no threat to the King, plopped down in the nearest available chair without being asked, popping one foot up onto the opposite knee.

"My father says I'll have to fight Horemheb for the throne after he's gone," Nakhtmin drawled, biting into an apple. Flecks of juice went everywhere. "That should be interesting."

"Yes, it should be," the Pharaoh replied. "Be careful, Nakhtmin. Just because he went on a peace mission doesn't mean that he doesn't make a dangerous enemy."

"Bring it on," Nakhtmin said, spreading his sticky hands in welcome. "I'd go toe-to-toe with that old man any time. What's the worst that could happen; have to wait a few more years til he gets killed in a campaign somewhere."

Tutankhamun shook his head. This kid had doomed himself. Someday that bad attitude was going to get him killed. And Tut was sorry for him.

"Just remember..." he said with a little sigh, "politics is a dangerous game." He paused, swallowing. "I learned that from your father."

"The Queen will have to pick one of us," the little General went on, taking another juicy bite of his apple. Slowly, the heavy perfume he always wore was spreading through the air of the bedroom like ink spilled on papyrus. "My father or I. What other choice does she have, if she wants to stay Queen?"

Tutankhamun's heart began to beat a bit faster, anger beginning to cloud his thoughts. Closing his eyes for a moment, he took a deep breath, letting it dissipate. He had a good reason to take offense... but only by being more mature than Nakhtmin would he win; be able to bring him to heel as he had Maya, as he had Horemheb, as he had Nakhtmin's own father. Although, as he had thought before, being more mature than Nakhtmin wasn't really that difficult.

The Pharaoh smiled sweetly at the sticky-faced General. And he dropped his voice to a gentle whisper. "Actually, Nakhtmin... she has quite a few options. She could marry you, I suppose, or your father..." Nakhtmin smiled smugly, but Tut pressed on. "Or General Horemheb or Treasurer Maya." He paused. "Or, she could write to one of our neighboring countries and propose to a Prince. Such as Prince Zannanza of the Hittites. Uniting Egypt with an enemy could strengthen both our countries and eliminate the animosity between us."

Tut smiled. Nakhtmin was listening to him with growing annoyance on his face; annoyance at the fact that the Pharaoh seemed to have thought through this thoroughly and was probably right. Which meant that Nakhtmin was not going to get to marry the pretty little Queen and sit on the throne.

"Or..." Tutankhamun said softly, "maybe she won't marry anyone at all. Maybe she will become Pharaoh and lead Egypt into the greatest Golden Age it has ever seen. Just like Pharaoh Hatshepsut."

He leaned back in bed and folded his arms, looking mildly at Nakhtmin. "So you see, General, the Queen has quite a few options. And you are just one of them."

"I just…" the little General stuttered, "just don't know how a girl is supposed to be King."

Tut chuckled. "Well, I suppose that's another philosophical difference between you and me," he said. "But you might want to look at your recent history. Both my parents were Pharaohs, and my oldest sister was Queen alongside my mother. I have no doubt that Ankhesenamun would be just as great of a King as she has been a Queen. But even if she did marry a Prince and make him Pharaoh, she would still be the one making the decisions. She is the wisest person I know."

"But—" Nakhtmin stuttered— "that's not what a girl is supposed to be."

The Pharaoh chuckled again. "Welcome to the future, Nakhtmin."

The General just took another bite of his apple and scowled. "I don't know what kind of future it's going to be. No slaves, no expansion, building expensive schools and lowering taxes at the same time. Wasting our precious gold on peasants who have been doing just fine as they are for years. Are these schools even necessary— are they really going to make a difference? How do you know what the peasants need to be happy? How do you know they aren't happy right now, with what they have?"

"Because I've seen it, Nakhtmin," Tutankhamun whispered, looking at the General with dark, kohl-lined eyes. He didn't put the thunder into them; he didn't need to. His whisper, and his words, would be enough. "And so has the Queen. We've seen those little mud huts. And we love our people enough to dream of a future where no one has to live like that. One meal can make a difference, Nakhtmin," he said, thinking of that long-ago day when he and the Queen had blessed that little girl with a meal and a shawl. That little girl who they still wondered about. "Imagine what an education can do."

The General just snorted, folding his arms with a huff. "It still seems like a waste… all that time, all those resources, when things are clearly fine the way they are. Why not put that energy to better use; expand our borders, obtain new resources? That would help us restore the economy that's still... struggling. And then we might have enough to think about building schools... or we might realize we don't need to."

Tut smiled. "We love our people more than we love gold, Nakhtmin. Enough to spend our gold on making their lives better. Through creating new jobs, making education available, lowering taxes. The more education people have access to, the better their prospects are, and the better their prospects are, the more the economy will continue to recover. And the happier they are, the better for their government. If people can support themselves, they won't have to beg for bread."

He smiled at Nakhtmin, raising his dark eyebrows. Now he did let just a tiny bit of the thunder rumble, growling softly behind his kohl-lined eyes. "Because no one likes that."

Nakhtmin gave an ugly sneer, his lip curling just like his father's did. He stroked his heavy, beaded necklace, his golden ring gleaming extravagantly in the lamplight, the sleeve of his fine, white tunic rippling. "Maybe my father was right. You and your naïve generosity *are* going to bankrupt the entire country."

Tutankhamun sighed heavily, letting it go. Nakhtmin certainly knew how to get under his skin. But although he reserved the right to do so, the Pharaoh was not going to have him thrown out... or executed. "Well, if you ever get your chance... you'll be the one making those decisions. And maybe you'll do a better job." He smiled sweetly. "We'll just have to see."

Nakhtmin gave a sigh of his own. He knew he was beaten for the time being... but that a crown might still be glimmering in his future. "Yeah... maybe someday we will."

Tut just looked at him placidly. "That remains to be seen."

"Well, I better go," Nakhtmin said, getting up and wiping his sticky hands on his tunic. "My father wanted to talk to me." He gave the Pharaoh a little wave as he left the room, forgetting to shut the door. The core of the apple he'd finished was still on the desk where he'd left it, and his perfume still hung heavy in the air. "Nice talking to you. Uh, life and prosperity."

"Nice talking to you too," Tut called after him. For the last time, he was sure. Poor reckless kid.

Semerkhet suddenly found himself sneezing as he walked back to his Pharaoh's room with a hot cup of licorice tea for his friend. Half a moment later, he figured out why. Nakhtmin's perfume was enough to give anyone an allergy attack.

"What did that little jackal want, Morning Star?" he asked as conversationally as he could, entering his friend's room and offering the teacup.

Tut reached out and accepted the cup. "To complain, mostly," he said, taking a sip. "About my naïve generosity and the economic ruin we're headed for."

Semerkhet rolled his eyes. "So, the usual, then."

Tut smiled. "Yes. The usual." He took another sip of tea. "Took care of him, though. Told him…" He sighed, shaking his head. "Told him that everything remained to be seen. It does, I suppose."

Semerkhet nodded briskly. "Well, reflections on the future aside, I think I'd better get rid of that apple core he left behind." He nodded at the desk, where further evidence of Nakhtmin's visit still remained.

Tut just chuckled.

39

Desperation

"Time is running out," Ankhesenamun said to her brother that afternoon. He looked at her with a heavy sigh, a touch of age on his weary face.

"I know."

"They're not going to wait for us to make a decision and then abide by it out of respect for us. We have to have a plan. And we have to get it going. Now. Or we will lose any power or influence over the future of Egypt. We have to mobilize."

Tut sat up a little in bed, looking solemnly at his sister. "Yes. We do. You wrote to the Hittites; that's a good first step."

"And I hid the letter with my makeup," she said with just a hint of a self-satisfied smile. "That's the last place they'll look."

"Well, what other steps can we take?" the Pharaoh said. "What are our options?"

"What would Mother do?" Ankhesenamun asked herself, tapping her chin.

"If the baby was here, you could become regent and rule until it grew up," Tutankhamun said, "and maybe take that opportunity to become Pharaoh yourself, like Hatshepsut."

She nodded. "Well... they don't know that I might be pregnant..."
Ankh smiled. "Meresankh, can you bring me Granny, please?"

"But if I'm so early, will they believe us?" Ankh asked Granny anxiously.

The old midwife smiled. "Dearie, if there's one thing men know nothing about, it's babies. They don't know it usually takes two or three cycles to be sure. They won't think anything of it. We'll just go from the date you gave me."

The Queen touched her belly. "Six days ago," she said.

Merneith nodded. "Well, a lot can happen in nine months."

"You'd lie for me?" Ankh asked.

Merneith gave half a smile. "There are times... when a lie can save a life." She reached out and took Ankh's hand, gently squeezing it in her wrinkled old fingers. "And we may not be lying."

So they set aside their precious tactical maneuver until it was ready to share with the man who had killed the Pharaoh. And they waited.

The Queen still thought of that little girl from the marketplace. Prayed for her, to Whoever was listening. And promised herself that she would fight for her til her dying breath.

Ankhesenamun had dreamed of that little girl every night for the past week. That brave child walking through Memphis, clothed in dirty rags, her poor little feet cut and callused, her poor little wrist-bones sticking out as she survived day by day without ever knowing what it was to have a full stomach. Each morning, those wide, brave eyes haunted the Queen. And even during her waking hours, sometimes she would blink, half-thinking she had seen the child disappearing around a corner.

She had to do something.

And as she pulled her warm, purple outer robe closer against the chilly day, she thought of what she could do.

The Queen smiled. Tomorrow, she would take action.

Ay still brought the Pharaoh daily reports of governmental activities. It was strange to receive them from him, the man who had murdered him, but it showed how happy the slippery Vizier was to, on the surface, appear as a loyal servant to the crown. Ever the politician, he would exploit that formality, concealing his crime from everyone who didn't already know what he had done, hiding behind the paperwork that made everything look normal.

But Tut knew he couldn't trust what Ay told him he had been doing.

As the nights grew cooler, Tut smiled to be able to find true pleasure in snuggling up under more blankets at night. Even with everything that was going on, that was one small thing that he could enjoy. That and wearing a cozy outer robe over his sleeping-tunic. He was also pleased that, at least when his fever wasn't high, he wasn't hot and sweaty like he had been all through the days of Epiphi, Mesori, and Thoth. And even when he was rolling around sticky with sweat as the fever radiated from his burning skin, the people around him didn't smell as bad as they had around the time of the Opet Festival. But when the fever was low, it was cool enough for him and his sister to want to get cozy under a blanket together, keeping one another warm as they cuddled. On these cool days and chilly nights, they would share cups of tea, feeling the cups warming their cold hands, the tea warming them up from the inside out.

The cooler weather also brought the rains. They saw little rain in Egypt; in a song he had written in the days of the Aten, a song no one was allowed to sing anymore, Tut's father Akhenaten had described the rain that was more common in other parts of the world as "a Nile in the sky." And that was what it was like; a source of water that fell from the sky, rather than snaking along the ground.

Other parts of the world, like the distant lands in the eastern reaches of Hattusa, got types of weather they never experienced in Egypt; sometimes, in the coldest parts of the year, they were said to find cold, white flakes falling from the sky. Tut could hardly imagine waking up to find the ground covered in white. Did it look like sand? Like feathers? And what would it feel like to grab a handful of it? He doubted he would ever know.

But on the long, chilly nights of Sholiak and Tybi and Meshir, it did sometimes rain in Egypt. It made for good sleeping weather, cuddled up in warm blankets, listening to the gentle pattering of the cool raindrops on the roof. Tut always found the strength to smile on rainy nights.

Small blessings to be grateful for.

Ankhesenamun drifted off slowly that evening as the rain pattered on the roof, wrapped warmly in her blankets, her chair made more comfortable with a few extra pillows. Into a warm, safe darkness she drifted, a place where she could rest until morning came with all its problems, mysteries, and decisions. Here, in sleep, she was safe.

She woke up in the depths of the night. And she rolled over in bed, toward a warm, familiar figure. She nestled into her husband's side, resting one arm across his chest. His beard tickled her forehead.

He shifted in bed, and Ankh smiled as he woke up, just a little.

"Love you, assiyant," he whispered. The Hittite word for "dear" or "beloved."

"I love you, my Hittite Prince."

And the Pharaoh Zannanza kissed his wife and went back to sleep as Ankhesenamun settled in, one arm wrapped comfortably around the baby who was to be born in only another month.

Ankhesenamun opened her eyes. They were full of tears. She was not in bed. She was in her chair. And there, in his bed, lay her beloved husband, her darling brother, whom she loved with all her heart. The baby, if their prayers had been answered, had not yet announced its presence. And she was not the wife of the Hittite Prince.

With a heavy sigh, the Queen lay back again, heart aching. She was betraying him; the brother she'd married according to centuries of tradition. By loving another, another whom she hadn't even met yet. But who was commanding more and more of her waking hours, visiting her in more and more of her dreams. The conflict... it filled her with doubt. Doubt that she was doing the right thing.

But she wanted to be married. Amid all the shame she was feeling, she wanted a husband. She wanted to know the true love shared by a real husband and a real wife in a real marriage. Was that so wrong?

And she struggled to go back to sleep.

While they waited for their ploy to germinate, they spent their precious time exploring other options.

"Usermontu is still on our side," Tut said as he and his sister cuddled under a blanket, enjoying the chilly day. "I don't know... Could we write to him, where he works now in Thebes? Bring him back to Memphis by the order of the Pharaoh; have him approve you as regent for, uh..." He looked down at her belly, and the question within. And the tactical maneuver they were about to employ.

Ankh chuckled and adjusted her arm around his shoulders. What would Ay think when they told him their news?

"I think we should," she said. "If there's anyone we can still trust, it's him."

The Queen prepared a letter to the old Vizier. And anxiously, she handed it to Amenmose, who was going as support on a visit to Thebes by some of the priesthood. Once they were there, he would find a way to meet privately with Usermontu. And he would deliver the Queen's letter.

The Pharaoh looked down at his hands. Even they were growing thin, his long fingers slender and spidery, his wrists knobby, his elbows pointed. His arms themselves were emaciated sticks, as were his useless legs.

I'm supposed to be a strong Pharaoh, he thought. *And here I am, thin as a ghost, about ready to blow away in the next breeze.*

Almost reluctantly, he picked up a nearby bronze hand-mirror. And slowly, he looked into it.

He barely recognized the person he saw. An old face looked back at him, the face of a man who had seen more of life than the boy who had looked into the mirror last. The bruises and scrapes of the battle at Kadesh were gone, and those on his torso and limbs had faded to no more than shadows, but the strain of the battles he had fought since his homecoming was visible. This was a thin face with the beginning of lines around the shadowed eyes, a weary face, a haggard face full of pain. The face of a man who had seen sorrow and pain, suffering and struggle… and had pulled through. A man who was brave and could endure… a strong Pharaoh.

He put the mirror away. He did not like what he saw in it.

But at the same time… it made him proud.

Ankh saw the mirror. And she took her brother's emaciated hand with a sad smile. She nodded at the mirror. "That face," she said softly, "is still you. You're still you."

He just blinked back tears as he smiled back.

"My Lady."

The Queen stiffened as she walked past the Vizier's office on a jaunt to the kitchen. Usually around this time she would be taking a ten-minute walk around the garden, but it was threatening rain, a sign of the month of Sholiak moving into Tybi. So instead she had decided to walk to the kitchen for a snack.

Until she had been interrupted.

"Yes, Vizier?" she asked coldly.

"My Lady," he said again, "I do wonder if you are considering… every possibility available to you. The future will come, no matter how hard we try to fight it. And you will have a decision to make."

The Queen gritted her teeth, resisting the urge to clench her fists. He knew about the letter to the Hittites. But he didn't know about the baby. Not yet. Surreptitiously, she placed one hand on her stomach, a gesture whose significance he would not guess.

"I have considered my options," she said smoothly. "All of them. And my decision is made. Good day, Vizier."

And she walked away.

Ankh pulled her warm robe closer around her body as the cold of the rainy day seeped into her bones. And she gave a tiny grunt of unexpected pain. She looked down at her chest. Why was her bosom so sore?

Ankh moped wistfully through the day, hoping, dreaming, waiting. Waiting to find out if Usermontu could help them... waiting for the plan she and Granny had prepared to be ready. Praying for their future. Thinking about the past.

And she could see her Mother's face in her heart. Wise, proud, courageous, Queen, Pharaoh, mother, wife.

"What do I do, Mother?" she whispered. "What do I do if this doesn't work? What do I do if it *does* work?"

And she knew what Nefertiti, Smenkhkare, would say. *Be everything you are, no matter what anyone else thinks. And do whatever it takes to protect Egypt.*

Somehow, Ankh found herself smiling. Because if her Mother had transformed herself into a Pharaoh, she could too.

And if she had to, she would. Whether she ruled from the throne or from beside it, she would be the leader Egypt needed.

The Queen summoned her handmaiden. And she sent her and Hannu into town with a mission. And with a gift; a bag containing ten loaves of bread, ten apples, three child-sized linen robes, a tiny pair of sandals, and two more warm shawls.

She was the Queen. And through her rank, her authority, the power she wielded, she could make a difference.

So Meresankh and Hannu set off. And they spent the rest of the day searching the city of Memphis, walking down all the back alleys, looking down each narrow, litter-strewn street. Walking past other people dressed in rags, other children barely older than the little girl the Queen wanted to find.

They would know her by her shawl, they had been told. The large, blue-and-purple shawl that the Queen had bought for herself, then given to the child. And they searched for that shawl.

The day was cold. And Hannu's knees were hurting him. Tough, strong royal bodyguard as he was, he spent the day complaining about the pain, whining that he wished he lived in Nubia where this part of the year wasn't as cold. And half-listening, Meresankh walked what felt like the entire length and breadth of Memphis, searching every street corner, every alleyway, every doorstep they passed for a tiny little girl in a blue-and-purple shawl.

Night fell. And they had not found her. So Meresankh and Hannu distributed the food and the shawls to the hungry children they had encountered; bestowed the robes and sandals on four little boys who must have been precisely the same age as the child the Queen had in mind. Because they knew that that was what Meresankh's Lady would want them to do.

Shivering in her own cloak, her feet dirty from the rough streets, her stomach rumbling, and her patience worn down to nothing by Hannu's grating grumbles, Meresankh made her way back inside the palace to her Lady's room. The Queen was taking a break, and stood up excitedly when she saw her handmaiden.

"Well?" she asked impatiently. "Did you find her? Where is she?"

Meresankh swallowed. And she fought down the annoyance that the Queen's insistence was awakening in her exhausted heart and mind.

"I'm sorry," she said, looking down at her dirty feet, "but we didn't find her. We were able to give the robes and the sandals to four little boys, though, and we gave out the apples and the bread and the shawls, so we made a difference today."

The look of expectation on Ankhesenamun's face melted into exasperation.

"What? You were out there all day and you didn't find her? How much of the city did you even cover— it's not that big. How hard can it be to find one little girl?" Her bracelet jingled as she gestured, the contempt on her face showing just what she thought of all of Meresankh's efforts.

Meresankh bit back her response, then gave up. Here she stood, announcing to the Queen that nearly a dozen children had been helped by the gifts Meresankh and Hannu had delivered, and the Queen was telling her that wasn't good enough.

"Well, I'm sorry," she said roughly. "We tried. And we gave all those things to children who needed them. Children who won't be cold or hungry tonight— because of what we did. And you're asking the impossible. I can't just magically find one random person in one of the biggest cities in the entire country just because you order me to. If you—" Her heart told her to stop, but she ignored it. "If you want a little girl, you can get one. Why does it have to be *that* one? She might not even live in Memphis anymore! And finding that one— finding that one isn't going to bring your little girls back."

The Queen went white. And Meresankh's heart dropped into her stomach, then slid down to somewhere around her feet. Silently, she stood there. Waiting.

Ankhesenamun stared at the floor, her hands clenched into fists. And without looking up, she told Meresankh,

"You are dismissed."

She had never been dismissed by the Queen before. But with a nod and a curtsy, she went.

Despite the peacefulness with which he had initially fallen asleep, Tut woke up in the cold, dark depths of the night, and Ankhesenamun and Semerkhet had to spend the rest of the night taking turns sitting up with him, trying to help him drift off for maybe an hour or so at a time. Something had changed...

And maybe he was right. *Maybe...* the Queen thought with a shudder, *this time... he was not going to pull through.*

Author's Note

The problem with history is that we don't know everything. When writing historical fiction, an author must choose what direction to go; which theories to take as one's premises. Many theories are built only on other theories, rather than on indisputable facts; as such, picking a "path" of events for my story to follow was a bit like a "choose your own adventure" story.

My description of Nefertiti's death offers a good example. A mummy believed by some to be Queen Nefertiti (and who has been genetically demonstrated to be Tutankhamun's birth mother and a sister or cousin of Tut's father) was found to have suffered a pair of severe, most likely deadly, injuries to her face and chest, possibly caused by a kick from a horse. Based on this data, this is how I tell the story of Nefertiti's death and explain her absence from the story. It is also possible, however, that the damage to her body represents a desecration that occurred after her death.

The Queen is also a candidate for the co-regent, and possible independent Pharaoh, Neferneferuaten, who reigned during and possibly after the reign of Akhenaten, as well as for Pharaoh Smenkhkare, a mysterious, poorly-documented Pharaoh who also reigned between Akhenaten and Tutankhamun. This is how I tell the story, following Kara Cooney's interpretation of events as outlined in her book, *When Women Ruled the World*.

In the murky years after Akhenaten's reign, it is also not entirely clear whether Smenkhkare, whoever he or she was, made Tut his or her heir. I answer this question by saying that the one way in which Akhenaten and Nefertiti bowed to tradition was by making their only son their heir after both of their reigns should be complete. My statement that as Pharaoh Smenkhkare, Nefertiti designated Grand Vizier Ay as regent for Tutankhamun in the event that she should die before Tut became a man, giving Ay the power to decide when to establish Tutankhamun in full authority as Pharaoh, is also completely conjectural.

There are many historical instances of Queen Mothers serving as regents on behalf of child Pharaohs, but even when a regency by a mother or stepmother was accepted as legitimate, regency was an unofficial position, and one almost never given to a male member of the royal court. Therefore, all of Tut and Ankh's desperate paperwork-preparation, putting their directives "in writing" and formalizing them with the royal signet-ring, is meant to underline the way that the Vizier, in the defiance with which I have written him, will refuse to honor verbally-expressed royal decisions that have not been signed into law, although the royal court would have been expected to honor either formal or informal royal directives.

Turning to other event that required me to "choose my own adventure," three of Akhenaten's daughters, Neferneferure, Setepenre, and possibly Meketaten, are theorized to have died in an epidemic during Akhenaten's reign, along with Queen Mother Tiye (Meketaten may also have died in childbirth). Another sister, named Neferneferuaten-Tasherit (Junior), may also have died before Tutankhamun took the throne, so I portray her as having died during this same epidemic. The epidemic seems to have lasted a number of years, and the deaths of the princesses may have taken place over months or years, but for drama, I have chosen to depict four of Tut and Ankh's sisters and their grandmother as having died on the same terrible night. It is not clear what illness had swept through Egypt (bubonic plague is a candidate), but I describe symptoms consistent with influenza.

I also portray Ankhesenamun as being five years older than her brother, and have made Tutankhamun the youngest child in the family for dramatic purposes. I have also adjusted Tut and Ankh's ages during the epidemic so both were old enough to remember it, and set the epidemic one year before Akhenaten's death, while the period between the beginning of the epidemic and the death of Akhenaten was actually about four years. The ages I describe for the sisters when Tutankhaten is born have been adjusted to maintain their accepted birth order while allowing for one child to be born each year without twins occurring.

It is not known how long Princess Meritaten, one of the only two surviving sisters, lived, or how she died, but she took the position of Great Royal Wife alongside Pharaoh Smenkhkare (who I see as her own mother) after Akhenaten's death. I do not touch on the hypothesis that Meritaten was Smenkhkare or Co-Regent Neferneferuaten, or that Smenkhkare was a brother of Tutankhamun or Akhenaten, or possibly even the Hittite Prince Zannanza.

As Meritaten's years as Queen alongside her mother would have made her an experienced politician, I realized that if she was part of the story, helping her younger siblings, they would defeat Ay and his entourage. However, I could not write Meritaten out of the story by simply having her retire from politics; whatever she had chosen to do with her life, and wherever in Egypt she was living, the political mayhem her siblings were facing would have drawn her back into the political realm.

Therefore, the only way to keep her out of the story was to kill her. In her death, I was pleased to be able to create a mystery that the King and Queen solve when Vizier Pentu's death is explained by Ay the same way as their sister's had been. Furthermore, although we have no specific evidence, we cannot rule out the possibility of the Grand Vizier having gotten both Tut's father and mother/stepmother, as well as his oldest sister, out of the way.

Ay, Pentu, and Usermontu, all of whom are historical figures, all held the title of "Vizier of the South" during Tutankhamun's reign. However, as Ay is sometimes referred to as the "Grand Vizier," I have described him as outranking the other viziers. I also follow the hypothesis that because of Tut's early death, he was placed in the tomb that had been prepared for Ay, who then used Tut's intended tomb.

Finally, to simplify some of the unknowns, I have chosen to describe the royal couple as splitting their time between Amenhotep the Third's palace in Thebes and another palace in Memphis. In this way, they can oversee the entire country, and it is possible for Tut to travel only 400 miles to Kadesh, rather than 800. A 400-mile trip is certainly far enough!

Politics and War

In this historical period, Egypt's main enemies would have been the Hittites. During Tut's reign, Egypt campaigned against them for control of the city of Kadesh. As I tell the story, I describe Amurru as a contested region in Syria that continually switches hands between the Hittites and the Egyptians, captured from Egypt by Hattusa during the reign of Akhenaten, and Kadesh as an independent city-state within that territory, taken by the Hittites only recently. Although the Hittites and the Mitanni could access one another's borders via a route to the northeast of Amurru, the region was, at a certain point in ancient history, positioned almost precisely in the center between the countries of Egypt, Mitanni, and Hattusa.

I link the campaign to recapture Kadesh from the Hittites to Tut's idealism and altruistic desire to protect Egypt's smaller and weaker neighbors from takeover, but also to his youthful inexperience in the arts of politics and war. In the words of Vizzini from *The Princess Bride*, he "[falls] victim to one of the classic blunders... never get involved in a land war in Asia," somewhat naïvely making Egypt into a "big brother" nation that enters into a strictly unnecessary war to protect a victimized neighbor from an aggressor through Egypt's superior armed forces.

According to my research, the Mitanni at that point were in no fit state to threaten Egypt, as they do in the *Spike* miniseries simply called *Tut*, a wild ride of a soap opera that partially inspired my saga. If anything, the Mitanni needed Egypt's help, her protection from the Hittites. Evidence suggests that Egypt, however, was strong enough to fight the Hittite kingdom for Kadesh.

It seems reasonable to imagine the Mitanni asking Egypt for protection against the Hittites, who represented a threat to both nations. In fact, as I mention, and as described in the *Encyclopedia of Ancient Egypt*, during the reign of Akhenaten, the Mitanni asked Egypt to send troops to defend them against the Hittites, but the Pharaoh does not seem to have sent any. Was this because all of his father's chariots and most of his soldiers had been lost in the Red Sea? In my telling, in Tutankhamun's day, Egypt's economy is still recovering in the aftermath of the Exodus, but its army, rebuilt after the large force sent after the Hebrews disappeared, is strong enough to start a campaign.

The main piece of evidence that Tutankhamun fought in Kadesh is found in a damaged carving dated to his reign, which shows the chariot of a Pharaoh riding into battle, literally smashing the Hittites under the wheels of his chariot. It may not be possible to conclusively determine whether Tut personally participated in this campaign, and whether he himself initiated it in his zeal to save the world, but a body of artwork suggests that he was a skilled bow-hunter. Six chariots, a set of armor, over fifty bows, and hundreds of arrows were found in his tomb, so if he could bow-hunt from a chariot, it is not impossible for him to have ridden into battle as an archer. Wouldn't a kid who had always been kept inside throw caution to the wind at the opportunity to actually ride into glorious battle, leading the troops as their commander?

Also, to clarify the potentially confusing use of the terms "Kush" and "Nubia," in this historical period, the province of Kush is the part of the region of Nubia that is controlled by Egypt. As such, the greedy Nakhtmin still wants to take over any remaining parts of southern Nubia that may not be under Egyptian control.

To sum up, I was glad to be able to tie these events and concepts together in Tut's decision to help the Mitanni: Akhenaten's decision not to help the weakened Mitanni deal with the Hittites, the encroachment of the Hittites on Egyptian territories, the possibility that Tut himself fought in Kadesh, Tut's "naïve generosity" and desire to save the world, and Ay and Horemheb's desire to see Tut laid in his tomb.

The Hittite Prince

Prince Zannanza and his father, King Suppiluliuma, are historical figures. During the 18th Dynasty, a widowed Queen of Egypt, often identified as Ankhesenamun, wrote to the King of the Hittites, asking him to send her one of his sons to marry.

The letter as I have the Queen write it is based on translations of two letters Suppiluliuma received, although rather than telling him that there was no one she could trust, historically the Queen told the Hittites that she had no son. Some say that Nefertiti, rather than Ankh, was the Queen who wrote to the Hittites, because of certain details, such as the time of year that particular events took place. But I believe that the evidence for her identification as this Queen is weaker. Even if she wasn't Tutankhamun's birthmother, she had a little stepson to carry on her husband's male line. And if she was Pharaoh Smenkhkare, she took the throne herself before passing it to Tut. Nefertiti was a widow, but she was politically strong and established. Her dynasty was secure, as a clear heir to the throne was present. Ankh, however, was a widow with no male heir. She was in a position of political desperation, facing a succession crisis.

If we assume that Ankhesenamun is the Queen who wrote to the Hittites, this gives us an important clue that suggests foul play in Tutankhamun's death. The fact that in her letter, the Queen seeks to remarry and says she is afraid implies that she does not trust Ay or Horemheb enough to let the throne pass to either of them and retire from politics herself. However, she also sees that she cannot obtain the leverage necessary to claim the next throne herself. She wants to retain some power, some control over Egypt, by remaining Queen, but not through marrying a member of her own royal court— a "servant," and a traitor.

In proposing to the Hittite Prince and attempting to bring an outsider into Egypt's royal family, the Queen also disregards the claim of Horemheb, who was historically Tutankhamun's designated heir when he died. Why would she have done this unless she knew Horemheb had betrayed their family? The Queen knows what she is doing. And she will do whatever she must to protect her country.

Powerful Women

I was glad to be able to contrast Queen Ankhesenamun's philosophy of gender equality and pride in her own political skills with the opinion held by her fellow wives that the purpose of being a woman is to marry a big, strong, wonderful man, become a sweet little trophy wife, and start producing little boys.

The Queens Regent and female Pharaohs of the previous dynasties described by Ankh to her brother are real, as are the achievements I mention. The exact titles they bore are not always clear, but all are women for whom there is evidence that they led their nation. Their accomplishments can be read about in more detail in the book *When Women Ruled the World* by Kara Cooney, and in an article by ThoughtCo. Two female Pharaohs reigned after the Eighteenth Dynast, Tawosret of the Nineteenth Dynasty and Cleopatra the Seventh of the Ptolemaic Period.

Hatshepsut and her fellow female sovereigns of Egypt should not be referred to as Queens after becoming Pharaohs. The Queen is the wife of the Pharaoh, so an Egyptian Queen Regnant can only properly be referred to as *Pharaoh*, which is actually a gender-less term.

I also chose to make a point in not including a female villain. I have my female characters straightforwardly deal with the conflicts they have with one another with respect and positivity, and then move on. The most female negativity comes from the character of Meryt. She decides to remain in her self-imposed prison of feeling like a failure for not having sons, and even tries to drag the Queen down with her, because she does not know how else a woman can be defined, other than as the mother of a little boy. In the end, Meryt is not a villain, per se, but is a sad character because of her fixed mindset and decision not to change her attitude and embrace freedom. Mutnedjmet and Amenia, however, quickly embrace the truths that Ankhesenamun shares with them.

I also made sure to underline how Akhenaten and Nefertiti were a formidable team, seamlessly sharing the duties of Pharaoh as equals. I also refer to Tut and Ankh's grandmother Tiye, who, alongside her husband Amenhotep the Third, served Egypt with her wisdom. She also seems to have demonstrated great diplomacy during the reign of her son, keeping up Egypt's relationships with its neighbors while the Pharaoh focused on his role as priest and Nefertiti, as Co-Pharaoh Neferneferuaten, quite possibly served as Egypt's main political leader.

The term "Effective for her Husband" was used by Nefertiti as Co-Regent Neferneferuaten, and, in my story, found its way into Ankhesenamun's efforts to continue moving things in the direction that Tutankhamun, under her guidance, had established. In an era of strong female politicians in the Egyptian royal family, I am proud to be able to portray Ankhesenamun, Meritaten, and their mother as women who held their country together using feminine strengths and the wisdom of women.

Names and Titles

Some of the poetic titles that various courtiers use to address the King came from Tutankhamun's royal titulary, and others I had fun making up. The grand "For Whom the Sun Rises" was inspired by a reference to Tut himself found in the tomb of the Viceroy of Kush, where he is addressed as "For Whom the Sun God Rises." The frequently used wish for "All Life, Prosperity, and Health" comes from the use of this phrase in the closing of a letter to a Pharaoh, or after his or her name. Also attested in Ancient Egyptian literature is the hilarious insult, "Your mind's like an empty room!"

The Egyptian palace had rather a hilarious bureaucracy, and nearly all the flowery, sentence-length titles of jobs and departments I refer to, including and especially Semerkhet's weighty titles, are real or only slightly rephrased. However, the *Washer of Pharaoh* may have been related to the laundry department, rather than referring to the servant who bathed the Morning and the Evening Star. It's hard to be sure…

I am also using the titles *Attendant of the Lord of the Two Lands* and *King's Valet* as synonymous, although it is difficult to say whether this was the case historically. One of the very few titles that I made up was related to beekeeping, although the Ancient Egyptians made extensive use of honey. Another one that I extrapolated was *Master of Cosmetics, Who Adorns the King*. And I found no reference to a *Senior Undersecretary to the Vice-Treasurer*, but in imagining such a role, the King certainly had the right idea.

The titles Tutankhamun bestows upon Semerkhet during the latter's trial of *Sole Companion, Favorite of the Pharaoh,* and *Unique Friend* are real titles possessed by courtiers throughout Ancient Egyptian history. Historically, Horemheb was Tutankhamun's Sole Companion, but I have chosen not to bring this into the story. My handling of "Sole Companionhood" as an approximate equivalent to knighthood is conjectural.

The existence of so many jobs to take care of one family might seem silly, but the extreme levels of specificity and specialization, with each funny job having its own sentence-length title, show that all these palace jobs were valued and that people took pride in being involved and making a difference.

However, even though I have tried to go all-out in terms of the sprawling excess that was the palace staff, there are places where I have simplified things by assigning more tasks to one servant than might have been historically the case. Semerkhet is the best example; most of his job titles are real, and his responsibilities do add up to a full-time job, but most likely would not all have been held by a single "Royal CNA." Meresankh may also fulfill more responsibilities than any one historical handmaiden, because I wanted to have the King and the Queen each bond with one of their servants.

Cup-bearers to the Pharaoh were responsible for protecting them from poison, but other roles Semerkhet fills in his position as "Chief Royal Valet etc." were inspired by courtier positions found in the English Monarchy, such as the *Lord of the Bedchamber*. Being close enough to the Pharaoh to be responsible for bathing and dressing him would have conferred great honor upon Semerkhet.

To be a Pharaoh was to be surrounded by help and support in day-to-day activities. Although for most of the Kings of Egypt, this level of care would have been largely ceremonial; an expression of worship toward the Morning and the Evening Star, it means that systems were in place that normalized the Pharaoh practically not having to brush their own teeth. Although most Pharaohs had more help than they actually needed, I was pleased to envision the ways in which one of Egypt's only special-needs Pharaohs would have had all the support he needed to accomplish his activities of daily living.

Sweet Songs

The lullaby warning ghosts not to harm a baby is my own rhyming paraphrase of an existing incantation sung over babies. Semerkhet's song for Meresankh is also my own slight adjustment of an existing love poem. Also, in Egyptian love poetry, couples referred to one another as "brother and sister" as an expression of intimacy. Therefore, it is ironically beautiful that the King and Queen are literally siblings. Turning from songs to stories, the fable of the magic fountain which, in flowing up instead of down, represents the "ripple effect" of *ma'at*, is fictional.

I must say that in all its creepy glory, the ghost lullaby is an early example of the longstanding tradition of lullabies being frankly terrifying. I'm glad that it helps Tut drift off even when he's feeling his worst, but it's not exactly something I would want sung to me in the middle of the night!

Medicines and Poisons

Poison made from peach-pits was known to the Ancient Egyptians—they contain cyanide, the same poison found in bitter almonds (although whether the Egyptians were able to determine that peach-pits and bitter almonds contained the exact same poisonous chemical is not known). Determination of guilt via this poison was known as "the Penalty of the Peach." As such, when Tut is given peach-pit "medicine," I describe him as suffering from symptoms consistent with cyanide poisoning at a nonlethal dose. It is true, however, that despite being poisonous when raw, peach-pits are also quite nutritious, and perfectly safe to consume if cooked.

In my description of Tut's experience of ague, I relied heavily on Laura Ingalls Wilder's detailed description of her own family's life-threatening brush with malaria, found in *Little House on the Prairie*. The overlap between the symptoms of malaria and those of cyanide poisoning also forms an important plot point in my story, and explains the selection of this particular poison by the doctor.

A slight adjustment I have made to the symptoms of malaria, however, is that I only describe Tut as experiencing full-on delusions during the very first fever, when he is also suffering from cyanide poisoning, as well as under the influence of opium, marijuana, and mandrake (all of which were used as painkillers in Ancient Egypt). I also describe his fever as recurring every three days or so, when the "rhythm" of a recurring malarial fever varies based on the specific type of malaria. *Malaria falciparum*, the type which Tutankhamun was affected by, is more likely to recur every 36-48 hours, or to remain constant at a low level. Malaria falciparum is also more likely than other types of malaria to immediately launch a patient into critical condition. Another adjustment I made is that malaria symptoms do not usually arise until ten to fifteen days after a patient has been bitten by a mosquito.

Family Trees

To simplify some of the unknowns and tighten up the plot, I have chosen to depict Tut and Ankh as full siblings, born to Akhenaten and Nefertiti, whom I describe as cousins. Although Ankhesenamun was the daughter of Nefertiti, Tut is more generally believed to have been born to one of Akhenaten's minor wives, whose genetic relationship to Akhenaten is equivalent to that of full siblings. Supporting the theory that Ankh and Tut were both born to cousins Akhenaten and Nefertiti, however, is the fact that three generations of first-cousin unions would result in a genetic similarity between Nefertiti and Akhenaten indistinguishable from that of siblings. Although evidence points against Akhenaten and Nefertiti having been siblings, we cannot say that they were not cousins.

Additionally, the main piece of evidence for Nefertiti not having been Tut's mother is the fact that they were not depicted together. However, as Aidan Dodson explains in *Amarna Sunset*, it was traditional in this period of history for the royal family to leave sons out of family portraits (until one of them became Pharaoh, as Kara Cooney tells us in *When Women Ruled the World)*. Since Tut would have been a fragile child, I wonder if he would have been kept out of the limelight for even longer than most royal sons. Therefore, the absence of any pictures clearly labeled "The Great Royal Wife Nefertiti and her son, Crown Prince Tutankhaten" cannot be used to rule out the possibility of Nefertiti having been Tut's mother.

Furthermore, in descriptions of Tutankhamun's reign, there are no reference to a Queen Mother guiding or supporting him. I believe that this serves as evidence that his mother was Queen Nefertiti, who eventually reigned as Pharaoh Smenkhkare, and that Tut succeeded her upon her death. Because she reigned before him, the only reason he would succeed her would be her death, leaving her unavailable to serve as Queen Mother.

The fate I assign to Nefertiti is according to a theory about the death of the unnamed woman identified as Tut's mother, as discussed above. I also simplified things by skipping Akhenaten's other wives. Furthermore, although Akhenaten had a sister named Hennutaneb, it is not known whether she had children.

It has been theorized that Ay was the uncle of Akhenaten, or even the father of Nefertiti. I have chosen not to get into this, instead, simply making Ay a courtier who has been an integral part of the Egyptian government since long before Tut was born. Mutnedjmet has also been theorized to have been Nefertiti's sister, but I have also not chosen to explore that line of reasoning. Another detail about Mutnedjmet that I have chosen not to include is the fact that by the time she died at around the age of forty, she had lost most or all of her teeth.

Turning back to the complexities of the Amarna family tree, although I have Ankh refer to her marriage to Tut having been their destiny from the moment of his birth, this may or may not have been the case. But whenever they were betrothed to one another, why did Tutankhamun marry his sister? For one reason or another, it appears as though marriage to the princess was necessary for Tut to take the throne. We see this same logic later in the story when Ankh offers to make Zannanza Pharaoh through marriage to her, and Ay seeks to take the throne in the same way, with Maya tempted to do the same.

As with a number of other historical cultures, the Ancient Egyptians valued the maintenance of a pure royal bloodline so much that marriage between siblings was not only acceptable, but expected, particularly during the Eighteenth Dynasty, in which Tut and Ankh lived. Whether their political marriage is right, wrong, or simply weird, Tutankhamun and Ankhesenamun only have each other, and their preexisting bond as siblings allows them to function as a highly effective team, helping one another as they walk side-by-side through all the storms of life.

The family trees of the Ancient Egyptian royal families may make us scratch our heads in confusion… or shake them in horror. All in all, I must say that the comedy song "I'm My Own Grandpa" sounds very Ancient Egyptian, although in three thousand years of tangled family trees, I am not sure if even they managed that particular arrangement! Ultimately, Pharaohs married their own sisters because it was traditional— because tradition was considered a good enough reason for just about any decision. Including incest.

So Many Questions

As many specific facts as I have been astounded to uncover about life in Ancient Egypt and Tut's life in particular, questions have remained that history cannot answer for us. At these points, I have carefully considered what "bridging materials" fit best into the gaps, choosing my own adventure as I've described. We can only imagine what details remain to be uncovered, and how the story of the Amarna Family will be told a hundred years from now.

Glossary

Ague: malaria, a potentially deadly, mosquito-borne illness that causes weakness, fever, and chills

Ammut: the crocodile-lion-hippopotamus beast who would devour the hearts of the unworthy dead, preventing them from entering into a peaceful afterlife

Bastet: ancient Egyptian goddess with a role related to various aspects of health, depicted as a lioness or cat

Diadem: a term for a type of crown with a lower profile than the white crown of Upper Egypt, the red crown of Lower Egypt, or the double-crown. A diadem would fit closely against one's wig, with the only protrusion being the *uraeus* in the front. Also referred to as a circlet.

Hemp: medicinal cannabis

Henna: red dye used in various cultures to decorate the skin with beautiful designs, and used by Ancient Egyptians to color nails and dye hair. Soldiers colored their nails red before going into battle.

Khepresh: the blue war crown worn by Pharaohs

Khonsu: Ancient Egyptian moon deity

Kohl: the eyeliner used by Ancient Egyptians to create the well-known cat-eye and to darken their eyebrows. Combined with blue-green "eye-shadow," it helped to protect the eyes from infection and from the bright sun. Both kohl and the "eye-shadow" were made from minerals.

Ma'at: both the name of an Ancient Egyptian goddess of truth, harmony, and justice and a term for these and related concepts. Upon death, Ancient Egyptians anticipated that their hearts would be weighed against the feathers Ma'at wore in her hair; if their heart was too heavy, it indicated that they were unrighteous, and their heart was eaten by the crocodile-lion-hippopotamus beast, Ammut. They would not have the opportunity to advance to a happy afterlife in the Field of Reeds.

Mandrake: a plant used as a painkiller

Nut: an Ancient Egyptian goddess of the sky

Palanquin: another word for a litter in which a member of the royal family might be carried, borne by servants

Pectoral: refers to a very large necklace that covers a portion of the chest

Poppy: medicinal opium

Seega: a board game played historically in Egypt

Spikenard: an essential oil obtained from a plant of the valerian family, long used in perfumery

Tawaret: an Ancient Egyptian goddess of fertility, depicted as a grandly pregnant hippopotamus

Uraeus: the cobra-headed decoration seen on the front of many Ancient Egyptian crowns

Vizier: a sort of "prime minister;" a high official responsible for supervising much of the running of the government

Locations

Akhetaten (Amarna): Pharaoh Akhenaten's capital city, which he had built to honor the Aten and to enable a "fresh start."

Amurru: Region in modern Syria and Lebanon historically subjected to both Egyptian and Hittite control

Avaris: Town in the eastern Nile Delta

Azzati (Gaza): Town in Palestine

Carchemish: Town in the region of Syria, taken from Egypt by Suppiluliuma I of the Hittites

Hattusa: Kingdom of the Hittites, located in modern Turkey

Kadesh: Town in the region of Amurru, which switched hands several times between Egypt and Hattusa

Khem (Letopolis): Town in the southern Nile Delta, just to the northwest of Memphis

Kush: Region of Nubia under Egyptian control from 16th-11th centuries BC

Memphis (Cairo): Northern capital of Egypt, in the southern Nile Delta

Mitanni: Neighbor of New Kingdom Egypt located in modern Turkey and Syria

Nubia: Southern neighbor of Egypt, comprising parts of modern Egypt and modern Sudan

On (Heliopolis): Town in the southern Nile Delta, just to the northeast of Memphis

Per-Amun (Pelusium): Town in the extreme east of the Nile Delta, on the Mediterranean coast

Per-Bast (Bubastis): Town in the southeastern Nile Delta

Thebes (Luxor): Southern capital of Egypt, on the banks of the Nile in the center of the country

Ankhesenamun's Queens List

Neith-Hotep: possible regent, possible Pharaoh (early first dynasty).

Merneith: regent for her son Den, possible Pharaoh (first dynasty).

Nimaathap: possible regent for her son Djoser (transition between second and third dynasties).

Khentkaus the First: possible Pharaoh or regent for her son. A title that can be translated either as "Mother of Two Kings of Upper and Lower Egypt" or "Mother of the King of Upper and Lower Egypt, *and King of Upper and Lower Egypt*" suggests that she may have become Pharaoh (transition between fourth and fifth dynasties).

Khentkaus the Second: bore the same titles as her predecessor, and may also have reigned either as regent or as Pharaoh in her own right (fifth dynasty).

Setibhor: wife of Pharaoh Djedkare. Her pyramid complex is larger, more elaborate, and "kinglier" than any other belonging to a Queen, and certain symbols and insignias were added to reliefs portraying her, which suggests that she may have succeeded her husband as Pharaoh or as regent for the next male Pharaoh (late fifth dynasty).

Iput: mother and possible regent for Pepi the First (beginning of sixth dynasty).

Ankhesenpepi the Second: sister of Ankhesenpepi the First, daughter of female Vizier Nebet, wife of Pepi the First, bore one of his successors (Pepi the Second), likely served as regent (sixth dynasty).

Nebet: vizier (sixth dynasty).

Nitocris: legendary female Pharaoh, considered to be final Pharaoh of sixth dynasty.

Sobekneferu: Pharaoh (very end of twelfth dynasty).

Tetisheri: mother of Ahhotep the First, powerful Queen and matriarch of royal family (transition between seventeenth and eighteenth dynasties).

Ahhotep the First: regent for her son Ahmose the First. Praised by her son for keeping Egypt in one piece, expelling rebels, bringing home deserters, guarding the country, and pacifying Upper Egypt (transition between seventeenth and eighteenth dynasties).

Ahmose-Nefertari: daughter of Ahhotep the First, mother of Amenhotep the First, may have served as regent for him. She may have founded the Valley of the Kings (early eighteenth dynasty).

Hatshepsut: Queen, then regent, then Pharaoh (eighteenth dynasty).

Tiye: wife of Amenhotep the Third, mother of Akhenaten. Worked as a politician to retain good relations with neighboring countries during her son's reign (eighteenth dynasty).

Nefertiti Smenkhkare: Queen, then co-regent, then possible Pharaoh (eighteenth dynasty).

Meritaten: Queen of Pharaoh Smenkhkare, who is speculated to have been her own mother Nefertiti (eighteenth dynasty).

Calendar

Season of Inundation (Akhet)

Thoth: 19 July-17 August
Paophi: 18 August-16 September
Athyr: 17 September-16 October
Sholiak: 17 October-15 November

Season of Emergence (Peret)

Tybi: 16 November-15 December
Meshir: 16 December-14 January
Phamenoth: 15 January-13 February
Pharmouthi: 14 February-15 March

Season of the Harvest (Shemu)

Pashons: 16 March-14 April
Payni: 15 April-14 May
Epiphi: 15 May-13 June
Mesori: 14 June-13 July

Holy birthdays

14th of July: Osiris
15th: Horus
16th: Seth
17th: Isis
18th: Nepthys

Lyrics

The Ghost Lullaby

Away, away, o ghost of night

My baby do not harm

Your face turned back, your nose behind

You'll wither at my charm

Have you come to kiss him, or sing him to sleep?

Have you come to harm him, or steal him as I weep?

I will not let you kiss him, or in the window creep

I will not let you harm him

And I'll sing him to sleep

Love Song

My one, the sister without peer,

Most beautiful of all!

Her face is like the rising morning star

At the start of a happy year

Selected Resources

The Holy Bible

Daily Life of the Ancient Egyptians by Bob Brier, A. Hoyt Hobbs

The Murder of Tutankhamun: A True Story by Bob Brier

Empire of Ancient Egypt by Wendy Christensen

Tutankhamun: The Exodus Conspiracy: The Truth Behind Archaeology's Greatest Mystery by Andrew Collins and Chris Ogilvie-Herald

When Women Ruled the World by Kara Cooney

Tutankhamun's Armies: Battle and Conquest During Ancient Egypt's Late Eighteenth Dynasty by John Coleman Darnell, Colleen Manassa

The Tomb of Iouiya and Touiyou: The Finding of the Tomb by Theodore M. Davis, Gaston Maspero, Percy Edward Newberry

Amarna Sunset: Nefertiti, Tutankhamun, Ay, Horemheb, and the Egyptian Counter-Reformation by Aidan Dodson

Monarchs of the Nile by Aidan Dodson

The Mysterious Death of Tutankhamun: Re-Opening the Case of Egypt's Boy-King by Paul Doherty

Egyptian Non-royal Epithets in the Middle Kingdom: A Social and Historical Analysis by Denise M. Doxey

Life in Ancient Egypt by Adolf Erman

The Medical Skills of Ancient Egypt: revised edition by J. Worth Estes

Oils and Perfumes of Ancient Egypt by Joann Fletcher

Growing Up in Ancient Israel: Children in Material Culture and Biblical Texts by Kristine Henriksen Garroway

"The Deeds of Suppiluliuma as told by his son, Mursilli II", *Journal of Cuneiform Studies, 10* (1956) by Güterbock, H.G.

The Golden King: The World of Tutankhamun by Zahi Hawass

Scanning the Pharaohs: CT Imaging of the New Kingdom Royal Mummies by Zahi A. Hawass, Sahar Saleem

Principles and Methods of Toxicology, Fifth Edition Edited by A. Wallace Hayes

The Pharaoh's Court by Kathryn Hinds

Conspiracies in the Egyptian Palace: Unis to Pepy I by Naguib Kanawati

Who Killed King Tut? by Michael R. King and Gregory M. Cooper

Powerful Female Pharaohs of Egypt by Jone Johnson Lewis (article published on ThoughtCo)

Sacred Luxuries: Fragrance, Aromatherapy, and Cosmetics in Ancient Egypt by Lise Manniche

Ghosts: A Haunted History by Lisa Morton

Ancient Egyptian Kingship by David Bourke O'Connor, David P. Silverman

The Hebrew Pharaohs of Egypt: the Secret Lineage of the Patriarch Joseph by Ahmed Osman

The Oxford History of Ancient Egypt by Ian Shaw

The Encyclopedia of Ancient Egypt General Editor Helen Strudwick

Chronicle of the queens of Egypt: from early dynastic times to the death of Cleopatra by Joyce Tyldesley

Tutankhamen: The Search for an Egyptian King by Joyce Tyldesley

Ancient Egypt: Its Culture and History by J. E. Manchip White

Acknowledgments

When I began working on this story in 2017, I had no idea that it would blossom into one of the most meaningful things I have ever created; the project I am the most proud of. Little did I know that I had begun the long pregnancy and labor that would bring my story into the world.

Let me thank the many people who held my hands, encouraged me, and coached me during this amazing process. To my mother, Anne, this story would not be what it is today if you had not let me read it to you out loud three times in a row. You have cured my dependence on paragraph-length sentences, you have helped me mature in my application of balance and pacing, and you have answered questions I could not answer myself. I will be forever grateful for your support, your willingness to serve as my sounding board, and your second set of eyes and ears. Thank you for being to me everything Ankh is for Tut. And thank you for playing *seega!*

To my brave friends, thank you for reading this saga before the rest of the world. Thank you for your questions and your comments; all your wonderful observations that helped me understand what was coming across well and what needed further clarification. Thank you for helping me make this story everything it has become.

And to the Pharaoh and his family… thank you for inspiring me.

CPSIA information can be obtained
at www.ICGtesting.com
Printed in the USA
BVHW041914221220
596290BV00006B/29